·HEROINES·

·HEROINES·

Demigoddess, Prima Donna, Movie Star

NORMA LORRE GOODRICH,

K.C., FSA SCOT.

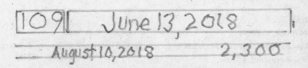

109	June 13, 2018	
	August 10, 2018	2,300

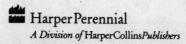

HarperPerennial
A Division of HarperCollinsPublishers

A hardcover edition of this book was published in 1993 by HarperCollins Publishers.

HarperCollins books may be purchased for educational, business, or sales promotional use. For information please write: Special Markets Department, HarperCollins Publishers, Inc., 10 East 53rd Street, New York, NY 10022.

First HarperPerennial edition published 1994.

Designed by Jessica Shatan

The Library of Congress has catalogued the hardcover edition as follows:

Goodrich, Norma Lorre.
    Heroines : demigoddess, prima donna, movie star / Norma Lorre Goodrich.—1st ed.
        p.   cm.
    Includes index.
    ISBN 0-06-016995-8
    1. Women in literature. 2. Heroines in literature. 3. Women and literature. 4. Literature—History and criticism. I. Title.
PN56.5.W64G66   1993
809′.89287—dc20   92-54746

ISBN 0-06-092502-7 (pbk.)
94 95 96 97 98 CW 10 9 8 7 6 5 4 3 2 1

Mr. Craig Nelson, Executive Editor,

HarperCollins Publishers,

with gratitude for his years of direction,

support, encouragement, and kindness

There be none of Beauty's daughters

  With a magic like thee;

And like music on the waters

  Is thy sweet voice to me;

When, as if its sound were causing

The charmed ocean's pausing,

The waves lie still and gleaming,

And the lull'd winds seem dreaming.

And the midnight moon is weaving

  Her bright chain o'er the deep;

Whose breast is gently heaving,

  As an infant's asleep:

So the spirit bows before thee,

To listen and adore thee;

With a full but soft emotion,

Like the swell of Summer's ocean.

From "Stanzas for Music,"
George Gordon, Lord Byron, March 28, 1816

•CONTENTS•

Acknowledgments		*xiii*
Introduction		*xv*
CHAPTER I.	LEGENDARY GOOD WOMEN	*1*
	Alcestis *(Alkestis)*	*3*
	Chaucer's Queen Cleopatra	*18*
	Shakespeare's Good Woman Lucrece	*20*
	Contradictions: Fitzgerald. Tolstoy	*25*
CHAPTER II.	LOVERS AND DEMON LOVERS	*31*
	Star-crossed Lovers	*31*
	The Love Story of Tristan and Isolde	*35*

The Demon Lover 52

The White Goddess 56

CHAPTER III. EDUCATING HEROINES 72

Earth Mothers 72

Heroines of Rousseau and Flaubert 79

CHAPTER IV. PROSTITUTES AND FALLEN WOMEN 98

Prostitutes 98

Phryne, the Greek Courtesan 103

Empress Theodora 109

Moll and Manon 111

Camille 118

Fallen Women 125

Electra 128

Antigone 131

Modern Times 133

Carmen 140

CHAPTER V. MOTHERS. DEATH QUEENS 150

Ancient Witches 150

Medea 153

Death Queens in the Modern World
(1833–1991) 156

Elizabeth Hunter, Heroine   171

CHAPTER VI.   HEROINES RETURN TO PAGANISM   174

Astronomers of the Old Stone Gods   174

The Story of Medusa   181

The Flight of the Heroine   185

CHAPTER VII. AMAZONS. STATUES OF WOMEN   193

Amazons. Women Warriors   193

The Great Queen from Ireland   196

Viking Heroines of Iceland and Norway   203

The Medieval Warrior: Saint Joan of Arc   209

CHAPTER VIII. THE RETURN OF THE GOLDEN AGE   218

Astraea   222

Goddesses of Justice in Historical Fiction   224

Sir Walter Scott   224

Aleksandr Pushkin   233

Charlotte Brontë and George Eliot   236

Conclusion   243

Appendixes   255

I   Prima Donnas. Grand Opera   255

II Demigoddesses   257

III   Modern Masters   259

IV   Modern Heroines   261

V   Movie Stars from Memory   263

Index   271

•ACKNOWLEDGMENTS•

The author thanks for their assistance and encouragement her husband, John Hereford Howard, Reverend John L. Higgins of the Arthuret Church in England, and the Arthurian Society there. She also thanks her Agent Mr. Harold Schmidt, Editor Jennifer A. Hull, and Assistant Editor Lauren Marino.

Special thanks go to Dr. Molly Ann Squire-Hanson for her tireless work on this book, and to Brigadier General Roger L. Rothrock for his gifts of books and for his patronage. Similar thanks go to President Thomas P. Salmon of the University of Vermont.

Thanks and gratitude to Clan Mackay Commissioner Barbara Paul Fanshier, to Grand Prior Andrew Mackie Davie, and to President Jean Hunt of the Louisiana Mounds Society.

Professor A. R. L. Bell, California State University, Long Beach, is thanked again for his continued interest and support, and his gifts of books and current publications.

Thank you to teacher Pat Higgins for her innovative work with deaf children. Thank you to Michael Cap de Ville, Beth Marble, and Director Ann C. Hope of the National Society of the Daughters of the American Revolution.

·INTRODUCTION·

This book is a study of the famous women who are now, and have been portrayed as heroines. They are heroines of history, of mythology, of fiction, of grand opera; and they remain our beloved heroines in the movies. Their names and their stories originated in ancient mythology, from which with slight alterations of place, and then disguises of name, they appear before us still, sometimes delighting us, sometimes challenging us to forget them if we can, and often troubling our sleep.

The significant role that heroines have played in our own lives is often overlooked because of their legendary status and their unique problems and characteristics. They are somehow unreachable and far removed from our own well-regulated lives. What is a Carmen to us? Or a Madame Bovary?

But if Carmen were to step off the operatic stage and speak to the audience in her own soprano voice, she might reproach us for false assurance. You never encountered a rival at work? she might ask. You never had to earn your own living, alone, in a big city? You never fell in love with a glamorous, but worthless lover? You never committed the slightest infraction, not even one resulting in a well-deserved speeding ticket? You never had to tell the man you love that since he struck you in the face, he may never come near you, ever again? You have never faced disgrace and lived it down? . . . Heroines have done so, Carmen would say. They give us one lesson after another in how to survive humiliation, discrimination, and defeat. None of us can afford to shrug them off. Why not? Because for centuries upon centuries uncounted, they have remained before readers and viewers, year after year, perennially. *They are still the foremost women of the world*.

Such a study as this, on heroines, relies upon ancient mythology, ancient history, and literature. These stories of heroines were first recorded in ancient Greek, in Latin, in ancient Norse and Gaelic before the year A.D. 500, which is generally agreed upon as the end of the ancient world throughout Europe. Our prime sources are ancient myths, which recount, by definition, rituals and rites of otherwise almost forgotten religions. But even after the general acceptance of Christianity by and after the year 500, the same, ancient heroines continued to delight, perplex, and instruct the generations just as they had always done. Each heroine was only modernized in name, dress, place, and language. Under perennially refreshed disguises, she still offered new readers and new viewers another chance to wrestle with her ancient set of problems. What is education, except practice in problem solving?

Hosts of specialists from various academic disciplines deal with these problems, which over the ages have beset heroines. The primary expert reads and interprets the most ancient of these texts written in ancient languages: scholars of Greek, Latin, Old Norse, Gaelic, and Old French, for example. At this level the tales call also upon specialists in myth, legend, and comparative religions. Teachers join ranks at all these levels, and they bring to bear upon the heroines' problems their training in psychology and pedagogy, and their data from years in the classroom. Teachers are well accustomed to hearing the problems of heroines erupt loudly at any hour of any working day. Most lately, and after the collected papers of Sigmund Freud were published in London in the 1920s, the new resources of psychoanalysis have provided the best of all methods and resources for solving human dilemmas.

Aside from the psychoanalysts, the persons most apt to deal with heroines and their problems are mothers, teachers, and authors. Objections come from the real specialists, of course, who properly remind the rest of us that the study of heroines falls into the soft-data category of the social sciences. History, which is literature, and literature, which consists of books, belong both to an area of imprecise observation, problematical qualification, and inevitable subjectivity, say the hard scientists. That is true. A heroine is an individual. She belongs usually to small groups of women who have already decreed absolutely how she is to act, behave, dress, speak, and think.

There are exceptions to this rule of life, however, and heroines have usually escaped the constraints of society, perhaps because they were outcasts from birth or by straightened circumstance. The heroine more resembles a contemporary university graduate in a large city where she has always remained free to join alternate groups of fellows and friends, than she resembles, for example, a student at a small woman's college where she must either conform or be ostracized. Conformity brings its real rewards: election to office in the small group, a rich husband who requires a feared, imposing, and socially acceptable wife.

Some authors seek those heroines who rebel secretly, like Madame Bovary. Other authors dote upon the declared rebel, a social outcast, like Carmen. Still others crave to disentangle the weird, inexplicable career of a Joan of Arc. Prostitutes fascinate the social scientists, the scholar, the jurist, the legislator, and the author. Great books about mothers, for mothers are probably the most problem-plagued heroines in our contemporary society, are usually crowned with a Nobel Prize for Literature. Warrior women, who are heroical by nature, still demand unsuccessfully to fly combat missions and take command in battle. In ancient days the Amazons fought the Greeks step by step from Syria north into Russia, and across the width of North Africa before they were forbidden combat roles. Ancient heroines also ran astronomical observatories and set up mathematical formulas just as modern gamblers bet fortunes on the same roulette wheels. The ancient witches are more fortunate; they have won a place in schools of medicine. Teachers and authors have won their doctorate degrees also and are prouder of them than of life itself. For what use is untriumphant life? Who does not need to conquer? The fun is in the testing of one's strength, says any heroine.

In studying heroines I, as both a teacher and an author, fall back upon my years of encountering girls and grown women in classrooms of public schools in Vermont, of private schools in Florida and New York City, of university classrooms in the United States and abroad, as demonstration teacher for colleges, and as the owner of a school in France. As a teacher of probably ten thousand female students to whom I was bound for anywhere from a semester to four years professionally and in strong affection—for teachers come very quickly to love their students, and subsequently to grieve over the loss of them—must now turn to literature. This teacher-author must now confine herself only to the great heroines of literature and do so in order to protect the confidentiality of the student-teacher relationship.

Even so, knowledge of real heroines met in classrooms over the decades of a teacher's career, from elementary schools to the privileged classes of doctoral candidates, and finally to the one-on-one hours with writers of dissertations, remains stored in the mind. Unfortunately, only the doctoral candidates remain lifelong, intimate friends of their professor. But the knowledge of thousands of young women remains in the mind as a real resource.

Experience, which lies in the past, is one of the surest reservoirs of knowledge. Professional knowledge remains a valuable source, for the experienced teacher can within ten or so minutes silently locate and identify those students suffering serious problems in any classroom. Within the first hour a teacher has matched every name to the person, and the person to the data in the principal's office. Within a week one can recognize the handwriting of every student in each class (eight classes per day in the public school, four per day in the private school, three per day in the college, two per day in the university plus two per week in its graduate school where the other office hours are one-on-one). Within a week also the state-certified teacher can surely read and identify all the handwriting, even that which is upside-down, as she stands before the class. Teaching affords the teacher all sorts of similar, private pleasures. Today she reads her students' poetry and goes to see the movies they have written or directed. They too had their problems, she recalls with a smile.

It is equally true that not experience alone lies in the past. History and mythology are also equal or greater repositories of knowledge. Heroines have fought harder for knowledge than they have ever fought for love and lovers over the ages. Our first mother, Eve, was expelled as was Pandora, from the Garden of Eden because she sought knowledge forbidden to woman, but granted to man for no other reason than his sex. Thus, the entire roster of a woman's behavior lies there, prostrate in her sad past. And upon her past all our presents rely for those decisions that will govern our futures.

As women and Americans we live now in a period of change at home, for women are entering politics more and more to improve the lives of the less able and less courageous among us. Women will become professional warriors and command ships, planes, battlefields, and the settlement of Mars. They will find better ways to combine education, family, and careers open to talent. They will learn how to join groups wider than the ones, like school and church, which have been historically available to them. More and more women will write books about our greatest problems: life-styles, human relationships, bonding of mothers and children, foreign aid, warfare, unemployment, and colonization. They will become more expert at making our institutions and organizations more useful and more answerable, from NOW (National Organization of Women) to AAUW (Association of American University Women) and to the NSDAR (National Society of the Daughters of the American Revolution).

All studies of women potentially benefit all women because all women face the same cluster of problems which, despite their bravery, heroines failed for the most part to solve successfully. A first such problem is the victimization of women, particularly when they are most helpless and most vulnerable, which is during pregnancy and the first five years of their child's or children's lives. A second, no less serious problem is that of self-sacrifice. Girl children are taught, or learn all by themselves, to refuse food at the table when there is not enough for their fathers or brothers. They also learn fast enough to cover cuts and bruises in order to protect the family honor, and to lie convincingly to teachers and doctors. Girls learn self-sacrifice and the sublimation of their own desires to those of their parents. It was for centuries the accepted norm for a young mother to lay down her life for her husband. To my amazement, when I asked various young, unmarried, working women in the United States over the last five years whether they would die for their future husbands, they replied "If I loved him. Yes."

Another thorny problem faced by all women is a sexism that calls for conformity without objection in dress, homemaking, wifely duties, parental obligations, sexual service, obedience, acceptance of male or majority rule. Female society leaders also rule through fear. They too wield power with soft voices and wills of iron. More than men, they relegate less wealthy women to subservience and require them to identify themselves, not by personal achievement, but under their husband's name, by his success and position, and by the number and ages of their children. The woman, as women see her, is usually an intermediary fleshpot linked by her services to the present, the past, and the next generation. As for herself, she is a smiling, speechless, overweight, and outwardly complacent nonperson. Not so, our heroines.

Woman's biological nature remains another troublesome problem, as the Sicilian author Grazia Deledda explored in her Nobel Prize–winning novel *La Madre,* as we shall see in chapter V. Faced with the biological imperative of motherhood, which cannot usually be denied, a young woman lies helpless, and at the utter mercy of lover, husband, and physician. Loss of power in such years is only compounded by loss of earnings, loss of identity, loss of self-respect and confidence, and finally, by the overpowering knowledge that her tiny infant is, in last analysis, alone in the world except for only herself—and she is ill and penniless. Many heroines have passed through, or fallen, during such experiences. Their beauty and lovability help them fall into the trap of their biological imperative, and thence to disaster more often than not. Our shelters are full of orphans and battered and beaten women. Powerlessness and dependence upon some other human being are not even the worst of a heroine's problems.

Such musings about a woman's life move finally to a consideration of terms. When in doubt, one looks in *Webster* to settle the mind about definitions. There we discover that a hero means both originally and primarily a "Greek warrior," an epic military man from that "heroic age" of Greece. Second, a hero is a man who has performed some noteworthy service to mankind, and through that accomplishment has advanced to honor, public worship, and posthumous glory. Third, a hero may also be the chief character in a work of literature, but in that case he is usually or must usually be of noble birth. Or, in a fourth instance, declares *Webster,* a hero may be so designated if he has lived a life of distinction, of great valor, or if he has demonstrated great fortitude. A hero is acclaimed, in a fifth definition, if he has been the central personage in an event, in an action or a deed after which he has become a *model* for other men and future generations.

Turning in *Webster* to the word *heroine,* one reads first that she is endowed with or has acquired in life *the same male qualities* which have made him named and universally recognized as a "hero." She too may be or must be a warrior, or one who has supplied some signal service to mankind, one who has acquired distinction, or one who has demonstrated conspicuous courage. A heroine is defined by her valor, fortitude, fearlessness, brilliance, and fame. Her achievements must be recognizably superlative. In danger she must transcend ordinary behavior and show a gay indifference to peril, bright mettle and spirit, superhuman address against odds, and gallantry in action.

A heroine may also have simply been chosen by an author to be the central character of his book, and so we shall consider these heroines and their heroical acts in the following chapters. One reservation here must be acknowledged, however, and clarified: Any heroine worthy of respect in this study must have demonstrated positive characteristics. This means that there must have been a considerable measure of unanimity between the author who chose her and this teacher-author in accepting her as heroical.

Any true heroine, it seems to me, must have made some remarkable achievement. She must have possessed and demonstrated her possession of an admirable personality and person. She must have proven herself more or less indifferent to danger and at some point able to triumph over it. She must have proven fearless before strictures which she has adjudged unfair or wrong. She must have scorned blind fortune and any hostile gods whatsoever. She must have acted positively in some situation calling for a cool head and a firm step. She must have shown magnanimity, which is the basic feminine and inborn trait of generosity common to all women who by biological determination are prepared to feed and nourish others. Being born also to mother a child, all heroines must demonstrate that endurance which our beloved author William Faulkner said characterizes American black women: they endure; they survive.

However tragically their lives may have ended—for both heroes and heroines too must eventually end and go to dust—they must both have received sympathetic portrayals from our greatest masters. These authors cannot be deceived by any human delinquency. Our chosen, modern, and affiliated heroines, descendants and sisters to the goddesses and demigoddesses of ancient Greece, remain in our view memorable all our lives. They may die tragically perhaps, like Carmen and Madame Emma Bovary, or they may pull themselves out of prostitution by their bootstraps, like Moll Flanders, and count themselves fortunate for having gone to live in Virginia. The French heroine of novel and opera, Manon, failed to receive the grace of God, explained her author, and for that reason collapsed in Louisiana. Greta Garbo/Camille died too, all white flowers and corruption, but not before the total offer of her love. The German heroine Marquise of O fared better, after she won the support of her noble parents and of her repentant lover. Madame de Merteuil was made of iron resolve. She was such as the thousands of French women who made no sound under the blade of the guillotine. Heroines of the historical novelists, Sir Walter Scott and Aleksandr Pushkin, were portrayed as young girls who appealed for mercy directly to their queens. Jane Eyre showed teachers how to survive happily. The Norse Viking Hjördis showed them how to choose death rather than dishonor as did Saint Joan of Arc. All appeared as true heroines. They live around us still and urge us onward.

Roget's Thesaurus, in a very constructive manner, grouped heroines for us into four understandable categories: actress, brave person, celebrity, and demigoddess. Various heroines of grand opera, and in cases where the opera bears the heroine's name as its title (see Appendix 1) bear out this categorization. Thus, we have another list of believable heroines: Leonora, Norma, Lucia, Traviata, Mignon, Aïda, Lakmé, Thaïs, Louise, and Madama Butterfly. When he came to heroic women, Roget could only name two: the Greek Amazon maiden Penthesilea, who was slain and then raped by Achilles, and Saint Joan of Arc herself. He had not heard of Virgil's heroic maiden, Camilla, who was so fleet of foot that she could run over a wheat field without bending the blades of wheat. Nor did he include Queen Cleopatra among his warriors, as he should have done, nor even the heroic Roman matron Lucrece. He failed also to mention any of the celebrated Northern heroines: Brunhilde, who died on her husband's funeral pyre, or the terrifying Empress Theodora of Byzantium, or the heroines of fictions written by Sir Walter Scott and Aleksandr Pushkin.

Roget fell short also when he gave no example of a noblewoman who in her person stood as "a choice and master spirit" of her age when so many historical persons come to mind at once: Queen Elizabeth I of England certainly was a warrior queen who even prepared to board ship for the battle against the Spanish Armada and who certainly represented the age which is named for her; Queen Catherine the Great of Russia, who also put her stamp upon her rule and age; Queen Maria Theresa of the Hapsburg Empire, who brought her kingdom to greater and greater glory; the Princess Maria Bolkonsky of Tolstoy's superlative historical novel of Napoleon I and his defeat in Russia; Madame de Merteuil from *Dangerous Acquaintances* (which is the correct English translation of *Les Liaisons dangereuses*); and the German noblewoman named the *Marquise* of *O,* in the novella of that name, who brought to his knees a gallant Russian army officer; and Queen Cleopatra of Egypt who fought gallantly also, but lost the war.

When Roget comes to his fourth listing of "mythical deities," divas, and "heathen goddesses," he allows us to name the very ancient heroines whose stories stood as models for medieval and modern heroines to come. We have Hecate, demigoddess and witch; Persephone, the daughter of Earth (Demeter or Ceres), who was stolen by the god of the Underworld and obliged to spend each winter below earth with him; the two demigoddesses whose statues we see: Liberty and Justice; the "good woman" Alcestis, who typified wifely love; Medea and Medusa, who could bring the dead to life and turn the living to stone; the Delphic Oracle who was the high priestess of the ancient world when no men claimed that right legally; and the young Irish princess, Isolde, who was wedded to aged King Mark.

Our method of operation, now that we know the names and estates of our major heroines, will be to repeat their stories in the ancient world and then move to the most celebrated authors who, in their modern works, repeated the stories and expanded them in a modern manner. These Greek and modern heroines will fall naturally and according to type into seven chapters:

    I. Legendary Good Women
    II. Lovers and Demon Lovers
    III. Educating Heroines
    IV. Prostitutes and Fallen Women
    V. Mothers. Death Queens
    VI. Heroines Return to Paganism
    VII. Amazons. Statues of Women
    VIII. The Return of the Golden Age

The modern heroines divide easily into groups. They are heroines of history and/or literature, or they are demigoddesses, or divas (prima donnas) of grand opera, and/or they are our most adored movie stars, signifying glamour itself. Only the word *demigoddess* needs classification perhaps.

The term *demigoddess* refers to any female deity less venerable than those whom the ancient Greeks placed so reverently in heaven: Zeus, Athena, Hera, Artemis, Ares, Apollo, Mercury, and Hestia.

They are our ancient women who once addressed the very problems faced by real, ancient, and medieval women in their lives. These women are still significant today:

1. Eve, Pandora, Rhea, and Phyllis are ancient names closely linked with our endangered planet, Mother Earth;

2. Hecate and Persephone, queens of death, and hell, reign in the Underworld;

3. Medea, Jocasta, and Medusa, priestesses or "witches" armed with magic, opposed their societies and disobeyed their rules and customs;

4. Antigone and Electra faced down corrupt rulers and dared to remain intransigent enemies of the State;

5. The uncompromising Norwegian Viking Hjördis and the Irish demigoddess Morrigu were invincible warriors who lit the way for Saint Joan of Arc;

6. The Irish princess Isolde remained virginal in marriage, and proved her holiness by a fire-walking ordeal;

7. Phryne and the Empress Theodora had been raped and prostituted since childhood and took sharp revenge upon all men;

8. Alcestis, Cleopatra, and Lucrece (Lucretia) were adored as ancient models of "the good woman."

Stories of demigoddesses remain from ancient mythology. They offer us heroines from remotest antiquity: victims, lovers, prostitutes, mothers, priestesses, witches, crones, and other models for modern women to ponder. It is worth asking now if problems facing ancient women were ever solved in their days, or whether those same troublesome issues remain to nag us in society today. They also constitute the treasury from which our greatest modern authors draw.

Victor Hugo, who was one such author, used to lament how few objects around us truly survived time. Even stones metamorphose, he noted. Nothing other than books survived obliteration. Only books prove indestructible. Powerful dictators have killed authors and have burned their books. The only thing needed was a single copy that survived in somebody's pocket, or in somebody's memory, in order to keep the stories alive.

Nobody has as yet explained the mysterious memory, much less the visual acuity of our great masters of literature who have drawn upon ancient myths from such civilizations as Israel, Persia, India, Greece, Rome, Africa, and America. The masters of literature guard this treasury of letters. They are the prime custodians not only of our culture but of our myths, our philosophy, our learning, and our history.

In the ancient world arcane knowledge was transmitted via established vehicles, or literary forms. Stories of great men as military heroes were rehearsed and memorized in epic poems narrating how a champion was selected to fight and die for his community. These ancient epics date from such works as Homer's *Iliad* and Iran's *Shah Nameh,* or Book of Kings. Epics remained popular genres well into the Middle Ages. Such works of art were reserved expressly for the celebration of outstanding heroes, and they always ended with mass expiation, wakes, or ceremonies during the hero's funeral.

The ancient world also recorded its worst scandals, and its worst crimes and problems such as matricide, incest, and rape, but told them in the form of tragedy for an audience to watch. Throughout the Middle Ages epic poetry continued to celebrate the warrior, or scape-goat hero. Drama and grand opera have continued to educate and enthrall their wealthy patrons. Both epic and tragedy have faded away over the centuries.

A new vehicle has gradually ousted both tragedy and epic as the principal vehicle for the transmission of ancient myths. We can understand why if we stop to consider how many persons among us, even with television sets, are barred from the enjoyment of city theaters and operas. The Middle Ages ended amidst an explosion of knowledge due to the intrusions of heroines demanding audience, and to the inventions of paper and the printing presses. Suddenly, rather than addressing a few privileged persons in the theater, authors found themselves writing for everybody who consented to learn to read the prose novel, the short story, and the longer novella.

It was Boris Pasternak in *Doctor Zhivago,* first published in Italy in 1957, who explained in this Tolstoyan novel why such modern literature must be recognized as containing, in its ancient as well as in its modern pages, a sometimes unrecognized treasury of problem solving. Literature deals principally with ancient myths because they are so human, he said, that they survive, especially in the novel today, as treatments of heroines.

Both Liberty and Justice were ancient women. One held aloft a torch which still lights up our lives. The other holds the scales upon which the souls of ancient women were weighed. Modern women look to both demigoddesses for enlightenment and justice. It is true that we must all feel free and be free to do so. When we all live in a society that grants freedom and justice to all, we shall have realized America's oldest dream.

NOTE TO THE READER

The reader will find at the close of each section of this book a brief list of texts for use in any continuing study. The lists include works of literature commonly assigned in both undergraduate and graduate classes in comparative literature.

A great work of literature is by definition multifaceted. It always solicits new interpretations, which give it renewed vigor and longer life. Reading and writing are both acts of generosity. Each new reader immortalizes anew the masterpieces of the world.

·HEROINES·

·CHAPTER I·

Legendary Good Women

Our examination of heroines commences with *the good woman*. She has come to us from so long ago that only her legend has been passed into the modern age. In tracing her story throughout the ages we will see what exactly constitutes for all time a good woman.

For about twenty-five hundred years, the story of the ancient Greek queen Alcestis (Alkestis) has passed from hand to hand, viewer to reader, author to composer, all of whom have considered her the first and foremost "good" woman ever to have lived, and to have shaped female behavior on this earth.

Homer mentioned Alcestis in the *Iliad* (II, v.711 ff.), Euripides (c. 480–406 B.C.) celebrated her around 438 B.C. in a tragedy, and Apollodorus wrote of her in his *Bibliotheca,* a book on mythology written in Athens around 140 B.C. Her fame continued down the centuries. Writers in the Middle Ages believed that life and the torch of learning in the Western world had been lit in Greece, passed to Rome, and bequeathed to France where it blazed the most brilliantly.

Many writers, supreme poets like Geoffrey Chaucer before 1400 and William Shakespeare before 1600, chose either Alcestis or her type of heroism in creating many heroines in their poetry. Sophocles started to write a tragedy based upon this lovely, young Greek queen. The ancient poet Pindar praised her at Thebes, as did the poet Robert Browning (1875) in England. In Paris the dramatist Philippe Quinault and composer Jean-Baptiste Lully wrote a lyrical tragedy (1674) in her honor. In 1767, when the Bavarian composer Christophe Gluck devoted the world-celebrated opera *Alceste* to this ancient heroine, his famous librettist was the Italian Ranieri Calzabigi. The American-born poet T. S. Eliot dignified Alcestis in *The Cocktail Party* of 1950. Both her story and its heavy symbolism have tracked down the ages via such talented persons that we must suspect any fictional, blonde heroine labeled "good woman," or any live "good" woman, or, indeed, any girl named "Daisy" is another Alcestis sprung from the brain and mouth of Apollo, god of poetry.

This heroine is supremely important to us all. Her story, or her legend, and the symbolism surrounding her has aroused masculine adoration for millennia. She has been the mainspring which has set the lives of women ticking. As we read her story, let us recall that the drama of *Alcestis* was always considered a problem play, even when Euripides first presented it in ancient Greece. Problems fascinate, but they also cry out for solutions. What was the problem with *Alcestis*? How could such a supremely good woman have a problem?

Let us commence by having a look at the play as if we were seeing it in the theater, with people coming and going mysteriously, as they do in real life. Euripides sometimes keeps us guessing, of course. That is why he is such a genius.

Alcestis *(Alkestis)*

_____

In the play by Euripides, Apollo begins as the narrator and says, I am, of course, the god of poetry and prophecy. You therefore understand that I foresaw all of this.

I am the god, Apollo told the old men listening to him, who once upon a time assisted this very King Admetus to capture his lovely bride.

That bride, now his wife, he told the mourners, was Alcestis. She was once upon a time the beautiful blonde daughter of King Pelias of Iolcos in Greece. Her mother was Queen Anaxibia.

In order to win the loveliest princess Alcestis, a hero had to hitch lions and boars to his chariot and drive them to Iolcos and back.

You probably realize, Apollo added, that it was not women, but ancient heroes who handily domesticated even the fiercest of creatures: the lion and the savage boar. So then this Prince Admetus seized his bride, won her, and carried her home in his chariot to distant Thessaly.

Prince Admetus, now King Admetus, took this bride home to his vast realm, which was entirely encircled by high mountains. His own city was Pherae, once ruled by the tyrant Jason of the Argonauts, who captured the Golden Fleece. So the now King Admetus captured this bride Alcestis and brought her up north into those mountains his tribe had defended since at least 1000 B.C. There are now Thessalian witches thereabouts, but they came in later. There were *no witches* while Admetus was king, Apollo added. The witch who tricked Hercules was over in Asia. But Hercules will appear in my tragic story too. Poetry and prophecy are closely allied arts.

There before you, Apollo told the Elders, rises the lordly palace of Pherae in Thessaly, and it is an oligarchy ruled absolutely by King Admetus. His wife is still the lovely Alcestis.

As my story begins, Apollo continued, you are now to understand that they have been happily married long enough for her to have borne him two little ones, a son and a daughter.

At this point in the drama, Euripides steps in as narrator, saying:

There in the lordly palace of King Admetus queenly, lovely, young Alcestis is approaching her death hour. Apollo has managed to save King Admetus from the death sentence laid upon him by the goddesses of fate. Apollo has intervened to persuade them, and they have been persuaded, to accept a substitute. Alcestis, the good wife, has volunteered to die in her husband's place. She now lies in her palace breathing her last. Apollo takes flight. All must avoid the pollution of death. Bowls of water stand ready for cleansing the rest of us.

Wrapped in his black plumage, wings outstretched, Death still protests the suspended sentence granted King Admetus. On the other hand, he agrees, he will increase his reputation by bringing down Alcestis, because she is much younger than her spouse.

The Elders still stand before the palace gate. They cry: What's going on in there? Is she dead yet? No, she still breathes, but fainter and fainter. Why don't they put some purifying water out here, before the gates? Where is the lock of her hair that is supposed to have been cut from her head and hung on the threshold? Where is the choir of keening maidens? Alas! How is this good lady cut down in her early youth!

The Elders advise against blood offerings. Blood sacrifices now will not help the lady. She is dying faster now. Could not somebody leave at once for the shrine of Zeus Ammon down in the Libyan Oasis? Would Zeus not save her? Could not ambassadors visit Apollo's temples in Greece, and beg for her life?

Suddenly a maidservant comes running out from the palace to bring the Elders the latest news. The handmaiden of Alcestis is weeping and reports to them that her mistress is dead. They suspected as much. The chorus of old men agree that she has been sinking fast. Her funeral robes lie ready for her to don as she enters Hades.

Her handmaid speaks and informs all: You should have seen how she prepared herself for the arms of Death. Who has ever surpassed this good lady? Is she not the best woman who ever lived? She may be already quite dead. She is sinking fast.

Alcestis prepared herself for death. She washed her body herself. She opened her trunk herself, took out her final vestments and her funeral jewelry, and robed herself alone.

Then she prayed to Persephone below to watch over her little children. They will be orphans soon, she told the Underworld Queen. See to them. Be sure to give my son a royal bride. Be sure to find my girl a husband to keep her, she prayed.

Then she crowned her own altars with sacred myrtle sprigs and said farewell.

Finally she apostrophized her wedding bed. Oh bed, she prayed, where I became a wife, remember me. Then she kissed the mattress and the coverlets. Only then did she begin to cry, and this set her young ones to wailing also. They clung to her garments finally and screamed. She could hardly pry them loose. But she tore them away, and embraced each one, and kissed them both good-bye.

I'll tell you what I think, concluded the handmaid. He should have died once for all and got it over with. Now our king has inherited an unforgettable grief. Maybe he didn't figure on the loss these two kids will suffer. Does anybody think they are going to forget the arms of this tender, loving young mother?

That's when I left, she told them, when King Admetus lifted the dead mother in his arms and raised her up. The choir of Elders agreed with her that in their view marriage is usually the pits, or leads to the pit where a good wife is concerned. Marriage usually brings more grief than bliss. They watch open-eyed as King Admetus comes towards them through the palace gates. What has our king inherited, they wonder, except everlasting sorrow?

The king half carries his dying wife in his arms. She wants to see the sunshine one last time, she whispers to him. In whispers, she asks to be laid down on the pavement. I see the skiff of Charon before me now, she says. He is drawing near to take me across the River Styx into Hell. There beyond him I can see the dark courtyard of King Hades where I am bound. . . . Please lay me down. . . . Farewell, dear little ones. . . . Now . . . you have no mother, now . . .

Do not go, Admetus begs his lady. Do not leave us.

Then Queen Alcestis speaks again: I die. Why? I die because I felt called upon to ensure your life, Admetus. The gods had condemned you to death, but Apollo appealed the sentence on your behalf. The gods amended their verdict by allowing you to provide a substitute. I am she.

Your old parents who, you thought, would die in your stead, categorically refused to do so. Unbelievably these two old persons refused this sacrifice to you, their only son. The gods were opposed, it seems. That left only me. I volunteered to die for you, my beloved husband. What else could a good woman do?

This is my last request of you, Admetus. Do not remarry. Do not bring in a new wife to our home. I fear an evil stepmother for my little children. She will hate them. She will burn with jealous hatred. She will slap them and whip them secretly.

Do you remember, Admetus? Do you remember when we got here on our honeymoon journey? What omen did we see when we threw open our bedroom doors? . . . The room was crawling all over with snakes! The bed was black with deadly vipers!

A stepmother would be such a poisonous snake to my dear babes. My little girl is the more vulnerable of the two. She would never get a husband to support her. I grieve not ever to be able to help her get a husband, or never to watch over her and cheer her up during her child-birthings. During those hours a girl most needs her own mother's kindnesses.

Admetus, I have been your peerless wife. Who will guarantee your behavior now?

The Elders speak to her, saying, We will.

Then Admetus promises her: I will not remarry a maid from Thessaly, no matter how glorious her genealogy is, not even if she proves to be the fairest maiden alive.

Second, two are enough children for me.

Third, I promise to mourn for you during the year, but actually more than required, forever, in truth.

Fourth, I shall despise my selfish parents forever.

Fifth, I shall forego all parties, wine, crown-wearings, music, musical performing, and will not sing any more to the accompaniment of the Libyan flute.

Sixth, I shall put a replica of you upon my bed.

Seventh, I unfortunately could not sing or play as well as Orpheus. Sorry, but I could therefore not go down into Hell after you, as he went down and brought back Eurydice. I would have proven unequal to Hades, Charon, and/or Pluto's many-headed, black dog Cerberus.

Finally, do go down to Hell yourself. Thus, you will prepare a home for us down below.

After he has finished his promises, he hears Alcestis warn her children to bear witness to his oaths, especially that of celibacy. For his part Admetus then addresses his household: I have known that her death was coming. Seeing that his wife is now a corpse, he continues: I am prepared and ready to carry off her dead body. I now proclaim general mourning for a period of twelve months. We shall all shear off our hair, wear black robes, silence all music, and cut the manes off all our horses.

The Elders then salute Alcestis and urge her to be happy in the dark Underworld. Announce your presence there, they urge her. Request the Priestess Muses to sing springtime songs in your honor every year in Athens. For you, and only you, have had the supreme courage to redeem your spouse from black Hades, which is a bargain you sealed with your own life. His gray-haired parents did not die for him. You died for him, Alcestis. You died moreover in your first youth and perfect beauty.

Then enters Admetus and our second, or successful, hero, the conquering Hercules.

Ah well, Hercules tells the Chorus of old men, I am about my Third Adventure, which is to capture the wild horses of Diomedes in Thrace. Their master has been feeding them on human flesh, as you know; and this wrong I must right. Seeing the face of Admetus more clearly, Hercules asks, Has somebody died here? Who was it?

Admetus replies: Oh, nobody important. Not a blood relative. It was only a stranger to this palace. The dead are dead. Please come in and make yourself at home.

He will be welcomed in my palace, Admetus advises the Chorus. Let there be no mourning to mar his pleasure in these halls! Close off the funeral area! Let us dazzle Hercules with our gourmet meals, our vast estates, our rich fields and pastures, our shepherds and flocks, our wild and domestic herds. Let the musicians strike up gay tunes!

The father of Admetus advances nonetheless to present condolences to his son and tells him that Alcestis's life was truly a noble example and shall stand forever as the noble example for all future persons of the female sex. He gives his condolences to his son, and says a marriage to an Alcestis is a blessing to mankind. Unless a man can marry an Alcestis, marriage is so costly as not to be worth it.

Prince Admetus is very angry and confronts his old father, telling him haughtily, You were not invited to come here. You are no friend of mine. We need nothing further here from you. Where was your sorrow at my death sentence? Were you not so old you should have died in my place? You refused. You thereby disclaimed kinship. I cannot believe that I was born out of you two!

You know what you parents are? A formula for cowardice. Think of it: that both of you, at the very verge of death, should have refused to die for your own son!

My wife was, on the other hand, actually a stranger to us, was not of our bloodline. But she died.

Look at the princely, long lives you have already lived! You have me as your son and heir. I have never dishonored you. Now consider my reward in return: mistreatment! This stranger woman became my savior, not you.

While the Chorus of Elders tried to quiet them both and urged peace and harmony between son and father, the latter replied: My son, you address me as if I were a slave. Who do you think you are talking to? This is your father, a Thessalian patrician, and no slave of yours. You are insolent. You are a braggart. That is no way to behave when I raised you to inherit and govern my House. All debts to you have been paid. We are even.

No law of this kingdom, the father added, requires me to die for you. No law of our ancient ancestors so stipulates. In fact, there exists no such custom either in any of the Greek states, that a father should die for his son. You must live or die as you can.

Son, you have already taken possession of your inheritance from me. Have I cheated you of any part thereof? As for me, my days on earth are short and sweet. Your wife has undertaken to die so that you can live out your allotted years. Do you still dare to call me a coward?

Admetus, my son, you are a weakling. You are unworthy of such a noble wife. To think that she has already died for such as you! . . . In truth, you cleverly manipulated her. And now in your guilt you come around taunting your mother and me with cowardice. Your words prove you the coward here. You had better shut your mouth; for, if you continue to speak ill of us, I will broadcast your crimes abroad.

Now the Chorus begs them to stop, but Admetus seeks to utter the last word. Too bad you sinned against me, he hissed.

His father replied: If I had accepted to die for you, I would have sinned more gravely. . . . Go get yourself some more wives—the more to die for you again.

Admetus cried, You ought to be ashamed of yourself!

His father, Pheres, retorted: Go bury the wife you have just slain! Murderer!

Admetus: Leave my house! Now I am fatherless! You have no son from now on!

Admetus has turned to see a famous stranger approaching his palace gates. He recognizes Hercules by his club, his bow, and his arrows. The great hero for his part now recognizes the signs of death before the door and wonders who has died there. He now sees that persons appear to be very sad, and he inquires of the servants whom they are preparing to bury. He is told at first that the corpse is that of a stranger woman. Not satisfied, Hercules asks another servant, who finally confesses that it was his wife that died. Then Hercules asks where her tomb is located. It is at Larissa, in the suburbs, they reply.

As soon as he hears that, the great hero makes up his mind to go to the rescue of the lady. If he hurries, he says, he can probably catch black Death while he is still drinking blood before her tomb. Perhaps he can even grab a hold of him. Failing that, Hercules decides, he will even go down to the dark Underworld and beg Queen Persephone and her husband, King Hades, to give up Alcestis. Perhaps he can persuade them that they should allow him to carry her home to earth again.

Hercules is still standing wrapped in thought when Admetus returns from Larissa and the tomb. Now for the first time Admetus seems to realize the extent of his loss. Weeping and lamenting, he crosses the threshold of his empty palace. Henceforth he will dwell isolated, he feels, and lonely at a widowed hearth which no dear wife will warm for him ever again.

I wish now that I were dead, Admetus laments. My mother gave birth to me at an evil hour. It was her fault. I envy the dead. I want to go to Hell where they are. This bright sunshine fails to warm me, or to cheer me up. My dear wife has been handed over to Hades as his hostage forever more.

Only his Elders agree with him, that now is the time for grief. And grief is here now, they lament with him.

Admetus asks his senators if he shall ever see his dear wife again. They think not. Weeping he cries Alas! and praises the dead Alcestis for her faithfulness. But why did I ever wed her? he wonders. Why did I father these kids? They only bring me grief too. Look at my empty bed henceforth! Why did Hades not take me? There he stood at her grave! Why did he not grab me too?

The Elders console him by reminding him how other people became resigned to loss, and that eventually he too will cease to suffer so awfully. But Admetus will not be consoled. Look at me, he sobs. I can't even go in the house. . . . Fortune has turned her face against me. What a reversal it has been when I think of my happy wedding. Our wedding party was so gay. We were so glad. Friends from all sides crowded about and congratulated us. . . . We were such a striking, handsome, young couple! We both wore white that day. We were both superbly gowned. We were both rich, young, noble, and lovely. Our wedding hymns were so appropriate and so sweet. Look at me now in my black mourning gown. See how ugly and barren it is around here.

The Elders cannot stop his tirade. He weeps and storms about in a frenzy of unhappiness.

At this point Hercules returns, leading by the hand a woman veiled in black. To Admetus he says, Keep this woman here until I have completed my present Labor. I won her in a contest for herds of oxen. She was too good to pass up, and so I took her too.

Don't leave her here, Admetus replies. She will only get deflowered here. And also, everybody will say she is my new bride. Take her away.

Hercules argues that she will be the new wife Admetus needs. When Admetus again refuses, Hercules argues that a new wife will console him for his loss. After considerable debate back and forth Admetus yields to Hercules. He then tells him to remove her black veil. Hercules does so.

Admetus sees that the woman is his wife, Alcestis. Hercules agrees. But Admetus still looks and wonders if it is a ghost, or whether it really is Alcestis. Hercules assures him that the woman is not a ghost. Admetus inquires if he may speak to her and ask her if she is Alcestis. Hercules replies that he may question her if he likes but that she cannot utter a word, as yet. She cannot speak until she herself has been purified, or after a period of three days.

Admetus summons his household and orders them to lay on a great feast and celebration.

The ever-present Chorus of Elders concludes the drama. In their summary they assert that life is powerful but that one never knows what turns the gods will give it. And furthermore, one never expects what actually occurs. What comes to pass is more often what was not foreseen. It has occurred thus here in Thessaly.

Finis.

The problem facing Euripides seems to have been his choice of vehicle. He had the story: time and place, characters, and plot. What created the problem was the outcome: tragic? comic? tragedy? comedy? Euripides above all people knew the format of tragedy: a brave hero falls irreparably, and through no fault of his own, from the glory and fame of a high estate to utter shame and the pit of disgrace, after which his death follows fast. The best, classical example is Oedipus, who was slated before manhood, unknowingly, to sleep with his mother and kill his own father at a certain crossroads outside Thebes.

The story of Alcestis is clearly, as has been seen, *not a tragedy*. Neither is it a comedy, because she appears to die but comes back to earth, is not disgraced, was not condemned by overruling Destiny, but freely chose her own fate and carried it through all by herself. She chose to die and did so, nobly and courageously. Then veiled in black she came, speechless for three days, back from the dead where Hercules had found her and rescued her.

Classical scholars have argued this problem play down the centuries. Let us suggest a novel solution and ask each reader to take the matter under consideration and make up his or her own mind thereupon.

If the reports of Euripides and Apollodorus are joined, as they were just presented, then the so-called "legend" of Alcestis proves its antiquity by more resembling a fairy tale. As we know, the fairy tale is most ancient. It too descends the ages in parallel progress with the ancient epic, and both originate in the one heroical pattern of primeval times. So in the Alcestis material we are able to discern the seven characters of every fairy tale that has survived as a complete entity. Our fairy tale characters here are:

1. The god Apollo, who acts to set the hero upon his assigned task (to wed the princess);

2. The god Death (Hades or Thanatos), who is the hero's antagonist;

3. Alcestis, the blonde princess, bride, and heroine;

4. Admetus, her husband, who is King of Thessaly, and our first hero;

5. The Donor, here Queen Persephone of Hell, who gives the heroine a magic talisman (a black veil) to save her life;

6. Hercules, who rescues the heroine after Admetus fails. Hercules is, then, the second hero, typical of fairy tales;

7. The heroine's father (absent in Euripides), from whose home she is abducted, or seized, or "won." Present in Euripides are the substitute Fathers, or Elders, or Chorus.

Thus, the morphology of an ancient fairy tale makes Alcestis the heroine for whom all male critics have expressed their utmost love and admiration. She is an heroic figure and is an exquisite creation of Euripides. Her gift of her own life for her husband, say they, is more eloquent that a thousand protestations of love.

But some critics demur. The great classical scholar Gilbert Murray hesitated. The play is somehow wrong, he thought, because of her husband. What was it on his part that let her die? You see, she couldn't speak for three days after her death (experience), said the great Erna P. Trummel, because her soul was deciding whether or not to return to her body.

We have one type of myth here, most scholars have agreed: a person (Alcestis), condemned to death, returns by favor of the gods. However, that does not satisfy the equation either, because she was never condemned to death. It was her husband, Admetus, who was condemned to death. Alcestis chose freely to die in his stead. She died and returned alive from the dead.

The story of Alcestis could understandably not be a tragedy, much less a comedy, which attacks society, berates, and admonishes. All the aura of the Alcestis legend is holy, reverent, and contemplative; not caustic, not berating us like the black humor of comedy.

Therefore let us suppose that below the fairy tale, and far behind the legend, stretches the more antique terrain of mythology. The story of Alcestis seems to derive originally from an ancient myth regarding the best feminine power on this planet: Mother Earth . . . Demeter . . . Ceres . . . Alcestis.

What Alcestis performed during the three days while she absented herself from felicity may have been to worship Mother Earth by descending into the Underworld. There the adoration Alcestis duly performed persuaded the goddess Persephone to give her a diploma, as it were, or the black veil, her passport, her visa for safe transit to the upper world again. For this permission Alcestis prayed so fervently to Persephone.

Alcestis had found snakes on her bridal bed. These creatures were sacred to Athena and Asclepius, who knew how worshipfully and silently they glided below the earth. They were sacred to the medical profession, then, and to women, who were its first practitioners. More than that, they were earth spirits like our heroine, Alcestis herself. As symbolized also by her name, which means daisy, Alcestis personified the nature goddess of flowers, Antheia.

Every year in ancient Greece women alone celebrated their private and utterly secret, absolutely tabooed religious festivals. Thus, Euripides trod very carefully, stepping across a deep river from stone to stone, never attempting openly to clarify, the gods forbidding the story of Alcestis to be told.

The religious ceremonies for Demeter (Ceres) were the most secret of all, and remain so today: the "mysteries" of Eleusis. Perhaps matrons recovered their virginity during those three days. The celebrants also quietly adored the mother goddess, Hera, for the three days of the Heraea Mysteries. Was not Alcestis their "Minister"?

Like heroes and kings after her, Alcestis descended for reinvigoration, and initiation as well, "under the stone," a phrase from megalithic ages. The significance of this phrase remains a mystery.

There Alcestis died and was reborn. In ancient Greece these daring persons, these initiates, these holy survivors of dark ordeals, became the mortal dead. Returned to life, they were the most revered Greeks of their day. Such was Alcestis, therefore best of women.

No "best of women" would have died for her husband if she had to abandon minor children in doing so, and certainly not if one child were a daughter, because the mother-daughter bond, psychoanalysts now claim, may well be the strongest tie in society.

Before the year 1394 Geoffrey Chaucer reintroduced Alcestis as Queen Alceste in his Prologue to *The Legend of Good Women* (v. 510 ff.).

Chaucer posited, as he began this poem in praise of the world's good women, that when he thought of Alcestis he thought of a flower. Above every celebrated meadow flower he personally preferred this red-and-white blossom which men call the daisy, or eye of the day. Every May, Chaucer rose early from his bed so he could walk in the fields and admire these pretty flowers.

In his chest at home he had a copy of the story of Alceste, he says (v. 510), who was a queen of great goodness that was turned into a daisy, or "dayesye." She was the one who chose to die for her husband and even to go down to hell in his stead. And it was verily Hercules who rescued her and brought her out of hell to the bliss of her life on earth. She is the "good Alceste," who is the red-and-white (English) daisy whose goodness, the poet feels, gives comfort to his heart. Even now, says the English poet, he can feel the goodness of this wife who after her death, as during her life, by her goodness doubled her renown and paid poets back for their affection.

So Chaucer too, after Homer, Euripides, Ovid, Boccaccio, and Froissart, among others in the fifteenth century, devoted his skill to continuing her "glorious legend" (v. 473). *The Legend of Good Women,* which Chaucer commenced but failed to complete, would have contained biographies of "good women, maidens and wives" who were *true in love all their lives long.* He would have celebrated them all even though their lives demonstrated how the very men to whom they remained faithful were false betrayers who spent their lives seeing how many women they could bring down to shame. Love is a game to such men. Love should not be sport. Therefore speak well of Love . . .

Chaucer did well to choose the English daisy *(Bellis perennis),* a member of the aster family, a flower with small white or pink rays and yellow disks. This particular daisy is also a relative of the chrysanthemum and of the wild aster which blooms on September 29, the day of the Archangel Michael. Chaucer was not referring to the Queen Marguerite daisy, white as a pearl of great price, which blooms on May Day. The daisy he ascribes to Alcestis, then, is a fall bloom associated with death and All Saints Day, festival of the dead in France where daisies, and chrysanthemums especially, are banned from the house and used only to adorn graves in cemeteries. Thus, Chaucer's choice affirms the subliminal connection between Alcestis and funereal Death.

The English poet Chaucer brought Alcestis's legend down almost to the end of the Middle Ages and established the context: All good women are they who die for Love. They are Cupid's saints and attendants who dying meekly become martyrs too, just like the Christian saints. Such a faithful woman, true to her man unto death, shone like clarity and very light in an otherwise dark world. She follows her god, who is Cupid, all the way to Hell, we are to believe.

The poet and god Apollo was, we know, the original harp upon which her memory was strummed. Queen Alcestis was in her person *The Guide and Sovereign Lady of the World,* Chaucer declared. All the old legends revered her. Queen Alcestis of Thessaly represented the Power of the Home.

Chaucer went on to celebrate other martyrs for love:

1. Cleopatra of Egypt (from Boccaccio's *De Casibus* and *De Claris Mulieribus*)

2. Thisbe of Babylon (from Ovid's *Metamorphoses*)

3. Dido (Astarte) of Carthage (from Virgil's *Aeneid* and Ovid's *Heroides*)

4. Hypsipyle of Lemnos (from Apollonius of Rhodes's *Argonautica*)

5. Lucretia (Lucrece) of Rome (c. 578 B.C., from Livy's *Histories*)

6. Ariadne of Crete (from Ovid's *Metamorphoses* and *Heroides*)

7. Philomela of Attica, or Thrace (from Ovid's *Metamorphoses*)

8. Phyllis of Rhodope (from Ovid's *Heroides*)

9. Hypermnestra of Greece or Egypt (from Ovid's *Heroides*)

Although some scholars have thought Chaucer must have been sarcastic when he claimed that Alcestis and her saintly followers were martyrs, the majority have overthrown this view and take the poet's claim seriously.

CHAUCER'S QUEEN CLEOPATRA

Queen Cleopatra of Egypt (69–30 B.C.) is one good woman in Chaucer's *Legend* easily recognized as historical. The case of Lucretia is less solid. The other seven, whose lives he touches, are all primarily mythological and/or legendary.

As Chaucer says (v. 580 ff.), this martyred Queen Cleopatra was born in Egypt (69 B.C.) to Ptolemy XI, who died in the Alexandrine War. She was married at age seventeen to her younger brother, Ptolemy XII, and later to another brother, Ptolemy XIII. She then married Julius Caesar from Rome to whom she bore a son, Caesarion. After the battle of Philippi in 42 B.C. and the murder of Caesar in the Senate, she married his advocate Marc Antony. The latter had already been married twice previously, first to Fulvia, who died, and secondly to Octavia, sister of the Roman Emperor Augustus. Antony incautiously deserted Fulvia and fled to Egypt where he and Queen Cleopatra became lovers and allies against Rome.

History records that this queen could not, according to Plutarch, hold a candle to the beautiful Californian, Elizabeth Taylor, who played her in the movies. Plutarch celebrated Cleopatra because she was a consummate politician, a very ambitious ruler, possessed of considerable personal magnetism; but she was far from having the ravishing beauty she is credited with.

Chaucer dwells at considerable length upon their defeat in the battle of Actium (31 B.C.). Queen Cleopatra killed herself the following year after her defeat and Marc Antony's, first at Actium and then at Alexandria. Their fleet was bested, reports Chaucer, because the enemy positioned themselves so as to keep the sun at their backs and not in their faces. The poet also reported correctly about the use of cannon, boulders as weapons, grapnels, cutting hooks to shear cordage, spears, dried peas spread on the decks to make them slippery, and pitch (or grease) on other decks, plus burning oil. The Queen hoisted her famous royal purple sail as she fled southwards from Greece to Alexandria. She had a mausoleum or shrine constructed for Marc Antony's body and decorated it with such gems as rubies. Spices were used profusely to embalm his body richly. She then staunchly descended into a snake pit and died there from the venomous bites of adders.

Chaucer contradicted history when he found Cleopatra as fair as "the rose in May" (v. 613). He knew that Marc Antony and his Egyptian queen were defeated by the same Octavian, or Augustus Caesar, whose sister Marc Antony had abandoned in Rome. Marc Antony, said Chaucer, went out of his head because of his military defeat and stabbed himself through the heart. Cleopatra, being a good woman and martyr, refused to live another day.

She made a covenant (v. 688), that Antony would never, night or day, be out of her remembrance, that she would feel what he felt, life or death. There never was, added Chaucer, unto love a more faithful queen (v. 695). . . . And so she went naked down into the snake pit where the adders stung her to death.

For love of Antony, who was "so dere" (v. 701), she died. Such women, in Chaucer's view, which is around the turn of the century in 1400, were as good as Christian saints. In fact, he says in his story of the Roman matron Lucrece (Lucretia) that wide as is the land of Israel even Christ Himself could not have found greater faithfulness than in such a woman (v. 1879 ff.). As for men, he added, see how they flaunt their ugly tyranny!

SHAKESPEARE'S GOOD WOMAN LUCRECE

In his poem *The Rape of Lucrece* (1594) William Shakespeare tells a terrible story of a good woman:

General Collatine unwisely, wrote Shakespeare, and publicly, before army officers, vaunted the peerless beauty of his daisy-faced wife, Lucrece (Lucretia). For pinkness she was a rose, and lily-white for virtue, was this Roman matron Lucrece.

But neither honor nor beauty can enclose a wife like Lucrece safely within a fortress. Beauty will draw men's eyes to her, and envy will light fires in men's hearts. Collatine bragged unwisely, said Shakespeare, around the campfire at night, on campaign.

Thus, an earthly saint of a woman was pitted against a devilish man—a dove (v. 360) versus a night owl. And the gentle dove stood high above such a man, being herself higher than him, and daughter of Roman patricians.

The Etruscan tyrant Tarquin was the owl who pawned honor for sex. He was obviously "brain-sick" with "rude desire" (v. 175), says our poet.

Tarquin took a torch. He forced her to yield. Conscience could not stop him.

The matron Lucrece was in bed, her cheek on her hand. At night her pretty eyes closed like marigold petals. She lay under a green coverlet (v. 386). Her golden hair lifted at each breath. He saw her blue veins, her coral lips, her dimpled chin. He loomed like some grim lion over prey (v. 421). She awakened and struggled to understand what was happening.

He said she had seduced him.

He warned her to lie still. If she struggled, he said, he would rape her anyway but then kill a slave and place him so her household would see the slave lying on top of her (v. 512 ff.). If she kept quiet, he would not make her husband a laughingstock or her children bastards.

The matron pleaded with him like a doe in a wilderness where there are no laws to protect a matron (v. 544). She appealed to the gods, his knightly rank, his gentlemanliness, their friendship, the laws of hospitality, her weakness, her tears, his princely hopes. He finally stuffed her mouth with the bedclothes and raped her.

Immediately afterward this lord of Rome felt disgust and nausea. He was afraid that "through the length of time" he would be disgraced (v. 718). He asked her how she was.

"I have become a living dead," she replied. Tarquin then stole out of her palace on tiptoe like any mongrel dog (v. 736).

With her fingernails Lucrece ripped and tore her flesh until the blood ran. She beat her breasts with her fists. She was frantic with self-hatred and grief. Growing breathless with pain, she apostrophized Night (v. 764 ff.). Can Night hide disgrace? No way, she cried, for even illiterates centuries hence will hear of how Tarquin polluted Lucrece like a drone in summer hunting for honey, like some "wandering wasp . . . that sucked on her" (v. 836 ff.).

He was more like a nasty worm burrowing inside the tender bud of a flower. He was even more like the ungainly cuckoo, greedy and hateful giant hatchling, that emerges in a little sparrow's nest, more like a poisonous toad polluting a clear spring, a disgrace among kings, a weed among flowers, a profligate son of a weakling father, an adder hissing when sweet birds sing.

Then she apostrophized Opportunity, that slave to Time (v. 939 for some 60vv. of tirade), who catches wandering souls, who makes Vestal Virgins break their vows of priesthood, who encourages drunkards, who stifles honesty, kills marriages, sows scandals, breeds wrath, envy, treason, rape, and murder. Then she apostrophized Time, calling for punishment to fall upon Tarquin: "Let him have time" enough to suffer (v. 981 ff.)!

My case, she concluded, *is past the help of law* (v. 1022).

Thus, Lucrece told herself: "For me, I am the mistress now of my own fate" . . . (v. 1069).

"My tongue shall utter all" (v. 1076). There is no remedy for me, and no excuse.

Therefore I shall tell of the abuse I have suffered, she decides. I shall not allow my husband to be tainted. Nor shall I allow Tarquin and the world to call my children bastards.

She felt herself fallen down into the pit of hell, into the deep trench of unalterable sorrow. She was like the Greek heroine Philomela who, when raped, turned herself into a nightingale or mockingbird that sings querulously night and day and avoids proximity to people.

When men become beasts, she believes, then only beasts feel grief for the doe who dies like a hunted woman.

Only my body has been polluted, Lucrece decided, and not my soul. Therefore she must peel her body off as if it were the rotten bark of a tree. Tarquin has spotted her body and spoiled it forever.

She will hereby bequeath her blood to Tarquin. She will put her body to the knife. Let her husband kill Tarquin.

Then Lucrece wrote a note to her husband and had it sent to his bivouac. She requested him urgently to come to her. While she awaited his arrival, she studied a painting she had in her chamber. It depicted the rape of Helen of Troy and the ensuing siege and fall of the great citadel.

Her husband and his officers arrived to find the Roman matron Lucrece clad all in black mourning and bathed in tears. He threatened to rape me, she said, and blame it on a groom he would then kill and place in my arms for all to see. Otherwise, he advised me to lie still and let myself be raped. Lucrece then asked all present to swear revenge before she named the rapist. They swore before she complied: It was our King Tarquin.

Then Lucrece raised her knife and stabbed herself so deeply that the blood gushed out on both sides of her body. Her father rushed to cover her body. Her husband knelt, dipped his hands, and bathed his face in her blood. Each man present swore she was his own: daughter, wife, sister, and all to him.

Noble Brutus said she should have slain Tarquin, and not herself:

> Thy wretched wife mistook the matter so,
> To slay herself, that should have slain her foe.
>   (v. 1826)

Brutus then calmly evaluated the situation: (1) the Capitol is disgraced, (2) the Roman gods are disgraced, and (3) Rome herself is disgraced.

Lucrece's body was carried through Rome for all to see. As for Tarquin, he was banished forever from the State.

Shakespeare strangely does not narrate the consequences of this crime, which forms Roman prehistory: Because of Lucrece's act of reprisal, the Etruscan kings were dethroned and their reigns ended. The Roman Republic was then established, to govern by elected Consuls who ruled and presided over the Senators.

Thus, due to a woman's sacrifice of her life, the long struggle for political representation in Rome commenced. Up until that time the only right of the common people, the plebeians, had been to serve as foot soldiers in Roman armies.

In sacrificing her own life, Lucrece was found by later Roman historians to have abided by the principal beliefs of their Roman civilization because she placed devotion to husband and children first. Second, she managed, by her handling of the situation, to preserve their family honor and her husband's family gods (penates) whom she as his wife was bound by law to worship exclusively after marriage. She also preserved from taint her patrician class.

Her procedure of arguing the case aloud to herself was the strictly Roman obligation of "right reason." Romans agreed with her: *"Mors ultima ratio"* (Death is the ultimate recourse). Thus, the Roman matron Lucretia and the Greek or Thessalian matron Alcestis became "Guides" for all women to copy forevermore.

Contradictions: Fitzgerald. Tolstoy

Thus far, we have seen the story of Alcestis and the other good women set forth in tragedy and in narrative verse. In 1767 the operatic composer C. W. von Gluck turned again to Alcestis as he laid forth the first theory for the grand opera to come. He had already composed a first opera, *Orfeo ed Euridice* in which a first heroine descended into the Underworld. For the first time, in *Alcestis* of 1767, Gluck made history with his overture, which set the mood for his lyric music. Suddenly upon the operatic stage the heroine Alcestis moved stage center in Act I as she volunteered to descend into Hell. She called out to the gods below earth in one of grand opera's most solemn scenes. One might argue that, in the person of this heroine, grand opera was created.

If tragedy died, then grand opera took its place as a series of tragic heroines, like Giuseppe Verdi's Aïda and Giacomo Puccini's Madama Butterfly, followed Alceste upon the boards. Another hundred years would demonstrate how the prose novel would rival grand opera in tragic and comic heroines easily available to masses of people who could not and cannot afford to attend operas.

Under her French name of Daisy, the heroine Alcestis becomes the beautiful Marguerite in *Faust* of Charles Gounod, Paris, 1857, and at the Metropolitan Opera in New York in 1883. In Act II she is the innocent girl exclaiming at her beauty in the mirror (of death). She is seduced and abandoned by Faust, and she dies in Act IV as she sings the immortal prayer to the angels whom she implores to bear her soul to heaven:

Anges purs, anges radieux,—
Portez mon âme au sein des cieux!

By 1925 both American men and women were being satirized and portrayed as careless, depraved, drunken, immoral, and faithless wastrels—from Hollywood to Long Island. Ironically the heroine of F. Scott Fitzgerald's most successful and best-known novel, *The Great Gatsby,* is named Daisy. This heroine could hardly be more removed from Alcestis, whose name and flower she bears. With bitter irony, innuendo, and clever sarcasm Fitzgerald unmasked the murderous, profligate, American society of the Roaring Twenties that followed the massacres of the First World War, in which he had served. Here his heroine Daisy has fallen absolutely from her ancient high repute as "Guide" and model for all good women. The wealthy, dark, cheating society she typifies lies halfway between the Atlantic Ocean and an ash heap.

Americans might well suppose that our age everywhere had set upon the vilification of young women except that the greatest master of world fiction had already portrayed one of the first of truly modern women, a dynamo of this or any century: Princess Maria Bolkonsky. Count Leo Tolstoy's *War and Peace (Voina i mir)* was written between 1864 and 1869, and was at least partially translated and readily available. His is a celebrated portrayal of a modern woman.

Tolstoy began his portrayal of Princess Maria as she was in 1805. Then she lived at home, a schoolgirl still being laboriously taught by her dictatorial father, whom she tended and loved until his death. The old prince died just as Napoleon Bonaparte and his victorious armies arrived at the Bolkonsky estate of Bald Hills. Maria's father sternly advised his daughter that the study of math would keep her from being silly "like all other women" (vol. I, p. 99 ff.). The young princess had already discovered that her low-church Christian religion would be the abiding consolation of her life. She condemned the approaching war.

Princess Maria's life parallels the catastrophic defeat suffered by Russia at Austerlitz, November 16–19, 1805. At the same time she discovered the treachery of her beloved fiancé, Anatole. She had wanted to marry him; despite her old father's warning, she had no intention of remaining an old maid forever. The sight of her beloved

Anatole making love to her own lady-in-waiting came as a great shock to the Princess. For some time thereafter she thought that religion was to be her only life. She thought that she would have to be satisfied to bring up her orphaned nephew. She therefore adopted the itinerant priestess Pelageya.

Maria provided for her especial protégée, whom she treated with all cordiality and familiarity. This preacheress is the Pilgrim Pelageya. This woman roams the countryside performing miracles of comfort and healing. Princess Maria housed, entertained, and funded these Friends, as Tolstoy continued to do until they were settled in Canada. It is a great honor for Tolstoy to place his definitions of war and peace into the mouths of these Quakers. Most historical novelists are stumped to define peace. Maria and Pelageya say that war goes on during God's daylight. It is obvious what it is. Silent catacombs of prayer and meditation are peace, therefore, let us descend into the depths.

Throughout the ensuing French invasion of Russia, Princess Maria bore the burden of raising the orphaned prince, of enduring her father's advancing senility and harsh despotism, of counseling her warrior brother and his friends, and of supporting her itinerant missionaries. Her father suffered his final stroke on the day of the battle of Borodino.

The day the French were less than seventy miles from Bald Hills Princess Maria offered her stores and her estate to her peasants. This young woman rose to command and administer the largest estate and greatest fortune in all Russia. Even then, she found the time to dress in her white gown of a priestess, as her father begged her to do. Therefore the dying man slipped into death with the joy of looking at his beloved and capable daughter. This young heroine, in a sense, has inherited Russia.

After the defeat of Napoleon, Maria wed the veteran and bankrupt Count Rostov. She assisted him in repairing his fortune, and they lived happily in marriage. In fact, he considered her "an angel." He saw only her "great moral beauty." Maria told him that love is life itself: Only love hinders death, she says.

This long drawing of the Princess Maria by Tolstoy contributed in no small part to making him the world's foremost novelist. Cynicism and misogyny do not take an author very far. His portrait of Princess Maria gives us his idea of what a young woman can become and what she can do in a lifetime. Readers may prefer Natasha Rostov to Maria, and that is their right, of course; but Tolstoy apparently thought that Natasha did not live up to her potential. Maria became a mother, a foster-mother, a wife, and an executive. She managed both a rich private life and a profitable career.

In such authors as Count Tolstoy the twentieth century laid to rest the ancient idea of a good woman as one who dies for her husband and who, in so doing, abandons her little children.

•READINGS•

EURIPIDES

For a recent translation, by Edward P. Coleridge, of *Alcestis* see the encyclopedia series, *Great Books of the Western World*. Vol. I (Chicago, 1952), pp. 237–247.

See, for an interlinear translation into French, *Euripide*. Vol. I. Translated and edited by Louis Méridier (Paris, 1961), pp. 56–102.

See *Euripides and the Spirit of His Dramas*. Paul Decharme. Translated by James Loeb (New York, 1906; Port Washington, N.Y., 1968), especially p. 211 where in footnote 1 Decharme quotes Plato's *Symposium:* "Alcestis is the wonder of mankind . . ."

CHAUCER

The Works of Geoffrey Chaucer. Edited by F. N. Robinson (Cambridge, Mass., 1933). See "The Legend of Good Women," pp. 480–518, and notes, pp. 839–854.

SHAKESPEARE

The Works of William Shakespeare. Oxford University Press (New York, 1938), pp. 1207–1224. I have preferred the Oxford Standard Edition, *The Complete Works of William Shakespeare*. Edited with a glossary by W. J. Craig of Trinity College, Dublin. See *The Rape of Lucrece*, pp. 1259–1280.

(It was the recommended text used at the University of Vermont by a celebrated Shakespeare scholar, Professor Frederick J. Tupper, and sold there in 1937 for $1.00. The verses are numbered in this earlier edition.)

Operas

See *The Metropolitan Opera: Stories of Great Operas,* by John W. Freeman, associate editor of the Metropolitan *Opera News.* W. W. Norton (New York, 1984).

Fitzgerald, F. Scott. *The Great Gatsby.* Charles Scribner's Sons (New York, 1925), 182 pp.

Tolstoy, L. N. *War and Peace.* 2 vols. Translated by Rosemary Edmonds. Penguin Books (Baltimore, 1957).

CHAPTER II

Lovers and Demon Lovers

STAR-CROSSED LOVERS

There have been many star-crossed lovers. Two of the most famous in the Middle Ages were Tristan and Isolde, who lived in Great Britain long before Shakespeare coined the phrase "star-crossed lovers." Others include:

1. *Orfeo ed Euridice* (Austrian opera of 1762),
2. *Paul et Virginie* (French novel, or pastoral idyll of 1787),
3. *Romeo and Juliet* (Shakespeare play of c. 1596, and French opera of 1867),
4. *Samson et Dalila* (French opera of 1877, from Judges 13–16), and
5. *Pelléas et Mélisande* (Belgian drama of 1892, and French opera first produced in 1902).

In each case one lover or both lovers die, but the heroine in each duo always dies in some sort of comedy of errors. Eurydice turns to look backwards into hell, and this triggers her relapse. Virginie so clings to her virginal modesty that she refuses to disrobe and swim when the ship sinks in plain sight of America, and so drowns. Isolde loses her protecting lover, Tristan, and returns to the wintry arms of her aged husband, where the first frost will kill her, if the old king's wrath does not sentence her again to torture and execution. Romeo and Juliet, in their youth and passion, kill themselves by mistake. In *Samson and Dalila* Samson kills worshippers when he tears down the temple. Historically speaking, it appears that heroines are unlucky in love, whether it is passionate or not.

The legend of Tristan and Isolde (Yseut, Isolt, Iseut, Isoud, Essylt) seems to have originated among the ancient Pictish peoples of eastern Ireland, whence the lovers move to another ancient Pictish kingdom in southwestern Scotland, home of the Nith-River or Niduari Picts. The reader is about to fall into a web of ambiguity.

The oldest text of Tristan and Isolde by Béroul specifies Dumfries in Scotland as home of Isolde's husband King Mark (from the Latin Marcus) and his realm as west of the River Nith, ergo contiguous to King Arthur's realm east of that river and called the "Lowlands of Scotland" then as well as now. The presence of King Arthur and Gawain in this Isolde legend would give us a date *ad quem* of A.D. 542. By the death of Saint Columba, who had by 597 united Picts and Scots, the ancient world had ended and the Middle Ages begun throughout Great Britain as well.

Thus, Tristan and Isolde are both royal personages from one of the world's oldest and most archaic cultures: Pictish and Celtic Ireland. That island remained pristine, untouched by the five-hundred-year Roman occupation of Britain, long ended by A.D. 500, except for certain Roman aristocrats and autonomous landowners like King Arthur and King Mark whose families had preferred to stay in Britain.

But nothing else is clear in this "love" story. Every reader must accept that we will never know. The story remains forever mysterious, just like life itself.

The French historian Alexandre Bertrand, writing a history of the Celtic Gauls (Paris, 1897), believed that Gaul also would have been another Ireland if it had not been totally crushed by the fiercest Roman invasion and permanent occupation. Gaul too, Bertrand decided (p. 313), would have remained faithful to Druidism, which celebrated sacred fire (Isolde), adoration of the sun (Tristan), worship of holy wells and springs, reverence for sacred stones (Stonehenge and Carnac), fountains, lakes, mountains, and rivers like the Nith at and below Dumfries, Scotland. Only Celtic literature mentions worshipping at such sites and embraces megalithic monuments. Only Isolde in western Europe is notably a fire-walking priestess. But Tristan belonged to a long line of classical and medieval solar heroes. He was a harpist, a musician like the original sun god, Apollo.

We see Isolde's fire ceremony as a magical and priestly charm for making spring sunshine return to warm a cold, northern land. By holding fire in her hand Isolde awakens the sun god from his long, wintry sleep. She performs the annual, Celtic vernal festival of fire, says the Scot Sir James Fraser in *The Golden Bough* (12 volumes, 1890–1915). The priestess doubtless performs, he added, on a day of the full moon, around the thirteenth day of April, when the sun crosses the equator on its path into the northern hemisphere again.

Like King Arthur's Queen Guinevere, called the "serpent with the golden head," Queen Isolde, the golden maid of Ireland, is so wedded to both summer (Tristan) and winter (King Mark) that she must be ritually purified twice a year, thus proving her virginity. Other Ossianic literature of ancient Scotland attests to such ceremonies by fire or fiery mantles which harm all except the sacred priestess. Isolde dreams of two lions (kings), and she wears the hair shirt of a holy person. Opposite the "white goddess" Isolde, we have her aged husband Mark who resembled Eire's even more ancient King Labraid Longsech because he too had horse's ears. In Gaelic Mark's name is *marach* (horse and rider), or centaur.

Isolde and Tristan are the original star-crossed lovers. Their story, as told in Scotland, Norway, France, and Germany, is perhaps the most famous love story in the world. Only that of Prince Paris and Helen of Troy would have been greater, but no one has ever told it. Tristan and Isolde enchanted and attracted eight or nine of the great writers of the Middle Ages. The following account treats only the high points of their story, which it interprets as it unfolds. The reason the interpretation is necessary as one proceeds here is that the Old French has been widely misinterpreted.

The reader may find a list of translations into English in the Readings at the end of this chapter.

THE LOVE STORY OF TRISTAN AND ISOLDE

King Mark of Scotland never trusted his young queen, Isolde, one of whose golden hairs a swallow had brought him from Ireland. That was a sign from heaven, as it were, that the then Princess Isolde, daughter of Queen Isolde of Ireland, was fated to be his long-sought bride. The golden girl was to have been wooed, won, and fetched for King Mark by his heir and nephew, Tristan.

There were two reasons, and both were explicitly proclaimed, why the hero Tristan in person was to act as King Mark's deputy, messenger, and ambassador with powers plenipotentiary. First, the young hero had already rid the kingdom, Ireland, of the giant Morholt, who had collected an annual tribute of a long ton of copper, gold, and silver, plus three hundred boys and girls who had just turned thirteen. Second, he had been healed by Queen Isolde of Ireland when she found him adrift after a shipwreck upon the Irish Sea. Then she had heard heavenly harps playing in honor of Tristan, the harpist.

Princess Isolde was fairly won, fairly given, and she wept fairly for herself who had no word in the negotiation, as the ship put out to sea that bore her, Prince Tristan, and the maid Brangane into the Pictish kingdom of Dumnonia. It was hot as they sailed east. Ireland dropped below the western horizon. Running out of tears, the princess asked for a drink. She knew her mother had prepared a flagon for the voyage.

Once at sea, the princess took the vessel and poured herself a drink from the liquid inside. She poured herself a drink, we are to know, and then poured one for Tristan. Afterwards she sometimes said, when she was sobbing bitterly and refusing to take any blame in the matter, and considering the misfortune that ensued, that Brangane knowingly handed them the philter.

It came out later that the Queen Mother of Ireland had prepared a philter, or a drug, called aphrodisiac because it arouses the young to the passionate worship of Aphrodite, goddess of Love and Beauty. This philter, or potion, provoked princess and hero also to suffer the sharp excitements of desire. They fell madly in love, we are to understand, which means Tristan became a great hunter of Venus, of Isolde, and of deer in the forest also.

For the two days of their passage each royal personage eyed the other, and shook and trembled, and burned. Before their vessel entered the harbor of King Mark's kingdom, they admitted before Brangane that theirs was a passionate love synonymous with the desire for death. Each knew that they were bound by a deathless love for which there could be no antidote or solution.

King Mark welcomed the pair, wedded the princess, made her his queen, thanked and rewarded Tristan, his nephew whom he had fostered to become his heir and successor upon his throne.

Love, however, cannot be hidden, especially at court where the sufferers pass close to each other day after day, where eyes meet and speak silent volumes, where fingers touch accidentally, where tears run down Isolde's cheeks at the sight of Tristan, and he stands redfaced, mutely agonized before her.

Such love, Béroul explained, drives a dying, wounded stag to the brook for one last sip of cool water. Such love drives the starving falcon to fold his wings and plunge through the air upon his fluttering prey. The red blood of Tristan and of Isolde fermented like new wine in a cask. Tristan's many rivals, who hoped one day to slit his throat and inherit the realm, observed all of this and stalked the lovers, all the while comparing notes, gossiping, and hoping to catch them *in flagrante delicto*.

Their enemies hoped to catch them under the pine tree, where the Irish hero Cuchulain, Charlemagne's nephew, and the hero Roland had all died. In summarizing the dangerous history of the pine tree, the author attempts to alert the hero that death lies in wait for the unwary. If Tristan is to meet Isolde in an "orchard" near a "spring" of cool bubbling water, beside an open, grassy knoll, he will also find his killer standing in ambush. This type of narration longs for the *stilus gravis,* the *solemn epic style,* which is better adapted to war and deaths of warriors and queens.

Behind King Mark's castle, which was called "Tintagel,"* stretched an enclosed orchard, Love's *hortus conclusus,* where priceless, noble maidens were permitted occasionally to stroll and take the air. Such was the splendid Roman garden which Julius Caesar willed to the Roman public as a park. Queen Isolde was allowed the use of King Mark's fenced garden surrounded by tall sharp stakes protecting fruit trees and grape arbors. Outside this palisaded safety zone rose a splendid fir tree with massive, dark, overhanging boughs. Beneath its trunk a crystal spring bubbled into a marble pool whence it overflowed into a brook. The current passed down the channel through the orchard and then alongside the women's quarters.

It was Tristan's custom evenings to cut twigs and with his knife cut messages in the ancient Ogham alphabet upon them:

B L F S   N H D T C   Q M G NG Z   R   A O U E I

He then floated the messages downstream to Queen Isolde who was thus informed of his whereabouts. She would then ask to meet him under the pine tree at a specified hour.

Thus, the sun-faced Irish god, Ogma Grianainech, who gave his Ogham alphabet to his people, smiled upon the sun-faced Tristan and his golden, secret sweetheart. Both lovers knew, of course, that their enchanted garden retreat afforded only the illusory safety of branches and palisaded fence. But Tristan also comforted the queen with the memory of Eire (Ireland) into which each would one day repair again to enjoy its fortunate isle forever safe inside the marble walls and

---

*The castle "Tintagel" of King Mark must not be confused with Tintagel in Cornwall, which is set atop a stony headland beaten upon by the sea. Tristan and Isolde furthermore could not have lived here, for the Cornish castle was not built until a thousand years after their deaths.

candlelit halls of the land whence no mortal returns except on Hallowe'en. Each lover understood how Tristan had already proved this by having passed from deadly wounds to health because he dared tread heroically upon the Here and the Hereafter, as she also had thus far done with impunity. The courses of their lives had been foretold at their birth hours by the learned astronomers of Ireland in their high, round towers.

On one such night, King Mark left his horse at the base of the towering pine, and clutching his bow and arrows with which he hoped to slay the guilty lovers, he climbed up in the dark branches overhead. It was a clear, moonlit night. The king had no difficulty identifying the slender hero who leaped the palisade, who then stooped to drop his Ogham twigs into the spring water. King Mark could even make them out as they bobbed, circled, and floated on down the little brook. But, as Tristan bent, still leaning over the silvery basin, he too saw, not the face of death which would have been his own, but the image of the king clearly portrayed in beneficent waters.

Motionless, Tristan heard the arrow fitted to the bow over his head. Still as death he listened intently. Yes, he heard her soft step. Isolde was coming to him across the still garden path. No! All was silent suddenly as the grave. She must have halted. What could have alerted her?

Isolde had sensed the danger, as a woman will. She felt the king's presence even before she saw his shadow. Carefully she stood still, barely breathing and forced herself to look only downward, at the dark garden borders. After a silent prayer and another admonition to herself, Isolde called out in a ringing voice: "What are you thinking of, Tristan, to call me to the garden in the dark of night? What is it you could possibly want of me, at this hour? Does the king think ill of us? I swear to God that we are innocent! May I be blasted if I lie!"

And so Isolde managed to deceive King Mark.

Servants, jesters, fools, and eventually his barons urged King Mark to put a tight surveillance upon the young queen, who they were certain was guilty of adultery with Tristan. The lovers were almost caught time after time as pits were dug for them by all and sundry. Once the barons set them up by persuading the king to send Tristan with dispatches to Carlisle, which was King Arthur's walled citadel where he often resided between campaigns. The barons figured that during the night Tristan would attempt to cross into Isolde's sleeping quarters to warn her of his imminent departure.

King Mark strewed flour on the chamber floors so that any person approaching the queen's bed would leave his footprints for all to see. Her bed was about a spear's length away. She too would leave footprints were she so hot with passion that she crept toward Tristan's bed. Then after the middle of the night had passed, the king crept out of the chambers. No sooner had he disappeared than Tristan rose from bed, and measuring the distance by memory, leaped across to the queen's bed. He had already returned safely, or so he thought, when in rushed King Mark.

There were no footprints on the floor, but there was a path of blood which had dripped from a wound on Tristan's leg. There was blood on the floor, on his bed, and on hers.

Tristan was bound and trussed up for execution next day. He threatened to kill any person who dared accuse the queen. By dawn a crowd of persons high and low had gathered in the streets around the citadel. The learned members of the court begged the king not to execute Tristan without due process of law, but King Mark wanted immediate revenge. He could barely wait for daylight.

The morning light found Tristan weeping and ignominiously tied up with ropes, and the queen offering to die in his place. When the king's officer saw the great hero tied up and humiliated, he cut the ropes at once. Tristan thanked him courteously and requested that he be allowed to slip into the small chantry, which was a replica of the chapel (cappella) of Saint Martin of Tours, France, where the revered saint's cloak (cappa, cappella) had been deposited. Tristan wished to pray there before his death. The king's officer allowed him to do this.

Tristan entered the sanctuary quietly, but very glad at heart that he now had a chance at least to avoid a disgraceful end upon a funeral pyre. Once in the chantry, he said his prayers, and then quickly ascended the single altar to the small window in the apse. Strong as he was, Tristan burst the window open easily. He climbed upon the sill, looked down the chantry wall, and leaped. He thought he would break his neck on the rocks below, but God upheld his cloak, doubtless in memory of the late Saint Martin (c. 316–397), whose feast day it was: Martinmas, November 11.

The fate of the lecherous Queen Isolde, who caused the noble Tristan to fall from his high estate and leap in chamber and chapel, was still to be decided.

One hundred lepers crawled from their hovels and crowded into the king's court. Their swollen faces were pitted, scarred, and scabbed. Some suffered from decay of their hands and feet and hobbled on crutches or crawled and croaked from agonized throats. Many were blinded because of red and swollen eyelids. They clamored to wreak vengeance upon the beautiful, richly clad queen who stared down at them. With Tristan gone, she had none but her female attendants to defend her. The poor lepers tried to rub the pus from their open sores on the lady. They claimed that their disease had made them furious with sexual desire. They panted to make her share their agony. They resented her youth, her splendid health, her proud demeanor, her cool behavior, and her clear, fearless eyes.

Down below her throne, the lepers moaned and tried to reach her. They stripped off their rags and showed her their suppurating lesions, their fingerless stumps, their skeletal ribs, their rotting bodies covered with nodes. If she felt pity for them, the queen looked down in silence and showed no feeling. Even if Tristan had been present, he would not have harmed them because great warriors never stoop to dishonorable combat.

Tristan was clever and infiltrated King Mark's citadel. With his

squire's aid he crept to the post to which Isolde had been tied upright.
He caught a glimpse of her poor, fallen head with the rope cutting
into her delicate neck. He quietly severed the cords which held her
upright. As he cut each loop he and the squire whispered to her and
gathered the poor, drooping girl in their arms. At first they had to
carry her through the halls where courtiers slept and snored. Then as
the blood started circulating in her numb limbs, they urged her on
faster and faster. All three took deep breaths of cold, fresh air, picked
up speed, and ran as fast as their young legs could carry them.

They didn't stop until they were in the deep cover of the forest.
They then stopped to get their bearings and settled down to a steady
pace that would cover the miles easily. Before dawn they were far into
the woods. As soon as it was daylight Tristan and the squire, Gover-
nal, cut branches and wove a bower for Isolde. They made a tiny
treehouse for her, with sweet ferns and bracken for a bed inside, and
mint from a brookside for her pillow. They spread one cape to
cushion her bedding and another to cover her tired body, and comforted her with soft words until she dropped off into a deep sleep. As
soon as her breathing became even and unlabored, the two stole away
to hunt game and gather nuts and apples for her dinner. Both were
skilled woodsmen, taught from earliest boyhood how to survive and
live off the land in great ease and comfort—and in total security. They
had learned from the hard teachers of their boyhood where they
could hide, the deep caves where they could take shelter in inclement
weather. They wouldn't set foot out of doors, or travel, without yards
of heavy camouflage tartan folded over shoulder and strapped to their
belt. Both were always well armed and bred up to the life of a true
forester, woodsmen at heart.

For her part, Queen Isolde, an Irish queen's daughter and king's
daughter, had also been brought up from babyhood to suffer stoically,
never to show the white feather, always to maintain the calm, dignified, and hopeful demeanor of a truly admirable woman. Thus, even
when tied to the post, trussed up like any criminal in full view of

censorious courtiers, Isolde drew upon her training to maintain her proud confidence in herself as a superior person equal to circumstance. Alone, far from home, unjustly accused, subjected to dire threats of personal degradation and lingering death, her girl's body subjected to filth, abuse, and injury, she bore it all without a tear or whimper. It was a relief to breathe forest perfumes, to walk on the soft forest floor, to be free among the dark, vaulted aisles where birds' stirring were the only sounds under the cool wind and rustling leaves.

The three began a new life inside the paradise of the "Morris" Forest, a woodland famous from Roman antiquity and the Roman legions and Roman commanders who a few centuries gone by had passed through and named it for the royal tribe of Celts who lived thereabouts: *nemus caledonium,* the Caledonian Forest of southern Scotland. The French translators modified the old Gaelic terminology only slightly:

Old Irish *mor* = great, and by extension, famous,

+

ros (rois) = "wooded" promontory in the ancient Gaelic of South Ireland, or "wood" itself, as *"promontorium nemerosum"*

The promontory here is the Rhinns (Promontories) of Galloway. *Morrois* is the famous Caledonian Forest, also of southern Scotland. The wooded promontory where the three fugitives sought refuge probably referred to this celebrated forest near the ancient and modern royal burg of Dumfries. The place name Dumfries (*dum* or *dunn* meaning fortress) occurs in French texts as the seat and residence of King Mark, whose citadel is called "Tintagel" (Dunn Dagel), its name repeated by the celebrated, later fortress now in ruins in Cornwall. The Latin *nemus* specifies that our heroine lived for a long time in a special type of forest: a wood with open glades.

. . .

Through the long summer Tristan and Isolde lived like Adam and Eve in Paradise. They were warmed by the sun, cooled by the fresh breezes, charmed by the perfume of flowers, delighted by the sweet taste of wild berries and the flavor of wild honey. The two woodsmen found pools where Isolde could freely bathe and play in waterfalls. They brought her fresh ferns for her bower, and Tristan, whose education had also consisted in imitating various bird calls of this Caledonian Forest, attracted rare birds to their bowers.

Only one sadness marred their happiness, and this was the words of the Christian hermit who also dwelled apart in the forest of penance and solitude. They paid their respects to this old holy man and told him their story. "You must repent," he advised both Tristan and Isolde. "Let me read you what our holy book commands."

Prince and queen both listened respectfully but came away unconvinced. Tristan refused to escort Isolde back to her revengeful master and the cruel death he had decreed for her. Isolde rejected Christian teachings and stubbornly preferred the ancient Druidical lore which had formed her and sent her there on her personal mission. On the other hand, both reserved the hermit and his counsel as a last recourse. For the moment, they failed to comprehend how either could be employed in any search for a definitive solution to their problems.

Tristan's greyhound caused a sudden upset which frightened both hero and heroine. Since puppyhood the dog had been Tristan's constant companion and closest friend. Before rescuing Isolde from the lepers, Tristan had hitched his dog securely to a stake and tied a block of wood to his collar so that even if somebody released him by accident, the dog could not travel far. Tristan had not counted on one of King Mark's keepers releasing the dog, freeing him from the block of wood, and ordering him to go get Tristan. Although the dog was much weakened from his long confinement and by his refusal to eat or drink most days, he still understood the keeper's command and loped off in the direction of the Caledonian Forest. Instead of whining and tugging at his ropes, he now stopped frequently to listen, and gave one long bark for Tristan. Then, not hearing an answer, he smelled the wind again and set off with every nerve alert for the scent of his master. It did not take him many days to find Tristan and arrive leaping and bounding for joy on his chest.

"You will have to kill him," the squire told Tristan. "He will lead them to us. Kill the dog, or we are lost."

Tristan realized that this was a serious problem. He could not refuse to sacrifice the dog, for Isolde's sake, and yet he loved his dog with all his heart. Tristan plunged deep into thought as he watched the dog make friends with their horse, examine their dwellings, and then softly approach Isolde herself. The greyhound stole closer and closer to the princess and seeing that she allowed him one familiarity after another, he gently licked her fingers. Finally he lay down quietly beside her, letting his master understand that the hound had assumed guardianship of Isolde from that moment forward.

"I couldn't kill this dog," Tristan told his squire. "What I must do is retrain him."

It took a long month for Tristan to teach the dog a new set of hunting instructions: never to bark, never to reveal his master's presence, to stalk game in utter silence, to mark the kill with grass or branches, to call his master without uttering a sound, and to hunt in absolute silence henceforth. Thus, the hunting dog added to their safety and their joy. The dog proved invaluable in deep snow or in the hard going of ice storms. It was the dog who found one of King Mark's foresters who had been bold enough to come prowling around their retreat. The squire silenced the forester, cut off his head, and hung it on the forest verge to swing there as a warning to others. The warning should have been understood as working both ways, for it rebounded upon Tristan and Isolde. One day Tristan returned weary from a long hunt. Under the warm sun of afternoon he lay down beside Isolde, carefully drawing his sword and laying the naked sword between them. The two fell asleep.

King Mark and his courtiers had set out that very day to celebrate May Day, which they knew not as Whitsuntide but as Beltane from the Gaelic *Bealltuinn*. This May Day, or first day of May, was always celebrated as a great Celtic/Druid Festival in honor of their god Belus (Baal). Fires were kindled that day on the mountain tops as a greeting and prayer to the returning sun god. Young folk congregated in the Highlands of Scotland, in the forest and moor. A ritual meal of custard and oatmeal cakes was prepared and eaten together. Tristan drew the unlucky piece of cake and was thus designated as the victim to be ritually sacrificed so that the coming harvest would be bountiful. Fortunately, because the kingdom could not pray to the sun god Baal and offer to sacrifice in his honor the solar hero Tristan, he was saved.

And so, on May Day, the lovers lay asleep in their bower with Tristan's drawn sword between them. The queen wore her gold ring set with emeralds, which King Mark had presented her on her wedding day. The lovers' lips did not meet and the drawn sword separated them.

Not a breath of wind disturbed their soft slumber. Silently one of King Mark's felons crept along the paths they had worn on the forest floor. Nearer and nearer he stalked them until his keen eyes separated their bower from the undergrowth and he saw them sleeping.

Like a snake unfolding, the villain turned and, careful not to break a branch or step on a dead leaf, he quickly fled. Breathless and panting from hatred and triumph he reported his discovery to King Mark. "I found them," he whispered in the king's ear. "They are not far away. In the Morrois Forest, asleep."

The king vowed revenge for the treachery of his beloved Tristan and for the adultery of his beautiful queen. Rising from his throne, where he had been hearing pleas, he called for his horse. With his spy leading the way, the king plunged from the meadow into the still darkness of the giant forest trees. Not a single bird sang, no creature darted from the underbrush before him. From time to time the king loosened his sword a bit in its scabbard, testing to be sure he could draw it out instantaneously. This day, he told himself, one of us will die a bloody death, either I or Tristan, my dear and beloved son of my House.

The foul traitor raised a hand in warning. "There," he said, and he pointed. Instantly the king dropped from his horse's back to the ground and crept towards the leafy bower. He let his rich cloak fall to the ground. He drew his sword as he crept closer and closer to the guilty pair. Without turning around, he waved the foul traitor away.

Not having disturbed their slumber, the king tiptoed along until, astonished, he loomed over them. They slept peacefully with slow, even breaths. There on the bed of leaves, but full length between the lovers, lay Tristan's sword. King Mark knew it well. That was the sword which he, as surrogate father and sponsor, had presented to Tristan the day of his investiture into knighthood.

The king saw at once that the pair were not lovers in any carnal sense for had they been lovers, Tristan would not have laid his sacred sword between them. Furthermore, this holy blade between them was a barrier he would never cross. The sword swore they were innocent of wrong-doing. The sword had served to guard her virginity. Their love was pure. They had fled because of the traitors at court. They had fled because King Mark and his heir had been pitted: the one old man against the youthful heir to his throne, like Prince Modred against King Arthur.

King Mark suddenly felt pity for the outcasts. They were, in truth, victims of an evil, worldly society. There in the savage wilds of the Caledonian Forest they had found more security, more peace, more tranquillity than among the ambitious savage hearts at King Mark's court. He felt relief that he had not slaughtered them both as they lay helpless before him.

All he could think to do, by way of reparation, was to draw off his glove and lay it on a branch so that it shaded Isolde's face from the ray of sunshine. He knew she would recognize the gloves she brought from Ireland when she first came to him as his bride.

He carefully slid the emerald ring from her thin finger and slipped on his own huge signet in its place, and then he raised up Tristan's sword and placed it in his scabbard, carefully laying his own sword in its place. He then wheeled and signalled his man to let loose his horse. Vaulting into the saddle, he shook his fist at the foul liar who had so unsettled him with his stupid allegations of adultery and promised him a speedy death for his pains. "Run as you can," he mouthed at him. "You are a dead man anyway."

Meanwhile, Queen Isolde was dreaming a vivid dream that she would always remember afterwards, and she woke up Tristan and told it to him immediately upon opening her eyes. She told him she had a vision of what her life is. She thought she was in a great, dark forest of the world. There were great trees over and around her. She was very afraid. She saw two powerful lions locked in mortal combat. She was so frightened she cried out, and it was her own alarmed scream that woke her up.

The two lions must have been two kings, she later understood, King Mark and the future King Tristan. The dark forest (Dante's *selva oscura*) is the world inhabited with savage politics and devouring men-beasts who deprive us of our wealth and leave us naked and fearful.

No sooner had she confided her dream than Isolde saw King Mark's large ring on her finger. At the same time she also saw his glove above her head. Tristan had already leaped to his feet at the sight of King Mark's sword. "We are betrayed," he cried. "Quickly, we must at once set out for the other side of the Forest and into another kingdom."

Passing by the Hermit's cell, Tristan began to feel considerable misgivings. He could no longer dismiss the Hermit's remonstrances. He realized that King Mark had undergone a softening which had led him to a change of heart. He still loved Tristan and appeared willing to take back Isolde and reinstate her as queen of his kingdom. When he had consigned Isolde to the hundred lepers, he had in effect authorized Tristan to rescue her and to safeguard her until further notice. His substitutions of ring and sword indicated his willingness to receive them both and make restitution for his suspicions and earlier judgments.

Also, the Laws of Rome condemned their exile together in the Caledonian Forest, as the Hermit had explained. This new religion also frowned upon priestesses, only recognizing women as maidens first and then as duly married wives expected to service their husband whenever and however he so commanded or desired. Tests for the continued virginity of Druid priestesses were, or soon would be, outlawed by Rome.

Furthermore, Queen Isolde did not thrive in the forest. She grew pale and wan and thin and her youth and beauty were being worn away. She needed to be restored to an easier life at court. She had been bred on silken cushions in tapestried halls with fireplaces large enough to house a troop of footsoldiers. She seemed to be pining away for a home and for her lady companions. She also saw that the king would never release his cold hold on her. Therefore Tristan prepared a contract for King Mark and left it by the path to his citadel. In this formal document he stipulated the terms by which he would restore Isolde to her lawful spouse. King Mark had his priest read it and rather than have Isolde return to her family in Ireland, the king agreed to Tristan's terms. He preferred to take her back rather than to fight Tristan, whom none of his champions had an earthly chance of defeating in combat. He sent word to Tristan.

The lovers agreed to part and enlisted the Hermit's assistance as a witness to the settlement. Isolde then gave Tristan her green jasper ring which in an emergency he could return as a token that whatever message he sent her was authentically his. Tristan reassured her that he would only pretend to leave the Forest and would hide until he saw that the safe return and reinstatement of all her honors had actually been effected.

King Mark broadcasted that the treaty would be ratified in three days' time at the Perilous Ford, to which citadel and famous site he instructed his vassals and his courtiers to come and assemble.

In tattered clothing Tristan escorted Queen Isolde, whom the Hermit had dressed in queenly dignity, up through the tents which Mark's vassals had pitched for the ceremony. He led her downhill from the citadel towards the swamp and white sands of the forest. King Mark greeted Isolde properly and had his Roman scarlet cloak of a royal commander thrown about her shoulders. He offered Tristan a princely compensation for his guardianship of the queen, but the princely hero refused it. He intended, he said, to take service under King Arthur of the Lowlands of Scotland. Peace between King Mark and his heir was announced. Tristan withdrew, but not to Carlisle. He went only a short distance away where, from a safe refuge, he could watch what would happen to Isolde, which turned out to be wise.

The politicians rebuked King Mark for his affection, more so for having accepted a runaway priestess-wife without testing her for virginity and for the veracity of her oaths. They decided that she must undergo the ordeal of fire. She would be stripped naked except for her shift, and be made to give away to the poor and to the lepers all of her earthly possessions. She would do this in plain view of the people, while she stood beside the burning firepot. Then she would walk forward for nine long paces while she held for all to see the red-hot iron in the palms of both her hands. God would then decide her guilt or her innocence. If she was not burned, she would be innocent of all charges. If she died, then it would be God's punishment for her corrupt behavior and adultery.

Queen Isolde agreed to do this only if King Arthur and his courtiers were sought from nearby Carlisle and requested to come bear witness to her ordeal by fire. Arthur would be asked to come to the Perilous Ford, which marks the demarcation line between his territory, the Lowlands of Scotland, and Dumfriesshire, or the Marches into Ireland to its west.

Queen Isolde's messenger reported this to Tristan and requested him to dress as a pilgrim and await the queen as she approached the marshlands adjacent to the Perilous Ford.

Everyone became nervous at the delay of seven days, for King Arthur was not in residence at Carlisle, but at his northeastern fortress of Stirling. He finally received Queen Isolde's request, to which he assented. King Arthur arrived at the White Sands seven days later to supervise the ordeal and bear witness that Isolde fulfilled her obligations as set forth in the treaty.

Tristan waited at the eastern bank where King Arthur's castle (now Caerlaverock) stood guard. Queen Isolde was rowed across the River Nith from the Dumfriesshire side to the western bank. She recognized Tristan and, rising in the boat, requested permission for the pilgrim to carry her through the mud of the riverbank to dry land up the shore. King Mark granted her plea. Tristan, disguised as a Jerusalem pilgrim, carried Isolde in his arms. "Now," she told him, "fall down upon this dry land with me under your body." Tristan appeared to stub his toe. He fell, with the queen under him. Courtiers rushed down to drive him away and lift up Her Majesty.

Then Queen Isolde proceeded to a rich, eastern cloth which had been spread upon the grass. On it were holy relics of the saints. King Arthur's retinue stood there as guards of honor over the holy bones. They bowed to the queen as she began to pull off her royal purple cloak, her gown, her jewels, her shoes, and her rings until she stood like a priestess clad only in her white slip, with the bare feet and legs of a holy woman.

Isolde looked at King Mark and swore her holy oath. "I swear," she said, "that no man has held me in his arms except my lord husband and this pilgrim who carried me today." Then she added the ritual words: "King Mark, do you accept this oath as legal?"

"God willing," replied King Mark.

"Amen," answered Isolde.

The crowd fell deathly silent to see her turn to the firepot where dried faggots sizzled and flamed. They saw how deathly pale she was. She stretched her bare arms into the fire and seized the red-hot iron bar. She lifted it up in her two palms. She walked forward counting one to nine, then threw the iron from her and raised her hands so all near her could see that the palms of her hands were pure white and not burned. All around praised God.

Years later Tristan married Isolde of the White Hands, over in Brittany, but he proved impotent and consequently unable to consummate his marriage. The potion or poison which Isolde of Ireland had made him drink was only supposed to have lasted for three years.

THE DEMON LOVER

In order to understand our virtuous heroine we need to disentangle from the ancient mythologies of Tibet, India, and Persia her antagonist, or demon lover. He seems to have originated in the Persian religion of Zoroastrianism where as the god Ahriman, spiritual enemy of mankind, he fought for eternity the god of light, Ahura Mazda. The belief of this religion of both Persia, or Iran, and India was that this dark presence warred upon daylight, goodness, and purity. He had to be subdued by goodness in works and deeds. Only then, after black was made white, could a new heaven and a new earth come to reign over the world. Deceitful and scheming as he was, Ahriman still fought as winter fights spring; and he remained a god.

Whenever the demon lover comes under the powerful pens of Judeo-Christian scholars, he is viewed in a very negative way and the names he has been given have come to connote evil: Satan, Baal, Beelzebub, Mephistopheles, Lord of the Flies, and Devil. To these widespread religions he is man's adversary, as well as the cause for woman's downfall. Satan remains for all time a chief spirit of evil in the world as enemy and tempter of both Job and Christ; and he will be expelled from heaven for the sin of pride. As Beelzebub, Matthew's "Prince of Devils" (Matt. 12:24), he had already been denounced by Elijah as Old Man Winter has always been defeated by spring. As Mephisto he became one of Christianity's seven chief devils, the one who persuaded Faust to sell him his immortal soul in exchange for everlasting youth. Ironically, Satan and Baal had once perhaps figured as ancient fertility gods. The prophets from Israel particularly chastised them and fulminated against their negative image as prefiguring the total corruption of female flesh, absolute destruction of a society, obliteration of the civilized world, and general depravity. The Jewish scholars would tolerate neither Scandinavian nor German gods of paganism under their animal forms, nor

Tibetan bat gods who swooped down black-cloaked to suck the blood of blonde maidens.

The Hebrew Isaiah also fulminated against a very ancient Greek and Roman god latterly named Lucifer: "How art thou fallen from heaven, O Lucifer, son of the morning" (Isa. 14:4, 12). According to ancient mythology of Persia, Greece, and Rome, however, Lucifer was originally a god. The Greeks understood that a great war had been fought many years before between the gods of Greece and the Titanic race, children of Cronus and Rhea. At the conclusion of this extensive war the Titans were expelled from this world and relegated to the nether world far in the west, beyond the western horizon where the sun disappears from sight every evening. While Greece and Rome are plunged into darkness every evening until the sun reappears the next morning as the goddess Aurora of the Dawn, garbed in her glorious gown of the sunrise, ushering it up the eastern sky, the nether world below the western horizon is bathed in sunlight.

That world hails Lucifer, Aurora's son, as their king. Many great heroes descended there to do heroic deeds and then returned to earth again. Hercules went there to rescue Alcestis. Theseus went down there and was brought safely back as he unraveled Ariadne's ball of twine. Aeneas went there in the footsteps of the priestess Sibyl, who led him there and back safely so that he was finally able to pay his respects and say good-bye to his aged father.

The Romans worshipped Lucifer gratefully as the morning star, our planet Venus. They hailed him as a light-bringer. They said he drove the silvery horses of the Moon. They looked at daybreak to see him streaking beams across the dark night sky. They also confused him with Pluto, who was the husband of Venus, or of Proserpine, who was daughter of Earth. Then they said Pluto lived with his darling bride in the Underworld where he had his forge. His forge and anvil sometimes caused earthquakes when he was hard at work hammering red-hot iron under Mt. Aetna in Sicily. Then he was alternately the hunchbacked Hammer King of the lower world, the dark, unseen, and mysterious ruler of the dead Titans, who so long before had been defeated and driven far into the dark west. The Greeks believed that the fallen Titanic race still lived there and were the giant children of Earth.

In his *Classic Myths* (1893) Charles Mills Gayley, of the University of California, spoke in Chapter IV (p. 47 ff.) of these "Gods of the Underworld" who were as well known to Homer and Virgil as they were to authors of Gothic fiction.

Homer specified in the *Odyssey* (Books 10, 11, 24) that the underworld lay on the "under side" or beyond the western limits of the known earth. Between these worlds lay ocean shrouded in fogs, not ever fully lighted by the sun. There the ghosts of the dead strolled on lovely shores beyond death, and rested in a necropolis surrounded by alders, poplars, or willows. Only the ancient Titans were forever condemned to this deep abyss of the lowest Tartarus.

In the fields above, called Elysian, or *Champs Elysées,* guiltless souls took their ease. Beyond Ocean stretched the lovely Isles of the Blessed where great kings and greater heroes rested after labor. There also lay the Fortunate Isles and the lost island of Atlantis. The ruler there was called the Father God, the *Dis Pater* well known mostly to the wandering Celts. He was an unseen god whenever he wore the helmet made for him by the three Cyclops, who were other brothers of the Titans. Under his helmet he remained invisible as did the later heroes of the Celts whenever they, like King Arthur, wrapped themselves in cloaks of darkness.

This same helmet of invisibility figures prominently in Horace Walpole's original or first Gothic novel. It was surely the Celts who, as they wandered west into Spain, France, and Britain, bequeathed to their future poets their preferred ancient mythology: the Titans, Pluto or *Dis Pater,* Tartarus, the Elysian Fields, the Isles of the Blessed, and Avalon, plus the concept of the "Nether World."

These radical departures from classical mythology have so marked the Celts as a people that they often claimed origins in the western world itself, on the western shores of the Atlantic Ocean. The Gauls in particular still say they came to France from America.

THE WHITE GODDESS

In scrutinizing ancient times it is amazing to see more evidence of ancient myths hard at work today. Before ancient Israel collapsed in A.D. 70, its ancient myths had been transmitted into Western Europe. There Christianity and Judaism overcame the native religion where women-in-white had been honored as high priestesses and, by A.D. 600, drove women out of their old position of honor and authority in their churches, and forbade them education.

It is still not known when patriarchy superseded the older reign of women, matriarchy, but it can only have been at a time prior by centuries to all recorded history. Some traces of matriarchy subsist, however, in myth, in law, in religion, and remain in the modern world. Jurists and professors of law have written many volumes which offer proof of all this, but few people read or even have access to their brilliant scholarship and professional argument.

It has been suggested that the heroines of Gothic fiction descend from the white goddesses of the paleolithic period. In historical times they reigned as high priestesses as long as matriarchy was tolerated in their societies, thus passing from Egypt into Greece via Crete, to Eleusis and the Eleusinian Mysteries of Alcestis, and to sacred Delphi where for untold ages they were the ultimate, highest religious personages in the world. From holy Delphi they passed into Rome where they met those like themselves coming out from Britain, Lapland, Finland, Scandinavia, and Germany as white-clad Druid priestesses. Dead by the early barbarian migrations, when women were forbidden both education and the priesthood by the Emperor Justinian, they still survived in medieval literature, or, like the heroines of other downtrodden peoples, they managed to cling to the popular imagination as supposedly harmless fairies, elves, dwarfs, and gnomes.

These ancient priestesses surface again and again from century to century. They appeared in prose fiction in France and Britain, places remarkable for their Celtic authors of long and unsuppressed memory. It was a resurgence of "Gothic" fiction. They then appeared again around World War I in another worldwide manifestation, again led by a Celt, André Breton, and called Surrealism. Gothic fiction made the same appeal to what lay beneath the "real," down in the depths of the unconscious.

It is not surprising that educated women have written excellent Gothic novels and also deep treatises on fiction. Women like the great scholar and Egyptologist Margaret Alice Murray or Pennethorne Hughes (Oxford University, 1928) have been the foremost authorities on witchcraft. The word *witch* is the feminine of the word *wicca,* or priest in Anglo-Saxon. Thanks to the books written by these women scholars, the last laws against witchcraft were finally repealed in England in 1951.

Women have also been foremost critics of Gothic fiction. Scholars like Edith Birkhead and Dorothy Scarborough at Columbia University in the City of New York have both written definitive works on that genre. Both agree that the witch used goddesses as role models: Isis in Egypt, Circe in Italy, Medea in Greece, Hecate also in Greece, and Diana in Britain. Like all submerged peoples, the witches practiced totemism, said Hughes, control of the body by psychic practices, the spiritual control of pain, and the detaching of consciousness by control of the *prana,* or breath.

The surrealists around 1914 added automatic writing to these earlier techniques. Just as King Arthur's Queen Guinevere was a high priestess, the great queens of the later Middle Ages were considered patrons of a women's religion. Saint Joan of Arc was considered one of their human sacrifices, and she was, of course, another White Maiden from the White (Celtic) Wood who, her accusers said, admitted to dancing about the (pagan) Maypole. Some Gothic heroines are etymologically named "white": Sir Walter Scott's Amy in *Kenilworth*, Dumas's Albine, Céline's Lily, Ann Radcliffe's Emily, and Faulkner's Emily also.

Many women were certainly priestesses in Western Europe before the advent of Christianity. Dame Margaret Murray wrote in *The God of the Witches* (Garden City, 1960), pp. 152–53:

> The Christian Church was organized in Rome when the status of women had so declined that the wife was merely the chattel of the husband. Therefore when the New Religion reached western Europe, women were strictly excluded from the priesthood.

The European persecution of witches, which had amounted to mass hysteria, ceased about 1650; it had already been supplanted by enthusiasm for witches and priestesses when Clara Reeve and Ann Ward Radcliffe wrote their masterpieces of Gothic fiction in 1777 and 1792.

Clara Reeve argued in her treatise *The Progress of Romance,* vol. I (Dublin, 1785), that the so-called Gothic novel may more properly be classed as a "romance." It is rather "an heroic fable," she thought, because it treats persons and events which are rather imaginary or fabled than real. Furthermore, as the novel treats vulgar persons often in appropriately vulgar language, the romance distances itself by portraying aristocratic and noble personages accustomed to lofty, elevated speech. In the novel we descend to ordinary situations, affairs, perils, persons, and happenstances; Gothic fiction, on the contrary, summons up dreams, portents, signals, prophecy, and other subliminal states of consciousness. All she lacked here was the word coined by the twentieth century: surrealism.

In 1777 Clara Reeve (1729–1807) joined her counterparts across the Channel who, like the Countess Stéphanie de Genlis, had also taken pen in hand to create Gothic fiction. The purpose of these stories in England was similarly to study theories of knowledge, and in doing so to rehabilitate the heroine. Clara Reeve speaks openly in her book entitled *The Old English Baron*. As an author she was regarded in England, notes her modern editor James Trainer of Stirling University in Scotland, as a maiden lady who was termed less frivolous than most other ladies of her time. Such learned ladies in France were then called "bluestockings." Reeve's purpose in following French precedents was also to oppose the marvelous to the merely probable experiences in life, to make an appeal for knowledge, to describe that which is ordinarily rejected as irrational and/or supernatural, and to pit her characters in combat against otherworldly powers.

Reeve proved she was not adverse to summoning a ghost in her introductory sentence, which set the stage for hers and for other Gothic fiction. Clara Reeve's introductory sentence sends a shock wave through the reader. The editor himself gives the reader a footnote because Clara Reeve has set her stage too craftily. This all took place, she wrote, during the reign of (the insane) King Henry VI of England, and during the Regency in France of the "renowned" John Duke of Bedford, and while Humphrey Duke of Gloucester was Protector of England. These were horrible people.

These men were the twice "renowned" murderers of Joan of Arc. The Duke and Duchess of Bedford were her jailers before and during her trial and execution and *neither lifted a hand to comfort her*. Gloucester was responsible for holding Charles of Orleans prisoner in England (1415–1440) and was eventually disgraced and ousted by Charles at his Pardon Ceremony in Westminster Abbey, 1440.

The ghost of Joan of Arc haunted the old English barons who had committed murder in England, concealing their victim's skeleton under the flooring of the castle, and usurping the true heir's property, estates, and revenues.

The needed approach to the Castle of Lovel commences this Gothic story and establishes a precedent all Gothic novelists will follow. Among those who will follow is Edgar Allan Poe, whose superb approach past the black tarn to the haunted House of Usher, and description of how the dead Madeleine's skeletal hand rises and reaches forth from her sarcophagus sends chills down the reader's spine.

As the story begins, we are told that Castle Lovel has fallen sadly into other hands, for in the fifteenth century the English loaded upon themselves a burden of guilt for their crimes in France, which caused them eventually to leave France forever and also to beg pardon formally of Joan's Duke Charles of Orleans in Westminster Abbey.

In a dream Clara Reeve's first narrator receives a message from the castle's true and legitimate Lord Lovel to the effect that injustice reigns within those dark stone walls. In his dream, or via knowledge by extrasensory perception, the narrator sees clearly blood-stained armor lying underground in some dreary, horrible pit, and single combat between the legitimate heir and the usurper. As he awakens, he sees young Edmund before him. There before him looms the dark Castle Lovel. There beside him stands the hero Edmund. The youth is pulled by invisible strings toward the dark pile.

The eastern apartments of Castle Lovel are haunted. Nobody can sleep there for all the groans and clanking chains thereabout. Young Edmund, who remains undaunted, undertakes an experiment: to sleep for three nights in the haunted eastern wing. By this time the reader has understood that the Gothic Castle Lovel is quadrangular, and that its secret knowledge is confined to its eastern side. In Judeo-Christian faiths, the most profound religious experiences also, always by revelation, occur at the east altar of a church. And, of course, these are Eastern religions, which originate in the Middle East.

When Edmund attempts to penetrate the locked eastern apartments, he finds that the lock proves to have rusted and the key is old and broken. The wind blows out his light. Courageously he enters the rotting woods and broken walls of these chambers where the hangings blow their tattered threads across his face and rats scurry to safety before his feet. He remains there anyway among complaining ghosts and more sad dreams. Soon Reeve will give us a heroine who is equally brave.

In his sleep Edmund sees two persons whom he recognizes but whom he has never seen before. A warrior and a wan lady predict he is close to what has been heretofore secret knowledge. Softly they bless their dear sleeper. Then Edmund sees in his next dream their funeral processions. Upon awakening he suddenly knows what he has never before admitted to knowing: that his own father was murdered there in that very chamber, that his dear, dead mother died giving birth to him. He has arrived, first via dreams and then by intuition, to the true knowledge of his birth and true identity. He understands furthermore that nothing can, in fact, be hidden from the eye of heaven. Heaven all by itself effects its own purpose. Providence, which is divine, works its own designs. Crimes committed demand retribution. No person escapes punishment. Ghosts will drink blood until revenge quiets them.

When young Edmund, fortified by his love for the Gothic heroine Emma, whom Reeve has properly named, declares himself heir presumptive to Castle Lovel and approaches its black walls intending to take possession of his title and his inheritance, he is expected. From nowhere he hears the ringing blast of the hunting horn. Then he is slapped by a gust of icy wind and before his startled eyes the castle gates fly open, all by themselves. No human hand had set them in motion. The outer gates stand ajar as if expecting his summons. Then the castle doors also burst open.

Before Edmund stands the old retainer, who announces: "The castle knows its true master." Because he is a simple, uneducated man, Reeve tells her reader, he is closer to true knowledge than we are. According to this new or old theory of knowledge, all black deeds of darkness (such as the hideous murder of Joan of Arc) will be uncovered and exposed to the light of day. The corpse will be reinstated. From inside the castle walls Edmund again hears the horn announcing that the guilty lord will be sent on penance to the Holy Land.

As for Edmund, he was recognized and loved at once by the Gothic heroine, Lady Emma. Before he enters the east chambers, Edmund prepares for self-hypnosis in the usual (fictional) way—by not eating or drinking. Both he and this colorless heroine, Emma, understand that down narrow passageways, stumbling in utter darkness, amid dire, rustling noises, and hollow groaning sounds, the hero or heroine must courageously advance. At the bottom of the dark, damaged staircase a dim light burns. Knowledge accrues from unknown sources. Just so, and before she went into labor, Lady Lovel saw before her the ghost of her murdered husband. Edmund also heard his long dead mother say: "This is my son."

Then "Goody" Margery, who was once his nurse, reveals her secret knowledge to Edmund and Emma. She tells how her mistress gave birth to a baby boy, and how she then was found drowned in the lake. Beside the child was a dress and the Lovel locket. Edmund's own intuitions are thus reinforced and endorsed. When the usurpers in their turn occupy the east chambers, they are ordered to depart thence. This instruction is given them by an unknown, armoured ghost. In such ways has Providence adopted the orphaned Edmund.

No crime of such magnitude as murder can be concealed from the eye of heaven. Heaven works in its own ways and times, without limit, to uncover and punish such human injustice: The fifteenth century heaped crime upon crime, but Providence looks out for the innocent victim, supports the injured orphan, remedies injustice and certainly murder. Edmund descends into darkness in order to find light. He learns there that retribution is certain.

In this romance, which was her first book, Clara Reeve took pen in hand to follow the lead of Horace Walpole and of the French lady writers who had shown the way. She guided her reader, as they had done, to knowledge by revelation. Extraordinary means of knowledge lie at hand, she was saying, and available to us all if we so choose: dreams, intuition, resemblances, lost knowledge, old patterns, symbols, and extrasensory perception. We may discover the hidden power of blood, the ties of birth and lineage, the uses of clan and family, and win our inheritances. Ideas of merit, nobility, and breeding may lead us to justice and keep us safely there.

What are the relations between magic and God? What does the castle symbolize? Why do its gates, portals, and doors swing open by themselves? What attractions move inert matter? Why must humans descend into the labyrinth of the Titanic gods? How could Edmund have acquired six fathers, all of whom stepped forward one after another to assist him when needed? What was the especial power of his mother, who clung to him from beyond the grave? How was a dead woman able to direct him? What powers accrued to the old nursemaid Margery? What knowledge prompted Emma to recognize and stand by Edmund? We never know.

Last of all, what relationships exist between magic, magicians, and religion? Are witches not priestesses? Should we not study all over again the new religious movements of the fifteenth century? Should we not calculate all over again the parts played by Celtic Scotland and Wales in the defeats of the English inside France? Was it enough to stand Joan's small wooden statue in Winchester Cathedral beside the gigantic sarcophagus of her cruel judge, Cardinal Beaufort? Religious ferment boiled below the surface in fifteenth-century England, where the atrocious crimes of King Henry V were publicly witnessed.

Thus in the capable hand of Clara Reeve, the Gothic romance, as she termed it, offered readers a program and much material for reflection. Her recent scholarly editor in Scotland agreed that the pioneer lady author, daughter of a curate in Ipswich, was a "high priestess." She actually sold her first book for £ 10.

In 1794 Ann Radcliffe, another English lady, born in London, brought her Gothic novel in four volumes, *The Mysteries of Udolpho,* to a peak of perfection which has never been surpassed in that genre. Writing in the *New Monthly Magazine,* vol. VII (1826), p. 150, on the supernatural in poetry, Mrs. Ann Radcliffe set forth the opposition which in her view raised Gothic fiction to the level of poetry. The opposition, she declared, lies between terror on the reader's part and static horror.

As the new, Gothic heroine descends into the dark castle at night, she experiences the terror which her readers will also feel; it is an emotion which "expands the soul and awakens the faculties to a high degree of life" while on the contrary horror "contracts, freezes, and nearly annihilates" the faculties. Neither Shakespeare, Milton, nor Edmund Burke before her, she admitted, "looked to positive horror as a source of the sublime," though they all agree that terror is a very high "source of sublimity in art." Radcliffe and the three predecessors she here claimed all looked to the celebrated, ancient Greek treatise on the sublime by Longinus:

By sublimity (Gr. *hypsos*) the author means "excellence in language," the "expression of a great spirit," the power to provoke "ecstasy" and to move the reader however often he reads the passage (*Encyclopedia Britannica,* vol. XIV, 1966, p. 300).

There in the waning eighteenth century, writing her fourth novel, Ann Radcliffe took her place, as she spoke through her Gothic heroine, named Emily, among the most beloved, first novelists of the world: Henry Fielding, Feodor Dostoyevsky, Leo Tolstoy, George Eliot, Jane Austen, Honoré de Balzac, Gustave Flaubert, Herman Melville, Theodore Dreiser, Thomas Hardy, David Herbert Lawrence, William Faulkner, James Joyce, and Jean Giono. She surpassed all minor writers by her superb command of her art and by the exercise of very great courage. In the depth and scope of her canvas, by the humanitarian love she displayed for her white-goddess heroine, by her freedom from hatred and jealousy, by her deep understanding of and sympathy for human life, and by her knowledge and command of her conscious and unconscious thoughts, she created the perfect setting in which to place her heroine.

Emily approached the Castle of Udolpho with a sense of melancholy awe. The nearer she drew, the more she perceived the Gothic greatness of its architectural features, its crumbling parapets of greyish stone, its deepening purple tint under the slanting rays of the sunset, the thin, ghostly vapors that rose about its foundations while its battlements were still tipped with gold. Emily wondered who would dare trespass inside this gloomy and austere pile?

Even as she looked, the castle sank before her careful gaze into the dark of evening. Silent, dark, alone, and sublime, it challenged her to advance down the mountainside to this chasm and sovereign mass from another time, another age, and other masons. Emily stopped in order to hear fully the heavy tolling of its bell. She later gazed astonished at the ancient servant who opened the portals to her. Gates clanged shut behind her. She entered bravely but halted over the threshold to consider the nighttime stirring of life within Udolpho. Carefully she measured it.

To think that this is a city author writing, who has never so much as seen Italy, to say nothing of an Italian castle, staggers the reader. But her fourth novel did earn Ann Radcliffe her one journey outside Britain, a trip to Holland and Germany two years later. Her marvelous descriptive approach-to-the-castle came entirely from castles inside England, plus the Glamis Castle she so admired in Scotland, and otherwise from landscape paintings in London Museums.

Her views of Udolpho are totally anthropocentric: the brow of the precipice, the clothed mountains behind it, the shaggy steps, the ramparts which spread themselves, the summits that rise above each other, and the (masculine) sun which shoots through an opening. Her narrator, Emily, maintains a consistently feminine view of all this. From passive eyes Emily illuminates each static scene until the reader feels he or she is there, looking back at Emily, passive and inactive.

Emily moves carefully along a series: (1) sunset, (2) road, (3) valley, (4) mountains (embellished by nine characteristics), (5) her eye's view of a vista, of the east, along a distant perspective, through images of grandeur, (6) awareness of a girl, a she-person, descending down and down, (7) the splendid sun (embellished with eleven details), (8) the wooded mountain summits all about her contrasted with (9) the castle spreading its towers, its black stone ramparts, more towers, and its black battlements.

This Gothic novel is a first and a prime example of a female consciousness at work, and a female exploration of the world clarified by a female understanding, by a third-person, female narrator under the direction of a woman author. The language throughout is poetic and aimed at sublimity: aesthetic paragraphing, idiosyncratic punctuation, tortuous and run-on sentences that duplicate the stream of Emily's consciousness, attempts to fracture grammar, and a Latinate syntax, for Radcliffe had studied Latin. She learned it well in order to prepare herself for authorship.

Emily's explorations of the interior castle are, like Radcliffe's symbolic of the states of consciousness: knowledge of the past, memory, intuition, darkness and ignorance, sleep and dreams, hypnagogic reverie, extrasensory perception, female sexuality, the return of spirits on earth, and now the survival of the twelfth century into the eighteenth.

"There," said the villain Montoni, speaking to Emily for the first time in several hours, "is Udolpho." It will take considerable courage, Emily warned herself, to invade this solitary, black domain.

The young woman explores a portrait hung with its black veil and the mysterious staircase descending from her chamber. Looking out from her casement the following morning, she begins to realize with terror, and then in frozen horror, that her fate lies in that castle which Montoni, the demon lover, cannot inherit. By nature Emily is a keen observer of others, which reproduces, of course, her author's creative personality. Like an angel of light Emily ceaselessly explores the castle by day and then, even in total darkness, by night. Seeking answers, she interrogates each turret: Whose castle is it? Who committed murder there? Who is the unknown person whom Montoni visits? Is the east turret the place of death? How can I learn the truth? Does not fear enter via the ear, and not through the eyes?

By volume three, Emily is ready to follow the porter at midnight from the eastern rampart down dark passages to a ruined chapel, and then down a terrifying, underground descent to subterranean vaults. She undergoes imprisonment in a cell furnished with an iron chair for torture, an iron ring, and iron bars. There she stumbles upon what could be the corpse of her murdered aunt, or perhaps her aunt dying in the east turret.

During the second watch of the night (p. 372 ff.), Emily was again on guard. She heard the sentinels on the ramparts above her. Darkening her lamp she stood at the casement watching. Above her head the moon appeared between heavy clouds, but below her all was pitch black except for an occasionally flickering light. The gleam of lightning showed her the lower terraces from time to time. Sudden flashes of blue fire lit up the landscape around her and then returned to darkness. Thunder rolled along the summits and down the pine slopes at the passes. As she watched and listened, the clouds turned red as sulphur. Then the storm broke. That was the night Madame Montoni died without transferring her property to her husband. Nor could he compel Emily to sign her property over to him.

> She saw herself in a castle, inhabited by vice and violence, seated beyond the reach of law or justice, and in the power of a man, whose perseverance was equal to every occasion, and in whom passions, of which revenge was not the weakest, entirely supplied the place of principles (p. 435).

Emily often thought in later years how similar her life had been to scenes of autumn: heavy mists, yellow leaves of beech trees underfoot, gray evenings in late fall, melancholy fears, and images of desolation. She had lived like the swallows tossed about on the wind when she sought calm skies and warmer sunlight. Emerging safely now and then, she soon fell again into the "stormy sea of misfortune" (p. 619). Even the bare branches above her head seemed to echo the distant lamentations of her heart. Here is a brilliant woman speaking about all women "beyond the reach of law and justice."

Emily was finally able to gain the shores of what her author termed at least a "rational happiness." Radcliffe ended her long novel (672 pages) with a brief encouragement to the reader, hoping he or she would come to believe with her that while vicious persons do occasionally pour misfortune upon the heads of the well-meaning, they only do so for certain, fixed periods of time. The dominion of the evil over the good is temporary and brief at best. Their punishment soon overtakes them. As long as innocence persists despite repeated attacks by the unjust, it will prevail. Patience will overcome injustice; women must be patient.

An author's pleasure comes from the hope that her weak hand has managed to leave on her paper words of hope and consolation. She hopes to have whiled away an evil hour for women, and diverted her reader for a moment from pain or sorrow. That is her only reward.

From the publication of *The Mysteries of Udolpho* the Gothic heroine became well established and necessary for the format Radcliffe had developed. This heroine was the white goddess in person. Her prime characteristic was her association with knowledge, with the pursuit of knowledge, and with the search for that knowledge which would solve the mystery of a crime, lay that crime open, and make its criminal liable to punishment. The heroine's purpose became always to defeat the evil hero, or demon lover, and end the mystery. By courageous exploration followed by reflection and observation of human behavior, the heroine makes good triumph. Although her skirts touch black, they remain white and unsoiled. The castle exists as a metaphor. It typifies the adult world of sexual fulfillment which the virginal heroine will enter as adult.

Charlotte Brontë's Jane Eyre of 1847 was certainly a development of Ann Radcliffe's Emily, and like her a searcher for knowledge by extrasensory perception, somnambulism, dreams, telepathy, hypnosis, and even by trance. Jane Eyre's dark lover, Rochester, was another vampire in a Bluebeard's castle. The eponymous heroines of *Delphine* (1802) and *Corinne* (1807) by the Baroness Madame de Staël also owe much to Ann Radcliffe's poetic imagination: Madame de Staël agreed also that, generally speaking, poetry and a highly poetic imagination are required if an author treats the realm of the extraordinary such as Gothic fiction deals with.

Even Jane Austen's Catherine Morland in *Northanger Abbey* (1818) falls under the Gothic spell long enough to realize that her married life will not earn emancipation for herself, as Emily won in Udolpho, but will consist of second best, of only a limited view henceforth, between the frames of narrow, Gothic windows upon the outer world of freedom and free choice.

Not surprisingly, and this despite her serious respiratory disease that probably shortened her life considerably, Ann Radcliffe actually dared in 1797 to publish a feminist declaration entitled *The Female Advocate, or, an Attempt to recover the Rights of Women from Male Usurpation*.

Such a brave but incautious lady as Ann Radcliffe could have taught us much more, if she had been so inclined. She could have added that before there was Gothic fiction, or the white goddess, there were the fairy tale names of hero and heroine: Beauty and the Beast.

•READINGS•

Lovers (English translations)

Béroul, *The Romance of Tristan and The Tale of Tristan's Madness*. Translated and edited by Alan S. Fedrick. Penguin Books (Harmondsworth, England, 1970).

The Romance of Tristan and Iseut as Retold by Joseph Bédier. Translated by Hilaire Belloc, and completed by Paul Rosenfeld. Vintage Books, Random House (New York, 1945).

Gottfried von Strassburg. *Tristan with the Tristran of Thomas*. Translated with Introduction by A. T. Hatto. Penguin Classics (Harmondsworth, England, 1960).

Thomas of Britain. *The Romance of Tristram and Ysolt*. Translated from the Old French and Old Norse by Roger Sherman Loomis. E. P. Dutton (New York, 1923).

Lays of Courtly Love. Translated by Patricia Terry, Introduction by Charles W. Dunn. Doubleday (New York, 1963). See "Honeysuckle" by Marie de France, pp. 11–14.

Sir Thomas Malory. *Le Morte D' Arthur*. 2 vols. Preface by Sir John Rhys, Everyman Library, E. P. Dutton (London and New York, 1906–1961).

The Demon Lover and the White Goddess

Birkhead, Edith. *A Study of the Gothic Romance* (New York, 1921).

———. *The Tale of Terror* (London, 1921).

Burke, Edmund. *The Writings and Speeches of Edmund Burke*. Vol. I. Little, Brown & Co. (Boston, 1901), pp. 110–115, 130–131, 208–209.

Graves, Robert. *The White Goddess*. Faber and Faber Limited (London, 1961; New York, 1948). See Chapter VI, "A Visit to Spiral Castle," p. 97 ff. (English edition).

Radcliffe, Ann. *The Mysteries of Udolpho*. Introduction by Bonamy Dobree; Notes by Frederick Garner. Oxford University Press (London, Oxford, and New York, 1970). The original edition dates from 1794.

Railo, Eino. *The Haunted Castle* (London, 1927).

Reeve, Clara. *The Old English Baron*. Edited with an Introduction by James Trainer. Oxford University Press (London, New York, and Toronto, 1967). The original editions date from 1722 and 1778.

Scarborough, Dorothy. *The Supernatural in Modern English Fiction*. Columbia University Press (New York, 1917).

Summers, Montague. *A Gothic Bibliography* (London, n.d.), published privately at the author's expense. This famous author could not find a publisher.

Varma, Devendra P. *The Gothic Flame* (London, 1957).

·CHAPTER III·

Educating Heroines

EARTH MOTHERS

These mythological mothers, from whom mankind and womankind are descended, have several names. However, each name duplicates the life, story, and reproductive functions of a Mother of Mankind. When she is murdered, as her son and daughter, Orestes and Electra, murdered her, she is in every way supposed to be wiped out of sight or mind. She belongs to the most ancient myths of the Middle East, long called the cradle of Western civilization.

By the ancient Greeks this Mother was called Pandora and Rhea. The former exacted reverence from all because she was the Earth, the only planet upon which most of us live, or she was called alternately Earth Mother, and Earth Goddess. She opened her womb as she gave birth, for we never gave birth to ourselves. When she opened her womb, she let flow her blood, which the ancient peoples of what is now Greece saw as the water of life. The womb remains her symbol because it represents her prime purpose: to bear children. In art the womb of Pandora is represented equally well by a "jar," which the artist moulds or sketches, or by an urn shaped like the uterus, and sometimes less graphically and less scientifically represented as a "box," or boxlike container.

Whenever Pandora opened her womb to push forth a child, she also brought into the world not only a baby son or daughter or twins, but also their human existences, which include death. Reasonably, then, the Earth Mother cannot save man from decay, illness, old age, and death. Thus, the Greeks admitted easily that Pandora also gave birth *to all the ills of life*. By extension she sometimes inadvertently gave some perfectly innocent husband a bad wife. She also bore children later called "bad seeds." Every time she opened her womb, then, there was the chance she might cause havoc, despite good wishes and honorable intentions.

In Asia, the Earth Mother was called Rhea rather than Pandora, whose name in Greek meant "the bountiful," "the giver of all gifts," or "gifts from all." Rhea meant simply "Earth," but earth understood as creator, just like Pandora. From the Asian side of the Mediterranean Sea the Asian Earth Mother Rhea, in a time of such great danger that mankind was soon to be wiped out in Italy, was imported into Rome. There she reigned subsequently as the Great Mother, *Magna Mater,* mother of Zeus (Jupiter). The Romans believed she had originally mothered them, and not necessarily the races of Asia Minor alone, and that she had originally sprung from their divine Titanic race. They said she had even been originally the reigning Titaness of Day Seven; and as such had defied the Kings of the Gods and had once ruled the planet Saturn.

It was Rhea, and she alone, who passing through ancient Greece, stopped at a warm spring near Argos, bathed and regained her virginity. Greek women were very blessed to follow Rhea's secret example.

The Mother Rhea married crooked Cronus, governor in her name of Heaven and Earth, perhaps also of the lost Atlantis. When she needed to communicate with her lord or with her children, Rhea sent a white dove. Thus, to her as to Queen Guinevere on her wedding day, the white dove, *colomba,* has remained the ancient symbol of Earth. The Mother saved Noah from the waters. Rhea called her children to worship by the beating of a tom-tom. This drum, still called a tom-tom, is Eastern in origin. The Romans also called her "Bounty" (or *Ops,* opulent) because all her original children were gods: Zeus, Poseidon, Demeter, Hera, Hades, and Hestia. In Rome they were known as Jupiter, Neptune, Ceres, Juno, Pluto, and Vesta.

The third most popular appellation for the Earth Mother was Phyllis, and especially when she was personified or symbolized by the vegetable kingdom. Thus, both the Virgin Mary and Saint Joan of Arc are represented symbolically by a white lily, the lily of Orleans, and France herself symbolized by the golden or silver lily, the fleur-de-lis. And the Virgin is the Rose of Sharon.

Phyllis, as *Mater,* stood tall before the worshippers and venerators of Mother Earth as a tree. Hers and ours now is the Tree of Life, for the green tree shades us, feeds us, cleanses our polluted air, and rests our tired eyes. From most ancient days great leaders were called lordly oak trees. The Druid priests and priestesses cut mistletoe from the sacred oak after which they were called Oak Men, or "Druids." And the Christmas spruce brings promise and perfume into our homes on the darkest day in the northern hemisphere.

Phyllis traditionally carried a casket made from the Tree of Knowledge, which when it loosed her children over the face of earth promised each one the privilege and the power of learning. None of the Mother's children, including her daughters—despite man's desire to exclude and sequester them—was to be consigned to the dead end of ignorance.

The trees of Mother Earth also symbolized knowledge. Both the almond tree and the walnut stood for learning as symbolized by their shells and the seeds of life contained therein. We still speak of wisdom as contained in a nut shell or a kernel. Like the Mother herself the almond breaks into flower and sets its fruit before it ever leafs out. In the same mysterious way the young mother sets in her soft body the kernel of each new life.

The fig tree, representing male sexuality by the shape of its leaf, reaches out to young adults as a lesson in forbidden sexuality. This is the truly forbidden knowledge allowed only after permission acquired by abstemiousness and proper ceremonies of betrothal and wedding. Promiscuous knowledge here can very well lead to permanent expulsion from the garden where grows the bountiful fig tree.

The apple tree also carries its well-known taboo, for it grows in the westernmost world where the sun disappears suddenly at end of day and plunges the civilized world into darkness. Thus, both the apple and its western isles represent the dark Underworld. Certain priestesses and goddesses like Inana, Sibyl, and Mary traveled safely there and back, as did certain heroes like Orpheus and Theseus, but only if they had received proper instructions beforehand. As easy as it was for them to go down into Hell's kingdom, it was very difficult afterwards to return onto the surface of earth. The one strict injunction had to be obeyed: never while down below to take even one bite of an apple. Both apple and pomegranate with its red seeds symbolized Phyllis's red blood of birth and conception.

Each tree gave Phyllis one of the letters of the alphabet and also its bark and its twigs upon which these letters were originally carved and the paper pages upon which they were later written, and the word "book" itself. Knowledge, then, came from woman. Inside her womb, which is variously termed urn, vase, jar, casket, or box, Earth keeps safe the knowledge of life. Inescapably woman and knowledge go hand in hand. When knowledge is personified, she is called Lady Philosophy. And in the Romance languages *philosophy* is a feminine word.

In ancient Israel Eve was also known as the Mother of All Life and similarly associated with the fig tree and the apple tree. Thereabouts she is recognizable despite her many variant spellings, such as Hepa,

Hepit, Hepatu, Hebe, and Hawwa. Both Old and New Testaments know the main line of her story: Genesis 2:4; Corinthians 11:3; Timothy 2:13. The Bible says Eve was the first woman on earth. She was made or created from Adam's rib, and she became his wife. She was the mother of Cain, Abel, and Seth.

Eve committed an unforgivable crime. Beguiled by the serpent or dragon, she ate the apple of knowledge, which was the forbidden fruit from the Tree of Knowledge. Then, compounding her crime, she persuaded Adam to eat the apple also. To "eat" is an Anglo-Saxon verb also meaning "to devour books," or "to learn." Because Adam and Eve acquired also the forbidden knowledge of human sexuality, they were both banished from the Garden of Eden.

The Roman poet Catullus beautifully expressed this: that while the Roman maiden was kept enclosed inside her parents' walled garden of fruit trees, she remained chaste and pure, a *"casta diva,"* a pure young goddess herself. Music lovers will never forget the Prima Donna Rosa Ponselle in 1927 singing the gorgeous aria "Casta Diva" from Act I of the opera *Norma*. The opera by Vincenzo Bellini of Sicily had its premiere at La Scala in Milano around the year 1832. The role of Norma in this aria presents the high priestess of Gaul praying to the Earth Mother. Crowned with verbena, the demigoddess Norma advances to cut sacred mistletoe. She stands in full moonlight in the sacred Druid grove. The tragedy of *Norma* by the French author Alexandre Soumet, and the opera by Bellini, have caught the worship by a demigoddess of the Earth Mother.

Thus, the White Goddess is Earth Mother, Philosophy, and Knowledge herself. And curiosity is the prime characteristic of young maidens, who conserve this inquiring mind long after childhood. That is par excellence the inborn female trait until or unless it is dulled and finally obliterated by hopelessness. If the girl or maiden fails to become educated, ergo self-reliant, and able to support or to support partially herself and her family, she has reached the dead end of hopelessness. Then she subsides into consumerism. The penalty for acquiring knowledge may be exile from the garden of her parents, which merely means Eve and her Adam will have to plant their own garden and erect their own wall around it.

The ancient Greeks explained that in the beginning was Chaos. Out of this nothingness that endlessly whirled, Earth emerged or was created. Then Earth looked about her and felt naked. Therefore she, the Mother of All, created Heaven equal to herself and wrapped herself in him. From Heaven and Earth sprung first the Race of Womankind.

One of the original male misogynists, a Greek poet named Hesiod, wrote his continuation in the *Theogony* (p. 42) of man's tender trap on earth: the race of woman. The race of women, hisses this old Greek pessimist, was created as the bane of man's existence. Man can neither do with or without her altogether. She hurts man. She is deadly. She spends all his money and keeps him a pauper. She eats too much. She is a dull drone in his honeyed hive. She conspires to do him ill. She eats all day long, in fact, and keeps filling up her belly. She toils not neither does she spin, added the French poet Jean de La Fontaine of the spendthrift (female) grasshopper's behavior when contrasted with that of the hard-working, thrifty (male) ant. She sucks man's treasures and gobbles them up. She is bad herself and doubly bad for man. She was the price tag allotted to man's gift of fire from heaven. She is forever the tender trap eternal; for if a man grows old alone, he has no tender, wifely hand to tuck him into old age's bed. Then all his property goes to even worse scavengers, his distant relatives.

Thus, from the ancient Near East, as from the cradle to the grave, woman has been blamed for having introduced man especially to this desire for knowledge. May one assume that as Mother Bountiful she bore man and therefore assumed responsibility for him. When a son failed her, as Oedipus failed Jocasta, it is true that he blinded himself, but she too committed suicide. When her husband failed her, as Agamemnon failed Clytemnestra when he sacrificed her younger daughter Iphigenia, Electra murdered their mother. Thus, the surviving sister, Electra, killed her mother Clytemnestra. When Antigone failed as surrogate mother to bury her brother Polyneices, and give him proper funeral honors—which is today considered a basic human right—she died for this right and for her imperfect motherhood.

In our modern days also, and especially after 1920 and the enforced acceptance by schools of misunderstood Freudian psychology, it has been common, if not universal, practice to blame the mother alone for all the shortcomings of her children. When any child of hers had to undergo psychiatric care, the mother too underwent, or was advised by the private school to undergo, the same psychoanalysis. The medical profession blamed her first and foremost, and so did her wayward or unsuccessful son, indiscriminately. His poor grades in school were especially his mother's fault, and hers alone. She was also blamed for his subsequent failed marriages. It is also a well-known fact that within the year of a divorce, one of the mothers of a divorced couple will die suddenly. Has she not shouldered blame until it killed her?

HEROINES OF ROUSSEAU AND FLAUBERT

Other, free searchers after the truth, especially in areas such as the relationship between women and knowledge, or the education of women, are preponderantly the great authors. They deal masterfully with words, sense oncoming events, explain us to ourselves, and teach us as no mere teacher can do. Both Rousseau and Flaubert, for example, felt the approaching crises: the unhappiness of woman in the modern world, *and* the approaching vindication of her demands for education, respect, fair pay, medical care, and equality.

The first modern author to be considered will be the celebrated French moralist and world-famous philosopher Jean-Jacques Rousseau (1712–1778), who wrote two majors works on education: a French novel called *Julie, or The New Heloïse* (1761) and *Emile* (1762), a treatise on the education of a boy he named Emile and a girl he also appropriately named Sophie (meaning "love of wisdom"). His novel *Julie* is presently not in print in the United States (1991), which does not make it a poor book but only a book written by another stern misogynist.

In the nineteenth century, Frenchman Gustave Flaubert's celebrated *Madame Bovary* (1856) created what the French were obliged to declare a "scandalous success." A few months after the book appeared serialized in the *Revue de Paris,* Flaubert was hauled into court, accused of obscenity and the corruption of public morals. Completely indifferent to this ordeal, which might have destroyed a lesser person, Flaubert expected to be acquitted and was acquitted of all charges.

His Chapter VI, a few pages from *Madame Bovary,* deals with Emma Bovary's education. This book is very much in demand and is in print here today. While *Julie* reads today as an archaic masterpiece by one of the world's most influential thinkers (Rousseau's ideas trickled down into progressive education), a man who still forms our ideas of women today, *Madame Bovary* can still be read, loved, reread, and seen in the movies at any time with the greatest of respect and admiration.

Today, in our waning twentieth century, the problems of women and knowledge, that of educating illiterate and unwilling masses, but most particularly the problem of offering education acceptable to women, have surfaced to alarming degrees. In the 1960s, which culminated in the Student Revolution concurrent with the refusal of many to serve in the Vietnam War, President Topping of the University of Southern California, preponderantly a graduate school, weekly asked his executive committee please to frame a curriculum sensitive to the real needs of women undergraduates. Why teach these future housewives Latin? The answers he received were: (1) The study of Latin will make them better mothers, (2) Who knows that they will not need Latin? When at age forty or fifty, their children then out of college, will they not need Latin in order to enter graduate school? (3) Are we not preparing them for longer lives and a longer old age when the leisure for learning will provide solace and pleasure? (4) Is not the study of Latin one of the keenest pleasures in a woman's life? (5) Do not women possess at birth the natural ability to learn foreign languages easily?

The great moralist and political philosopher Jean-Jacques Rousseau was by all accounts notoriously antifeminist and this, despite the fact that he, and Flaubert after him, was faithfully befriended by the greatest woman novelist of their days in France, George Sand. Rousseau revealed his true opinion of women as he disclosed all his opinions, frankly and freely for the benefit of mankind, without regard for the countless enemies he made on both sides of the English Channel. He found the two sexes antithetical in every regard: Men were both active and physically strong while women were, he declared, both passive and physically weak. This first declaration falls presumably counter to medical opinion of the twentieth century.

Men, further asserted Rousseau, are easy to educate because they are open and frank in all their dealings. Women are, on the contrary, difficult to educate because they are secretive, false, lying, dissembling, and sly. Men are often poets because they possess from birth an elevated nature, while women think mostly about sex and are flirtatious by nature. Women control manners and regulate private society while men become masters of community and governors of nations. Thus, men must teach women what and how to see the world into which they are born, while for their part women only instruct their menfolk in how to eat, how to behave properly, or what to wear or do on certain, lesser occasions important only to family and friends.

Education for both sexes should be based upon natural principles and must obey the laws of human nature, decreed Rousseau. Education is more an art than a science. The purpose of educators is the same as that of parents; not to keep a child from dying, but to help each male live and experience life as fully and as widely as possible. All females are governed by certain innate principles such as the acceptance of suffering. All men have learned in childhood that man must be a soldier, and they accept this as a part of every man's fate. Girls and women are always inferior to men because they do not accept heroic ideals. Women, unlike men, remain great children all their lives long. They prefer to cry and blame others rather than grow up and accept responsibility for their own lives. Girls need not follow a curriculum designed for boys. Girls are consumers, and are better at menial labor anyway.

Because they are being prepared for leadership of communities and nations, as for careers in industry, commerce, business, law, the army, and religion, men must follow a rigid curriculum of studies. Rousseau sees this program of studies as following logically three separate areas: (1) natural studies, (2) industrial studies, and (3) studies related to mankind. By studies of nature he means cosmography, geography, physics, meteorology, botany, and zoology. By the second category he understands both industry and commerce as man's relations to man and resources. By the highest of all academic pursuits, last, and those reserved for the highest achievers in school, Rousseau reserved those disciplines relative to man himself: history, politics, and religion. One is to understand that by history he means the distant past, and by politics he understands the recent past, such as the last hundred or so years.

In *Emile,* Rousseau studied the education of a fictional hero named Emile whose studies he followed from birth into manhood, and then the education of a fictional heroine named Sophie. In his novel *Julie* he referred his reader back to medieval times. His celebrated heroine Julie, who in her novel of the same name is being educated in the home of her wealthy family by a handsome, young upper-class tutor, brings Rousseau's reader down to a finely delineated, fictional autobiography of a girl by a male author, Rousseau.

More specifically than that, however, Rousseau warns his reader by the very title of his novel *Julie, or The New Heloïse* that he is referring to the most celebrated scandal, or cause célèbre, of the Middle Ages. Heloïse was, we are asked to believe, a French girl being educated by her tutor in Paris in the Middle Ages. Thus, Julie duplicates the experience of another girl, then famous as Heloïse, who is still fairly famous even today.

Rousseau believed sincerely, and there seems no grounds for argument here, that Heloïse really lived in the Middle Ages, was probably historical, and really was tutored by a young scholar who was also probably historical, and that their story also was true, and happened as a series of letters from one to another truly related.

Such beliefs are, in my opinion untenable, for the so-called letters exchanged by Heloïse and her tutor bear all the earmarks of a fictional device fairly commonplace in French letters and furthermore one repeated in Rousseau's lifetime by a book called *Letters from a Portuguese Nun.* These were, in fact, fiction and written clandestinely by a man. The author was again a French aristocrat. In this attack on a Catholic nunnery he had every reason in the world to maintain strict anonymity. Rousseau claimed in his *Confessions* that women, who were the principal purchasers of books in his time also, fell so wildly in love with authors that he could have had any great lady of his century if he had wanted so much as to snap his fingers in her direction.

Voltaire had said of *Julie,* however, that one of the greatest infamies of the century was the way the public applauded Rousseau's "monstrous" novel. For his part, Choderlos de Laclos, who also hated women, found it "the premier work of the century." The Madame Roland who became famous for her active role in the French Revolution, claimed: "When I am with Rousseau, I would like to stop the sun in its course." "Ah," cried Rousseau, "the book is about Julie's being and her nothingness. That's why they love it." And I resemble her, he also wrote (because he wrote volumes, all in longhand, and copied them all five or six times on blue paper for several great ladies in Paris), in that like Julie I have always felt hypnotized and near dying around lakes and water.

Very adroitly Rousseau pegged his novel around an exchange of letters between Julie and her tutor. He used the same device, letters to and from Heloïse and the celebrated church scholar Peter Abelard (died April 21, 1142).

These medieval letters constitute such a scurrilous attack on a great scholar, and are so defamatory that today one hesitates, in fact refuses, to believe them true. In 1116 Peter Abelard (as his name is now spelled in English) became not only Dean of Notre Dame in Paris but also full professor at the Sorbonne, University of Paris. He was also a likely target for attack in that he was not French, but a Celt from the poor province of Brittany on the west coast, and the poor son of impoverished Bretons.

When this celebrated, talented teacher Abelard was thirty-seven years of age, he was asked, says our improbable scenario, to tutor Heloïse, the daughter of a minor clergyman attached to the medieval cathedral. It appears that she wished to learn to read and write. Such is not totally impossible, of course, since a few women over that period of a thousand years are known not to have been illiterate. There apparently was such an Heloïse, and such a woman entered the church and died on May 17, 1164. During her girlhood she bore an illegitimate child whose father was later said to be the still very renowned church scholar Peter Abelard. These illicit lovers are said, today still, to be buried in the same tomb at Père Lachaise Cemetery in the city of Paris. This so-called authentic correspondence has been widely edited (Paris, 1616; Paris, 1797, in three volumes; London, edited anonymously in 1722; Paris, 1841; with publication of recently discovered, new letters).

Rousseau keeps close parallels between Julie's letters and the medieval letters. Rousseau eventually names Julie's tutor Saint-Preux (meaning in pseudomedieval French "Sainted or Holy Proud Hero"). He mimics the exchange of the scandalous letters between Abelard and Heloïse.

One notes that the real Peter Abelard was one of the most disputatious and most feared of medieval dialecticians, still considered today the real founder of the University of Paris. His enemies included the even more famous Saint Bernard of Clairvaux, who founded the Knights Templar, preached the Crusades, and managed in 1121 to have Abelard's works declared heretical. This renowned medieval professor Abelard's most bitter enemy was among the champions of the Church, but to his eternal credit the most brilliant of French and English scholars among his devoted students there at Notre Dame, at Saint-Denis in the northeastern suburb, and elsewhere. Among his students were the worshipful Peter Lombard, John of Salisbury, and Arnold of Brescia.

After Abelard founded his last monastery inside Brittany, he also founded a house for holy women nearby. This last act probably gave some impertinent, obscene, and jealous rival the idea to write the series of letters still attributed to Abelard and Heloïse. Before it draws to a sad close, their "love affair" became more and more scurrilous.

It is even claimed that for his sexual relations with the future nun Heloïse, Peter Abelard was attacked in Paris one night and emasculated.

Part I of *Julie* narrates the gradual capitulation of the rich, privileged heroine and her lower-class tutor obliged to earn his meager living in the luxurious Swiss estate of his pupil. Julie endearingly, as pretty, simple, little girls are charmingly endearing, calls herself his "servant," his "child," his "wife," and his "sister." In the spurious letters Abelard calls Heloïse *"soror mihi in seculo cara in Christo carissima"*—"sister dear to me, most dear in this century of Christ"—in silly Latin, which the real, learned Abelard would also, long before us, have chastised any student of his for uttering.

Silly, vapid Julie writes Saint-Preux that between them no possibility of marriage could ever arise since her father would never condescend to the thought that a working commoner could ever dare love his daughter. "Will not love have more power than marriage to keep our hearts firmly united?" she sobs.

Saint-Preux has Julie's picture in his room. She has Abelard's picture in her suite of chambers. As the lover in either case falls more and more out of love, the so-called student in either case becomes more and more infatuated. By the end of Part I, Julie arranges the circumstances of her own seduction. Her child by Saint-Preux is stillborn.

Rousseau is largely responsible for the theory of "deathless love" as attributed to the twelfth century. Love, repeats Julie, over and over, ad nauseam, is "the hideous precipice" down which a girl "falls in love." Love is the *"funeste passion,"* passionate and death-dealing, and funereal. It is *"le fol amour"*—madness in love. It is *the sacrifice* of one's maidenhood. It is the fateful down-slope into death. "Sensual love," she preaches, "cannot live without sex and dies with it." "True love" lasts as long as the foreplay, she (Rousseau) dares add. Love is not necessary before marriage. As for poor Saint-Preux, whom she soon tires of seducing in her bedroom, he goes mountain climbing in the

Alps and traveling with an English Lord, by which he manages to calm down. Julie commits suicide. She fell or slipped into a Swiss lake where, not so very sadly, she drowned.

Unlike Eve, Julie expelled herself from the lovely lakes and mountains of Rousseau's beloved Switzerland, which was the lesser of her major crimes.

Her story otherwise resembles Eve's. Julie adheres as Rousseau did also, to the classical Judeo-Christian myth of the sexually active woman who corrupts man by eating, or biting into, the apple of knowledge. Thus, she expelled herself from Paradise.

Julie presented to the modern world the Talmudic and Christian view of sinful woman who has reached out for knowledge, or whose tutor has essayed in vain to persuade her to do so. Like all daughters of Eve, however, Julie here succumbed to her own naturally unbridled sexual appetites. She was not raped by Saint-Preux of the ancient, noble name. She seduced him, tired of him, and killed herself. Rousseau found her as evil as Eve. As for himself, Rousseau abandoned his own children. He found sex evil. He had early adopted rigorous Protestantism, exchanged this faith for Roman Catholicism, and later returned to Calvinistic Protestantism.

Jean-Jacques Rousseau's *Julie,* since Romanticism rose to fashion, has been gradually dropped out of sight after more than two hundred years and is out of print in the United States. As far as fiction went, Rousseau's novel was ousted from public consumption by the generation of masters born between 1845 and 1852. Their very names read like a roster of the blessed: Dostoyevsky, born in Russia in 1845; Gustave Flaubert, born in Normandy, France, in 1849; and the two great and highly educated noblemen born in Old Russia in 1852, Tolstoy and Turgenev. By this time the eyes of France had already been opened wide by the person of Mérimée. In middle age Prosper Mérimée decided to begin his education all over again by learning to read and translate Russian. Thus, he introduced France and Western Europeans, who all read French anyway, to a great new master of world letters: Alexander Pushkin, or Russia's first black poet and novelist, Aleksandr Sergeyevich Pushkin (1799–1837).

Immediately after Mérimée's translations of Pushkin, Europe understood that a new view of the world, of woman, and of society was about to snatch their laurels away from French authors, formerly the crowned heads of Western civilization. Their crowns had already fallen. Mere words now cannot express the general respect and gratitude to the four new Russian masters of the novel: Pushkin, Dostoyevsky, Turgenev, and then Tolstoy, who outlived and out-produced them all, and who personally entertained and taught the world until his death in 1910. Although Count Leo Tolstoy traveled widely in Western Europe, spoke French as his first language, and read avidly in French and Belgian historians, he never resided in France as Turgenev did.

Both the French Flaubert and the cosmopolitan Turgenev were friends and colleagues, and both endorsed a new impersonal style in literature called "art for art's sake." For five years Flaubert agonized to expel his own persona from his great, first novel *Madame Bovary* (1856). And yet when he was accused of using the life and death of a real Frenchwoman as model for his heroine Emma Bovary, Flaubert quipped: *"Non. Madame Bovary, c'est moi."* Emma is me. But her bovine husband, Charles Bovary, was Everyman. In actuality, Flaubert distanced himself even better than Mérimée had done in writing *Carmen* (1852). While Mérimée stashed Carmen's story between two pseudoarchaeological frames on Spain, Flaubert totally obliterated his authorship of *Madame Bovary*.

It is essential as we line up heroines from one major presentation of them to another, to admit national bias in their cases. Nationalism and patriotism play large parts in these modern centuries where major world wars erupt, calculated the English historian Arnold Toynbee, every seventeen years. A new generation of soldiers, said Toynbee, arrives at maturity every seventeen years. Thus, each new generation of novelists is conditioned by wars and terribly scarred by them.

Gustave Flaubert, for instance, was a young schoolboy during the Revolution of 1830, a frightened refugee during the bloodier Revolution of 1848, and completely broken-hearted, as was Victor Hugo also, by the massacres of French armies, one of which had surrendered and was starved to death by the Germans in full sight of French people on an island in the river at the collapse of France to Germany in the Franco-Prussian War. Flaubert died of overwork and a cerebral hemorrhage at age fifty-eight.

He was only thirty when he commenced writing *Madame Bovary:* six hundred pages written over a period of five years. Bargemen coming down the Seine River from Paris used to take fixes upon Flaubert's writing light, which was sometimes lit all night long. In daylight, Flaubert roamed the streets of Rouen, where Joan of Arc was burned, and the paths around his country house, collecting those salient details which authenticate Emma's tragic story.

Gustave Flaubert was born in Rouen Hospital, where his father was chief of staff, on December 12, 1821. As a boy he adored the old French evangelistic author Rabelais, who is France's equal or superior to Shakespeare. But he also worshipped the British Romantics: Sir Walter Scott and Lord Byron. Flaubert spent his summers at Trouville, as Marcel Proust was later to do. Like Proust, Flaubert suffered from ill health and became a semirecluse. Like Turgenev, who foretold the end of Russian aristocracy, Flaubert foretold the liberation of women in the coming century. Thus, French critics sarcastically adopt the verdict of Emma's husband, Dr. Bovary, when after viewing his wife's dead body, he declared pontifically that she had killed herself by swallowing arsenic and that it was not her fault. "It is the fault of fatality," he opined. Women are supposed to sacrifice themselves.

When French critics ape Dr. Bovary by calling the heroine's book, *Madame Bovary,* a "novel of destiny," they speak with tongue in cheek and know much better. Flaubert has, in his Chapter VI, made it very explicit that the fault lay in Emma's unsatisfied thirst for knowledge on the one hand, and the almost total poverty of her education on the other. Thus, Emma repeats in her fictional characterization the faults of her education. She did not succumb to a blind desire for sex, as Julie did, or as Tolstoy's Anna Karenina will do: all three heroines who sinned and therefore committed suicide. Emma died of boredom, of suffocation, long before she swallowed poison. Julie fell from her high cliff of passionate love and drowned in a lake, or committed suicide. The adulterous Anna Karenina threw herself before the locomotive as it pulled the train into the railway station.

Emma Bovary killed herself only after all her attempts to be happy had failed: school, husband, marriage, adultery, and spending money, running up enormous debts.

Emma's life unravelled slowly but progressively as one escape route after another proved futile. Her prison in a dull country town closed about her tighter and tighter. She died where Dr. Charles had brought her, in his dark, cold, small, poor, and cheerless stone house level with the narrow sidewalk and wet gutter flushed down, along with the town's refuse. She had progressed only toward her own dead end. Any girl raised in such a dreary town without a chance by education to escape someday to a better place where lights glow, libraries are open, theaters bring sparkle, and music is heard everywhere can know Emma's long, dreary agony—each day a live entombment. Thus, the first emancipated and modern heroine must soon follow Emma's hobble skirts.

On May 27, 1795, the French government had passed three decrees against French women: (1) They must henceforth remain indoors, and are forbidden to congregate in any group consisting of more than five women; (2) women are forbidden ever to attend any meeting of a political nature; and (3) all women suspected of fomenting, or of having fomented sedition, are to be minutely investigated. These laws brought in a new style of feminine apparel, which was a light sheath over a slim chemise. One summer defiantly *undressed* women died in masses from bronchitis. Even so, and despite the "hecatombs" of women killed earlier during the Reign of Terror, Napoleon Bonaparte still declared that what he feared most under his absolute rule was the influence and power of women. Under his Consulate, French women dressed outrageously, walking along the avenues of Paris with their breasts totally bare and their bodies stark naked under a chiffon sheath. Suddenly, and perhaps due to the aristocratic woman journalist George Sand, trousers on women also became the rage.

Even today, women who dare brave public censure by wearing pant suits recall that Saint Joan of Arc died for wearing them and for her so-called lack of femininity. The first charge against her, and which brought the death sentence down upon her head, was that she wore trousers under her suit of armor.

By a sudden leap the European novel between 1790 and 1814—during which years between four and five thousand novels were published inside France alone—arrived at preeminence as premier shaper of public opinion. By the time of *Madame Bovary* the big four literary countries had arrived at total mastery of their art and language, positions only these four have gained and still hold: England, France, Russia, and the United States.

Every novelist in these four lands knows all the great novels of his competitors. Each great book is one statement in a continuing dialogue for the betterment of both mankind and womankind. All Romantic heroines succeeding Emma Bovary lodge protests against discrimination and female oppression. Romanticism itself under the pens of the great, from Sir Walter Scott to Count Leo Tolstoy, via Gustave Flaubert, is active Insurrection. The charges are: Civilization is evil; war has been declared by the lone individual versus society; man's laws and manners are absurd; the rights of love cannot be legislated; society and power perpetually distort human justice; rebellion is therefore legitimate, necessary, and ongoing. Women too must declare war.

Emma married Dr. Charles Bovary, so incompetent a practitioner of medicine that he was honored by the bestowal of the Cross of the Legion of Honor. Before she married him, Emma thought she was or would be in love. Afterwards she strove to comprehend what the usual words could mean: love? bliss? happiness? passion?

Flaubert's seven or so pages of Chapter VI lay the blame for Emma's impoverished spirit squarely at the door of educational practices. Before age thirteen the poor girl had only read the "American" novel *Paul et Virginie,* which Saint-Pierre had set in the Caribbean islands. Paul and Virginia were raised in one cradle by their widowed mothers, and as children were inseparable. In adolescence Virginia was sent to France to finishing school. Upon her return to the New World her ship foundered in sight of its harbor. Paul cried to Virginia to jump into the surf from which he could manfully rescue her. She refused modestly to uncover her body and was pulled down to death by her heavy garments. Such a novel, mawkish in the extreme, gave Emma her first and only source of knowledge for those years of girlhood. At age thirteen she was placed in a convent.

During the first years of her stay there Emma enjoyed meeting the sisters, going to chapel with them, and walking the long corridors to the refectory. She studied her catechism and answered the vicar during his interrogations of the students. She fell under the white, mystical spell of the quiet life and loved the pretty lambs, sacred hearts, and crucified Christs on her prayer book. She tried to go whole days without food, like her mentors. She tried to take vows not to do this or that. Sooner or later she fell into somnolence.

Later she began to devour the lurid, stupid love stories smuggled in by her fellow boarders, but being of a sentimental rather than of an artistic nature she sought thrills only. Thus, handy in her apron pocket in those days she kept all these titillating details of solitary pavilions in Gothic gardens, horses spurred to death by impatient lovers, skiffs floating down moonlit streams, nightingales in the shrubbery, heroes brave as lions, gentle as lambs, and tearful as leaking faucets. She loved Sir Walter Scott's stiff, wooden Ivanhoe. She saw herself as bride in his Saracen knight's arms or as Mary Queen of Scots awaiting the executioner's ax. Or she led troops like Joan of Arc, wrote her homework for Heloïse's tutor Saint-Preux, died with the Protestants on the Saint Bartholomew's Eve massacre. She preferred, when given a choice, romances written by viscounts.

Before her father withdrew Miss Emma from the convent, he might have learned, had he asked, that the sisters were heartily sick of her. And she of them. They recognized Emma for what she was: "limited."

At first she enjoyed being home again and assuming charge of the small household after her mother's death. Within a few days she wished herself back in the convent. The exchange of one incarceration for another depressed her. Now she had not even the few books to reread and occasionally a new one to peruse in stolen moments.

When Dr. Bovary began to call on Emma, he brought, at the least, a new face into the one, cold downstairs room. She was not sure whether his presence excited her by its novelty or irritated her that he did not transform her heart into some splendid, rose-colored dove which must be love. Or was the stillness of her person love?

After living as his wife for a few days, Emma began to withdraw completely into herself. Her next recourse was escape into a cruel, outer world where she fell victim to one sex-starved man after another, as to one circumstance after another. Emma had no power over either world, nor over herself. She had no notion of her own person.

Had Emma Bovary attended school in France today, she would have been separated by age twelve from those of her classmates able to continue into high school and even college. Flaubert's evaluation of his heroine as a girl shows her low degree of intelligence. As she proceeded in school, she dissociated herself more and more completely from the pursuit of knowledge. Contemporary France would not have wasted on such a girl an expensive education in Latin literature, for instance. She would have been educated in areas that appealed to her, and in skills or some trade which she probably would have enjoyed pursuing all her life long. With an education acceptable to her, she might even have earned a living wage.

We must admit, thus far, that both Rousseau and Flaubert present pessimistic views of woman's possibilities.

It is one warning to have Rousseau demonstrate how girls fall into the medieval pattern of Heloïse by being seduced instead of taught or, as in Julie's sad case, by seducing their private, lower-class tutor, and then killing themselves. It comes as a second, even more dire warning to have Emma Bovary gradually lapse from attention to her kind teachers, fall out of love, take to adultery, slide into consumerism, and finally swallow arsenic. A third injunction had already appeared in *Dangerous Acquaintances*.* There Madame Stéphanie de Genlis (1746–1830), who was a real teacher of elementary school subjects for the children of the Duke of Orleans, composed the following cautionary verses:

Change donc, ma fille,
Ta plume en aiguille,
Brûle ton papier;
Il faut te résoudre
A filer, à coudre:
C'est là ton métier.

(Therefore, my girl, change
Your pen for a needle,
Burn up your paper;
You must make up your mind
To spin and sew:
That is your life work.)

*Choderlos de Laclos. *Oeuvres complètes,* Pléiade, p. 495.

Madame de Genlis died in 1830, however, during another major revolution. Even before she passed away, the social leader, La Marquise du Deffand, was in 1766 entertaining demon lovers and all famous authors in her Paris salon. English intellectuals, in particular the patrician Horace Walpole, thronged to Paris to discover what innovations were brewing. Jealousy between French and English novelists has always spawned new fiction. The results of this rivalry amaze us today.

Rousseau's adoption in 1761 of the medieval legend or fiction of Heloïse was seen by high society as a very innovative Gothic "tone," *"ce ton gothique."* Three years later Horace Walpole published in England the first "Gothic" novel, *The Castle of Otranto*. He was followed immediately by Clara Reeve and Ann Ward Radcliffe, who have already been discussed, and who improved upon his format and offered the world very exciting reading and, what is not surprising, *real, heroical heroines*.

Most successful novelists of Gothic fiction, as launched most brilliantly in those years (1764–1794), came finally to fix upon the castle, or château, or house as the title of their novel: Sir Walter Scott, Edgar Allan Poe, Alexandre Dumas, Nathaniel Hawthorne, Jules Verne, Franz Kafka, Jean Giono, Louis-Ferdinand Céline. Others chose the demon lover as hero: *The Monk, Frankenstein,* and *Dracula*. Some even chose a heroine, who was always a White Goddess: *Jane Eyre, Carmilla, Nadja,* and William Faulkner's Emily in "A Rose for Emily."

While revolutions continued to terrify Europe throughout the nineteenth century, the Gothic novel increased in popularity because it was and has always been a novel of terror. This horror, this sublime terror felt by the heroine as she enters the dark castle at night reproduces the historical heroines of the French Revolution's Reign of Terror. Women then, many of whom were great aristocrats bred to live fearlessly and proudly, died fearlessly under the public blade of the guillotine. Similarly, in the Gothic novel, demigoddesses descended fearlessly, but trembling, even into the subterranean vaults of the

Gothic castle. Why? What were they searching for? Rousseau to the contrary, they were searching for knowledge. They repeat ancient mythology.

These women in white, who have been for centuries by now, our beloved, brave heroines always seek to unmask, dethrone, catch out, and punish their would-be demon lovers. While the heroine is easy to study, being young, adventurous, idealistic, pure, and enterprising, her demon lover is more difficult to pin down. In some cases he actually kills her, so that the author is obliged to double his heroine. In Bram Stoker's most famous depiction of *Dracula* (1897), the hero wants mainly to bite her in the throat and suck her blood.

This demon lover also occurs from very ancient times in literature: in a French miracle play of the thirteenth century, versus Faust, who sells his soul to the devil, seduces the maiden, and abandons her; in Spain and the Mozart opera as Don Juan, bound to hell for similar crimes of the 1,003 rapes and abandonments of noble señoritas.

Ironically the white goddess, who is the most successful heroine in fiction, seeks knowledge, and this despite Rousseau and Flaubert. Flickering candle in hand she seeks to discover and remedy some awful crime committed once inside the dark, medieval castle. Thus, she anticipates Agatha Christie's elderly Miss Marple, who always becomes more agitated when girls and women have been murdered.

The bravery of another woman novelist who does not flinch from a close portrayal of the terrible depression of 1840 in the Five Towns of industrial England, and including Glasgow, is Mrs. Elizabeth Gaskell in *Mary Barton* (1848). It was her first novel, just as *Madame Bovary* was Flaubert's first novel, and one which unfolded during the same depression in France. Gaskell was a vicar's wife in Manchester. She saw people freeze and starve by the hundreds and look towards America, not as Moll Flanders's get-rich paradise or Manon Lescaut's penal colony, but as a future home where a working family could live honest lives, toil, and educate children.

In the Manchester of 1840 Mary Barton had only two careers open to her at age thirteen: servant or apprentice seamstress. But she becomes a truly heroical heroine in defense of her fiancé.

Protected by her husband, Elizabeth Gaskell is always called her husband's wife rather than an author. She is "Mrs. Gaskell" to this day, and never Elizabeth Stevenson (1810–1865).

Poor George Eliot (dismissed as "a woman writing under a man's name") never dared soil her family by calling herself by her own name: Mary Ann (Marian) Evans. But in *Adam Bede* (1859), a mere ten years after Gaskell, she pleaded like an angel silver-tongued for women's rights. When the girl heroine Hetty found herself pregnant, and realized she was not wed as she had thought, she gave birth in the woods alone. She stuffed her child under the root of a tree and wandered desolately away, hearing its feeble cries in her ears. She was, of course, sentenced to life in prison. When she hid her baby, all she had in the living world was the rest of one crust of bread. Oh, never to be born a woman, a heroine can only cry even today!

◆READINGS◆

EARTH MOTHERS

Gayley, Charles Mills. *The Classic Myths in English Literature and Art,* illustrated. Ginn and Company (Boston, New York, Chicago, and London, 1893).

Graves, Robert. *The Greek Myths*. Vols. I and II. Penguin Books (Harmondsworth, England, 1955).

Hesiod and the Theognis. Translated with an Introduction by Dorothy Wender, Penguin Classics (Harmondsworth, England, 1973).

THE HEROINES OF ROUSSEAU AND FLAUBERT

Flaubert, Gustave. *Madame Bovary*. Presented by Henri Troyat of the French Academy, Editions J'ai lu 103 and 104 (Paris, n.d.). (English editions in print, Signet Classic, New American Library/ Dutton.)

Rousseau, Jean-Jacques. *Julie, ou La Nouvelle Heloïse,* illustrated. Classiques Garnier. Introduction and Notes by René Pomeau (Paris, 1960).

———. *Emile, ou de l'Education*. Edited by François and Pierre Richard, Classiques Garnier (Paris, n.d.).

CHAPTER IV

Prostitutes and Fallen Women

PROSTITUTES

Some decades ago critics in our own century spoke widely of a fictional character they named the "antihero." They meant he was the chief male character of a book, usually a novel, who could in no way be seen as heroic. He exhibited, on the contrary, very unheroic characteristics. We saw him in the movies, playing the various like-able roles assigned to Caspar Milquetoast: a poor fellow, a cute guy, but a weakling and utter failure. He became the new hero for the twentieth century—one who defied traditional heroic standards and was admired by many.

In dealing with the isolation of heroines, especially when these women characters live in the demimonde, or are prostitutes, we could as easily call them antiheroines.

The Old Testament forbade prostitution and laid down the law as seen in Genesis 34.31 (a harlot is not a sister) and Proverbs 7.27 (her house is the way to hell). The New Testament agreed, as in I Corinthians 6.18 (flee fornication) and Revelation 17.5 (harlots are abominations of the earth). Judeo-Christian teachings have always castigated any connections between prostitution and religious observances and all sexual orgies reportedly practiced along with worship of such pagan deities as Mylitta, Baal, Moloch, and Astarte.

Historians have observed from their studies of Egypt, Phoenicia, Persia, Assyria, Babylon, and India that when prostitution is tolerated in a society, moral depravity and debauchery are the consequent signs of the self-destruction of that society.

Prostitution, then, is widely recognized both by theologians and by historians as signaling decadence. The deterioration of morals and abuse of women, announces an oncoming collapse. Women who see themselves as victims and who choose prostitution as a way of earning their living are said to love excitement and danger. Their sexual appetite is said to be as large as is their taste for drugs, crime, leisure, and luxury.

After the problem of prostitution was referred to the United Nations, such generalizations surfaced globally. The external conditions which were given as excuses for girls and women turning to prostitution appeared to be identical worldwide.

The cause of school drop-outs and of subsequent prostitution must be considered serious. The *Los Angeles Times* staff writer Denise Hamilton reported in a feature article on prostitution (H3, November 12, 1991) that high-priced, well-dressed prostitutes in Russia today, and one such is pictured in Kiev's Intourist Hotel, denote "the depth of the economic and moral collapse." Hamilton reports that "60 percent of schoolgirls in Russia today" said they wanted to be high-priced prostitutes when they grew up. Prostitution now ranks "8th among the top 20 preferred professions."

Some blame democracy for the "big problem" of prostitution in Russia. It appears to be true that women are highly respected only in aristocratic societies, England, for example.

In the following pages five famous, epoch-making studies of prostitution, in Greece, Byzantium, England and France, will hopefully open our eyes to this terrible sign of the collapse of modern civilizations, including our own. The prostitute Phryne from ancient Greece is mythological because she was worshipped as a human manifestation of the Cyprian goddess of love, Aphrodite. The Empress Theodora (died A.D. 548) was a real woman whose dark and drooping face we have all seen on photographs of the Ravenna Mosaic where she stands crowned beside her husband, Emperor Justinian. They lead into memorable literary characters: Moll Flanders, Manon Lescaut, and the Camille that Greta Garbo immortalized on the screen.

The reader is requested now to arm himself, and especially to arm herself, with one piece of protective equipment from philosophy and theology. Prostitutes are usually looked at from one of two philosophical/theological points of view. These mindsets can be defined, as can prostitutes, as either free or predetermined. We see Moll Flanders, who is a prime example, as a fallen woman working her way slowly and with courage up the social scale until she has cleared her skirts of all the dirt of prostitution and her person of disease and poverty. The alternate view of life comes from French literature in the two last cases: Manon Lescaut and Camille.

When the French theologian Jean Calvin finished his *Institutes of the Christian Religion* in 1536, he posited predestination, or determinism, as a fundamental doctrine of Calvinism. He then took his analysis to Geneva, Switzerland, where it passed to John Knox in Scotland, then to the Puritan Revolution in England, then to the Plymouth Rock and Massachusetts Bay Colony in 1630.

By extension, the theory that a woman's life is already predestined even before she is born explains why certain women, and all prostitutes, are considered *totally depraved*. They can be neither helped nor cured, certain people think. They are, according to this theory, irremediably lost. Many modern American novelists and dramatists hold Calvinist views.

We shall see one example in the following pages, the Byzantine Empress Theodora, whose character and deeds are narrated with no allegation of any extenuating circumstance. In her case, said Suetonius, there could have been none. She was *totally depraved,* totally evil. She deserved to die ignobly, and so did Manon Lescaut, *atque idem* Camille. Theodora's hideous behavior and her reign of terror were never explained in ancient times.

Such violence could be the result of guilt, which could have commenced building in Theodora as early as age two, until her hatred of people turned her into a monster once she laid her hands on absolute power. Her violence could have stemmed, psychologists now say, from a load of guilt transformed into hatred.

This evil empress once showed great courage, however, in the face of revolutionaries. Her behavior otherwise betrayed her suffering: frequent hot baths and her repeated retreats from Istanbul to the Asian side where tourists still go today to bask in sunshine and enjoy the gorgeous flowers.

The reader of the following pages, however, is now again requested to accept or reject this theory of total depravity. Does such a condition exist in a human being? Are some women and girl children totally evil? Were their parents "demons" in human form?

Such questions exist today as thorns in our side because so many contemporary American writers, and cinematographers especially, have done their best, said the famous critic Edmund Fuller, to persuade us so. The consequences direct us to accept and tolerate evil or to legislate, control, and abolish prostitution.

The reader is referred to two famous and sympathetic works of fiction: Somerset Maugham's short story "Rain," with its chief character Sadie Thompson; and the tragic American indictment of prostitution, Theodore Dreiser's *Sister Carrie,* which this author considers one of the world's greatest novels. Publisher Frank Doubleday's wife asked her husband to withdraw *Sister Carrie* from publication. It took seven years, or until 1907, for Dreiser's novel to be published in the United States.

The cleverest short stories of our century have flowed, probably, from the prose of William Somerset Maugham (1874–1965), appearing after 1921 in many collections such as *Collected Short Stories* (4 vols., Doubleday and Penguin Books, 1951). Maugham's most famous story is "Rain" (vol. I, pp. 9–45). Like the surgeon he was, Maugham here slices live tissue not anesthetized. He lays open his agonized human specimens, piths their brains, severs veins and arteries until his creatures satisfy his unquenchable desire to see *how,* as Dr. Zhivago has explained, they became whore and lunatic missionary. He ferrets about like any freshman in Zoology I and actually sees *how* the last heart throb dies. Unlike Boris Pasternak, Maugham allows his reader to wonder forever why Sadie Thompson was sentenced to jail in California, and why the missionary became sexually repressed, if repression was his hang-up.

In "Rain" he juxtaposes the hero's unsatisfied lust to copulate alongside the prostitute's terror of his returning her to three more years in penitentiary. His white goddess of whoredom is Sadie Thompson, played in the movies, and unforgettably, by Joan Crawford, against the cruel, equally agonized missionary Claude Rains.

Maugham blames this ancient Greek tragedy on the "malignant," "primitive" monsoons in Pago-Pago. The hot, tropical downpour brought out *the ancient evil* of their human hearts. Fiercely malignant is the surgeon's diagnosis, and "all too human" (p. 38). Succumbing to seduction, the missionary bows to extinction, but the vulgar whore triumphs. Right has won, she exults, over such a "dirty pig" as him.

Notable also is Maugham's "The Mother" (vol. I); but also the many heroines in Vol. II are "dogs" ("The Round Dozen"), whores again ("The Man with the Scar" and "The Closed Shop"), murderesses ("Footprints in the Jungle"), and dreamers of murder ("The Dream"). Giulia Lozzari kills her lover in Vol. IV. Another woman is caught in "The Letter" (Vol. IV), which stands alongside "Rain" as probably Maugham's second most shattering story.

Maugham said he traveled to "see men," but in his Preface to the film *Quartet* (1948) he adds: "My stories fill out the pattern of life I made for myself." In Vol. IV "fiendish" murders by a woman appear five times (pp. 317, 321, 322, 324, 336–7). Men do not murder, says Maugham, because they do not feel passionate love as women do. This is another example of Rousseau's sick doctrine. To think that in Italy a prostitute advised Rousseau to "leave off women and stick to mathematics," as he reported in his *Confessions*.

Phryne, the Greek Courtesan

When the celebrated lawgiver Solon was elected to govern Athens around 594 B.C., he established legal houses of prostitution, called *dicteria*. There girls and women were confined and forbidden to enter the better parts of the city. They were policed by being assigned other disabilities such as the obligation to wear a certain costume by which they could be quickly recognized and avoided. They were also forbidden to attend religious services, which other women could share, even if only on special days of the year. The state police assumed responsibility for enforcing the laws of this Athenian *democracy*.

The world's most famous prostitute worked in Athens some two hundred years after the death of Solon. Her name was "Toad," and the description of her face has characterized the celebrated prostitutes of literature ever since about 300 B.C. Her name Phryne, meaning toad, described a pale face which had acquired this lack of color because she sold her loathsome wares at night and was rarely allowed out of doors in sunlight. Phryne was born in Thespies, and her father's name was Epicles. It is not known if he was the person who first sold this beauty into prostitution, or if it was, as it usually was, the girl's first lover who did this.

Phryne became well known in Greece and was patronized by only the richest of politicians; she was not called "prostitute" (which is a

Roman word anyway). She was called "courtesan," which is the French equivalent *(courtisane)* from the Italian "court mistress." Thus, as *courtesan* or *courtezan*, Phryne is still recognized as having been sexually and illicitly associated with courtiers, men of the highest political power in the state or courts.

The New Testament associated harlots and publicans (Matthew 21, 31). Jewish men are said to be forbidden to frequent harlots, or, worse yet, to hire her sexual services. Thus, Israel has this further distinction of having been, it is said, along with Lucrece's republican Rome, the only nation to have successfully controlled, even from the Old Testament centuries, disease-ridden prostitutes.

The much uglier English word *whore* is of Scandinavian *(ware, hoare)* and German origin, which explains its special repugnant sound to us native speakers of modern English. It is our own native, Anglo-Saxon word of scorn and hatred.

The word *harlot,* which sounds anodine enough to our ears, came rather late from Normandy, France, into our language. It appears to have derived from propaganda artfully invented to disparage and humiliate the Norman Duke William after his lightning conquest of Anglo-Saxon England in 1066. Behind his back after that date, and softly if they did not want their tongues cut out, his enemies called him "bastard" and his mother "harlot." They thus felt better by calling King William I of Britain a nothing, an upstart of a prostituted mother, a *homo nihili*. Duke William's mother was a "washer-woman," they said. Her son was a "guy," a "fellow," a "nothing man" of a mother named Arletta, or "Arlotta," a "harlot." Thus, the word *harlot* originally designated a man, some low fellow of despicable, low-class family. Prostitution is also known to originate from a poverty-stricken, "low-class" background.

For her part the Greek courtesan Phryne, even though she was pale as a toad, became very rich from "servicing" the mighty, wealthy rulers of Athens. Her beginnings were also very humble. It is still said she came originally to Athens as a flute player in a band of homeless street musicians. She was, however, a woman of such splendid beauty that she was able to amass a huge fortune.

During her lifetime the Greeks once undertook to rebuild the walls of Thebes, a project that, like all such community actions, degenerated into political rows and male contests for power and money. Phryne insolently offered to fund the project personally. The city of Thebes had sided with the Persians against Athens in the Persian Wars, and was punished for its pains. Thebes had also at first joined the Spartans against Athens in the Peloponnesian War. However, when Philip II of Macedon invaded Greece, the Thebans joined Athens to defeat him at Chaeronea in 338 B.C. It was Cassander and not Phryne who rebuilt Thebes in 315 B.C. Phryne's offer was, of course, refused. But her insolence is remembered.

Although she lived under the ban of social and religious ostracism, Phryne at least once attended the festival of the sea god Poseidon at the sacred women's center of Eleusis. There, in plain view of a pious throng of worshippers, the Athenian courtesan stripped naked and daringly stepped down into the ocean waves.

It is thus that the famous artist of Cos (336–323 B.C.), Apelles, painted Phryne. This picture was the Phryne also called "Anadyomene," which was the epithet of Venus of Cyprus: She who emerges from the sea *(Anadyomene)*. Phryne also worked as model for the world-celebrated Greek sculptor Praxiteles who made in her image his Cnidian Aphrodite (Venus). The statue once stood at Cnidos (Gnidos), a town in the Asia-Minor province of Caria.

For this, or another illegal invasion of the temple at Eleusis, Phryne the Courtesan was hauled into court, charged with having by her bawdy presence and her overt actions polluted the sacred Eleusinian Mysteries.

These were the same, highly secret rites which Alcestis also may have attended, and those also which Euripides was either charged with revealing, or suspected of having revealed in his play. The sentence was death if pollution or revelation was proven in court. Phryne was more than insolent.

One of Phryne's regular customers was the defense attorney Hypereides (Hyperides), a friend and contemporary of the greatest Greek orator Demosthenes. He defended Phryne. As his closing argument, he strode up to the beautiful defendant. In plain sight of the Court he reached across, grabbed her gown, and ripped it down the front, thus exposing her beautiful bosom to all eyes. Phryne was acquitted immediately.

Phryne's arrogance apparently knew no limit. She even tried to seduce one of Plato's great admirers and disciples, Xenocrates, a native of Chalcedon, a town opposite what was later Byzantium. In addition, Xenocrates was then the august rector of the Athens Academy (339–314 B.C.). As admirer of Plato's *Timaeus,* Xenocrates worshipped especially the three Fates, goddesses who must have protected him here; for Phryne never hitched his scalp to her girdle.

Praxiteles stood her statue as Aphrodite in marble at her home town and furthermore gave a copy in gilded bronze to golden Delphi, throne of the most revered of all priestesses, the Delphic Oracle. The favorite subject of painters remained, however: Phryne displaying her bosom to the Tribunal. A fresco discovered at Pompeii near the volcanic Vesuvius portrayed Phryne consulting the god of love, Cupid or Eros.

Thus, to the ancient Greeks, the prostitute Phryne connoted noble, godly love. To republican Rome and the Jews (Judges II, 1) immemorial prostitution was considered ignoble, a selling of the body for money, an offering of the self for sex and for pay, the promiscuous unchastity of "lower-class" women for gain.

Christianity has had no success in eliminating prostitution. The only success has been experienced by isolated areas, or countries like Scotland and Israel, where men are forbidden to frequent prostitutes.

Thus, men are ordered there to subordinate passion, or the instinct to reproduce anywhere at any time, to the needs of the race, and ordered to preserve the purity of the blood. Thus, Israel and Scotland have maintained not only a pride of race, but also a high regard for public decency.

Early in the Middle Ages King Louis IX of France attempted to declare prostitution illegal, and in 1945 France as a nation did so, but was obliged to repeal this law a year later. Down the centuries women prostitutes everywhere were whipped publicly, shaved, pilloried, branded, imprisoned for life, burned as witches, deported to America and other colonies, and banished for life . . . to no avail. No measure against fallen women has served in any way to stop prostitution or halt the spread of sexually transmitted diseases. Again, the French seem to have worked hardest, forcing prostitutes to carry identity cards and report for medical examination weekly by policemen. Pope Innocent III (1198–1216) urged men to marry and reform such women. By the end of the Middle Ages the epidemics of venereal diseases were so widespread in Western Europe that people there blamed them on Columbus and declared that their infections had been endemic to the New World, a charge that was totally false.

The rise of proletarianism caused Lutherans, Calvinists, and other Puritans to make a concerted but short effort to stamp out prostitution:

Germany 1531
Basel 1534
London 1546
Paris 1560
Nuremburg 1562

By 1892 French scholars were pointing to the standing army as the principal cause of prostitution and the resultant epidemics of venereal disease:

Nation	# of Soldiers	# of Cases, Venereal Disease
England	193,336	52,455
France	524,719	46,214
Russia	872,560	77,832
Germany	434,680	14,637

Survey of 1900

Prussia	. . . . . .	500,000 new cases per year

In both France and Israel laws forbidding prostitution continued down the centuries. The Jews allowed it with foreign women only. France in 1635 condemned all men proven to have had intercourse with a prostitute to the galleys for life. Ancient Israel went so far as to forbid women to enter Jerusalem. Their punishment for prostitutes was death. If a betrothed damsel was unchaste, she was stoned to death. Venereal disease was recorded in this same ancient world (Lev. 25). At the other end of the spectrum, Kings Henry II, Richard the Lion-Hearted who was one of his sons, and Edward III passed laws to protect prostitutes. However, the English King Henry VIII abolished the English houses of prostitution in 1546. He called venereal disease the "infirmity" most to be dreaded, most loathsome: *infirmitas nefanda*.

In America prostitution is centered, as elsewhere, in our large cities; but here as the twentieth century draws to a close prostitutes are much envied for their earnings, and much admired as "call *girls*" in our metropolitan centers. In Las Vegas they are adored by men, and even more so there by American females of all ages. Prostitution is illegal in the United States, though what appears to be slack enforcement or tolerance may make it seem otherwise.

Empress Theodora (d. 548)

The daughter of an animal trainer in the circus, an actress, dancer, and prostitute by age seven, Theodora married Justinian in 523. When, four years later, he became Emperor of the Byzantine Empire at Constantinople, she soon became his joint Empress. His passion for her made Theodora's pale face feared from one border of the empire to the other, as torturer, thief, murderess, extortionist, before whom all persons were obliged to lie face down on the ground. Only then did she allow them to kiss the sole of her bare foot, at the instep. Her secret torture chambers, said the historian Procopius in his *Secret History*, lay under her palace. They were kept so dark that her prisoners, whose fortunes and property she had not yet finished transferring to herself, eventually lost their sight, becoming also as white as toads in underground caverns.

All the women who came in contact with Theodora became depraved, claimed Procopius, her eyewitness. Her crimes, he wrote, were inhumanity to man, fierce animosity to other people, unapproachability, brutality to her own slaves, murder of a queen, castration of men, exile of ministers, and immediate murder of her own grown son when he arrived from overseas at her court.

Both she and Justinian were not human was the only theory Procopius could evolve to explain these tyrants. The pair of them were demons. The empress spent inordinate amounts of time on her bodily needs, always eating, bathing, and sleeping for excessively long periods of time. As soon as she awoke, she fell to ordering vessels burned at sea, men mutilated, estates annexed, letters forged, treasures looted, girls married, governors, generals, and elders defamed, jailed, and killed.

Two great historians, Edward Gibbon in England and the jurist Baron de Montesquieu in France, were very interested in the decadence of Byzantium under the rule of the empress and prostitute Theodora. Gibbon points out that Justinian was not a Roman, but a barbarian from Sardica, now Sophia in Bulgaria. This youth from an obscure race of savage tribesmen in what was then a wild and desolate country had journeyed on foot to join an older Justin. The latter had done likewise, come on foot, joined the Byzantine army, and mounted the throne at age sixty-eight. He had his relative Justinian raised to follow him on the throne. The youth was taught how to rule: by the circus (to placate the populace), the churches (to gain adherents), and the senators (by putting them deep in his pockets). Justinian adhered to the orthodoxy, encouraged the populace to crave parades, and enriched the senators. Acceding to the throne at age forty-five, Justinian played a double game with Theodora, and he ruled for almost thirty-nine years. They were the two inhuman demons, Procopius urged, who presented a united front for the purpose of destroying mankind.

As an alumna of demons, Gibbon explained, Theodora surpassed the other evil females we have heard about from Israel: Eve, Dalila, and Herodias. Her elevation to supreme power, he added, "cannot be applauded as the triumph of female virtue" (vol. IV, Chapter XL, p. 160). What could be expected from a girl raised in the circus, her father a "master of the bears" from Cyprus? In early childhood Theodora was the comic in pantomime. All her life her sexual charm kept hundreds of men fighting for her body. As a lovely Cyprian wearing only a narrow belt, she was exhibited for sale night after night on stage. At any banquet she sold as entertainment her favors to as many as ten youths and thirty slaves. In order to wed her, Justinian actually repealed existing laws which forbade anyone to marry a slave, a prostitute, a degenerate, or a libertine.

No jurist could be surprised, Montesquieu believed, at the general collapse of civilization in what became Constantinople during the long reign of Justinian and Theodora. Decadence in a civilization, he taught, always follows great wealth and the collapse of morals. Depravity and decadence go hand in hand. What causes the collapse of morals? Corruption in the heads of the state when rulers are corrupt; depravity soon descends through all the citizenry.

The prostitute empress died of a cancer that had spread throughout her whole body: *"toto corpore perfusa."* She died after twenty-four years of marriage and twenty-two years of an absolute reign of terror. She encouraged massacres, riots, the rape of matrons, the seizure of noble boys for prostitution, the forcible marriages of little girls, and night raids by gangs robbing and kidnapping the rich and powerful.

When Theodora went abroad once to take the baths, she required the roads over which she would travel to be repaired, a palace to be built to receive her, and four thousand attendants to serve her.

Moll and Manon

The three most famous, or at any rate best known, prostitutes of the modern world are heroines of the works of literature: Moll Flanders, whose fictional memoirs were written by Daniel Defoe, England (1722); Manon Lescaut, adventures recorded by the Abbé Prévost, France (1731); and "Camille" or Marguerite (Daisy) Gautier, also called *The Lady of the* (white) *Camelias* (Paris, 1852), star of a five-act drama *(La Dame aux camélias),* by Alexandre Dumas fils. Daniel Defoe died the year *Manon Lescaut* appeared, but the French priest Abbé Prévost was a herculean translator of English fiction. He either knew or translated *Moll Flanders.* As for Alexandre Dumas fils, son of his most prolific, loving, and indulgent father, who was also a major Romantic dramatist, novelist, traveler, benefactor, historian, and close friend of Paris courtesans, he knew the major works of art in the Western world. He even refers to Phryne in his plays on prostitutes, libertines, and other *débauchées* of the Paris demimonde.

Several neologisms, such as *demimonde,* coined by Dumas fils to designate the Paris underworld, have passed into modern languages from these three heroines: a *Moll* or a *Marguerite* who is as pale-faced as a white "camelia," or any other prostitute called "Toad." All these minor connections lead us to very influential personages, all of whom were discriminated against because of sex, profession, life-style, or race:

1. Alexandre Dumas, because he was a wealthy author, but remarkable in any day, because he was a rich, black author.

2. Alexandre Dumas fils, illegitimate son of this celebrated black author, doubly stigmatized because of birth *and* race.

3. Daniel Defoe, who, although imprisoned and pilloried, created a lasting sensation with *Moll Flanders,* only one among his 370 works. He is even better known for the less controversial *Robinson Crusoe.*

4. George Sand (also illegitimate), who wore men's pants and dared to become a socialist, journalist, and prolific author (eighty novels alone) in a day when she should have stayed home and starved while her stupid husband squandered her fortune.

5. George Eliot (Mary Ann Evans), from whom "George" Sand took her name, also a social novelist, but persecuted by English society because she lived with her editor, who was unable to divorce his wife and wed her.

6. Abbé Prévost, who was so notorious that even now he is known by his own name for himself: The Exile. He was at various periods of his life a French Jesuit under sentence by the Courts, a French Benedictine, an English journalist, publisher, translator, novelist, and then refugee in Holland.

7. Daniel François Esprit Auber (1782–1871), rector of the Paris Conservatory of Music, composer of the first opera on the Abbé Prévost's novel, *Manon Lescaut* (1856).

8. Jules Massenet, whose opera *Manon* of 1884 remains one of the most popular musical compositions of our day also.

9. Giacomo Puccini also wrote a famous Italian opera, also

called *Manon Lescaut* (1893). It is also very much admired and a very somber treatment of the heroine.

Moll Flanders reads depressingly, as must any social novel which succeeds in decrying the depravity of a young woman. The housemaid Moll had been seduced by her employer in his mansion, and forced later to transfer her body to his younger brother. She was then abandoned, penniless, without even the hope of a letter of recommendation. Thus, Moll Flanders was a young girl debauched, corrupted, a castaway adrift in eighteenth-century London. A mere girl, she had become a pauper in danger of immediate starvation and death, if not by hunger then by cold or murder, disease, or despair. To save her life she turns to the only means instantly available to her, which was, of course, crime. Eighteenth-century London had neither many social services nor much money to spare for a weeping, homeless waif turned out in the city streets.

But this waif was a Protestant, like her author and champion, Daniel Defoe; and Protestants then believed that to her that hath, it shall be given, and to her that hath not, it shall be taken away. That was also in her case the much-plugged morality of the Spanish fictional hero of the Renaissance, the first *pícaro,* Lazarillo de Tormes. How can a young and destitute vagabond get ahead in the cities of this world? Well, there are several sure ways. A girl or a fellow can serve a master and rise to wealth and honor by following his example and robbing him gradually by the way. Then he or she can pick out a richer master who keeps books less carefully as he goes about his transactions. If worse comes to worst, the *pícaro* can always begin with the easiest crime requiring only a sly hand and fast legs: pickpocketing. In a city like London there are always, Moll Flanders found, rich louts looking for brief intercourse and able to pay in advance. As always, prostitutes came from the "lower classes." Destitution and expulsion from home were the initial events which set youths on the road to crime. Prostitution also provided entry to more serious criminals: gangsters, white slavers, drug pushers, addicts, gamblers.

Moll Flanders had several ideas working for her, and slowly and painfully she learned to survive in the big city by the use of her brains, her youth, her courage, her optimism, her hope, her industry, her lack of scruples, and her faith in God. One wonders if she was not the original working woman suffering from inequality, as American working women suffer discrimination silently today, without recourse or hope of justice.

Moll Flanders knew that she was a sinner, which is Virginia Woolf's evaluation of this heroine: "The old sinner!" Moll accepted sin for all the decades during which she was sustained by means of sin, largely that of prostitution. But all the time Moll knew that the wages of sin is death only for those who die. If you don't die from sin, then maybe you can accumulate enough experience and cash so that you no longer dress like a prostitute.

Nor did she have to *dye her hair yellow* as all prostitutes from ancient Israel and ancient Rome were obliged to do so that they could be instantly recognized as whores.

In other words, like a good Protestant, Moll believed in divine Providence; for God helps those who help themselves. Therefore Moll helped herself to money freely and without regret. She studied her victims. She worked hard to please her male libertines. She put aside a little bit of cash every day. She practiced the manners and dress of respectable, middle-class women and was determined to one day repent her days as a guttersnipe. In the words of Jesus: "Neither do I condemn thee; go and sin no more." It is as if she had read the noble Roman Cato: "If at any time women are allowed to became legally equal to men, they will at that instant become superior to men."

When Moll was ready, she went back to church, repented her sins, and felt forgiven. She went out in the city to the offices of the London Company and plunked down her savings on the desk and purchased a passage to Virginia. Everybody in London for a hundred years had heard what happened so tragically at Roanoke Island, but now a shipload of maids had arrived safely there in Virginia (1620). Everybody in London heard of the "much-vexed" Bermuda and of the storms off Hatteras. Everybody remembered Pocohontas and Powhatan. They all knew Virginia because in 1624 it was the first royal and English colony in the New World.

And so Moll Flanders and her life savings embarked for Virginia and also arrived safely there after a long and fearsome ocean crossing. Moll was not a "purchase bride." As soon as she walked down that gangplank, she became an American at heart, the proud owner of fifty acres of rich, bottom land, free and clear, in royal Virginia. By age seventy Moll Flanders had become even wealthier and a very respected property owner, a great lady of old Virginia in the New World of "freedom and justice for all."

Manon Lescaut was not as fortunate as Moll. Abbé Prévost's book details utter depravity on the parts of hero, heroine, and the heroine's brother, who is her procurer. Modern readers may make a far more severe judgment than those made by such male critics as Prévost's French editor Pierre Mac Orlan (1959) and our late, beloved Professor Donald M. Frame of Columbia University, who made the marvelous, modern translation of *Manon Lescaut* (New York, 1961).

Mac Orlan of the Académie Goncourt in France identified Prévost himself as debauched and malicious, and yet saw him as the honest author of this "honestly human" book (Preface, p. ix). Of course, Manon is a Moll Flanders in Paris, he agreed, a charming if immoral young tramp. Her nobleman lover enjoys their tender and illicit love affair because he is an indigent truant from his class and a dropout from his schools. She is no more than a tender-hearted, common little "bitch" *(garce)*, said Mac Orlan, no "daisy" but sentimentally sweet like lilacs, lilies of the valley, chrysanthemums for All Saints Day, and mistletoe for New Year's.

Professor Frame was one of the world's foremost experts on Renaissance Studies, Montaigne and Rabelais, among many others of their time. In his Introduction he did not belabor the real point but merely, slyly reminded his French readers to study Paul Hazard's religious analysis of *Manon Lescaut*. Clever music students maintain that the three *Manon* operas thrive because of their latent spirituality derived from Prévost's own understanding of "grace," a prime theological dispute of his age. One would also maintain that it was this argument over divine grace which sent Prévost running madly from France to England to Holland, and from the Society of Jesus to home finally among the Benedictines.

Prévost's novel presents a quadrangular structure of four characters: (1) The sexual pervert Manon who prostitutes herself repeatedly because she can only live either in bed or on the lap of luxury; (2) the degenerate, idle nobleman Des Grieux, who descends into crime and prison, after having spurned his father's pleas and exhortations, in order to live off Manon's earnings; (3) their spiritual friend, priest, and would-be rescuer Tiberge; and (4) Manon's brother, the rake, cardsharp, and soldier Lescaut, who provides customers for Manon. "A girl like her ought to be able to support us," he tells the lover.

"If you can deliver yourself from sexual love," says Prévost, "I shall know you are a virtually perfect person." But his novel presents not only a picture of contemporary society, but a paradox for the reader to break his heart on: "the contradiction between our philosophy and our behavior."

Their comfortable circumstances all end where Europe fails them and Louisiana begins. Manon was accused by one of her dissatisfied Romeos and sentenced to be deported in chains to the New World, where she dies.

Manon, adds Prévost, represents the incomprehensible nature of womankind. He can do no better than that.

His century, that of Pascal before him, labored mightily to define a doctrine of Divine Grace that would be, as Descartes said, so "clear and evident" that it would be accepted as true by all Christians. Manon Lescaut had received superabundantly at birth the natural graces: the gift of life, health, and radiant beauty. What she never received were the supernatural graces which would have given her sinful self enjoyment of eternal life. No prevenient graces freed her will to choose good from evil. French Jansenists thought that grace was not given outside the Church. French Calvinists thought that God's grace was offered only to those persons predestined to receive it. Did the sacraments confer grace? Or were they merely signs of grace?

Manon died in Louisiana without ever having requested, much less received, divine mercy and forgiveness for her dissolute life. She never achieved a state of grace where she was pleasing to God or responsive to His grace. She altogether lacked Christian virtue.

The sentimental music of Massenet's opera *Manon* is heartbreakingly beautiful, even Manon's silly lament to her little supper table at the end of Act II. "Adieu," she sings, "notre petite table" where Des Grieux and she were so happy! And Des Grieux's lovely tenor replies that in dreams, eyes shut, he can envision for them some humble retreat in the country where they could be so happy: *"En fermant les yeux je vois là-bas une humble retraite . . ."* The librettist here is oblivious to irony: Manon would never be happy in any "humble" lodging.

In Act III Des Grieux's tenor rises to the heights of Tristan's operatic love for Isolde when he sings *andante*, "Oh, go far from my thoughts, sweet girl, too dear for my soul./ Respect the repose I have so cruelly won./ And know if I have drunk from this bitter chalice,/ That my soul will be repaid for what it has suffered here . . ."

The French language (translation just given) is one of the world's most literary, and exquisitely, musical:

Oh! fuyez, douce image, à mon âme trop chère;
Respectez un repos si cruellement gagné.

Et songez si j'ai bu dans une coupe amère
Que mon âme gagnera de ce qu'il a souffert.
Oh! Fuyez, fuyez . . .

Fortunately for him—poor, young lover—Des Grieux earned merits in heaven because he suffered so much in prison. Manon is not capable of rehabilitation. Neither beauty nor youth has excused her. She is a wanton, a juvenile delinquent who has deserved deportation in chains, said the French Court, and death in the Louisiana "sands."

Camille

In 1849 a young French author, son of the great black writer Alexandre Dumas of *The Three Musketeers* and *The Count of Monte Cristo,* wrote a five-act drama which has made history. Alexandre Dumas fils finally saw his *La Dame aux camélias*—which Greta Garbo immortalized in her cinematographic role of *Camille*—presented in Paris on February 2, 1852. The Paris censor had caused a delay in production. "Camille," or Dumas's name for the heroine, Marguerite (Daisy) Gautier, is another Phryne, said Dumas fils. In his Preface (December, 1867) he added: "This is not a play but a legend."

Marguerite Gautier, our prostitute heroine, is not named Daisy when she sings the soprano role in her opera, but Violetta, probably because violets from Parma, Italy, suggested feminine and perfumed beauty to the librettist Francesco Piave of the opera *La Traviata* (The Strayed Woman). Giuseppe Verdi's operatic telling of Dumas fils's story has played worldwide, year after year, since its first presentation in Venice, Italy, on March 6, 1853. One presentation at the Old Metropolitan Opera House, New York City, on November 29, 1941, saw the debut of Jan Peerce in the tenor role, with the lovely Jarmila Novotna singing Camille-Marguerite-Violetta, and the American tenor Lawrence Tibbett singing the hero's father Germont.

Dumas fils meant to tug at everybody's heartstrings when he conferred, or alleged, that he really took *La Dame aux camélias* from a live Parisian prostitute. Her real name was Alphonsine, and not Marguerite, and like the heroine of drama she really died of tuberculosis at age twenty-three and was interred, *comme de juste,* in Montmartre (Mountain of Martyrs), Paris.

The pale, delicate beauty of Garbo and Novotna was perfectly suited to the tragic story of Camille-Marguerite, camellia and daisy; for both are white or pale flowers, and both are fragile. The European violet too is highly perfumed, which is not the case for the American purple violet found growing wild along the margins of our brooks. Novotna's delicate beauty and glorious voice convinced her audience in the tremendous finale of Act I that she truly was happy and always free *("Sempre libera . . .");* as long as she did not fall helplessly in love with some young weakling. After the pattern of Prévost's Des Grieux, she would be as carefree and gay as Manon. But even as Camille-Marguerite concludes her aria, flitting from pleasure to pleasure *("di gioja in gioja"),* she also hears her future lover Alfredo extolling his love from under her balcony.

The audience realizes that Marguerite-Daisy-Violet will die of a broken heart and tuberculosis. It is strange how these flowers, and the flower itself, are so closely associated with lovemaking. Little girls also hold daisies, tear off the petals one by one, chanting "He loves me . . . he loves me not," until they come to the last, decisive petal. Thus, fate, love, and cruelty continue closely linked in our Western cultures.

Because he has revealed in his Preface his good will towards women and his good intentions for his play, Dumas fils invites us to look at his masterpiece, act by act. The first act contains the exposition, and Marguerite Gautier takes center stage promptly. She is very pale-faced, we learn at once, like the Greek prostitute Toad, or Phryne. Her acquaintance Armand is among her guests at supper, and he wishes to care for her. She says that she is ill, for which reason she must live frenetically until she dies.

"Have you no heart?" Armand inquires.

"Heart?" She replies, "That's the only thing which causes ship-wrecks in the crossing I'm making."

Thus, early in the play, Dumas fils has stirred subliminal memories in his audience. What beautiful, young, lovelorn prostitute made a transatlantic crossing? Manon Lescaut, of course, and from the port of Le Hâvre de Grace, from the harbor of mercy from the peril of the sea *("del péril de la mer")*. Ever since the conclusion of Prévost's *Manon Lescaut,* Le Hâvre has kept this symbolic and literary significance of a jumping-off port, of a departure harbor, whence one leaps into the unknown, or into the death of the western, terrible ocean. The winds from America that blow across the Atlantic to France are prevailing westerlies. They increase travel time from east to west. And the worst storms that strike Britain and flood the exposed coasts of France drive in from the vast Atlantic.

Marguerite tells Armand with a laugh that he can't afford her. There is no way, she says, that he can raise what she spends every year—upwards of 100,000 francs. Her advice to him, she continues, is to get married to a rich girl, or to go love somebody less expensive than herself.

Marguerite warns Armand not to fall in love with her. I have never been in love, she says, and I thank God for that blessing. In any case, she says, he would fall out of love with her before she even had the good fortune to die, and her death is coming on very quickly now. She is already gravely ill.

Act II finds Marguerite unaccountably disposed to grant young Armand a sufficient taste of her favor. She proposes that they take a country house for the summer, which was Des Grieux's sorry dream when Manon's fate also had already been determined. For his part, Armand refuses her offer. He would not dream of going to the country at her expense. Have you not read *Manon Lescaut?* he asks her. Manon always used rich lovers so she could earn funds year after year in order to support Des Grieux. Marguerite shrugs off his objections.

Look, she advises him, you say you are madly in love with me. Then dismiss your scruples and chalk it up to love, why don't you?

In Scene V of this act Marguerite defines herself not as a woman, not as a human being, but as a mere animal, *"une créature du hasard"* (p. 96), created haphazardly, by a freak of luck. Nobody desired her to come into the world. She was just a freak happenstance, a worthless commodity.

Her soliloquy, paraphrased here, which she delivers standing alone on the stage, explains it all to the audience: Who could have said, eight days ago, that this man, whose existence I never even suspected, would to such a degree fill my heart and thoughts? . . . Does he even love me? . . . What am I but a creature of luck? Then let Lady Luck take me wherever that will be! It's all one, whether I am any happier than I have been up until now. It makes no difference, as far as I can see, and maybe it's a sign of danger ahead, for me as a woman. Women always see into the future; we always envision that some man will fall in love with us. But *we never plan ahead* for the other contingency, the other possibility, that we will fall in love with some man. So, when that misfortune strikes us, even during the first symptoms of this oncoming infection, we don't know what's coming over us, or where we are, or what to do about it.

Love is *"un mal imprévu."* Love is, as she defines it, an unexpected disease.

Look here (and we paraphrase again), Marguerite tells Armand later, be reasonable. We could have spent three or four months in the country. It is lovely there in summertime. Then we could have returned to Paris, shaken hands, and called it quits. The love we feel, once this first passion is spent, can never be transformed into true friendship between you and me. . . . And furthermore, the country might have given me one last chance to recover my health there in the sunshine and pure air out of this city. Here in the polluted air of Paris I grow worse daily. . . . But now, of course, you have made me send away my former lover, who was willing to provide for me lavishly, not only clear up my present debts here, but also fund a few months in the country for me.

Between this confrontation and Act III, Marguerite has decided to go away with Armand, funds or no funds; and Armand has also decided to throw his scruples to the wind. As the Act III curtain parts, Marguerite is telling her chums how she plans to provide for herself and Armand during the next three months. At this point our fourth character, the antagonist, who is Armand's father, asks the courtesan to receive him. Monsieur Duval pleads with Marguerite to sacrifice her happiness so that his errant son may be placed back in his studies, and so that their family may not suffer loss of reputation because of this unfortunate association with a common woman of low life. Marguerite agrees. Her words aloud tell what she really thinks and feels:

Ainsi, quoi qu'elle fasse, la créature tombée ne se relevera jamais.

So, whatever she may do, the fallen creature shall never raise herself above that position.

Act IV is the famous, splendid ball scene where Marguerite arrives with her noble, wealthy lover, Monsieur de Varville, as her handsome escort. Armand erupts suddenly in the throng of dancers and confronts Marguerite. He makes a scene, calling her foul names in a loud voice and finally damning her. Marguerite pales even more before him, reels, and falls on the dance floor in a dead faint. Monsieur de Varville calls Armand a coward.

Act V is justly famous throughout the world. The curtain parts on a dark stage. Dumas fils had instructed his set designer to create the following scene: Marguerite's bedroom chamber, her bed at stage rear, drapes closed halfway, fireplace stage right. Her loyal friend Gaston is stretched out on her divan, set before the fireplace. No other illumination at all except for Marguerite's night light. She is asleep. It is 7:00 A.M., New Year's Day. New Year's gifts are being brought in for Marguerite. Her friend Prudence enters to beg or borrow money. Marguerite manages to rouse herself and hand it to her from her purse.

The doctor enters to consult with his patient. Then Marguerite is handed a letter of sympathy and apology from Armand's father, who also thanks her for her generous sacrifice and for loving his son. Then Armand himself creeps into the dark chamber.

Armand tells Marguerite how he plans to take her out of Paris once more and forever. He asks her to rise and dress. With her maid's help the dying woman manages to do this, but then discovers that she cannot walk. In halting words from damaged lungs Marguerite manages to thank Lady Death for having allowed her one last visit from Armand.

As Marguerite dies, and Armand falls weeping over her dead body, the maid concludes: "She will be forgiven because she loved him so much."

Dumas fils wrote in his preface to the play *Le Demi-Monde,* a comedy in five acts first presented in Paris on March 29, 1855, an explanation of the phrase. Below polite society, and above professional and other working people, stretch high born "interlopers" who wish to rise above what reality has afforded the rest of us, and wish to stay there permanently. So the demimonde consists of princesses metamorphosed into owls, bats, and other nocturnal creatures. The women at this intermediate, social level are those who perhaps earlier deserted their families, unwed girls who became pregnant, or dissolute women who live with one man after another. This is a separate class of classless women, who may once have been inscribed in the Social Register but who have fallen to a level where they are more comfortable and neither regulated nor curbed in any way. Once they were not only respectable, but honored. Most fell from their high estate because of love, love of a man and/or of money. Occasionally and finally they became paupers, then destitute, and then naked like

Theodore Dreiser's fallen woman, Sister Carrie (1900). The men at this level end by being separated from the wives they once knew, frequently as the result of public scandal; and eventually they are separated by lack of money even from the courtesans.

From Phryne to the Empress Theodora, and from Manon Lescaut to Camille, heroines were ruined by the pleasure of love as well as by the love of pleasure.

FALLEN WOMEN

Notions concerning honor have varied only slightly over the long centuries from the ancient world into our own. Both Electra and Antigone, in ancient Mycenae and Thebes, ancestral sites antedating Classical Greece, felt obliged to defend family honor. The former heroine displayed such a psychopathic attachment to her father that she urged and abetted murder of her mother. Antigone persisted, despite law to the contrary, in burying her warrior brother. For this act of filial devotion she was herself put to death by the state. The modern world, however, has seen a remarkable change in attitudes towards a woman's honor, or towards what various heroines perceive, just as Electra and Antigone only perceived, what it was honorable for a woman to do and not do.

The Romans considered honor the crowning glory of a woman's mortality. Her honor was her glory, her fame as a Roman lady. She and her husband went to pray at the Temple of the goddess of Honor, which adjoined the Temple of the goddess *Virtus* (Manliness) near the Porta Capena in the city Rome. Roman women were respected *honoris causa* as women in the academic world may or should today be esteemed in the United States.

French people today define a woman's honor as her sense of moral dignity which controls her behavior; for example, an unwed daughter must obey her parents, dress with all modesty, and assist her mother in offering afternoon tea to her mother's lady friends. A French girl of honorable family *(une jeune fille de famille)* does not dress immodestly or cut her hair until after her wedding. In French, one speaks commonly of "my word of honor," "the field of honor," "a point of honor," "a seat of honor," and of that hightest commendation: The Legion of Honor. In France, but not in the New World, women too are elected, to the high rank of *Chevalier* (Knight) of the *Légion d'*

Honneur. Madame Eve Curie and Madame Jeanne Lanvin were both in our time so honored.

Webster's Dictionary, which gives us common American usage, defines honor differently, as *esteem paid to worth,* or due to worth. Honor to us means respect shown to a person. That respect may include a civil title which labels a person as worthy of honor. These nuances tend to indicate, it seems, that here honor accrues to an individual from some person or body of opinion outside herself. Authors in the modern world do not study honor in this American way, and do not accept this reading.

The first great modern works centered around a woman's honor define this concept quite differently. These authors understand honor as a woman's self-respect, a self-esteem which they find not only laudable, but necessary to a woman's life. These authors of masterpieces which give us the French Marquise de Merteuil in *Dangerous Liaisons,* the Marquise of O in Germany, and *Carmen* in Spain build the characters of these women, for good and evil as the case may be, upon the respect which each woman has built to shore up her own person. Each heroine is both self-sufficient and unique; a separate, modern individual who somewhere along the lengthy and hard road of childhood learned to trust in herself. When Don José slapped Carmen, he lost her love. He had attacked her self-respect.

Of course, the three modern authors of these heroines, Laclos, Kleist, and Mérimée, each wrote on the eve of one of the great revolutions of the late eighteenth and early nineteenth centuries. Thus, the three authors lead us, bewildered as we still are today about the definition of a woman's honor, from the American Revolution through several French Revolutions, and towards the Russian Revolution and World War I.

Our three authors who lived through revolutions were profoundly affected by the swift revenge taken upon French women who had been revolutionary leaders. Their portrayals of three women derive from these reprisals taken upon women specifically. France passed the hideously repressive Code Napoléon, for instance. The French novelist Honoré de Balzac cried loudly that the passage of this Code of Laws in France signaled the end of freedom there forever. Women cannot be so persecuted, he cried. The three authors portray three fallen women.

By the term "fallen woman," let us agree to designate a heroine who has, either intentionally or accidentally, fallen from her honorable estate in society. Some are truly tragic heroines, like Electra and Antigone, while others rose only to fall, or just simply fell and were perhaps redeemed. To say "fallen women" is to speak kindly, of course, by means of an euphemism.

Dreiser's *Sister Carrie* portrays a fallen woman whose "passive soul" (p. 144) utterly lacked sympathy for a life of toil in such an "underworld" as a Chicago shoe factory. She lost her virginity to a salesman named Drouet (from the French *roué,* or reprobate) in exchange for three rooms to share with him and some glad rags for herself. Her craving for comfort ensured her fall, "his conquest" having been "her loss" (p. 85), but no way his fault; for the tiger is not responsible, writes Dreiser (p. 70).

Her second and final conqueror is Hurstwood (Emily Brontë's Heathcliff) whose lack of pity characterizes him (p. 127) in his dealings with family, girlfriend, and pauper alike. After stealing Carrie, whom he says he considers a "Lily" and/or a white goddess (p. 132), and after having tricked her into eloping with him, he falls from being a business executive in Chicago, who absconds with company funds, to a tramp in New York City, and finally a beggar supported by Carrie.

Thus, Carrie is the fallen woman, whom her lovers literally call "Caddie," "Cad," and "a little daisy," or Alcestis. She at least forces Hurstwood to marry her. Then she supports him for quite some time, as she rises in the music-hall world to become not only independent but able to spurn both Drouet and Hurstwood. *Sister Carrie* winds down as not so much her story as Hurstwood's. His steady, tragic decline from wealth and success leads him to dirty, dissolute beggary. *Sister Carrie* stirs up an American's worst nightmares, however. Dreiser must have had Emily Brontë's tragic Heathcliff in mind, from Brontë's celebrated *Wuthering Heights* (1847).

Electra

The renowned Greek heroine Electra (Elektra) fascinated three great masters of tragedy: Aeschylus in 458 B.C. *(Oresteia)*, Euripides in 415 B.C. *(Elektra)*, and Sophocles in 411 B.C. *(Elektra)*. She was the daughter of Agamemnon, the Greek commander who was so long absent fighting the Trojan War, and his Queen Clytemnestra, who awaited his return equally long. Electra's sister was the priestess Iphigenia, whom her father had sacrificed in order to expedite the Greek departure for Troy. Upon Agamemnon's return he was murdered in cold blood by his wife and her lover Aegisthus. Electra's younger brother Orestes was sent away from the first-degree murder scene but Electra stayed on.

The story of Electra takes no account of any extenuating circumstances in the case of Clytemnestra's murder of her husband. It concentrates upon Electra's dire hatred of her mother, her mournful love of her dead father, and her longing for the return of her brother Orestes. The personal name "Electra" derives from the Greek word for Amber, which is *elektron*. Amber is a yellow resin now used as a jewel, and virtually priceless if it is cherry-colored; but it was long known and used to store and to excite electricity. A necklace of amber will lift paper, for example, from a jeweler's velvet pad. Thus, Electra was able naturally to motivate her brother Orestes.

Soon after his return to ancient Mycenae, Orestes was persuaded by his vengeful sister Electra to murder both his mother and her second husband in cold blood, as they had done to his father. This premeditated murder, in which Electra was his accomplice, was excused by the Courts on the grounds that Clytemnestra was no blood or clan relative of Orestes. Both he and Electra were recognized by law as children of the father only. By Greek law a mother was not a person but only the uterus which for nine months bore a child.

Only the female death goddesses, the Furies, pursued Orestes to Athens, where despite their arguments, the Areopagus acquitted him of what the Furies called matricide.

This story, however, turns not upon Orestes, but upon Electra as the moving force behind the new order, although she too was exculpated from any taint of crime. It was not until the advent of modern psychology by Sigmund Freud that her role was stigmatized as an "Electra complex," meaning a system of negative oedipal memories which dominated her personality. She drove her brother to commit a double homicide because of her overwhelming passion for her dead father and equally consuming hatred of her living mother. Electra managed to electrify her brother Orestes even as she saw him for the first time, a grown man at their father's tomb.

In the *Oresteia* of Aeschylus (*Choephoroe*, v. 882 ff.), Electra informs the Chorus that all she asks for is justice, honor, and payment for her father's unjust murder. Since she has inherited her mother's lupine soul, she roams the world relentlessly in search of prey. After her father died so unexpectedly, his death left her shut indoors like some rabid cur. She wept inside her heart, thus managing to dissemble and wait for a time to strike back. Meanwhile she sat like a naked fledgling upon her father's monument. The dead are not dead to a loving daughter like herself. Such girls bob about like corks on a fisherman's net. They sink only to pop up again and plot revenge. It is no wonder Clytemnestra dreamed of a snake while she was carrying Orestes.

It is Orestes who takes charge, once his sister has set him upon murder. He dispatches her indoors, and advances towards his mother consoling himself that justice demands this revenge. He disguises his accent and pretends to be from sacred Delphi. He will only be killing murderous monsters such as abound on land and sea. He will be murdering only a female beast overcome *like all females* with hatred disguised as love, with evil designs against all ties created by marriage rather than by blood. The crimes of Greek women fill books, and Orestes cites them by name and foul deed.

Justice is the anvil upon which lies the sword of Fate which Orestes will draw forth. "Ah," cries Clytemnestra as she first glimpses her son, "here is Orestes whom we thought to keep clean of all the mud of murder." Those present praise Orestes and Electra.

The Chorus wraps up the tragedy by noting that murder has now come fully round to entrap the third generation of this royal family of Mycenae. The view of Aeschylus is too somber for words.

Sophocles manages to present the accomplice Electra as a less grim female monster. It was not her fault, as he sees it, that her girl's bosom became stained with her dear father's blood (v. 92 ff.). Agamemnon fell like a lordly oak chopped by a woodcutter's axe. She who weeps for him is the (raped?) nightingale Philomela, and her own words here betray the depth of her obsessive father-love. Or she lives, she adds (v. 147 ff.), like Niobe weeping for her dead (unborn?) children. Is there no justice to regulate human lives? Has a royal daughter deserved this kind of existence? She prays for revenge and begs the Furies to answer her pleas.

Electra also resents her condition of old maid, that of any unmarried woman in her childbearing years. She demands that her honor be restored to her by the hand of her brother. She informs the world that no woman has managed to steer her off course, neither her mother nor her sister Iphigenia.

Here we are to believe that the latter was not actually sacrificed but that Agamemnon only intended to sacrifice her. The goddess Artemis in fact snatched her away from his knife to safety.

Electra pleads war as her final, extenuating circumstance. This occurred, she argues, due to the Trojan War. That war acted upon females as upon males. Even a girl like herself grew up during a war which made her also just as warlike as her heroic father. She too became a warrior who must uphold honor. She too is devotedly warlike.

For his part, Orestes pleads a manly duty to eradicate evil. Clytemnestra must die. Aegisthus too must die although he was not actually the murderer of Agamemnon, but the accomplice. Being a man he must die more painfully, however, and suffer a slower death. Murderers, says Orestes, must all be put to death immediately. It is only in this way that the spread of evil will be halted.

Antigone

The second Greek heroine who upholds her honor beyond the point where Electra subsides is Antigone. In her case again the greatest masters of Greek tragedy notably plied their profession: Aeschylus in 467 B.C., with his *Seven Against Thebes,* followed by two tragedies of Sophocles's *Oedipus at Colonus* (ante 401 B.C.) and *Antigone* (c. 441 B.C.). The personal name "Antigone," says Robert Graves in his *Greek Myths* (Penguin Books, 1955), means "in place of a mother." And, in fact, Antigone serves her family as surrogate for her dead grandmother Jocasta. Antigone is the royal princess of Thebes, as Electra was royal princess of the other most renowned very ancient city state of Mycenae. As the daughter of Oedipus, she followed her father into exile and led him from one refuge to another after he had blinded himself in expiation for sins the gods caused him to commit: murder of his father and incest with his mother, Jocasta.

After the war of the seven against Thebes Antigone wished to uphold the honor of her family by giving her last dead brother a proper burial. The new Regent or King of Thebes, who was her Uncle Creon, had forbidden this funeral and burial. Creon had no birthmark of the serpent on his body, which signified to Antigone that he was not the legitimate king. Antigone, because she loved her dead brother, and must for honor's sake assuage his ghost, refused to obey Creon's law.

Antigone prowled about the royal palace at Thebes, a town which still stands today high on the side of Mt. Parnassus and near the holy Delphic Temple. She had survived the awful curses laid by the gods upon her innocent and beloved father Oedipus, and had followed him like any devoted child.

Her story begins when she faces Creon, who has unwisely decreed that any person covering the body of Antigone's brother will be stoned to death. Oedipus has long since died an outcast and a ragged beggar. Jocasta long ago hanged herself. Antigone's sister now begs off, saying that she is only a woman and that women cannot fight men. This leaves Antigone alone faced with the dilemma and crux of this tragedy: to do or not to do. Firm in her resolve, she resolutely buries her brother in the dark of night.

The next day, when accused of anarchy, she confesses her guilt openly. If burying her brother was a crime against the state, then she accepts death as her penalty. But it will be, she says, death with honor (Prologue). She has truly hovered *like a mother bird* over her dead brother's corpse and buried it with dust.

Antigone argued that God's justice takes precedence over the justice of the state. God's laws are above manmade laws. God has decreed those laws which human beings must obey as just. Such law tells all that the dead are to be honored by the living. The heroic dead deserve honorable burial. Antigone's brother died honorably in combat. Therefore she felt obliged to bury him, and she did so. Her sister, Ismene, did not feel so obliged, and was therefore innocent of crime in the eyes of Creon. Sophocles sympathized with Antigone. He agreed that Fate usually works ill.

Creon argues that he is the state. He makes all the laws. He therefore locks Antigone in a stone vault. When the Prophet Tiresias berates Creon and brings him to his senses, it is too late. Antigone has hanged herself. Her fiancé, who is Creon's son, has also committed suicide. Creon's queen has also stabbed herself before the altar. Thus, with Antigone's death the line of Theban royalty is forever extinguished.

Modern Times

The political implications of *Antigone* reminded French women as late as World War II that they should join the secret army of the French *Résistance* and fight underground the Nazi Occupation of France. In 1942 Jean Anouilh wrote and presented his new *Antigone* to Paris theatergoers.

The greater popularity worldwide of the opera *Elektra* (Dresden, 1909) by Richard Strauss has far overshadowed the law-abiding Antigone. Writing in the *Los Angeles Times* (November 28, 1991), the distinguished music critic Martin Bernheimer calls this newer *Elektra* "terribly modern, terribly meaningful, terribly daring and terribly exciting" (pp. F6–7). Elektra herself receives in this "musical masterpiece" no glimpse of sympathy. As woman and royal daughter she is evil personified amidst a nightmarish and grotesque modern scenery of death and revenge, goons, ghouls, ghosts, corpses, and carcasses over which Elektra rules, a white-haired, screaming, hideous, old witch.

Women in defense of feminine honor were not always so hated and reviled, however. Early in the nineteenth century the view of women such as Antigone once prevailed with a light touch far from the grotesqueries of our own, ghastly, twentieth century. Once upon a time not a terrible Richard Strauss but the aristocratic and sophisticated German dramatist Heinrich von Kleist (1777–1811) wrote a novella called *The Marquise of O*. Kleist was born at Frankfurt-an-den-Oder on the Polish border. As a dramatic poet he was very successful despite his other career: seven years' service in the army. Personally unhappy, he committed suicide at the age of thirty-four. Like the Greek dramatists before him, Kleist was fascinated by the idea of justice and fallen women.

Like Electra and Antigone the young German poet Kleist sadly found this an imperfect world of monstrous disorder where wickedness reigned and heroes were unjustly beheaded. However, despite his own physical ills, Kleist admired and preferred Antigone to Electra. Being himself a German officer and a gallant gentleman, Kleist also appreciated the difficulty such a person encountered close to a desirable, aristocratic, and sheltered German noblewoman. Fortunately for such a lady of honor, with due respect, he wrote in 1806 his justly celebrated prose novella, *The Marquise of O*.

In this work Kleist seems consciously to have attempted a correction of that novel which had since 1782 held world attention enthralled: *Dangerous Acquaintances,* which is a translation of the French *Liaisons dangereuses* by Choderlos de Laclos. Here then are two illustrious works of fiction in which aristocratic ladies, each one a Marquise (Marchioness), lodge claims in protection of their honor. Rather strangely, both authors wrote from similar backgrounds and similar professions. Both were born into privilege and high estate, both aristocrats, both very young, and both wealthy. In addition, both practiced that career which their high birth required noblemen to follow, military service in the army. Kleist was a German field officer, and Laclos, a French artillery officer. The latter's name alone indicates his lofty, aristocratic position: Pierre-Ambroise-François Choderlos de Laclos. He rose from lieutenant to general in Napoleon Bonaparte's armies. Neither military nor career officer ventures, however, upon the field of war as Stendhal, Tolstoy, Victor Hugo, and Thackeray will soon do in attempts to disentangle history and law from the brutish grip of Napoleon I.

What Kleist does in his utterly charming story of the *Marquise of O* is to depict the struggle of a Russian officer, who is a wealthy aristocrat, caught in the toils of an equally highborn German lady. Kleist points out that he is guilty and has broken the code of his society. He has wronged the lady, and he sweats blood for fear she will discover his crime. Thus, from Germany, comes this problem novella which points to lapses in morals among the highest and supposedly most noble personages of that society.

Choderlos de Laclos still shocks the world today just as the film version of his novel, *Dangerous Liaisons* starring Glenn Close and John Malkovich, shocked and sometimes disgusted many Americans in 1988. Laclos's novel *Liaison dangereuses* (1782) was an immediate success which ended the century of *Manon Lescaut,* Rousseau, and Voltaire. The philosophers Rousseau and Condorcet had pleaded all those years for popular sovereignty. Then like a massive cannon blast came this inflammatory novel of Laclos which was read, not only by intellectuals, but by ordinary, working people—consumed avidly by popular demand. Therein lay a blow-by-blow depiction of the aristocracy. Suddenly everybody knew what a French aristocratic lord or lady was beneath powdered wigs, beauty spots, bare bosoms, and tight corsets: a lustful, hideous, corrupt, and evil sexual pervert. Lord and Lady, Marquis and Marquise, indeed!

In 1782, seven years after the appearance of young Lt. Choderlos de Laclos's novel *Liaisons dangereuses,* the first stage of the bloody French Revolution burst forth. The erstwhile French hero of the American Revolution was the highly esteemed Marquis de Lafayette. He set about organizing a National Guard for the purpose of defending the King of France and his Queen, Marie Antoinette, the royal Austrian princess who observed, when Parisians ran out of bread, "Let them eat cake." Descended from France's greatest lady novelist, Madame de Lafayette, the Marquis was sadly unable, when blows came to blows, to defend the French monarchs. They were guillotined and their children were executed also, as would happen to the Russian royals in 1917.

Unlike the American hero Lafayette, Choderlos de Laclos (1741–1803), it is said in France, altogether missed military service under the

American Colonies. This came about through no fault of his own. He too had embarked to serve under General George Washington, but he did so without parental consent. The story goes that his noble mother, who still held the pursestrings, entrusted to the captain of the vessel upon which Laclos had taken passage, a letter and payment. She instructed the captain to call upon a French port and there to put ashore her noble, young son for the duration. The captain put Choderlos de Laclos ashore on the small island which France had traded, along with Guadeloupe and Martinique, for that unknown territory the French called *Canadas,* which we now call Canada. Young Laclos cooled his heels on St. Pierre and Miquelon while Lafayette was winning glory and beating the English.

Choderlos de Laclos, who most improbably wrote his novel, it is said, while awaiting return passage to France, was a professional and career officer in the French Army. He had graduated at age nineteen from the very selective Royal Military Academy as a lieutenant specializing in artillery. His business, like his novel, was violence. Throughout his entire lifetime he remained a career officer in the Corps of Engineers. As a French aristocrat he fulfilled his obligation in this feudal military elite. Understanding this commitment to service to the Fatherland, *la patrie,* and this wide gulf between ordinary men and this hereditary aristocracy bound by the ancient principle of *noblesse oblige,* one grasps the motives behind *dangerous liaisons:* attack and destroy.

When Queen Marie Antoinette, daughter of the majestic Queen Maria Theresa von Hapsburg of the Austrian-Hungarian Empire, was ignominiously guillotined in full view of a bloodthirsty mob, at the Place de la Concorde, Paris, in October of 1793, Choderlos de Laclos did not lift a finger to rescue her. He was, on the contrary, a member of the radical left along with other notorious and violent radicals and members of the Jacobin Club: Mirabeau, Robespierre, Danton, and Marat. Through all this period and into the Reign of Terror, when the radicals ended by guillotining thousands upon thousands of noble children, *girls and women* especially, Choderlos de Laclos pursued his brilliant military career: Revolutionary wars commenced after 1792 against Italy, Germany, and England, establishing the Directory in 1795, serving Napoleon Bonaparte after 1799. By the time Napoleon I acceded to the absolute rule of France, Choderlos de Laclos had become one of his generals. Our infamous author lived to help inaugurate *total war*.

Never to be outdone by the English, the French dispatched Laclos to govern their interests in India, where the English had sent their humiliated Lord Cornwallis, after his surrender at Yorktown, to become Royal Governor. Laclos wrote another book meanwhile in which he attacked the system of fortifications erected in France a hundred years before his time by the celebrated military engineer Vauban, and he cooled his heels again in prison for such temerity. France has always respected its Maginot Lines.

Laclos's novel anticipates the politics of Napoleon I with his invitation to men to aspire higher and higher if they have the will and the force to take advantage of the Emperor's "career open to talents." Hand in hand with this encouragement to men went the Emperor Napoleon's curse upon women, established legally as law: the Code Napoléon under which France was to be and is governed. Here retaliation laid its heavy hand especially upon French women, who had for a short while gained the right to divorce, and the right to have their own income and bank accounts, and the right to raise their minor children, if the mother was widowed. Their part in the Revolution reduced them, as both Victor Hugo and Balzac wrote, to female slaves and widows living at the level of starvation.

For long decades it was believed that the heavy executions of girl children and women during the Revolution was due to the demands of Rousseau and Condorcet for their full representation as citizens equal to men and possessed of equal rights. That opinion has now changed for the simple reason that prior to the French Revolution the egalitarian books and tracts of Rousseau were not in print inside

France, and virtually not available to any readers of any level in society. What was abundantly available and superabundantly consumed were the original four volumes of letters of Laclos's epistolary novel about dangerous liaisons.

Laclos's novel contains several series of letters to and from persons in the French Social Register who work upon each other, seduce and betray each other, corrupt and deprave each other for the purpose of sexual delight and amusement. If the reader makes a diagram of these exchanges between thirteen or so major characters (including "Anon."), he will soon discover who is the major mover and promotor and archfiend among these personages, and what their precise relationships are emotionally. Drawing a series of arrows between these major correspondents, one ends up constructing a polygon with the nobleman Valmont (played in the movie by John Malkovich) at the center. He exchanges letters with the six other major characters of the book, most frequently with the two women who have loved him most and whom he will most cruelly betray, one to her death and the other to mutilation; the latter vows very early to outdo Valmont in evil. So the letters reveal this primary battle between a man and a woman (Valmont versus Madame de Merteuil), each determined to out-flank, defeat, humiliate, scar, wound, destroy, break down, and obliterate the other. No holds are barred. It has become between individuals what it is nationally: total war. Before Laclos, it was called only a "battle between the sexes." In and after Laclos, the battles are waged to the death. Madame de Merteuil refuses to remain powerless. Woman has declared herself equal.

When he edited *Les Liaisons dangereuses* in 1952, the modern novelist and late, great statesman André Malraux called the book "a mythology of the will." Such a heroine as Madame de Merteuil reproduced her ancestresses Electra and Antigone. She refused to surrender her honor or to devote her life to the service of a man. She declared total war against the evil Valmont and furthermore set about matching him: evil for evil. The book is about the will and the uses and abuses of willpower, declared Malraux. There the ancient antitheses come once more into full play: goodness versus evil, angel versus devil, black versus white, beauty versus corruption, witch versus society. Since over the millennia philosophy has disagreed entirely about the will, psychology has in our days taken it over and broken it down into such components as adjustment and maladjustment, conscious mind and subconscious, motivation and the lack of it, attention span and degree of intelligence, endocrine glands and aggression.

No such complications exist in the 1806 novella of Heinrich von Kleist (1777–1811), who served in the Prussian Army and who also studied mathematics. His story of the same aristocracy that Laclos found utterly depraved and deserving the guillotine depicts another elegant lady holding the field after the battles were won. She is the Marquise of O. We are never allowed to know more of her name. Such a lady is, in the view of Kleist, to be honored and shielded. But his heroine is the alter ego of Madame de Merteuil. Master of irony, Kleist proceeds tongue in cheek to entertain us with what never became a topic of open gossip.

A widowed mother of "several" (or "two") young children, the Marquise of O was once set upon by a band of common soldiers intent upon trashing her town house and raping her. In her terror, the Marquise screamed for help, which brought to her rescue a gorgeous young Russian officer. He carried the poor lady, who had fainted away, safely to her bed, and then had the soldiers shot. Peace returned to Prussia, except that the lady, within a few days, began to experience the usual discomforts of morning sickness. For weeks she ignored them because she had lived a perfectly virtuous life since the death of her beloved husband.

To make a short story shorter, the handsome Russian returned to call upon the lady and make her several offers of marriage, which she haughtily refused forthwith. Her family finally forced her to retire to the country. Nobody understood the disconsolate and spurned Russian officer who kept falling on his knees in drawing rooms, insisting he must wed the Marquise and repair his one dishonorable deed.

Neither she nor anybody else in her family spoke a single word to the distressed Russian officer upon his wedding day to the Marquise of O. Nor was he thanked for having dowered the bride with all his love, estates, possessions, revenues, income, and future expectations. Only after the birth of her son did the Marquise apparently feel that she had removed any stain upon her reputation and had upheld to the *n*th degree her honor unblemished. At that point she and the Russian nobleman were wed a second time, after which he was received like a long-lost son into her father's house.

Heinrich von Kleist was fond of saying that in these days of newspapers people live out their lives in the eyes of the world, and not necessarily only according to their own choices. He usually added that consequently Folly rules the world, at least until a staunch and stalwart lady sets about refurbishing her honor. A fallen woman, if she is a German lady, will rise.

As it turned out, the Marquise of O had merely inserted an advertisement in her local newspaper, calling for the person who made her pregnant to step forth and declare himself. And so he did, many times over, married her twice, and publicly upheld her honor.

Carmen

More integral to all our lives and more well-known is the novella entitled *Carmen* and written, all sixty pages of it, in Paris by Prosper Mérimée over a period of six months. His formula for a literary masterpiece was to write ten pages a month and to write it over twenty times.

Those of us who have not seen twenty times over the lyrical drama or grand opera *Carmen* (Paris Opera, March 3, 1875), which offended France at the time, have probably seen the superb Spanish movie *Carmen,* of 1983, directed by Carlos Saura, and starring the dancers

Antonio Gades, Laura del Sol, and Paco de Lucia. The opera, with music written by Georges Bizet, probably plays in snatches of such commonly hummed numbers as the Toreador Song on radio or TV programs every day.

Carmen offended France, which was shocked by the ending. London and New York adored it, as they adore all ancient myths made modern. The French called the author of the book *Carmen* a cold fish. London agreed that Mérimée must have lived inside an "envelope of ice." How else could he have let Carmen die? It is only true, however, that Carmen dies just like Antigone, for the sake of her honor.

Mérimée's sixty pages fall into four narrative sections. The novella is cleverly plotted so as to disculpate the author from various charges, such as falsehood, prejudice, slander, ill will, and malevolence. We therefore see by his successful maneuvers that Mérimée fully intended to champion both ancient and modern heroines. Just as nobody else stood up for Antigone except her fiancé, who died with her, Mérimée alone stood up for Carmen, dead or alive.

Mérimée remains a threat to us all for two reasons: (1) because he is a successful author, still held in high esteem, a hundred years after his death, and (2) because he belonged to the opposition party doubly, as creative artist first, and as Protestant sympathizer inside a Catholic country second. France very wisely enforces their rule to leave creative artists alone while they are alive, because their major function is to attack society. In his historical fiction, as in *Carmen,* Mérimée protested ill treatment of underdogs. Carmen was an enterprising, heroic girl from the lowest class of society, and from the feared and scorned race of the gypsies. Carmen was also a magician and a witch.

In his Parts I and IV the author eases himself into and out of the masterpiece, which only he knows he is writing, with seventeen pages of blather about the archaeological placement of battlefields in Spain. As for himself, he wants humbly and merely to tell a story about Spain. He is far from France. He claims that he is no scholar and that for nothing in the world would he belittle Spain. He just wants to tell a little story about a Basque, named Don José Navarro, and his gypsy love, named Carmen.

In Part II the narrator tells how he went to Cordova to study but instead watched the girls undress and bathe in the Guadalquivir River at sunset. One of them took a smoke, ate some ice cream, admired the narrator's alarm wristwatch, and introduced herself: "I am Carmencita." The narrator describes her as being probably a witch, certainly a magician, certainly not a maiden, surely some servant of the Devil calling up spirits from the shadows, some *gitana,* some Bohemian, but one who fulfilled the Spanish criteria for beauty: black eyes and brows, delicate lips and fingers, lovely copper-toned skin, slant eyes, white teeth, blue-black hair, savage, fierce, and voluptuous beauty, and great charm. He called her eyes cat's eyes, or Electra's wolf's eyes. Reaching in her pocket she pulled out certain secret objects and for a penny told his fortune.

Then the narrator met Don José (Part III), who had come from his native Basque country in the north of Spain down to Seville. Here Mérimée employs another narrator, Don José himself, to recount his own story. He tells how he found work in the big city by enlisting in the cavalry, and how he now stands guard along the "ramparts of Seville," which became, under the pen of Georges Bizet, one of the most famous arias in the opera *Carmen*.

Don José stands guard near a factory that manufactures cigars and employs four or five hundred women workers. Don José met Carmen there. He could not have missed seeing her darling, little red shoes of Moroccan leather, or her beautiful lace mantilla, her nosegay of currant blossoms placed low in her *décolletage,* the sprig between her pointed teeth. He stared at her performing before him, rolling her hips like a filly in heat, fists akimbo. She strutted straight up to him, closer and closer. All he could think of was a female cat you haven't called to come and certainly don't want.

Then one day Carmen fought with a coworker whom she stabbed

with her cigar knife. The wounded woman lay on the ground, screeching bloody murder, "four hoofs in the air," with red crosses of Saint Andrew that Carmen had cut upon the woman's cheeks. They had called each other a witch, or Carmen had started by calling the other woman a witch. Don José arrested Carmen.

On the way to jail Carmen offered Don José an aphrodisiac if he would let her go. As soon as she discovered he was Basque, she claimed to be Basque also, and spoke Basque to him. He knew she was lying, but continued to listen to her anyway which was part of her magical charm. The name *Carmen* means charm, not only charming but able to work a magical spell, or charm, or a Latin *carmen*. So he let her go.

Don José let Carmen go free because he couldn't resist her. Even when she lied to him, as she lied every time he ever saw her, he still believed every word she uttered. He could never forget her. He asked everyone he met where she had gone and was told she had gone to Portugal on business.

He met her again one night while he was assigned to guard duty on the city ramparts. Suddenly she appeared beside him in the dark, begging him sweetly to let her pass into the sleeping city. When he hesitated, she threatened to go ask permission of his colonel. Don José yielded and let her and the band of smugglers she brought behind her into the city. He saw they were illegally transporting contraband from England. Carmen was their guide and business manager.

When he scolded her, she blamed him for begrudging her favors, and flew off in a rage. A few hours later she returned and invited him to her lover's nest. He knew then in his heart that her loving arms and her bright smile resembled a sunny morning in the Basque mountains. That clear sunshine tokened a sudden, vicious storm. He soon sees Carmen taking his lieutenant to the same lover's tryst. Madly, Don José kills his own officer and then runs wildly along the dark streets. Again, it is Carmen who finds him and saves his skin. Cleverly she disguises him as a peasant, bandages his head, and gives him a sleeping pill. He will do better, she whispers, to become a member of her smuggler band than face a firing squad.

Don José reflects upon this turn of events, concluding that Carmen was a "devil of a girl." She had ended by enrolling him in her life-style and her occupation just as simply as if she had plotted to do so from the minute she first laid eyes on him. He sees it all, now that the die has been cast, irrevocably. He decides then to amend his original theory: Carmen had planned none of it beforehand.

Carmen lived, as it were, from hand to mouth. She went actually from one chance encounter to the next, willy nilly (p. 221). In actual fact she lived the life of a true rebel. She rebelled continually and always: against contemporaries, against restrictions, against society, against law and order, and against her outcast condition. To the rest of her world she proudly maintained her own idea of a woman's life. Above all, she sought to be free. Although that was hard to enunciate or disentangle, she followed her own sense of honor, defending her own person as best she could in whatever manner she found at hand. She was proud, self-reliant, and self-supporting.

As she often told Don José, she loved him truly, but in her own style. He should have known it, for she had never once asked him for money. From all others, she not only asked for payment, she demanded it and got it. She also enforced her own rules of proper conduct.

Once Don José saw Carmen on the arm of a superb English Lord down at Gibraltar. Her band was unloading cargo from an English ship tied up in the harbor. Don José admired how she manipulated the Englishman and drove a hard bargain for the sake of her own men. Don José began to relax and enjoy the freedom, the journeys, and the excitement of his new life. He felt that Carmen had mended her wanton ways and that she loved him only and truly.

She jolted him awake from this dream of bliss when she confessed that she was married to a blackguard named García whom she had just managed to free from prison. No sooner had Carmen's husband taken command of their band of eight or ten smugglers than their morale worsened. Don José was horrified to witness García finish off a wounded comrade rather than help him escape with the others. When Carmen failed to protest, she showed herself as cruel and as depraved as her foul husband. Don José told her: You are the devil. "Yes," she replied, "I know it. I am the Devil. I live under Him, and under nobody else. My life is ruled by blind Providence."

From this conclusion mutually agreed upon their life takes a bitter turn. Carmen begins to laugh at Don José every time she comes close to him. She laughs at her tricks, at her clever retorts, at her secret orders, at dupes, and at Don José. She says he resembles the dwarf who thought he was a big man because he could spit far.

Finally Don José kills García and Carmen stays beside him for two weeks to nurse the wounds he received in the fight. As soon as he regains his strength, Don José asks Carmen to marry him and emigrate with him to the New World. She refuses. She tells Don José that she was not born to plant cabbages in America but to live richly off those who couldn't do much else but plant cabbages.

Their relationship continues to deteriorate after Carmen takes up with a picador from the bull ring. Don José forbids her to frequent this boastful fellow, and warns her:

Si tu ne m'aime pas, je t'aime.
Et si je t'aime, prends bien garde à moi.

(Whether you love me or not, I do love you. And if I love you, you better watch out for me.) Here again is one of the great arias of the opera *Carmen.*

At this moment, and for the first time, Don José actually strikes Carmen across the face. His threat and insult mark the turning point of the violent drama. Don José has suddenly impugned her honor, which to Carmen is intolerable. From this point on, Carmen is openly the enemy of Don José. No compromise will ever be acceptable to her. He has crossed a line which he can never cross back over.

Don José finally delivers his ultimatum. He gives Carmen one last chance: Will she go to America? No, she says, she will not go. Intent upon a magic ceremony, she hardly notices his presence anymore. She prays to Mistress Maria Padilla, queen of all magicians, and learns her destiny.

Then, throwing away the ring which Don José had given her, Carmen rises and carefully folds her mantilla about her face.

Everything is over between us, she tells Don José. I can never love you again. I will never live with you again.

She has been truly a demon, Don José concluded. Raising his knife he stabs her deep in her chest. She makes no sound at all. He pulls out the knife, raises it, and stabs her again. She falls to the ground. She still made not a sound but stared at him full in the eyes with her big, black eyes a long time until death blanked them for her.

Mérimée's *Carmen* derives in many ways from *Manon Lescaut,* but Mérimée said he first heard her story from a friend of his, a Spanish lady in Spain. There really was such a murder of such an enchantress there in 1830. Mérimée did not know the German dramatist Georg Buchner, nor his play *Woyzeck,* written circa 1836, about a soldier who is driven by poverty and injustice to murder his wife. This work too has become widely acclaimed as the opera *Wozzeck* by Alban Berg.

In fact, when Mérimée was once asked why he wrote *Carmen* and if his motive was not to celebrate this errant gypsy who died in order to sustain her honor, Mérimée declined all praise. He maintained that he only wrote *Carmen* because he needed the money to buy himself a new pair of trousers.

•READINGS•

PROSTITUTES

General

Fuller, Edmund. *Man in Modern Fiction*. Vintage Books, Random House (New York, 1949). See "The Female Zombies," essay on total depravity of women, pp. 94–121.

Miller, K. Bruce. *Ideology and Moral Philosophy*. Humanities Press (New York, 1971). Professor Miller was my learned colleague for several years at the University of Southern California, Los Angeles. I have much enjoyed his conversations and his book.

The Empress Theodora

Gibbon, Edward. *Decline and Fall of the Roman Empire*. 6 Vols. See Vol. 4, chapter XL, p. 146 ff. J. M. Dent and E. P. Dutton (London 1910–76; New York, 1976).

Montesquieu, Baron de. *Considérations sur la grandeur et la décadance des Romains* (Paris and London, 1734).

Procopius. *The Secret History*. Translated by G. A. Williamson. Penguin Classics (Harmondworth, England, 1966).

Moll Flanders

Defoe, Daniel. *Moll Flanders*. Cardinal Edition. Pocket Books (New York, 1951). Edited by G. A. Starr. Oxford University Press (London, 1972).

Manon Lescaut

Abbé Prévost. *Manon Lescaut*. Presented by Pierre Mac Orlan. Livre de Poche (Paris, 1959).

―――. *Manon Lescaut*. Translated with an Introduction by the late, beloved Professor Donald M. Frame, of Columbia University. Signet Classic, New American Library (New York, 1961).

Camille

Dumas fils, Alexandre. *La Dame aux Camélias* from *Théâtre*. Vol. I (Paris, 1858).

―――. *Le Demi-Monde* from *Théâtre*. Vol. II (Paris, 1858).

FALLEN WOMEN

Electra and Antigone

Aeschylus. *The Oresteia Trilogy and Prometheus Bound*. Translated by Michael Townsend; Introduction by Lionel Casson. Chandler Publishing Company (San Francisco, 1966).

Four Plays by Sophocles. Translated by Theodore Howard Banks. Oxford University Press (New York, 1966).

Sophocles. *The Oedipus Cycle*. English versions by Dudley Fitts and Robert Fitzgerald. Harvest Books, Harcourt Brace (New York, 1939).

Laclos

Les Liaisons dangereuses. Preface by André Malraux. Livre de Poche, Librairie Gallimard (Paris, 1952).

Les Liaisons dangereuses. Translated by Richard Aldington; Foreword by Harry Levin. Signet Classic, New American Library (New York, 1962).

Kleist

The Marquise of O and Other Stories. Translated by Martin Greenberg; Foreword by Thomas Mann. Signet Classic. New American Library (New York, 1962).

Mérimée

Carmen, from *Romans et Nouvelles*. Vol. II. Presented by Jean Mistler. Livre de Poche, Librairie Gallimard française (Paris, 1973).

Carmen. *Colomba*. Translated and with an Introduction by Edward Marielle. Penguin Classics (Harmondsworth, England, and Baltimore, 1965).

CHAPTER V

Mothers. Death Queens

ANCIENT WITCHES

In ancient mythology Death Queens were revered as infernal deities of death and doom. Named openly, Hecate, Proserpina, the Furies, they were glimpsed only obscurely because they preferred wandering the earth at night lurking at crossroads and in graveyards, because they unveiled their faces and dark-gowned forms only intermittently, like the moon emerging from cloud cover, or they were not even seen at all but only sensed by dogs. Any sudden, furious barking by watch-dogs at night alerted mankind to the hovering Death Queen there-abouts.

The Romans believed the Furies were goddesses who lay in black beauty on splendid, golden couches. When the ancestor of all aristo-cratic Rome, the goddess' son Aeneas, offered sacrifices to the Furies, he heard a roaring clamor sweep the earth. The woods on the hilltops shook madly, and dogs took up the cry from all sides of him. Aeneas knew that in order to approach the Death Queens, he would need the only guide available. This was the white-clad Sibyl from her shrine on the Bay of Naples. He never would have persisted in his request to descend to "under the world," "below the sunset" without her. When he approached the threshold of this darkened realm, he met the fearsome attendants of Proserpina: many-headed Hydra, black River Styx, and the Ferryman Charon upon whose skiff only those allowed by the queen could hope to set foot.

The place where one must descend in order to enter the Underworld has moved since the days when Aeneas managed his daring exploit and returned safely, thanks to the Sibyl and her Golden Bough. The green meadow one crossed before the descent into death, as Plato explained in *The Republic,* later became the Champs Elysées of Paris, and then farther west the death isle of Avalon in the Irish Sea, and even farther west, volcanic Mount Hecla in Iceland, and, much farther west, the Isle of Avalon off the Los Angeles Airport. In place after place, mythology continues to instruct us, just as that strong, unkempt boatman Charon bowed low before the Sibyl's Golden Bough. He obeyed her unspoken instruction, docked his skiff, accepted his passengers, and crossed the water. Before the Death Queen, silent in her presence, the black dog Cerberus sat alert on his haunches, and at attention.

Antigone feared so much for her brother Polyneices that she gave up her own life. He should not have to wander eternally up and down the near shore and every day beg passage of Charon. Without this transportation over the narrow strait he could never leave that weeping throng of the damned and win his everlasting repose. Nor could he, without funeral rites blessed by the Death Queen, ever cross the lovely, green meadows of the Elysian Fields. It was Antigone's bounden duty to release Polyneices from any intermediate stages in Hel's Kingdom.

These Death Queens kept the list of the nine Ills of Mankind, and they personally supervised the ninth: (1) grief, (2) worry, (3) illness,

(4) old age, (5) terror, (6) starvation, (7) labor, (8) poverty, and (9) death.

The Greeks recognize the Queen as the murderous witch Medea, who assumed her person once on earth. She starred in the tragedy of *Medea* by Euripides. Thus, contemporary man sees her now also, agreeing with viewers that our great American operatic and concert star Jessye Norman, often impersonating both *Carmen* and *Medea,* is another such majestic and queenly woman. "She's strong in the face of death," said her interviewer, on December 22, 1991, on national television ("60 Minutes"). We all know, have known our lives long, Agatha Christie's elderly Miss Marple, the unassuming death-dealer, a ferret from her English village, nonetheless revengeful Fury, doom-sayer, judge of murderers.

MEDEA

A perfect reconstruction of a service performed by Medea and her husband Jason as they honored and worshipped the Death Queen survives in the Medea story. Their service was a mystery rite. Our word *mystery* also deriving from the Latin word for church service: *ministerium*. Jason and Medea had pledged their troth at Hecate's altar. In memory of these vows they enacted their ritual "mystery."

Medea first instructed Jason, as he performed the function of high priest, to cast a stone in memory of the one he cast before enemy warriors. As she handed her husband the stone, Medea may have recited, "Cast this stone among them. They disperse!" Then, she instructed, you may offer the dragon this potion (Isolde's *poison*). He will sleep or become impotent. Then Medea cut up pieces of raw flesh, which recalled how she had cut up her own brother and cast his flesh upon their trail as they fled south into Greece. The pursuers were bound to recover the pieces and give them proper burial and funeral honors, which delayed their pursuit so well it allowed Jason and Medea to escape.

Then Medea enacted her search for the plant of immortality. For nine days and nights she journeyed (into ancient Sumer?) in order to pick the flower(s) of eternal youth so that she could make Aeson forever a handsome adolescent. After she had descended from her dragon chariot, and stepped down upon the lowly earth again, she and Jason erected a new altar to Hecate. Then they sacrificed a black sheep to the goddess, for each family and each flock has a young one potentially discardable. Then the officiants at the altar offered prayers also to Pluto and Proserpina. Then they laid Jason's father, Aeson, to sleep on a bed of powerful herbs. He lay still as a dead man. No person was permitted, at that still point in the rite, to look at either him or them. Medea meanwhile unloosed her lovely hair. She stooped to dip certain twigs in blood. She laid them then upon a fire. She observed them burning.

Medea then prepared her brew and the cauldron containing it which appears in all mythologies, from Asia west to the poet Taliesin of the ancient Celts. In her magic cauldron she placed seeds and herbs, and the bitter flower(s) of youth, such as Inana in ancient Sumer or Titania in the *Midsummer Night's Dream,* gathered. In token of the world's uniqueness she then put in her kettle stones from Asian mountains and sand from Atlantic beaches. One by one, she placed in her concoction one token contributed by each sacred totem creature: (1) wings from the funereal owl, bird of death because his wings are so silent they give no warning to his victim; (2) shell of a tortoise because it clings to life so much more stubbornly than most other creatures on earth; (3) entrails of a wolf because it has the guts to continue the chase in silent harmony with its own kind, and stay there running mile after mile in ice and snow until it triumphs at the kill; (4) liver of a stag for two reasons, the stag is recognized as the noblest of all animals, and the liver acknowledged to be the seat of all prophecy; (5) head and beak of a crow (raven) because that bird speaks truth and outlives the tenure span of eight human generations, and into the ninth. Medea then turned her back as Ceridwen did later among the Welsh, and added the remaining ingredients, one drop of which upon the lips of a child would turn that child into a poet. The poet is most sacred of all persons.

She then stirred the brew with a dead and brittle branch from an olive tree, for the crown of olive signals the courage of warriors, just as the wreath of laurel nominated and crowns the great poet. The dead branch served as a successful test for her brew, for it burst into fresh, new green leaves. As Medea watched it closely, her branch blossomed and then set fruit which matured even as she observed them. The drops which fell accidentally on earth sprang into grass and flowers. Whatever else Medea dropped in her cauldron must remain forever unannounced. But the recipe survives despite its secrecy and is not lost.

By this time Aeson's body had been totally drained of blood. Medea proceeded to administer to his corpse a transfusion from juices in her cauldron. Before their eyes his white hair turned black, his white skin turned pink, his slack veins swelled, his flesh plumped up, his limbs began to move; and finally a youthful Aeson rose from his couch. There he stood, before their altar, not as an old man of sixty but as a young man again, twenty years of age.

DEATH QUEENS IN THE MODERN WORLD (1833–1991)

After having been massacred as witches by the millions in the sixteenth century, usually for having practiced medicine without an M.D. degree, old women suddenly became unpersecuted and even fashionable. From 1833 until this date of writing (January 1992), Death Queens themselves appear in those vehicles which celebrate and/or feature women prominently, indeed, in vehicles which could not exist without prominent women delineated: the historical novel, the novella, the movies, and grand opera. Interestingly, in the cases everybody has either read or seen, and certainly in what we in the twentieth century call "classics," defined as a work of art studied in our classes, the author or creator has been almost always male. Notable exception must be made for the greatest actresses and singers of our century, women of the stature of Jessye Norman, Glenda Jackson, and Eleonora Duse.

It will perhaps be simpler to list those most outstanding of modern classics which feature an old woman who is recognizably a Death Queen:

Author	Date of Publication	Title of Work
1. Alexander Pushkin (1799–1837)	1833	*The Queen of Spades*
2. Fyodor Dostoyevsky (1821–1881)	1866	*The Gambler*
3. Gustave Flaubert (1821–1880)	ante May 8, 1880	*A Simple Heart,* from *Trois Contes*
4. James Joyce (1882–1941)	ante 1905	*Clay* from *Dubliners*

Author	Date of Publication	Title of Work
5. Grazia Deledda (1875–1936)	1920	*La Madre* (1926 Nobel Prize Award)
6. William Faulkner (1897–1962)	1930	*As I Lay Dying* (1950 Nobel Prize Award)
7. Federico García Lorca (1898–1936)	1936	*La Casa de Bernarda Alba*
8. Jean Giono (1895–1970)	1949	*Mort d'un personnage* (*Death of a Character*)

Although he actually wrote *The Queen of Spades* between October and November of 1833, Pushkin had been planning it for four years, since 1829. He was all prepared, with his useless epigraph which disingenuously tells us nothing: Bleak weather in autumn leads to Russian officers playing cards for money. He does not help us much either with his gratuitous information that the Queen of Spades wields the evil eye, and that she is the Death Queen.

The English translation of 1962, through no fault of the translator Rosemary Edmonds, does not help us either in the matter of names: Queen of Spades. Is she a queen because a spade digs the officer Hermann's grave? Or her grave? Is she Queen of Spades perhaps because the queen is the most powerful piece in chess? Is she the Death Queen because she wears black?

If the playing card Queen of Spades came via the Moors into Spain, then *spade* is derived from the Spanish word for *sword: espada,* as in Italian, *spada.* In Spain the matador Carmen paraded herself with an *espada* used to kill the bull. But French historians writing in the fifteenth century claim that playing cards were invented in France for the express purpose of whiling away the sad time during the last illness of their King

Charles VI. This Charles the Beloved was proven beloved of God because, struck on the helmet by a beggar in the Forest of Mans, France, on a very hot day, King Charles had fallen from his horse, become insane thereafter, or intermittently insane, and soon died. He much enjoyed playing cards. He died finally in 1422.

In the French language the Queen of Spades is called *La Dame de Pique* because she holds in her right hand a lethal weapon or blade shaped somewhat like an arrowhead. Either way, armed with sword or, with the French *pique* (lance), she is the murderous warrior, the lancer, and thus, the Death Queen.

Sixty years prior to the opening of Pushkin's story, a Russian countess, who had frequented Jewish counts, Casanova, and the Duke of Orleans at his gaming rooms in Versailles Palace, once chose three cards with which she won enormously. She also revealed the secret of the three cards to one gentleman alone, and he duplicated her wins. The story begins when this Countess is eighty-seven years of age, residing in Moscow, continuing to frequent its aristocrats, and raising a poor orphaned maiden, Lise, in her household.

Young Lise foolishly admitted, upon returning from a ball one evening, an officer named Hermann, who she thought loved her. Hermann waited not upon Lise, but in the old lady's chamber for her return. There he bearded her, and demanded to be told her secret of the three winning cards. Shocked at the sight of him and at his tigerish manner, the old Countess fell back dead in her chair. Who was Hermann but another Napoleon Bonaparte, another Mephistopheles who had sold his soul to the devil. "You are a monster," Lise told Hermann.

Although this officer had never gambled before that time, he fell so thoroughly under its spell, and under the charm of the old Countess, that he dreamed she came to him as a woman-in-white. He clearly heard her as she revealed her precious knowledge: three-seven-ace. Madly, Hermann rushed to the most exclusive, private casino in Moscow, and there twice won enormous sums on the three and the seven. Then, already half mad, he bet it all on his third card. He called for the Queen of Spades! She herself from the underworld had dealt him this death blow, after all. He could not even remember what he knew. Ironically, Hermann never knew what he should have suspected, that the reason she had found her way to him in his dream was that the old Countess was his natural mother.

Some thirty-three years later Dostoyevsky continued along the same vein with his novella, *The Gambler*. His ghastly crone is a seventy-five-year-old Russian Grand Duchess, a second such great lady from Moscow, and reputedly on her deathbed. Her family, enthroned in a German resort they cannot afford, await their inheritance breathlessly. Each of her heirs desires to wed some impecunious French person.

But lo and behold, the old Duchess appears in person, "enthroned," active, lynx-eyed, erect, harsh, and imperious. "Blockhead" and "Donkey," she yells at the hotel employees. Power-loving, greedy, impatient, and intolerant, she frightens everyone except her favorite, who is the real gambler and our narrator, Dostoyevsky. Dostoyevsky has moved the reader one generation back in time to a grandmother, and probably in an attempt to distance himself, hide himself from the accusation that the most insane gambler is himself, out of control from time to time.

"Cette pauvre terrible vieille," as the grandame is often called, or "this terrible poor old (rich) woman," obstinately sets herself down at the gambling resort to try her luck. She became immediately obsessed with roulette, and she is "fair game" for croupiers and onlookers too. After a first win, which she shares with servants and strangers, she settles down to serious play. With what Dostoyevsky terms "calm madness," she first loses 15,000 roubles, and then 90,000 roubles in six to seven hours. Why? Because "Tomorrow, tomorrow it will all come to an end" anyway (p. 162). She has lost her fortune.

Young Dostoyevsky was once placed before a firing squad and almost miraculously spared after others had been executed before his eyes. Then he spent years of exile in a Siberian death camp, which he described in his book originally entitled *Letters from a Dead House*. His narrator in *The Gambler* is a barely disguised Dostoyevsky who also tries to recall where he has been and what "madhouse somewhere" (p. 114) he still inhabits. Consulting his collected "pages of notes," he tries to separate past from a present reality that only seems to happen. The German town falls into his own yellow melancholy: ugly, strange, and tragic.

His old lady "grande duchesse" (p. 73) has now lost her "terrible" and immense fortune by plunging down drunken into a vortex which jolted her as much as life jolts all of us, which whirled and spun her so wildly that she lost her balance. Reality proved finally to have been a toboggan run where for the ancient sin of pride she finally divested herself and her fawning, starved relatives of all security. Dostoyevsky has personally seen and endured far worse.

Why does he write? To give form and structure to what otherwise is the meaningless, slippery reality of an old woman's life. What truth can tragedy teach us all? A very sad truth, indeed: That all people enjoy observing and learning about the humiliation of their friends, but that best friends enjoy it the most. This is an old truth, Dostoyevsky observes, and well known to all intelligent people.

These two Russian women who lodged in Western consciousness, and whose stories have long since become classics, were supplanted around 1880 by Flaubert's servant woman, Félicité. The French master had her before him as every resident of France sees her at homes, in the markets, lugging produce down the streets, and hanging up the wash. Everyone in France has always been able to employ such a live-in servant as Félicité, whose monthly wages thirty or forty years ago were about the equivalent of fifty dollars a month.

Doubtless because she was such a common sight, or because of his terror during the French revolutions of the nineteenth century, ending with the Franco-Prussian War that commenced just the few years before World War I in 1914, Gustave Flaubert seized upon his poor, illiterate, work-horse Félicité as a heroine. We drop suddenly from

Russian nobility and wealth to abject poverty, ignorance, and the benightedness of this broken female laborer in the affluent bourgeoisie. Such a woman, so commonly seen trudging down the rainy stone pavings of France, walks with her shoulders sagged almost to her waistline from the burdens she has carried in each hand, and since girlhood when her bones were still pliant. Her huge, red hands, swollen with rheumatism from washing linen every week out of doors and always in cold water, hang like raw paddles beside her knees.

Félicité, Flaubert writes with bitter irony, was merely a mechanical, wooden woman, and never, to the people around her, a real, suffering human being. And yet only she protected the two little children of her mistress against an angry bull in the pasture, setting herself as its target until the two little ones could slip through the fence. Thus early on her bravery has made her an heroical heroine.

Heroical also was her self-deprivation before every person she ever knew: her mistress, her nephew Victor, the two children, neighbors and passersby alike. While she was still young, Félicité spent herself to exhaustion and knew no better. Flaubert allows people to treat her even more savagely than he treated Emma Bovary, for whom he had at least a small, soft spot in his heart. In the case of the aged Félicité, Flaubert castigates society, all of us, everyone, for our cruelty toward old women, and for our utter heartlessness towards the ignorant and the innocent poor among us.

Félicité's life unravels through the years, much as Emma's dreams vanished painfully until she killed herself. As a younger woman, escorting the child Virginie to her catechism lessons and ceremony, Félicité loved Christianity for its little lambs and white doves. After Victor died of yellow fever in Havana, Félicité walked miles to see where Victor's ship was tied up and pored over a paper map to see if she could find him lying dead of malpractice in some place called Cuba; and after she had sat sleepless for two days and nights beside Virginie's body, when she died of consumption in her convent, the old woman finally rebelled against God. In the streets outside her mistress' town house, and looking down from her dormer window in her unheated attic bedroom, Félicité saw the populace take to the streets and rebel against the government of 1830. Having no longer anyone to love, Félicité took advantage of her kitchen and her marketing to befriend, dress, wash, and feed all the poor people who came begging for scraps at her kitchen door, and including drunks, and the cancerous.

To her astonishment, one day a "Negro from America" rang her back doorbell to bring her the gift of a parrot from her long-dead nephew Victor. She named the bird "Loulou." For the next years, as Félicité lost her faculties slowly and surely, she lavished all her unsatisfied love upon the parrot, cared for it, talked to it, caressed it, and finally *worshipped the bird*. To her, the parrot became what Christ becomes to devout worshippers. One terrible day it escaped and flew away. The poor, aged woman went mad looking for it and almost died of grief and exhaustion. Suddenly Loulou landed on his usual perch—Félicité's shoulder. The feeble old woman never recovered from this trauma.

To her, Loulou became a son. His was henceforth the only voice she could hear. Then he became the lover she had never had (p. 75). Loulou died of cold in Félicité's garret during the terrible winter of 1837.

A frequenter of her mistress suggested Félicité have Loulou stuffed. The poor, old woman set out on foot from Trouville to Honfleur, which in her day would mean traveling a narrow, dirt road from one coastal and resort town on the Seine River estuary to the latter seaport (of Samuel de Champlain). Going down the long hill into Honfleur, Félicité was whipped and wounded by a postillion driving the stage coach. She had not heard it coming behind her and therefore had not given them right of way. During her last illness she kept seeing Loulou soaring overhead, looking just like the Holy Ghost about which Virginie had been taught, and her along with Virginie, in the catechism lessons.

Gustave Flaubert died in 1880, or twenty-one years before the first Nobel Prizes were awarded; but an American author who received the Nobel Prize in 1950 spoke words in acceptance of that great award which Flaubert might earlier have said. If Flaubert and Turgenev felt that by endorsing an aesthetic doctrine called "art for art's sake," each achieved anonymity, they were mistaken. Flaubert was unable to hide his true purpose, which was to reason with his readers and try to warm their hearts by appealing to their better impulses.

When he wrote *Madame Bovary,* and even more daringly when he wrote Félicité's story *Un Coeur simple,* Gustave Flaubert launched another full-scale and frontal attack against the French social system that had created poor Félicité. His immediate successor was James Joyce from across the English Channel and the Irish Sea. Joyce came, like Flaubert, from a nonnoble and nonroyal family; and he knew, as Flaubert knew from the hospital his father worked in, how badly and how hopelessly poor people suffer, and more so in a small and impoverished island like Ireland. After Flaubert's "A Simple Heart," he was exiled forever from his homeland. He had apparently infuriated everyone. With money from the first successful book he ever wrote, William Faulkner departed for Paris so he could at least sit at the feet of James Joyce.

Joyce's story "Clay" from *Dubliners* is only ten pages long, and yet one ventures to claim for it the title of best short story in the world. Joyce begins, "The matron had given her leave to go out as soon as the women's tea was over and Maria looked forward to her evening out" (p. 123). Abruptly Joyce leaves the reader without further clues. What "matron"? What "leave"? What "women"? One "evening out"? What establishment is this? What is Maria's status? Who is she? Is this a prison?

The reader, whom Joyce calls "you," does arrive at answers of a sort. Maria is the maid in a laundry that employs women only. They apparently either reside there like inmates in a prison, or they work there all day long, quarrelling amongst themselves. But Maria is herself an inmate like Félicité. She escapes one evening a week in order to spend her meager wages on cakes for her nephew Joe, a cruel drunkard, and his wife and their two callow and stupid girls who eat her cakes and give her short shrift. In order to get through Dublin to Joe's house, Maria has to travel in crowded trams. This night one kind gentleman in one of the trams quite unusually offered Maria a seat. Upon arriving at Joe's house the poor woman discovered that he had stolen the better part of her goodies.

Because it is the evening of Hallowe'en, the family, or the children and Maria, play a blindman's buff game to see which one will win the lucky prize or (engagement) ring. One wins the prayer-book, three touch only water, but one girl wins the ring. Then Maria is blind-folded. Laughing and joking she approached the table until her hand found the saucer. She felt a soft, wet, cold substance; then she heard a great scuffling of feet in the silence. The girl from next door was sent home. Maria was told to begin again. This time she touched the prayer-book.

The party ended with Maria making an error as she sang a familiar Irish melody. Joyce offers no other explanation. Nor is there any mention of clay in the story, but the reader shudders to realize suddenly what has transpired. Maria has touched clay, or felt her own imminent death. She is a second-class, poor working woman who will have lived deprived of someone to love her, although she will have loved virtually everyone else. That night she touched her own death. The thesaurus enlightens us: A corpse is dust, ashes, earth, clay, tenement of clay.

The 1926 Nobel Prize went to the Italian novelist Grazia Deledda (1875–1936) for a novel called *La Madre,* translated by Mary G. Steegmann as *The Mother* (New York, 1923). Deledda tells the story of another poor working woman who toiled all her life to raise her son for the priesthood, and who slaved for him even after he became a priest and took a mistress. She died alone and uncomforted so much did she fear disturbing this son, Paul, who had always been mortally ashamed of her ignorance and her poverty.

Perhaps those Nobel Prize judges had read the *Collected Papers* of Sigmund Freud, which had recently been published in London; and perhaps they realized that the person of an aged woman, mother or not, but more so if the mother of a son, would be one of the major and most painful concerns of twentieth-century psychiatrists, psycho-analysts, school teachers, and mothers.

In 1930 it was the turn of William Faulkner (1897–1962), who had not as yet received much attention and little or no acclaim. In fact, when he was awarded the Nobel Prize for literature in 1950, not one of his books was in print. Generally speaking, it takes about one hundred years after death for a major author to be discovered. And major American authors are often "discovered" abroad: Herman Melville for *Moby Dick* (London), Edgar Allan Poe in France by the poet Baudelaire, and Faulkner in France also.

William Faulkner, who was not a wealthy gentleman like Flaubert, but only a relatively unknown American, declared in Stockholm in 1950 that an American author also believes mankind will not only survive but triumph. Man is immortal, Faulkner said, because his voice cannot be silenced, because every man has a soul, because he feels compassion, because he endures, because he willingly sacrifices himself. Therefore an author's real purpose is to help persons live better lives by reminding them to be hopeful, proud, compassionate, and brave. Pity for the poor and the unfortunate and care for the homeless are the only traits which have made mankind's past glorious. Such persons are the truly heroic. Faulkner's black heroines owe much to Flaubert's Félicité.

In 1930 William Faulkner published *Tandis que j' agonise,* his novel *As I Lay Dying*. It is such a strange book at first sight because it is narrated in spurts, as it were, by family members of a dying mother.

But the reader grasps it easily enough just the same. Monologue after monologue by Anse and by her children build her story: Her son Darl speaks first, he whom she does not love but who worships her, followed by her son Jewel whom she loves but who does not love her, followed by her pregnant daughter Dewey Dell, who is frantic to find ergot of rye for an abortion. Another major voice comes from the deeply religious neighbor Cora, another from the Doctor, and several monologues are spoken by the youngest son, Vardamon. The mother, Addie Bundren, speaks only once, to repeat her key word "quiet."

> In the afternoon when school was out and the last one had left with his dirty snuffling nose, instead of going home I would go down the hill to the spring where I could be quiet and hate them (p. 161).

Addie Bundren is dying of a broken heart, principally because there is no love among this tribe of Bundrens. The only reason at all for living, Addie says, is so one can prepare to remain dead "a long time." She hates her own father for having seeded her. She has always longed to whip her children more than occasionally. Like the prototypical American heroine, Addie was originally a school teacher who could not find an educated husband, and married the disgusting, ignorant Anse, a country man so self-centered and so vicious that he deserves his name: anserous, anserine from *anser* (goose), or *anse* (curved handle), or gooseneck (a curve, a clamp). Like some morons, he is only crafty, wily, and cruel. He manipulates everyone in the family, cheats them, deprives them of their earnings, steals the horse Jewel and Addie have earned so painfully, deprives Addie of proper burial, cuts off Cash's leg, forces Dewey Dell to give him her ten dollars of abortion money, which her seducer has given the child, with which he buys false teeth for himself and a new wife carrying a victrola.

Today, which is only a few months short of thirty years after Faulkner's death, his dissection of American heroines remains almost too unbearable for words, but so very true. Only French University critics and translators like R. N. Raimbault call it what it is: a study of American *paysans,* peasants, by a native American educated at the University of Mississippi (1919), but already a veteran of the Canadian Air Force (1918).

American professors of English brought tears to their colleagues' eyes, as did the late Professor Arnold at the University of Southern California, when they read Addie's words on "motherhood" (pp. 163 ff.). Somebody who never went through it, she said, made up the word. Somebody who never felt the *fear,* she said, or the *pride,* let fall the word as a spider falls, faster than the eye can catch it sometimes, which dangles dangerously by her mouth on her own filament. Her first child, Cash, violated once for all her separateness, her distinct and previously inviolate individuality. At her second pregnancy she considered killing Anse in some way that would leave him unsuspecting. She visualized him flowing into her, the handle of her vessel, as cold molasses drips into a jar. The neighbor Cora knew that Addie was no true mother, and told her so.

William Faulkner's immediate admitted master here was James Joyce. In 1925, after the publication of his first novel, *Soldier's Pay,* about a soldier returning from World War I, Faulkner traveled abroad and spent part of four months, September–December, in Paris, 26 Rue Servadoni. Daily, it is said, he passed his mornings on the Left Bank near the Sorbonne at the authors' café of *Les Deux Magots,* where James Joyce was also known to go. It is said in France that Faulkner took his usual seat at a point across the room where he could face and observe Joyce. Faulkner never walked over and introduced himself, however, which one understands. He did not achieve success as a writer, or earn any substantial sum of money, until 1933, when he published *Sanctuary*. While in *As I Lay Dying* he had zeroed in on the prime dreaded and/or joyous experience of every American woman, motherhood, in *Sanctuary* he focused on every American woman's worst nightmare and/or worst nightmarish experience, rape.

It is certainly true that William Faulkner is, like Flaubert, a woman's novelist in the sense that complicated, as well as the most wonderful, heroines dominate his books. Raimbault, who was his first French translator, noted Faulkner's own words of love for women when he declared that *his books resulted* from this admiration for the courage and the sheer endurance of women. The raped Dewey Dell, afraid, alone, and penniless, is repeated in other characters such as the poor, penniless, pregnant Lena Grove walking along the dusty dirt roads of the South in *Light in August*. The author reserved his greatest love for American black women, however, because they *endured* terribly hard work and sacrificed themselves silently and nobly, and because they did so proudly, in the face of universal loathing and hateful discrimination of all sorts and from all sides.

The French, prize-winning novelist Jean Giono (1895–1970) is another direct heir, in his post–World War II novels especially, of William Faulkner. His autobiographical novel, *Mort d'un personnage,* or *Death of a Character* (1949), studies the aging and death of Giono's own grandmother, whom he had represented earlier as a young, adventurous heroine, thus the title word *personnage,* which in French means a fictional, literary character. His grandmother used to trace a line on the little boy's forehead, designating Giono as future, creative personality and author. The phenomenon of the Jocasta mother, who programs a son or a daughter from earliest years to achieve superabundantly, both academically and creatively, is commonly recognized by such modern professors of psychology as Anthony Storr, Oxford University. From Provence, Giono returned to the Greek legends of Oedipus and Jocasta to underline his own pseudo-autobiographical battle against the dying old woman. He tried in vain to restrain her as she plunged headlong into death.

Even more interestingly, Giono, in an unforgettably poetic passage, envisioned this aged, frail grandmother, as a young, black-clad Alcestis standing in the green window, or rather sunken hip deep in

Alcestis's daisies in that same green meadow which stretches mytho-logically just this side of the entrance to the Underworld. Up until now Jean Giono is known mostly for his ravishing short story, "The Man Who Planted Trees" (Vermont, 1963). As soon as an expert translator appears, or reappears in his case, Giono will become one of the greatest writers of fiction of the twentieth century.

Major masters of cinema have already adapted and treated superbly the elderly heroine from ancient mythology, Hecate, goddess of the dead, or the Death Queen. Mention should be made at least of a recent play and film by the English scenario writer Steven Poliakoff: *She's Been Away*. The movie was shown twice (December, 1991) on public television in Los Angeles. It was notable, but not for its repre-sentation alone of the Death Queen. At the end the old woman saved the life of her pregnant young niece after she, the Death Queen, had been rescued from the insane asylum where for the past sixty years she had been incarcerated. It was also memorable because the late Peggy Ashcroft played the Death Queen. It was her last performance. Like the younger Glenda Jackson, Peggy Ashcroft remains one of the most beloved and most accomplished actresses of our century.

Praise should also be lavished upon the late Spanish master of letters Federico García Lorca (1898–1936) from Andalusía, who was so sadly murdered young at Granada, during the Spanish Civil War. His *La Casa de Bernarda Alba* (1936) was played by Glenda Jackson in the title role as a film on public television (Los Angeles, December 20, 1991), which also starred Joan Plowright as Señora Alba's housekeeper of some thirty years.

This brutal and widowed Señora Alba had sequestered her five daughters in her airless stone townhouse. The eldest daughter of a previous wife was rich and therefore, although already forty years old, engaged to marry a young suitor. The youngest daughter, Adela, loved this fiancé and expected to wed him soon. Her oldest sister had such a narrow pelvis that Adela was certain she would die in childbirth after nine months of marriage. Another jealous sister reported Adela's escapades out after dark with her older sister's fiancé, which caused the two girls to roll in desperate combat.

In the grim, hot, stark, Greek classical, and claustrophobic downstairs room, where the action unfolds, Señora Alba and her repressed, stifled daughters hear from the streets outside their shuttered window that an unwed village girl has been discovered. She had delivered her own baby, killed it, and buried it. But dogs have dug it up and eaten it. The young mother screamed at the sight, which let the villagers know what she had done. They catch her and she cries for mercy as Señora Alba leads her daughters in their chant: "Kill her! Kill her! Kill her!" Only the youngest girl, Adela, had cried over and again as she clutched her abdomen, "No! No! No!" We have guessed what she was doing undressed and out of doors at night.

When Señora Alba threatened to shoot Adela, this youngest daughter hanged herself. The old mother, the bitterest of all Death Queens so far, gave out the report for village consumption: "My youngest daughter died a virgin. I will allow no tears."

García Lorca has caught not only the stark and unrelieved tragedy as it may have been played in ancient Greece, but also the human passions which move us all to love, bear, and rear children. Bernarda Alba, and this is all one could ever think of to say in her defense, realizes that her daughters can never, with the means at their disposal, attract suitors. Therefore she has cloistered them for their own good.

ELIZABETH HUNTER, HEROINE

The Nobel Laureate for 1973 was the Australian novelist Patrick White for his ninth novel, *The Eye of the Storm,* which the Nobel Prize committee called "epic and psychological." The fascinating heroine of this great book is Mrs. Elizabeth Hunter, a dying woman, aged eighty-six. While the story of her life is told almost entirely in the last months of her life, it finally grows by months, weeks, days, and then minutes, to her death. It is true that this is an "epic" novel if one agrees that novels dealing with two generations of a family are epic, and psychological if one agrees that a descent into the depths of a woman and a plumbing of the depths of her two children, her nurses, cook, lawyer, and other attendants is enough Freudian psychology to fill twelve chapters and close to six hundred pages.

What White seems to have done is to contradict Faulkner's novel of 1930, *As I Lay Dying.* It is not so much a tragedy that mothers now wonder if they love their offspring, but it is a tragedy when children hate their dying mother. In the last days of her life, the children of Elizabeth Hunter come to claim from her their inheritance, and to will her to die immediately so that they can henceforth live at ease with her money. The son is an alcoholic actor, and the daughter is a sterile old maid filled to the brim with hatred for her mother. Neither attends her funeral. Both attend the reading of her will. Mrs. Hunter leaves almost everything to them. *The Eye of the Storm* could also be called a murder story.

This novel wraps the reader in all the awe and majesty of ancient Greek tragedy, and all its fear before the evil and weakness of human beings. Over all sweeps the eye of the cyclonic storm symbolizing the "natural" shambles of human relationships. Her children never once look their mother in the eye. Stoically they ignore and resist her aged tears . . . until she yields and dies. Her children will prolong their lives with her murder, which only her chief nurse resents and objects to.

To others the crone Elizabeth is an idol and "source of oracular wisdom" (p. 364). Even the mother's lawyer steals her star sapphire ring and this even though she has dowered his wife royally. One must agree that this is a family novel, a genre which the English excel at writing. White is English and a fourth-generation Australian. English critics found this novel not necessarily Australian, but "universal." In any case, its style is universal.

The Eye of the Storm provides a classic example of the style of fiction called *nouveau réalisme* from 1950, or "New Realism." The book is a long study of reality which steadily advances to death, the ultimate reality. The method is stream of consciousness via a destruction of grammar, pronominal ambiguity, upset chronology, flashbacks, and symbolism. The author speaks through each of his many characters as he attacks the immorality, insensitivity, coldness, and loneliness of modern people. White foreshadows the ending twentieth century by his return to paganism, reverence for this old woman idol, priestess, oracle, and demigoddess. Her death ceremony is a "mystery" play, and a drama where God is absent.

Elizabeth Hunter is the most memorable heroine of them all. She is also the most unforgettable mother in fiction.

•READINGS•

Dostoyevsky, Fyodor. *The Gambler*. Translated with an Introduction by Jessie Coulson. Penguin Books (London, 1966).

Faulkner, William. *As I Lay Dying*. Modern Library Edition, Random House (New York, 1930).

Flaubert, Gustave. *Trois Contes*. Edited by Bert M.-P. Leefmans. Collection Internationale (Garden City, New York, 1962).

Giono, Jean. *Mort d'un personnage*. Grasset (Paris, 1949).

Joyce, James. *Dubliners*. Introduction by Padraic Colum. Modern Library Edition, Random House (New York, 1926).

Pushkin, Alexander. *The Queen of Spades*. Translated with an Introduction by Rosemary Edmonds. Penguin Books (Baltimore, 1962).

Storr, Anthony. *The Dynamics of Creation*. Secker and Warburg (London, 1972).

White, Patrick. *The Eye of the Storm*. The Viking Press (New York, 1973).

·CHAPTER VI·

Heroines Return to Paganism

ASTRONOMERS OF THE OLD STONE GODS

A knowledge and understanding of ancient history, myth, and ritual is important in interpreting the roots of modern customs, views, and ideas. This phenomenon persuades us to halt again and comprehend what that means. Ancient myths have to a high degree informed and inspired modern fiction, as we have seen in the preceding chapters. Astronomers have long told us how very ancient our knowledge is, and especially our knowledge of the heavens. Theologians have also long since explained that our religious ceremonies were once called "mysteries." Thus, modern fiction, astronomy, and religion have served not only to advance our knowledge, comfort, and to safeguard mankind, but also to preserve ancient knowledge.

When such arcana appear in the modern fiction of our acknowledged world masters, and recipients of their highest awards such as the Nobel Prize for Literature, then we may suspect that novels and novellas have also served to conserve this same, archaic knowledge, both astronomical and theological, of our ancient and even prehistoric past.

In casting another backward glance at certain strange rituals, we can come to understand an otherwise inexplicable and peculiar documentation made by some of our greatest modern authors.

The ancient Greeks, at their prime oracular center in Delphi, Greece, used a strange calculating machine to determine the lines of latitude of the globe, lines such as we see today on our maps. The same lines of latitude also gave them the distance of Delphi from the equator, or 38° 28' north of it. They, then in ancient Greece, also calculated they were three-sevenths of the distance from the equator to the North Pole. Another sacred site at Sardis in Asia stood also on that same parallel, they knew. They figured out that the great temple at Thebes in Egypt lay at two-sevenths of this distance, temple to pole. Their calculator was, said Peter Tompkins in *Secrets of the Great Pyramids* (New York, 1971), an apparatus closely resembling our modern roulette wheel (pp. 349–50).

Their wheel stood in ancient Delphi, which is not far from Athens, on top of their sacred stone at Delphi. This oval white stone was and is called the navel of the earth, or *omphalos*. All visitors to Delphi today will have seen it.

The wheel which the Greeks then used to calculate latitude had thirty-six spokes. Just as in a modern roulette wheel, a ball was spun around the wheel. The ball stopped at one of the spokes, which were both numbered and lettered. From this apparatus and action, which resembles our gambling apparatus and activity, ancient Greeks computed latitudes, seasons, and their calendar. Theology is also based upon an accurate calendar of both the seasons and the centuries. Travel and navigation, agriculture, education, government, and labor, and our very lives depend equally upon an accurate calendar.

Furthermore, the Delphic calculator gave oracular replies to the questions asked by millions of anxious persons of the Delphic priestess, or Oracle, as we saw listed in *Priestesses* (see Readings at end of chapter). Thus, the major religious center of the ancient world depended for its authority to rule upon an archaic roulette wheel.

Oracular answers to questions posed by worshippers, who incidentally came prepared to pay for information received, somewhat like a visit to a modern fortune-teller, were also derived from playing cards, adds Tompkins, and derived also from Ouija boards: The roulette wheel of Delphi originally was, it appears, a special kind of abacus used for calculating in terms of angles.

The correct angle of shadow from a Maypole or from a mountain peak would also give the viewer the first day of spring, time to plant peas in New York, for example, and first day of fall, or time to harvest corn in ancient Mexico. Both native American and Mexican peoples also knew these dates, as well as many others.

Silbury Hill in Great Britain is a great mountain of earth and stone, a tumulus which drivers to and from Bath to London always have to circle because of its vastness. It is at least four thousand years old. It also was originally used as a calculator. This truncated pyramid, resembling the three great ones in Egypt, required laborers to move by hand some million tons of earth and stone in its construction.

Scholars in England have long known that the area from Avebury and Stonehenge west to Silbury Hill contains an agglomeration of megalithic sites unequalled except for Carnac in Brittany, France. A Maypole of a certain height, erected on the flat top of Silbury Hill, would cast a shadow down its sides to the foot of the pyramid and exactly reach the base at the four crucial days when the sun crossed the equator twice a year and when it crossed the Tropics of Cancer and Capricorn once each year: two equinoctial days, and the two solsticial days, the ends of June and December, and the ends of April and September. These four days still mark today our prime religious festivals. They have done so over millennia: Midsummer's Night and Christmas Eve, Easter and Hallowe'en.

Every 2,150 years the heavens revolve and alter the present calendar considerably, but the zodiac we know will remain stable in our days. It is valid from the years A.D. 350 to 2500.

Today the spring equinox falls in Pisces, the summer solstice in Gemini, the autumn equinox in Virgo, and the winter solstice in Sagittarius, as calculated by Peter Lum in *The Stars in Our Heaven. Myths and Fables* (New York, 1948). We recall how Joan of Arc was burned at the stake by her chief prosecutor, the Cardinal of Winchester, England, which place is adjacent to both Stonehenge and Silbury Hill, because he said she danced about a Maypole. This constituted one of her English tribunal's or kangaroo court's principal charges against the maid of Orleans. In other words, she allegedly participated in a pagan ritual which had survived contumely and time, and which originated in some megalithic age. The stones which Medea placed in her cauldron may possibly have come to her from Stonehenge itself, or from Carnac.

A great astronomer and historian of ancient mythology published in London in 1894 a magnificent study of worship in ancient temples and astronomy in prehistoric times. Without specifically mentioning Medea, her cauldron, her witch's brew, and her rite of open-heart surgery, tranfusion, and revival of the patient suddenly restored to the vigor of youth, Sir Joseph Norman Lockyer in *The Dawn of Astronomy* pointed out that such an inverted cauldron, as Medea's from the Black Sea Coast and of Ceridwen's in ancient Wales, represented the heavens above us.

The stars seem to revolve in orderly procession around the inverted cup or cauldron of the North Pole. The four major stars cross our nighttime sky every six hours. Only these major stars tell time for us with accuracy. Stonehenge, or its megaliths, give us solar time. Stonehenge points to the sunrise at the summer solstice.

We speak not only of four stars, but also of the four quarters of heaven just as did prehistoric astronomers in Persia. The ancients gave long ago our familiar, zodiacal names to the four major stars:

Regulus (Leo the Lion) and star of Summer; Antares (Scorpio the Scorpion) and star of dreaded Autumn; Fomalhaut (Aquarius the Water Carrier) and star of winter's rain and snow; and Aldebaran (Taurus the Bull) and star heralding spring. These stars, but also constellations that appear minor to those of us who live in northern latitudes, certainly figure prominently in modern treatments of ancient mythology.

Peter Lum puts it clearly: that much "of the knowledge and thought of the earliest astronomers was not in the language of science but of mythology" (p. 9). Thus, we may even now reconstitute pieces and bits of ancient science from those same ancient myths repeated by modern authors as well as earlier by ancient storytellers. Philosophers who are experts in epistemology will still have to tell us all how modern authors knew what they knew.

Studies of the author's creativity are very recent. How did Giono's aged grandmother know, as she traced the circle upon the small boy's forehead, that he would, because of his superior creative talent, be able to plumb the depths of human consciousness and human memory also to supernatural levels? And Giono was, like Rousseau before him, self-educated, which is the case of everybody, of course, whether he has sat in schoolrooms or not. Most of us like to forget what is unassailably true: No teacher can teach anyone anything if that individual refuses to learn, or cannot learn. Perhaps Giono's grandmother only stimulated the small boy to want to learn and to want to create. It is more likely, however, that he inherited superior intelligence. The refusal to learn, and/or the inability to learn, which is often seen as stubborn or sick behavior, more probably indicates low intelligence.

This brief review of astronomy, as it is related to mythology, has been done in order to explain mankind's worship of stones and of stone monuments. How many of us have journeyed to see stone calculators and stone monuments at Delphi, Stonehenge, Carnac? On summer Sundays English tourists come by busloads to walk the miles of megaliths at Carnac, France, and purchase postcards. England has had to close off Stonehenge, for fear of the land itself subsiding. Historians report that the uses of stones, and the very transporting of stones, which characterizes us all as human beings, were ancient, religious exercises.

We place beautifully carved stones above the graves of our beloved family members, and come from afar to sit beside them and commune. We touch the stone gratefully because it serves as a real memorial, just as the stones in Arlington Cemetery and the Vietnam Memorial, and the millions of stone markers in Normandy, along General Patton's Highway, commemorate the American and Canadian soldiers dead in World War II. Stones mean more to us in the twentieth century because this century has seen the greatest holocaust in the world. We have killed other human beings by the billions in this century, and worse is to come in the next hundred years.

Thus, in the twentieth century stones mean more to us than ever before because they speak to us, who fear our own extinction, of our long ages upon this earth. These stone monuments in England and France not only predate the findings of classical Greece but even anticipate the discoveries of Pythagoras, by a thousand years, says the late Alexander Thom. This English engineer explains how to calculate the date of such megalithic stone constructions as Stonehenge from the sun at the vernal equinox: *Megalithic Sites in Britain* (Oxford, 1967, '72, '74, pp. 1–5). There are, he reported, some four hundred fifty such huge stone, or megalithic, sites inside Britain. Thom personally surveyed three hundred of them.

In her new book, which includes a Foreword by Alexander Thom, Jean Hunt, who is president of the Louisiana Mounds Society, believes that the last survivors among these megalithic builders "were submerged or exterminated during the years following 3000 B.C." *Tracking the Flood Survivors* (Shreveport, 1991), "In a nutshell" (n.p.), she dates Stonehenge I at 3000 B.C. (p. 3). She promises a new paradigm, that at least once before 1991, an advanced civilization disappeared, leaving behind them such stone monuments as Stonehenge itself (p. 11). The scholar's task, she concludes, must remain this: to find the truth (p. 12). Therefore we study ancient myths as repeated in modern times.

THE STORY OF MEDUSA

Medusa's story seems to occupy the foreground in one of the world's oldest accounts, that of a long and bitterly fought war between prehistoric Greece and northern Africa. The vague recollections of such a war surface at various levels and were credited by Greek poets and historians. In the western Mediterranean, for example, we hear even now of an Ethiopian dynasty from southern Egypt, which founded the Greek Delphic Oracle. That temple and priestess were subsequently guarded by an African giant, some warrior prince named Python. Little more now than these definitions remain:

Pythia = the Pythoness, or Delphic priestess, who uttered the responses requested of her by worshippers at Delphi; Python = The Serpent guardian of this priestess called Pythia. He was slain by Apollo, who adopted his name, and became Apollo Pythius. The Greeks wiped out an African people.

The python is itself a nonvenomous African snake which crushes its prey and which is often thought to be the largest living serpent. These facts of size and African origin remind one immediately once more of the old war Greeks waged against the unknown giants called Titans. The Titans too were killed and/or expelled in the west of the known world.

Medusa was also a giant, one of three gigantic, one-eyed sisters. She was herself killed by a Greek warrior. Even after she was beheaded, however, Medusa struggled to give birth to her sons, one of whom was the winged horse Pegasus, who was later captured by the Greeks. It was her second son, Chrysaor, or Golden Sickle, who bore the sign of her power.

Thus, Medusa's African peoples only lost the war and their queen, but survivors were able to move north and west. Medusa herself is associated with northwestern Africa, and specifically the Garden of the Hesperides on the coast south of modern Casablanca. She is also closely related to that same area behind which rises the lofty range of the Atlas Mountains. Medusa is further associated with the western or Atlantic Ocean itself. Robert Graves writes in his *Greek Myths* (I, 8, 2) that Africans then also migrated to Crete and Greece as early as 4000 B.C.

The Greek hero Perseus, who killed Medusa, hoped to annihilate her race of Gorgons in Africa. A vial of her healing blood was saved and given to Asclepius, father of medicine in Greece. Her face was used to defeat the giant Atlas, who turned to stone at the sight. Her skin was flayed from her body and presented to the Greek goddess Athena for her use as double protection on her shield. The remains of Medusa's body were then transported to Greece for burial.

Both Medusa and Python remain conspicuous in mythology because both were Africans, then called Libyans, and both were serpent deities dedicated to the moon, doubtless garbed as serpents, and wearing the usual raised cobra, or Pharaonic crown, on their heads. In addition to this crown, which proclaimed Medusa, and Cleopatra after her, queen of the reigning "great house," the African Queen Medusa wore her hair in dread ringlets said to be snakes themselves.

Since her story in so many words exists only in Greek and the Roman version rewritten by their poet Ovid, Medusa is seen typically through the eyes of her conquerors alone. What was curly hair to Africans easily became coiled snakes to their foes. We forget that the best priestesses had long, curly tresses.

Medusa's race became extinct, claimed the Greeks, which claim is also suspect. Literature in both Spain and France particularly recalls the race of Gorgons who, they say, were truly giants. These giants, said François Rabelais in the sixteenth century, were genial and even highly educated. One of them preserved Medusa's family name of Gorgon in his French name of Gargantua which meant in French, wrote Rabelais jokingly, How-Big-You-Are. Since Gargantua, like

Medusa, was mountainously big, many mountain peaks around the world were named for these ancient ancestors, and called Mounts Gargan, Gorgonio, and so on.

Robert Graves believed that Medusa was a Mother goddess of the moon, worshipped on rocky mountain tops, many of which bore her name or her clan name Gorgon for that reason. She was certainly associated with megalithic stones. She petrified men and even turned a giant named Atlas to stone. Her myth therefore recalls megalithic builders and their heirs, who devoutly hauled giant megaliths unbelievable distances—from the mountains of Wales to Stonehenge, for instance—and who erected the thousands of dolmens and menhirs across the world.

By the years 1160–56 B.C. the high priests of Egypt had ousted high priestesses, however, and thus obliterated almost all memory of such earlier ages when, as in the lifetime of Medusa, the older matriarchy was also ousted by Aryan sun gods such as Perseus and Apollo. These warriors spread patriarchal rule gradually over Western Europe as well.

Some squadrons of Amazons still remained in Africa into modern times, however, and served in modern European armies. In the same way memories of matriarchy, of goddesses, women warriors, priestesses, and the peoples who built the megaliths survived total destruction.

Inspiring fear and horror perhaps, and always awe and dread, ancient queens like Medusa and Cleopatra were inseparable from the worship of animal forms. They too represented numinous forces outside man and beyond his comprehension: the viper, the python, the cat, and the cow, for example.

People still climb there and stand in awe of high mountains like the Atlas range in North Africa. They also still feel the power inherent in stone and in the untamed cat so secretive and aloof even when imprisoned all its life long. The sacred stones of bygone ages and lost civilizations still attract millions every year.

Medusa's people remain only names today, but in the days of their defeat by Greeks, they furnished to that poor land all the rich produce for which Morocco has always been famous. North Africa still supplies Western Europe with the first fruits and vegetables of spring. Both the olive tree and the grape vine were exported from the African Garden of the Hesperides. Despite these riches, Africa remembers Queen Medusa because turning men to stone releases them from the sorrows and fears of life. Medusa made men virtually unforgotten. Thus, she belongs among the old stone gods whom she continued to worship, who continue to worship her even out of the Mediterranean Sea and across the Atlantic to Britain and Brazil.

THE FLIGHT OF THE HEROINE

Certain heroines who cannot make an accommodation with contemporary society, or who are ousted and abandoned within that framework, opt out. One could perhaps claim that the twentieth century opened fictionally with a novel by Thomas Hardy (1840–1928): *Tess of the D'Urbervilles* (London, 1892), which later became an American film by Roman Polanski (December 1980 review in *Newsweek*, p. 73). Tess was played by the teenaged Nastassia Kinski. *Newsweek* applauded this three-hour film as "magnificent cinematography," but called it "Victorian tragedy." The costumes by Anthony Powell were indeed Victorian, and very ugly.

From a strictly literary point of view, Hardy's tragedy was a repeat of "Beauty and the Beast," except that the fairy tale ends happily with hero and heroine at the altar. In Hardy's novel Beauty is innocent and appealing enough, but she is no queen's daughter besieged by suitors. Our Tess is an impoverished, uneducated peasant girl sent to labor at menial, back-breaking, farmyard jobs on the estate of a heartless landlord who may even be her distant and aristocratic relative. There Tess is remarked for her beauty, seduced, jilted, and abandoned. Even her illegitimate baby is refused a Christian burial. She weds another love by whom again she is abruptly deserted. Cast out again destitute, she hooks up with her first seducer in order to save her family from starvation.

When her true love, or husband, Angel Clare, returns to claim her, he triggers all her welled-up grief. Without a thought or a word, she takes a knife, kills her lover Alec D'Urberville, and sets off on foot after her dearly beloved.

All this unrolls rather tiresomely in the film, but heartbreakingly in Hardy's savage novel. This English novelist knew true tragedy when he saw it, even in the case of a wretched, throwaway girl milking cows in a barn, pitching hay in a meadow, or out in the cold digging potatoes. In Hardy's pages, just as in Theodore Dreiser's scandalous masterpiece, *Sister Carrie* (1900), a poor country girl rises to the equal of the tragic Queen Medusa.

The Beauty named Tess commits murder. Then she slogs along the forest paths of southern England in the wake of her learned gentleman, and then amorously and forgivingly hangs on his arm until, days later, they reach an empty country mansion. There in relative comfort, Tess falls into bed with her beloved Angel Clare, for the last days of her young life.

Her real husband Angel has some vague idea that they can escape pursuit by the police, reach some seaport, and emigrate, like Manon Lescaut and Moll Flanders before them, perhaps to America, or Australia, or Canada. If that is Angel's plan—and Tess is too ignorant even to plan any course of action—then he is traveling in the wrong direction. The deserted mansion where they take refuge for a few sweet days of loving has provided Hardy's successors with a chapter to be equalled.

Beauty has fallen utterly victim, now and once more, to the same two beasts: Alec D'Urberville and Angel Clare, the former a country squire or lout, and the second, a weak-kneed, pallid pseudointellectual. Hardy, however, knew his countryside well. What final refuge will this gorgeous country lass stumble upon, but the megalithic temple her countrymen still worship at the day of the spring equinox: Stonehenge . . .

Here the film falls apart, showing us what are too clearly, not Stonehenge, but some cardboard rocks.

The novelist, on the other hand, delivered a telling blow against each wrong done Tess-of-the-aristocratic-name, accusing both Christianity and society for her ignorance, poverty, enslavement, rape, the general beastliness of males, and the do-nothingness of women in positions of power. Hardy also asserted strongly that the fairy tale of Beauty and the Beast is absurd, immoral, and useless as a cautionary device meant to keep girls submissive, passive, exploited, and yielding. Thus, Thomas Hardy is a most successful, powerful, and outspoken champion of women in the beginning of the twentieth century. What is Victorian about that?

Great Master that he was, and as he remains, Thomas Hardy could not and cannot hold a candle to the greatest Masters of the even more modern novel: David Herbert Lawrence (1885–1930), predecessor of William Faulkner. The English D. H. Lawrence came from a family of poor miners in Nottingham, England, but he prepared himself for his most glorious career in letters by becoming first a brilliant scholar and by teaching school for a while. He became successful immediately as a writer of widely acclaimed stories, of controversial fiction, and of literary criticism, translations from the Italian, volumes of poetry, paintings, and wonderful theology. He was exiled, or he fled from his homeland during World War I, which he opposed because war, as he wrote, leads men into savagery and their women into depravity. He spent his few, short years of life in Italy, Sardinia, Australia, Mexico, and fortunately for us Americans in Taos, New Mexico. He was befriended by an American heiress with whom Lawrence and his wife resided for some time. Both are buried in beautiful Taos, which is a shrine to Lawrence, and well worth the pilgrimage. All American women especially owe him an immeasurable debt; for he, along with Faulkner and Giono, is the greatest champion of woman the world has ever bred. He is therefore very much despised and maligned by some American critics.

Lawrence's novel, *The Plumed Serpent* (1926), *la serpiente plumada,* may very well be the best novel not only of the twentieth century but of all time. It is not only mysterious and fascinating, but actually unforgettable, terribly spellbinding. The story itself is the least interesting component: An Irish woman named Kate leaves Mexico City for the interior where she gradually becomes not only an ancient Mexican Indian, but a goddess chosen by the Aztec god Quetzalcoatl as his bride, Malintzi. Two Mexicans of wealth and power, Ramon and Cipriano, choose her to complete their trinity of the old, pagan religion of the Aztecs. Kate's flight reproduces that of Tess, not in the few, final pages of Hardy, but in close to five hundred pages of learned, fascinating, and complex ancient mythology.

The Christians, says Cipriano (p. 292), treasure their "centipede power" over all frightened persons, "especially over women." Cipriano desires a new return to the pagan gods, a worship of such goddesses as Astarte, Freya, a revival of Thor and Wotan in Germany, of the "Druidic world" among the Celts, of the Tuatha De Danaan in Ireland, of Hermes and Quetzalcoatl. He wishes "natural aristocrats" everywhere to become again "Initiates of the Earth" because only they can bring nations and races together into harmony. People must make a new religion (pp. 273, 292, 289 ff.) "that will connect them with the universe," or we shall all perish on this earth. Women especially resemble rabbits, alike in the hand of God, nonetheless at the mercy of men.

Ramon and Cipriano sought to recover the ancient rhythms of "aboriginal America" (p. 283): the old dances of the Aztecs, the bird-steps "of the Red Indians" to the north of them. They dreamed how beautiful the American plains were when inhabited only by native peoples and wild animals as at "Atlantis and the lost continents of Polynesia" (p. 454). Kate was elected to the priesthood because she was Irish and therefore had inherited the "Aboriginal Celtic or Iberian" lore of prehistoric days which Irish people themselves have never forgotten (p. 455 ff.). Hers was not a common blood but aristocratic like that of Tess of the D'Urbervilles. The present earth, full of humble, writhing Christians, is to Ramon *a place of shame* (p. 301).

In his Chapter XXIV, entitled "Malintzi" (p. 423 ff.), Lawrence attempts a definition of woman not as an isolated individual, not singular in herself alone, but reciprocal in marriage and flowering together. While Kate had believed that each man and each woman was a completely separate and unique individual, a belief that has held in the western world since its inception around 1500, she now came to agree with Ramon and Cipriano that people before marriage are merely halves or fragments of persons. Cipriano restored her virginity each time they made love.

Thus, Kate or Malintzi came to identify herself with a "great cat," equally voluptuous and lustful, roaming gratified in a new sense of power (p. 480). Lawrence quotes a "woman writer" to the effect that women have suffered much more from loss of ego than from sexual frustration (p. 481). In Mexico henceforth and forever Malintzi will sacrifice herself in order to wear the green of a priestess with the proud eyes of a conqueress.

Lawrence had once been even more explicit in his treatment of the modern woman. His famous and celebrated short story (1922) called "The Woman Who Rode Away," picks up another story in Mexico where a woman lives near the abandoned silver mine owned by her husband. This woman of thirty-three has been morally downed, says the author, by her husband. He keeps her enclosed and invincibly his slave. With her children away at school, the woman has no outlet, no escape, no hope, and no diversions.

Therefore she dreams of what can lie beyond the bare hills which surround her. Indians live there. They are perhaps naked. They wear flowers in their hats, she knows, and carry bows and arrows. Their religion is very old and consists of secret rites called "mysteries." Two tribes, the Navajo and the Yaqui, are still free to roam their own prehistoric realms.

Therefore this woman, originally from California, leaves her much older husband and her home, rides off on horseback without a word of farewell and without leaving a letter of explanation.

She rides on, camping at night beside a small brush fire, mounting up next morning, and following trails that led her finally to an elevation of 9,000 feet.

When she comes upon Indians in the Chilcui country, she joins them quietly and replies to their first questions: "Yes, she comes to them of her own free will. She comes to seek their God." The Indians seize her and lead her, like a prisoner, up the mountains to their hidden village. They realize that she looks without seeing, replies without evaluating consequences, looks like a human person to her own race perhaps while to them she is little more than a huge, white ant.

She found their village far more attractive than she had imagined and their rulers far more qualified, and personally far more clever and more authoritative. She was treated well there and well cared for. She realized from the first day in the village that she was being drugged. Various men undressed her and attended to her bath, then robed her in splendor. Once or twice she was shown to the populace there, and also allowed certain requests, such as to stroll among flower beds. Various low-level officials interrogated her, then referred her to chiefs, and eventually to medicine men, and ultimately to the very aged cacique. All inquire whether she is dedicated to their religion, if she has brought her heart to their god. She replies yes to their questions, feeling more and more that she has lost all will of her own, even that she has died to the world.

The woman grasps the inevitable: *that her type of dependent woman will and must be obliterated*. She realizes finally the utter ferocity of males. The Indians believe that when they were conquered by white men, they lost the power with which their own sun god had endowed them. Simultaneously their womenfolk lost their power, which had for eons come to them alone from the moon. Both sexes now have a chance to regain this lost force which so long had kept them proud and free. This mastery, it is their belief, passes from one race of people to another. It must be regained, or the Indian will vanish from the earth.

The heroine begins to note that fall has passed, that the days are growing shorter and shorter. She was sacrificed as the setting sun struck the altar within its cave on the day of the winter solstice. Her heart was cut out of her chest and offered to the sun god.

An even more recent story of this kind is Callie Khouri's film of

1991, *Thelma and Louise*. Two American working women, both ordinary persons, only one of them married, and to a beast, ride away gaily one day to get away from their drab, workaday lives, feel young and pretty again, and have some harmless fun for a change. They have in mind a carefree weekend away from work, and toil, and bosses. Their lark turns sour when one of them is beaten badly and almost raped by a drunken lout in a roadside bar. They flee after the other young woman kills him to save her friend. Then the two continue upon the course adopted by Angel Clare for Tess of the D'Urbervilles: a mad escape. Soon they have committed such crimes, such sheer folly, that they too can neither surrender, they feel, nor be accepted in society ever again.

While Tess was arrested quietly and hanged with some privacy and some dignity left her, Thelma and Louise are the prey of bands of ravening, male, motorized police lusting for the kill.

In this crisis, hotly pursued, or rather hunted down like poor vixens tracked by dogs and riders, the two terrified women burst into the red splendor of the Navajo's Monument Valley. They have returned like Lawrence's two heroines, the one Irish and the one Californian, into the prehistoric, monolithic world of America when it was still beautiful, splendid, and unpolluted. The moment is breathtaking as their automobile glides silently between the mountainous red buttes.

The women stop momentarily. This beauty has strengthened them. What shall we do? They understand, and they agree. They are women who ride away from modern America, permanently. They shift into high gear and drive off the cliff into obliteration.

Behind them vast numbers of police vehicles come to screeching halts. Now we know that young women are also hunted down by dozens of policemen in twentieth-century America; their only means of escape is apparently for them to vanish into the prime and pure landscape.

•READINGS•

Goodrich, Norma Lorre. *Ancient Myths*. NAL, Viking Penguin (New York, 1960).

———. *Priestesses*. Franklin Watts (New York, 1989); HarperCollins Publishers (New York, 1990).

Hardy, Thomas. *Tess of the D'Urbervilles*. Laurel Edition, Dell Publishing Company (New York, 1962). Includes Preface by Hardy to the Fifth (English) Edition, dated July 1892.

Lawrence, D. H. *The Complete Short Stories*. 3 vols., but see Volume 2 for "The Woman Who Rode Away" (pp. 546–81). Viking Compass Edition, The Viking Press (New York, 1971). First Copyright 1922.

———. *The Plumed Serpent*. Alfred A. Knopf (New York, 1926); Vintage Books (New York, 1955).

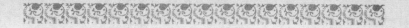

CHAPTER VII

Amazons. Statues of Women

AMAZONS. WOMEN WARRIORS

Matriarchy once ruled as *the law* among civilizations and peoples in Asia Minor and North Africa. It spread westward as tribes moved west across northern Europe into lands where it almost surfaces today: Finland, Scandinavia, Scotland, and Ireland. Tales and legends of heroic warrior women remain in these countries as evidence of this ancient body of laws.

Doctoral dissertations on matriarchy from Finland and Scandinavia today, where women professors are routinely funded by the state to explore these ancient rights of women otherwise forgotten and staunchly denied, prove their antiquity. Christianity came late into these northern lands. Where it spread quickly, as in France, Italy, and Spain, for example, all or almost all traces of matriarchal rule had disappeared, as did also traces of indigenous warrior women.

France, astonishingly, has almost no mythology, as a result. Only

Rabelais in the Renaissance stamped, with his great genius, memories of giants upon the public memory, thus reviving lost literature in disparate fragments from total oblivion. Rabelais is generally considered, for his pains certainly, a mere writer of medical pornography that is largely scatological. Closer reading proves the contrary, however. His giants were ancestral warriors from the lost African race of Medusa the Gorgon Queen. Otherwise, the eager acceptance of Christianity inside France completed the almost total massacre of the Celtic warrior aristocracy there by Julius Caesar (c. 55 B.C.). Armies of aristocratic warrior women took to the field against Roman Legions and were slaughtered along with their children by the hundreds of thousands. A native French/Celtic population was wiped out.

To read a very rare epic where women play central roles as queens, warriors, and sacred priestesses, one might turn to the Finnish *Kalevala,* visit Finland today, or recall its magnificent defeat of Russia in World War II. To trace this heroical tradition of armies made up entirely of warrior women trained to combat from early girlhood, one can go as far back in time as the *Iliad* and other such prehistoric works of mythology. There one finds records of Amazons, women raised in a matriarchy, in what is now Turkey and southern Russia, that is, around the shores of the Black Sea and also along the African coasts of the Mediterranean.

The two major movements which dethroned women, or which toppled them from active roles of leadership, were certainly democracy, on the one hand, and Christianity on the other. The weapon used was pregnancy and motherhood taught as obligation and sacrificial way of life. The woman must stay at home where she is assaulted by commercials into becoming a consumer, heart, body, and soul. Christianity wiped out the ancient heroical mode for women and demoted them to service, subserviency, and impurity.

Therefore only the northern lands today strive to remember, and pay women to remember, recall, and prove what were once far better days for women. Literature comes to the rescue, for despite his stalwart efforts Saint Patrick did not succeed in burning all the ancient records of Ireland. Our first warrior queen—in the image of Pallas Athena of Athens, and the warrior goddess Minerva of Rome, and the Winged Victory, and all warrior queens named Victoria—comes from Ireland. The second heroine comes from Norway, who at the first sign of Christianity, committed suicide.

The story of the third warrior is the saddest story the world has ever seen and has, like our own American mysteries of death and political assassination, proven a mystery impossible to solve. She was called Joan and raised to the nobility as "d'Arc," or Joan of Arc. Nobody has more than mere clues as to who she was, where she was born, or when and if she died in Rouen.

What is apparent are her mythological ties to the ancient warrior ethos from across northern Europe. She was called the *puella* (maid) *gallica* (of Celtic Gaul), from the *white wood* (Druid temple in the forest). She was certifiably virginal. She dressed in white. She rode a white horse. She carried a white banner with white lilies on it. She had second sight. She prophesied correctly: This Englishman will die now; this troop will surrender now; this fort will surrender now; this supply train will arrive safely today; this city is now safe enough for us to enter; this prince will be crowned King of France; the English will now leave France; this war will be won.

She spoke with the authority of an ancient Druid priestess whom she resembled in every detail. Hers was a voice from the distant past.

THE GREAT QUEEN FROM IRELAND

The ancient Celtic Queen of War was named *Morrigu,* which means exactly that: great and queen.

> *mor* in Irish, and also in Welsh *(mawr),* German, Norse, Slavic, and Latin *(merus).*
>
> -   +
>
> *rigan* from *righ* or *rig* (ḳing), as in *regina* (Latin), Sanskrit *raj* or *rajah.* Gothic *reiks,* and English *rich.*

The Celtic Morrigu was a battle queen, but also a death queen. When on the battlefield she was a young death goddess called Valkyrie in Scandinavia and Germany, but she was usually seen as an aged crone among the Celts of Ireland. The Greeks had called her Athene or Pallas Athene. The Romans worshipped her as Minerva. To the Celts she descended from an even more ancient source, their totem animal, the crow or raven.

Edgar Allan Poe spoke of her as the raven, as sitting by the "pallid bust of Pallas [Athene] just inside our chamber door," and croaking "Nevermore." She always spoke in riddles when she prophesied with forked tongue. Local superstition in Vermont says that if a crow's tongue is slit, she will speak like a human being. When the black bird of death is a magpie, which flits black-and-white over hedgerows, she is still recognized as a goddess called "Daisy" or "Marguerite." The raven, crow, or magpie is an oracular bird delivering utterances in veiled fashion, or with forked tongue. She is also goggle-eyed because she descends from Magog, the Mother. Shakespeare's Regan recalls her presence: *regina,* goddess and queen.

Arthurian legends in Scotland recall the symbolic presence of the Great Queen in Perceval narratives. The hero Perceval set out on the

Grail Quest. He went west from Arthur's Camelot; on a morning when the ground lay deep in snow, suddenly Perceval saw a black bird fall on white snow where it lay spurting red blood. Perceval fell into a trance and was struck dumb. In other words, he too worshipped the Celtic Great Goddess. King Arthur sent an emissary to bring Perceval back to his senses which was difficult; in other words it took a long time for Christianity officially to supplant paganism. One might not show the white feather. But black feathers were worn on battlefields by lovely Valkyries as they sorted through corpses. The raven ate the dead as does the carrion crow.

Charles Squire says that Morrigu, the Great Queen, reigned supreme over all other goddesses of war because she represented the worship of the moon, which was sacred to women. As goddess of the moon she would have been another aged crone, mother of the native American fertility god Hiawatha. Moon worship preceded that of solar deities and their cults of young, male heroes. Morrigu, Squire says, was usually thought of as going to war fully armed, like a later solar hero. She carried two deadly spears in her hand. Her death cry as she declared war was as loud as that of Greek heroes before Troy. She often disguised herself as a carrion crow and descended shrieking over the warriors' heads. As she leaped like a ghastly wraith over their upright spears, they saw, even so, that she was a tall, skinny old hag with streaming gray hair. Relentlessly she fluttered and divebombed young men until she inspired them with battle frenzy.

The celebrated warrior Queen of western Ireland, Maeve (Mebd) of Ireland (Connaught), once fought a long war against Ulster for possession of the bull of Cooley (Cuailgne). That dreadful affair started as pillow talk between Queen Maeve and her husband. It started about which one was superior and which one was better before and after the wedding. Queen Maeve asserted as the talk became serious that she was better than her husband in gift-giving, counsel, battle, with weapons, in fights, in armed combats, in number of warriors, in Irish provinces which she alone ruled, in offers of marriage, and in wedding presents. She then declared herself the richer of the two.

The last bragging so angered her husband that he challenged her to prove it. The two of them leaped out of bed and started an inventory of their possessions down to the last object and the last animal. At the end of the tally the Bull of Cooley was found to have wandered from the queen's herd to her husband's, which made him the winner. Queen Maeve was beside herself with wrath to realize that her husband now had possession of the best bull thereabouts. What was she to do? (Lady Gregory, vol. II, p. 141 ff.)

Since warrior queens of Ireland usually win their disputes, Queen Maeve sent her herald Mac Roth to ask if she could, upon a huge payment, borrow the Brown Bull of Ulster for a year. Ulster agreed, and then broke their contract. Queen Maeve unhesitatingly declared war on Ulster. It took her two weeks to call up her three bands of six thousand warriors, consult her Druid, get her daughter ready to go, and hear her priestess Fedelme's prophecy. Although he was the greatest of all heroes, Cuchulain was still only a boy. He cut off the heads of Queen Maeve's scouts, however, and stuck them, for the whole world to see, on tree stumps. Then he cut off more heads from more of her men, and really angered Queen Maeve by killing her pet dog. Cuchulain sent word he would absolutely not ever live under the reign of a woman, and certainly not under hers. He also cut off her daughter's braids.

Then the Great Queen Morrigu herself swooped down upon him. This was "The Great Queen, the Crow of Battle," said Lady Augusta Gregory (vol. III, pp. 85–86). She dated from long before the Gael (Celts) even invaded and settled Ireland at all. In those most ancient days the Great Queen resided at her royal palace of Tara (Teamhair), where she dined on raw meat, butter, and other meats cooked on a spit (vol. III, p. 85 ff.). She gave nine ribs to nine rascals, and three hearts to her son. She also taunted the future hero Cuchulain when he was lolling about in boyhood. "You couldn't kill a shadow," she probably hissed at him because he got up and also struck off the head of the shadow that had loomed over him. She roused up Cuchulain too whenever cattle raids were held, for Morrigu was a superb reiver herself, always angering the cow chiefs by stealing their prize cows. She also had a pillar stone of her own, and if anyone happened to sit on it, he would go crazy. She drove heroes crazy by flitting in raven's feathers over the battlefield to blur their eyes until nobody could tell friend from foe.

In the same way, the Irish saw harpers coming from Ulster and heard them harping their sacred war songs to stir up the host. They got up a war band and chased the foe away over hill and through swamp. But the Morrigu had tricked them. What Queen Maeve had thought were Druidical harpers turned out to be a herd of deer. As if that happenstance, caused by the Great Queen was not foolishness enough, she also incited Cuchulain to sling stones at Queen Maeve. He fitted sharp stones into his sling and took aim at the queen's shoulders where her pets always sat close to their mistress' cheeks. Cuchulain killed her pet marten with his first shot. She loved her little tree weasel, or stone marten, from the pine trees and the beech trees. Her grooms hunted every day for berries, nuts, and honey to feed it. Queen Maeve had loved stroking her little creature's sable fur like the hunting fisher's brown-black coat. With his second, cruel shot he killed her dear little bird.

The death shook Queen Maeve to the quick, for her pet wren was the soul of her ancestors reincarnated as they flew out from their barrows, or stone tombs. Their souls were thus seen as light as the feather against which they had been weighed in the old, Egyptian ritual given in the *Book of the Dead*. Thus, Cuchulain signaled to Queen Maeve that it was New Year's Day in Ireland when she needed only one wren's feather to carry in honor of the Moon goddess Morrigu, and in warning of her own approaching defeat and death. "Hold a wren's feather," he was telling her, "and the truth of this battlefield shall be seen."

Queen Maeve confronted the Morrigu a second time; for, as her army approached Cooley, she heard that the Great Queen, Crow of Battle, had seated herself upon a stone at the royal palace of Tara and had croaked a dire warning to the Brown Bull which Queen Maeve planned to drive off into Ireland. As a result of this notice, the Brown Bull herded his heifers far away into County Londonderry. Meanwhile Queen Maeve's troops herded all the other cattle they could find.

Bad events occurred frequently, and they stemmed from the black-feathered crow. One evening as Queen Maeve's lady servant went down to fetch water from a brook, she wore her mistress' crown because she was serving Her Majesty. Cuchulain shot her dead. He thought she was the queen. Then as they tried to cross a tidal estuary, several men and chariots were swept out to sea by the tidal race. The queen halted to cut a wide swath, a broad path through one of their best mountains. It is still there today.

Queen Maeve realized that when Cuchulain reported he met a red woman driving a red chariot pulled by a red horse, he knew it was his protectress Morrigu. She had red hair, indeed, and red eyebrows. She wore a great red mantle that swept along behind her. She drove standing up tall and holding her two spears. If he didn't correctly report her as the young Great Queen then, he did so later after he had taken a lunge at her. Even as he jumped, he saw how foolish he was. She was not even there. She had vanished, along with her red horse and her red chariot, her red cloak and her evil spears. When Cuchulain looked over his shoulder, all he saw was the black crow croaking loudly on a dead limb overhead.

The invasion of Ulster went from bad to worse now. It showed Queen Maeve that nobody in her whole host was safe from death, not even horses nor dogs. Once the Morrigu herself stalked the troops of

Queen Maeve, was herself wounded, and then went to Cuchulain to be healed. He knew it was she wanting magical medicine, for she ambled up to him like any peasant driving a cow with three teats to her udder, and not the ordinary four. Cuchulain asked for a drink from each udder, and he blessed it each time. Then her three wounds were healed for the Morrigu, who was three-in-one: Virgin, Mother, and Hag. Thus, the three ages of woman are the same as the three phases of the moon, the trefoil, and the three sacred colors of religion which Perceval saw: red, white, and black.

It is no wonder that Queen Maeve's war with Ulster came by and large to defeat. First of all, who could win a war when the Morrigu championed her dear Cuchulain? Second, who could win a war when her other darling Fergus got hold of Excalibur? Obviously the tiny Moon cannot win over the Sun.

Excalibur ascended from the Underworld itself, for it was originally forged on Ynys Afallach, the Isle of Avalon, ruled once, later, by King Urien whose wife was Queen Morgan le Fay. That fact was sung by harpers even before the year 431, and in both Ireland and North Britain before King Arthur was even born.

Excalibur belonged to the Celtic world. It was their common property: *gemeinkeltisch*. This sword was the sacred fire of the lightning and related to the wheel, chariot, ring, ship, horse, bird, golden cup, and eye of heaven. The Underworld god, who was sometimes a salmon and sometimes a serpent, had forged Excalibur. The Romans called it "Excalibur," but the Celts understood it came from *calad* (hard) and *bolg* (lightning), which gave late Latin its spellings: Caliburnus and Excalibur. The great woman warrior Scatha on the Isle of Skye, who taught Cuchulain his martial arts, once gave Excalibur to Cuchulain. Then Morrigu gave it to the hero Fergus. Then the Lady of the Lake, who was Arthur's teacher and Lancelot's, gave it in turn to them. Welsh poets said this sword had two golden serpents on it which spat two tongues of fire whenever these heroes drew it from the scabbard.

Queen Maeve may not have defeated Cuchulain, but she did kidnap the Brown Bull of Cooley and drove him into her own wider kingdom, which he very much enjoyed. And so he bellowed with such glad fury that the White Bull of Connaught came at him and was killed some days later. But the Brown Bull gave such a victory bellow that he burst his own heart altogether within him.

Ancient Ireland was not the only home of ancient, warrior women. Their preserve was often heralded in Scotland as when a giantess 192 feet long washed ashore there once on a beach. As early as A.D. 500, say some, ancient Viking warriors, who were huge women, raided and conquered the island of Eigg in the Hebrides, off Scotland's western coast.

Thus, both Ireland and Scotland have preserved records and stories of warrior women just as the Greeks recalled their Amazon queens and Amazon warriors whom they conquered and killed. Penthesilea was one such famous woman warrior.*

Virgil in Rome also recorded praise for the heroic woman champion, beautiful runner, and warrior maiden Camilla. Her successor, said Jean Gerson, chancellor of the University of Paris, in the fifteenth century, was Joan of Arc.

But living after Camilla and before Joan were two other celebrated women warriors: the only Druid priestess to be historical, Velleda of Gaul, and King Arthur's warrior Queen Guinevere. Her life resembled that of the earlier British warrior, Victoria, or Queen Boudicca, who had defeated a Roman Legion. "Bud" and "Buddy" come from her name.

---

*Willis Cunning, President of the Clan Cunning in Iowa, and author of *The Clenconnan* (1991), writes me that he has found references to a Viking woman warrior called "Queen of the Pirates," who conquered the island of Eigg in the spring of the year 617.

VIKING HEROINES OF ICELAND AND NORWAY

In the year 1230 the Icelandic author Snorri Sturluson probably composed *Egil's Saga*. In this great history or epic he attempted to give life to the bare facts of Norwegian and Viking history. These heroes and heroines of ocean navigation and exploration remain among the great personages of the Dark Ages. One of their chief personages was the Viking hero named Egil. He was a daring explorer and a raider who lived around the year 910. It was he who set out from his far northern land on several long voyages back and forth from that coast to England and Ireland. The corroboration of dates comes from internal evidence, that Egil visited the English King Athelstan who, it is well known, ruled from 924–940. Athelstan had conquered Northumbria, a northern coast also well known to Viking raiders. In fact, the chronology of *Egil's Saga* is also confirmed by the visit of King Haakon (Hakon) at King Athelstan's Court, and Egil visited him too around the year 950.

Taking various Scandinavian sagas, including the Icelandic *Egil's Saga,* the brilliant Norwegian dramatist Henrik Ibsen (1828–1906), in the course of his association with the Norwegian National Theater in Bergen, wrote a first lofty tragedy entitled *The Vikings at Helgeland (Haermaendene paa Helgeland),* in four acts (1858). The major character in this play is a very fierce woman warrior named Hjördis. Ibsen's tragedy of this warrior, and of her adopted father Ornulf, and her husband Gunnar, possesses all the pride of nationality that one could hope to find in a Norwegian author, descendant himself of Vikings.

In Ibsen's world of Helgeland, which is northern Norway beside North Cape itself, we are plunged into this cold, grave, distant, and lofty tragedy from ancient heroical days. Far in the western distance, across mountainous breakers, lies England ruled by an Anglo-Saxon king. In Norway of this time rules Eric Blood-Axe. The four Vikings who hold center stage for the four acts of our tragedy live in the lands of a rich yeoman named Gunnar. His lands are Helgeland, and his wife, who does not love him, is the barbaric warrior woman Hjördis. She in her turn desperately loves and adores the heroic, young Viking chieftain named Sigurd the strong. But Sigurd has married Dagny, a mild housewife, a mother, and no warring heroine. Thus, Ibsen has presented another quadrangular structure anchored at its four corners by the husbands, Sigurd and Gunnar, the former a warrior and the other a rich farmer. The other two corners are held by Sigurd's sweet and wifely Dagny, and Gunnar's fierce and warlike wife Hjördis. The remaining character who holds these four together is Ornulf of the Fjords, an old Icelandic chieftain. He is father to Dagny and stepfather to Hjördis.

During a blinding snowstorm, deafened by roaring waves that came thundering across the shingle, the players live out their confrontations. Fights arise between the fierce Viking warrior Hjördis and the other persons connected by ties of blood or fosterage. Brandishing a spear Hjördis cries above the howling storm that Fate, and not she, rules their conduct. Fate has already decreed, she screams, that what will be will be. As for me, she announces, I prefer death to any cowardly settlement. Only Hjördis, she says, accepts no ties of loyalty or blood. Dagny humbly follows father and husband. Sigurd owes service to his father-in-law, his wife, and his friend Gunnar. Ornulf has met only disobedience, defeat, and rejection from his foster-daughter Hjördis, whom Gunnar abducted. Thus, Hjördis still lacks the official and honorable title of wife. She wedded Gunnar because he performed the bravest, single feats in the world: to kill the polar bear before her door, and to take her virginity by force.

The brave Viking Sigurd offers his ship, his treasure, and his life if Ornulf will only return peaceably to Iceland after relinquishing his oath to fight Gunnar. But Hjördis has continually insulted, incited, and threatened the men. She pits one against the other and longs to join their melee. There she will deal even more confusion. "Fate alone must be allowed to decide," she insists. The others fear that in the dark of this low midnight sun, which continually glows red on the horizon, peasants will burn down Gunnar's homestead and kill everybody in it. Then the survivors will likely freeze before they starve to death.

Sigurd wants to board his ships and leave at once for King Athelstan's court in England. Fearing combat and terrible slaughter, Gunnar has sent his small son safely away by ship. Ornulf fears that the ship will be overtaken and the lad slain.

This complication leads to the original misunderstanding which has set their five lives off course. This was the confusion as to who killed the white bear. This echoes an old Scandinavian myth that has persevered: Siegfried, and not Gunther, defeated Brunhilde, and it was Siegfried who forced her subsequently to lose her virginity. But Brunhilde alone failed to recognize the perpetrator of these feats of arms.

Eventually, Hjördis will unwittingly confess as much to the simpleminded Dagny. Hjördis enjoyed sexual relations only once, immediately after the white bear's death and it is this man alone that she has always loved. Eventually she will learn, and so will the pliant Dagny, who took Hjördis's virginity, and who killed the white bear upon whom the whole community depended for winter food and furs.

Sigurd confesses at last to his wife, Dagny, that it was he who killed the white bear. Hjördis had already vowed to wed that man alone. Sigurd killed the bear moreover as a favor to lovesick Gunnar, his friend. He said his drawn sword lay between them, or that he was Tristan to this unlikely Isolde/Hjördis. Sigurd took her gold bracelet, which is the symbol of lost virginity. He gave Dagny the bracelet as a wedding gift, which was thoughtless of him. He suggests she now throw the bracelet in the sea if they are to feast at Hjördis's home farm. Dagny refuses to throw away the bracelet.

Hjördis welcomes Dagny to her banquet, but the two disagree at once. Hjördis cannot understand the subservient, gentle wife of Sigurd any more than Dagny can understand the woman warrior. Hjördis says she lives like an eagle caged when she longs to tear flesh and drink long draughts of war. She will sew her small son's flesh to his tunic to see if he can bear pain like a man, without even flinching. She has felt love only once, the night her lover came to her after having killed the white bear. Since that wonderful night she has lived like a ghost in her new home. She has to sit beside the fire while she longs to ride the whales' backs on the sea. At night she prefers to crouch in her cold boathouse rather than huddle close to the hearth because there beside the waves she can hear the jangling of harness bells as dead warriors on black steeds ride overhead towards the northern icy hell of the slain. They are the men and women who turned their backs on the slavery of domesticity. They were not tamed, she tells Dagny, like you and me.

The banquet scene allows all tempers heated by ale to break forth into bragging, boasting, insulting each other, and finally into challenges to combat. All secrets are finally openly revealed. Passions rule their hearts: love of war, admiration for physical achievement, lust for money and treasure, conquest of foes and women as the proof of male superiority, and the use and abuse of children for the ends of power. Murder, rape, and slaughter are the means used by men to humiliate and destroy their foes. And every man is eventually seen, as every wife and child is seen, as a means to one such end. This is the world of the barbarian.

These are the Northmen and their nephews who also and repeatedly devastated northwestern France, killing, looting, plundering, and kidnapping the women and children of the Franks and Celts until in 911 the Viking Rollo, or Rolf the Marcher (so-called because he could not ride horseback, so long were his legs) accepted the surrender of the province still called the Norseman's, Normandy, from King Charles the Simple-minded of France. These are the same Norsemen and their sons and heirs who in 1066 conquered England where their Duke William "the Bastard" killed King Harold at Hastings, and then was crowned King William I on Christmas Day in London.

As this terrible banquet and orgy end, the old Icelander Ornulf enters carrying Gunnar's son, Egil. He overtook his craft and rescued the little boy from pursuers. In that sea engagement Ornulf lost his own six sons, however. Since Ornulf is himself a bard, he recites verses to his dead sons:

> *Wherever you ride now, my brave sons, I*
> *greet you. The massive gates of bronze will*
> *not slam shut on your bare heels. You*
> *shall arrive at the head of a great host when*
> *you enter Valhalla.*

As she hears him, Dagny tells Hjördis the truth: Her beloved husband, Sigurd, and not Gunnar, killed the bear and slept first with Hjördis. Taken aback, Hjördis swears to kill him for it. Her notion of heroism requires her to kill him. Dagny must die too, she cries, for having insulted her.

Along the seashore Ornulf sets to building the funeral barrow which will contain the bodies of his six sons. Memories of Beowulf crowd down upon the viewer, and his barrow and lighthouse also somewhere along such a frozen coast. Hjördis turns to Sigurd for an explanation of his cruel behavior towards her and towards his wife, Dagny. Sigurd has no explanation. Hjördis agrees with him. We have no choice and no power over our own lives. Why not? Because cruel Fate rules our world. All we can do is fight its decrees. I myself choose to fight until I die. I hope to master Fate. Therefore I shall braid bowstrings from my hair, and kill.

The web of wretched Fate has held us all, Sigurd confesses. He too, he tells Hjördis, has loved only her. His story, like hers, has therefore been as sad as his life has been. Fate has spun its wretched, hateful web to entangle them both. Hjördis pleads with Sigurd to allow her to join his troop as their Valkyrie and fight alongside them so Sigurd can rise to become King of Norway. It is too late, he tells her. And besides, he no longer loves her.

At nightfall Dagny persuades poor Ornulf not to die beside his sons' funeral barrow. Why should he live? the old Icelander asks. Dagny comforts him by reminding her foster father that he is a skald. Only his poetry can heal his wounds, no matter how deep. He takes comfort from her and writes the funeral dirge.

Hjördis consigns Sigurd to perdition as she stabs him. But before he dies, he tells her that her vengeance has gone awry because he is Christian and no longer subject to a pagan death without resurrection.

Hjördis then leaps into the ocean. She has been pursued long enough, she cries, by the red-eyed wolf, phantom of her death. The survivors plainly hear overhead dead heroes riding towards Valhalla.

As soon as day breaks, they will embark for their homes in Iceland.

Henrik Ibsen's translator explains in his Introduction to this play (vol. II, pp. 1–26) that the playwright amalgamated here four ancient sagas: *Egil's Saga, Volsunga Saga, Laxdaela Saga,* and *Njal's Saga,* because he wanted to present general, historical possibilities which once characterized his ancient, Norwegian people. In an archaic setting he sought to portray the spirit and temper of the Viking Age. By way of plot he moved towards the three surprise revelations: (1) Sigurd killed the white bear, (2) Sigurd really loved the heroine Hjördis, and (3) Sigurd had become Christian. So doing, Ibsen opposed the ancient Viking virtues of Hjördis (strength, courage, will power, domination) against the Christian virtues of Sigurd in the modern world (duty, obligation, discipline, and loyalty).

THE MEDIEVAL WARRIOR: SAINT JOAN OF ARC

After reviewing the known facts concerning Joan of Arc, reexamining eyewitness testimony given when she was first tried by the English conquerors of France who condemned her to death for witchcraft, and recalling the eyewitness testimony at her retrial where judges appointed by the Vatican found her innocent of all charges made against her, modern historians have wisely consigned Joan to theologians of the Catholic church. In our own century she was elevated to sainthood, which was the only honorable course possible. Joan of Arc belongs not to history alone but also to theology, not to the epic, although she was a girl and a victorious warrior, but to adoration as divine.

This great French military heroine has stumped historians because of the confusion surrounding her origins and contradictions in the telling of her story. Noble French families in the twentieth century, and including General Charles de Gaulle, have still claimed her. Some still deny that she was burned at the stake, this despite eyewitness testimony to the contrary by her confessor. It would make a difference to those attempting to situate her in the French royal family, if they could be certain that she was twenty years of age when she arrived miraculously at the besieged and apparently doomed city of Orléans, but perhaps she was only seventeen then and eighteen when she was executed. Eyewitnesses said she had never menstruated. The English ladies who examined her reported that she was still virginal. The Duke of Alençon said at his trial that he saw her naked when she had taken off her armor, which she had worn uninterruptedly for several days, and was trying to wash herself in the river. He saw plainly then that she was a very young, immature girl. Her figure was not that of a woman. This Duke of Alençon, her constant companion during her raising of the siege of Orléans, was one of the few eyewitnesses still alive and still willing to testify at her retrial. The artillery officer

Count Dunois was another exception. Most of the witnesses who testified at her English trial died suddenly, became alcoholics, or are known to have been murdered. Alençon too became an alcoholic. Recent claims have maintained that Joan was an illegitimate daughter of the French monarch, or his queen Isabeau, and thus half-sister to her Dauphin, the future King Charles VII.

France was badly shaken for decades after Joan's execution in the Norman city of Rouen in 1431. Women claiming to be Joan of Arc abounded, claimed damages, demanded respect, and asked to be ennobled too. For his part, the King of France passed a law stating that henceforth inside France no woman, witch or not, was ever again to be burned at the stake. Thus, no French woman was among the six million women put to death for witchcraft during the sixteenth century.

France trembled with hatred for the English for fifteen years before Joan's execution at the hands of the Cardinal of Winchester, Henry Beaufort, sometime Prime Minister of England. This hatred might explain Joan's coming, for after the battle of Agincourt (Azincourt) in 1415, after King Henry V had, according to the laws of warfare and code of medieval chivalry, accepted the unconditional surrender of the French nobility, he inhumanly ordered them all to be beheaded. One French prince close to the throne regained consciousness the morning after the carnage and was held for ransom. He was the French king's nephew, and the husband of King Richard II's French queen: Duke Charles of Orléans, the poet.

Joan of Arc said she came in 1429 to ransom him. Ever since 1415 Duke Charles had been held in various English prisons where he paid heavy, if not completely exorbitant, sums for his keep. His own daughter, Joan of Orléans, was born the same year as Joan of Arc, if the latter was aged twenty in 1429. Thus, Joan of Arc might, indeed, have been noble, educated, trained in horsemanship, familiar with weapons, and the Dauphin's first cousin. This would also explain why she carried in combat the Banner of Orléans, and why she was so dead set on liberating her father's duchy.

On the other hand, Joan could have been a commoner, but one wonders why then she would have come from Burgundian and enemy territory. The French used no commoners in their battles of the Hundred Years War, but only noble and royal warriors. The English, on the contrary, used commoners as crossbowmen at the battle of Agincourt. Caught in their crossfire from either side of a wood while they descended a steep hill deep in mud, the French nobles poured down on their heavy Percherons, each rank riding over the fallen and mired knights in front of them. Most French warriors who did not survive to be beheaded, died of suffocation, their faces deep in mud and unable to open their visors.

Most troublesome are also acrostic prophecies which announced the coming of Joan. They leave little doubt that she fulfilled a propaganda war which left the English so terrified of her that they mutinied and surrendered at the sight of her in white armor on her white horse. Her coming to Orléans on February 12, 1429, was heralded far and wide on slips on paper, bark, and parchment in capital letters some of which, being Roman numerals, could be added across the line to total 1429. People knew who she was. They knew she was coming. They expected her to scare the English to death. They also expected her to deliver Orléans at the Loire River, and at Blois Castle, and to free all of northern France. At Cadillac in 1453, twenty-three years after the maid's death, this feat was accomplished. The English were entirely driven out of France except for the ferry port of Calais.

If Joan of Arc, as Shakespeare suspected, was really Joan of Orléans, daughter of Duke Charles of Orléans still imprisoned in England, then the maid burned at Rouen was a substitute. The Duke of Alerçon would not have let his wife burn. Nor would the artillery expert Count Dunois, Bastard of Orléans, have allowed his half-sister to be burned at the stake.

If Joan of Arc was a shepherdess from Champagne, and if she saw the visions of the Saints Catherine and Marguerite, then she was the girl burned at Rouen. In that case the Duke of Alençon did not lie about her adolescent body, but he still had plenty of reasons for becoming an alcoholic. In either case, he was saved from death and disgrace by Duke Charles of Orléans released at Westminster Abbey in 1440. This great duke, who is the best, most celebrated, and most beloved French and English poet of the fifteenth century, arranged with the papacy to destroy England by alienating their chief ally, the Duke of Burgundy, and then to humiliate them forever by having the Vatican's legate travel all over France to vindicate Joan of Arc. The Vatican legate proved the English judges who condemned Joan to death false, hateful, monstrous, immoral, and inhuman demons.

What has survived superabundantly from Joan of Arc's short year of life as a warrior, 1429–1430, is not so much the controversies she raised by her military victories and her daring rescue of the duchy of Orléans, but her brilliant repartee depicted in the stained glass at the Holy Cross Cathedral in the city of Orléans. If Joan was really the daughter of the greatest French and English poet then living in the world, and even more so, the recipient of his inflammatory verse brought back every month as his ambassadors carried his moneys, books, and court documents back and forth across the Channel or Straits of Dover, and Parliament recorded all these, then her words can be explained. Otherwise, it is very hard to imagine such verve and such acumen in an illiterate shepherdess who heard voices and was said to have danced around a Maypole.

Her brave words are given us on each window of her Holy Cross Cathedral in the city of Orléans, and she is pictured above them:

Window 1 shows a pale Joan, eyes closed, dressed in silver mail, and Saint Michael with her. He wears golden armor, has blue wings and a wide-brimmed scarlet hat. Below the stained glass are the words in French: then (she) fought at the assault on the Baileys, saying, "All are ours. So, enter!"

Window 2 shows a pale Joan on horseback, her gauntleted right hand raised, her eyes lowered, her face composed, her lips smiling slightly. She wears a gray tunic embroidered with gold. Her white banner on a golden staff is displayed on her right side; her words are only a prayer: "Jesus Mary."

Joan's white horse is caparisoned completely in sapphire-colored silk embroidered in gold leaves. With her hands raised in supplication, a woman kneels before Joan. With clasped hands, a man reverently touches her armored knee as she rides past.

Window 3 displays Joan wearing what seem to be boy's garments. She has a short haircut. She wears a sword. She is kneeling before a prince. He must be the Dauphin because the text reads: "And was presented at court saying to him: 'King, God is sending you succor.'"

Window 4 depicts Joan mounted on her white horse but looking back towards the Dauphin. She is waiting for him to join her. She says: "And went by reason of her great pity for the Kingdom of France to find the king."

Window 5 bears these words: "How Joan the Maid heard her heavenly voices and their commandments." The window portrays Saint Catherine and Saint Michael finding Joan as she tended her lambs. They raise her head and whisper in her ear.

Window 6 pictures Joan kneeling before the altar. She wears silver armor over a golden tunic bordered with white fur. Her face is very pale. She has light brown hair. The words say: "And the VIIth day of May entered most piously Holy Cross Church to give thanks to God."

Window 7 depicts the Dauphin's coronation at Rheims Cathedral, where all French kings, if they are to be considered holy, sacred, and untouchable, must be crowned. Joan stands smiling and looking down at the Dauphin crowned King Charles VII. Joan wears blue and silver armor, a blue cloak, and carries her white banner. It bears on its white field the golden lilies (fleurs de lis), which are the armorial bearings of French monarchy. The prayerful words again are only "Jhesus Maria."

Window 8 shows Joan dressed in silver chain mail covered with a gold brocade tunic. Her sword is raised. Her horse is caparisoned in blue brocade. The words explain "How it happened that Joan was handed over treacherously into the hands of the English."

Window 9 shows Joan in her prison dungeon. She wears violet trews, a pea-green tunic, and she slumps down on a bench. Her feet are wrapped in heavy chains, her ankles in wide leg irons. Two ugly soldiers and an English lord in a royal purple robe stand over her, the latter holding a pike. Women saints stroke her brow. Above them Saint Michael prays for her. Joan's hair is now quite long. The text reports: "Gentle even in prison, she suffered much violence."

Window 10 depicts Joan being tried before four judges seated on the bench inside a rather high wooden enclosure. Joan stands before them. She wears a white robe. Her wrists and her waist are tied with a rope. Her hair is very long now, almost down to her breasts. Three saints are present. They are bowed in prayer. Cardinal Henry Beaufort from Winchester Cathedral in England is the high magistrate present. He wears a royal purple velvet robe with a taffeta collar and the red velvet, pointed hat of a Cardinal. The words say: "And was burned at the stake by the perfidious English. Her voices saying: 'Do not bewail your martyrdom when you shall come in time to the Kingdom of Paradise.' "

Joan held her own and put down various lords of Britain. A French princess might be expected to do as much, or better. The royal princess Catherine was forced to marry King Henry V, a butcher if there ever was one. King Henry V had hoped to wed the child widow of King Richard II, but he was deprived of both her person and her dowry, unfortunately misplaced somewhere in England, probably at Windsor Castle. King Richard's widow, still a virgin, was married post-haste to Duke Charles of Orléans, then fifteen years of age. Her daughter, Joan of Orléans, was born in Blois Castle, in an upstairs tower room still shown to visitors today.

If Joan of Arc did not say the stunning words attributed to her, and if they were not said by Joan of Orléans, who was perhaps her same age, then were they sent over from Duke Charles of Orléans along with the Scots Lords who won the major battles alongside Joan, Alençon, and Dunois?

These words of Joan have been as carefully preserved as have the French and English poetry in his own handwriting of Duke Charles. In fact, his personal library formed, by his will and last testament, the founding volumes of the National Library: Bibliothèque Nationale de France, in Paris.

Very possibly all we can know for sure of Joan, and what has made her beloved beyond the frontiers of France, are her apt words. Our last opportunity to have known her, identified her, and understood her was lost shortly before her execution. That man who was the most trusted chronicler of the age had succeeded in acquiring authorization to interview her in prison. He was Georges Chastellain, whose eye-witness *Chronicle* remains as one of the most dependable sources for events, and for personages also, of the fifteenth century. His last written words were entered the night before he was to meet Joan of Arc. Apparently he met her in fact the next day. But all his pages beginning on that day were cut from his manuscript. Thus, we shall never know the real Joan of Arc. After her death several women claiming to be Joan haunted France for years. Reading what twenty witnesses said about Joan shows how terrible was their collective guilt. This sense of having been guilty of an unforgettable crime haunted her century from the day of her capture, at her one defeat, on May 23, 1430, to her execution on May 30, 1431, and thereafter.

Thus, at Holy Cross in Orléans we also leave Joan to heaven.

•READINGS•

IRELAND

A Celtic Miscellany. Translated by Kenneth Hurlstone Jackson. Penguin Books (Harmondsworth, England, 1951).

Cuchulain of Muirthenne. Vol. II. Translated by Lady Gregory; Preface by W. B. Yeats, Foreword by Daniel Murphy. Colin Smythe (Buckinghamshire and New York, 1975).

Early Irish Myths and Sagas. Translated and annotated by Jeffrey Gantz. Penguin Books (Harmondsworth, England, 1981).

Gods and Fighting Men. Vol. III. Translated by Lady Gregory, John Murray, 1904; Colin Smythe and Macmillan, 1976.

Goodrich, Norma Lorre. *Medieval Myths*. NAL and Penguin Books (New York, 1961).

Squire, Charles. *Celtic Myth and Legend*. Newcastle Publishing Company (Hollywood, Calif., 1975).

SCANDINAVIA

Egil's Saga. Translated by Hermann Palsson; Introduction by Paul Edwards. Penguin Books (Harmondsworth, England, 1976).

Goodrich, Norma Lorre. *Medieval Myths*. NAL and Penguin Books (New York, 1961).

Ibsen, Henrik. *The Vikings at Helgeland*. Translated by James Walter Mac Farlane. In *The Oxford Ibsen* (London and New York, 1962).

JOAN OF ARC

Goodrich, Norma Lorre. *Charles Duke of Orleans*. Macmillan (New York, 1963).

————. *Charles of Orleans. A Study of Themes in His French and in His English Poetry*. Librairie Droz (Geneva, 1967).

CHAPTER VIII

The Return of the Golden Age

Other powerful ancient myths of heroines have also enchanted the world. By promising an end to wars and other sorrows which afflict mankind these myths have always, and continue to, assure us that the Golden Age will again return to earth.

In his *Eclogue IV* the beloved Roman poet Virgil explained predictions made from earliest times by pastoral poets. Virgil (70–19 B.C.) said his years were witnessing the last of the greatest prophets. They were the Sibyls, or high priestesses, who prophesied from their underground temple at the Bay of Naples. These Sibyls, who over centuries had composed *The Sibylline Books* foretelling the future, were closing their oracular center.

Now, wrote Virgil, we are seeing the last era of prophecy. The Iron Age of war and weapons is drawing to an end. The three Fates have spoken. The sequence of ages is about to recommence.

When the pastoral age does begin again, the prophetesses declared, the greatest of our ancient heroines will reign royally once more to usher in a new world of peace. The name to conjure upon is Astraea the Virgin. Her task will be to reestablish on earth the reign of justice. Astraea is herself Justice: "Already returns the Virgin," *"Iam redit Virgo"* (v. 6), wrote Virgil.

Under the coming reign of Justice herself, Virgil explains, iniquity will vanish from the hearts of man. These nights of war and horror will draw to an end. New men will read about the achievements of their ancestresses so that they will learn anew what true virtue is. Even though some wars on the periphery will still be fought out, they too will fizzle out under a new heroine's watchful eye.

More daring than killers, a new breed of men, smiling at the dear mother who bore them, will rejoice to discover new lands, a new earth, new oceans, and the most distant skies. Creation all over again will be glad and rejoice.

In such verses ancient poets of Greece and Rome perpetuated this myth of a lost Golden Age towards which mankind looked back in sorrow, as an adult looks in sorrow to his or her infancy when a sweet, young mother turned him away from her breast, urged him out of his cradle, and encouraged him or her to look forward, grow up, and leave home.

The demigoddess Astraea has come to be Justice personified. Her statue still stands outside our halls of justice just as it stood in ancient Greece and Rome. When she appears as a character in literature, we say she is Justice personified. When she lives and acts and speaks in literature, where other abstractions are also personified, we call it allegory. While allegory has long since gone out of fashion, novelists still celebrate its distant memory. Perhaps we even remember that Beauty's name is Rose and that in her *Romance of the Rose* she resides safe inside her garden surrounded by a thorn hedge guarded by Danger. To reach the person of Rose, the lover must defeat Danger and penetrate the maze correctly. He must beware of Bad Luck called

Mala Fortuna when she helps Danger win the chess game. Lover must duel with him. Care, who has such lovely eyes, but who is blind, often troubles Lover. But *Espérance,* who is Hopefulness herself, often steps in to comfort him. Fair Loyalty herself steps forth at the defeat of Danger to stand defending the portal of Beauty's Castle called Pleasant Joy, or Joyful Pleasance. This is a familiar allegory.

Another such heroine is Liberty. The ancient Roman or Latin goddess of Liberty *(Libertas)* continued to appear in this same medieval allegory, Chaucer's *Romance of the Rose,* which he translated from Old French; or her name was Loyalty, which originally meant "legality," that is to say, "religious law" from the Latin words for law *(lex, legis).* All are feminine words, feminine concepts, and are thus personified and allegorized.

Poets of the Middle Ages visualized Loyalty as guarding the final entrance to Beauty's Castle, as witnessing and putting her seal of approval upon Beauty's betrothal and marriage contract, and elsewhere as drawing up all written family laws and contractual agreements. Before she became the Goddess of Liberty enlightening the world, Loyalty supervised Law as does our one Lady Justice of the Supreme Court.

Nowadays Loyalty has regained her Latin name from ancient myth: She is now called Liberty. We Americans are grateful to the French sculptor Frédéric Auguste Bartholdi (1834–1904) for his bronze Statue of Liberty at the entrance to our greater New York Harbor.

While in allegory the Death Queen was called *Aage,* or Old Age in medieval versions, she functioned as harbinger of death. She personally announced the message of approaching death to each individual. Philosophy also was personified and especially in that work by the philosopher Boethius (c. 480–524) as he sat in his prison cell awaiting execution. His only visitor there was Lady Philosophy whose gentle conversations with Boethius he entitled *The Consolation of Philosophy.* She taught him how not to fear death, and this book has remained for fifteen hundred years now one of the greatest achievements of man and lady.

But the greatest, most wonderful of ladies has over the ages still been named Astraea, goddess of justice, Justice personified, and the Starry One. We see Astraea in our nighttime skies overhead. She is a star in our heaven. Her only rival is the goddess of Liberty, which is her name in French, and/or Freedom, which would be her name in English.

ASTRAEA

In most ancient times Astraea was born to the goddess Themis, or Order. As Justice, Astraea's role was to spread justice throughout the western Mediterranean. She married King Evander of Arcadia, which Greek land ever since has represented the pastoral world of harmony and prosperity. The members of her husband's family were Arcadian shepherds and nymphs. Daughter of Themis and Zeus, Astraea spread justice during the Golden Age. After its demise she mounted into heaven to become a star. In fact, as the Golden Age declined, but before the ages began to unroll all over again, Astraea reluctantly left earth. She was the last person to abandon fallen mankind. As the constellation Virgo, Sixth House of the Zodiac, she lies near the ecliptic, watching us carefully.

As this faint but large constellation of fifteen stars, the Virgin Astraea appears to our eyes to move east to west in the southern sky from March to July. Because she became a grain goddess, she holds her brightest star *Spica,* sheaf of wheat. Astraea also holds below her feet *Libra,* the Scales of Justice, upon which souls are weighed against a feather as they live up to or qualify for admission to heaven. The one green star among the six stars of Libra represents the gown of this high priestess.

Heroines on earth were named for Astraea: Joan of Arc, who was referred to as warrior Maid, the Virgin Queen Elizabeth I after her, and the Vestal Virgins or last priestesses Rome ever anointed, each of whom was called *Virgo filia* (Virgin daughter). Some Christians say that the Archangel Michael supplanted the goddess of justice in early Christian churches.

However that may be, the ancient pastoral world where two heroines, Justice and Freedom, stood head and shoulders above a less-than-perfect world to ensure the happy reign of gold, has never faded from the consciousness of our authors. For centuries certain authors followed a prototypical novel called *Astrée* (French for Astraea), which a courtier Honoré d'Urfé, born in Marseilles in 1568, wrote and had published in five volumes between 1607 and 1627. In this novel, no longer read except by painstaking admirers of literature, the heroine Astrée requires many proofs of love before she grants full pardon to her suitor, who has been accused of infidelity. Thus, championing justice, she effects finally a Renaissance, return of the pastoral and Golden Age.

French critics hastened to point out that the novel *Astrée* was both pastoral and ancient in theme, but modern and historical in its depiction of a French courtly world. And so, it is agreed, *Astrée* really depicted under the disguise and dress of shepherd and shepherdess, the only French Protestant King, Henri IV of France. There is no doubt but that this king was one of the greatest peacemakers, economists, and organizers France ever crowned. He granted religious freedom to all persons, including the Protestants in 1598; revived agriculture, industry, commerce, and prosperity; and sent Samuel de Champlain to found Quebec in 1608. The point here is that *Astrée,* or Astraea, and her pastoral and Arcadian world very early turned to history for its documentation, evidence, argument, and proof.

GODDESSES OF JUSTICE IN HISTORICAL FICTION

Sir Walter Scott

The historical novel always chooses to depict heroes and heroines from actual history. Joan of Arc ought to remain a principal source of such case histories. In fact, what is most historical in this fiction are characters.

The historical novel was invented by Sir Walter Scott (1771–1832), who was himself a magistrate regularly dispensing justice in Scotland. Between the years 1814, when Scott published his first historical novel *Waverley,* which dealt with the reign of King George II (1745), and 1831, when he finished his last book, *Castle Dangerous,* which dealt with King Edward I and events of 1306–7, Scott composed twenty-nine historical novels. All but the first were translated immediately into French.

Scott achieved unparalleled success virtually worldwide. His works covered history from 1090 to 1798, including King George III, who declared war against the American colonies.

Sir Walter Scott also originated the structure or format followed carefully by all historical novelists for the next hundred years in his tenth and best-known novel *Ivanhoe* (1820). A critic once asked Scott why he called that book *Ivanhoe* when it was not about Ivanhoe. And Scott answered correctly, in what has since become standard practice for historical novelists: because it is not about Ivanhoe.

Astraea appears, as she surveys her old domain and exercises her old prerogative to require that justice be done, in four novels by Sir Walter Scott: *The Heart of Midlothian* (1818), *Kenilworth* (1821), *The Talisman* (1825), and *Ivanhoe* (1819). Midlothian is the region around the city of Edinburgh; Kenilworth Castle in Warwickshire, England, was once given by Queen Elizabeth I to her favorite courtier, Robert Dudley, Earl of Leicester. And thereupon hangs the tale of *Kenilworth* and the castle, now in ruins. *The Talisman* deals very romantically with King Richard I in the Holy Land, and *Ivanhoe* treats Crusaders at home in Britain, but Anglo-Saxons versus their French rulers after their 1066 conquest of England.

The Heart of Midlothian deals with an actual occurrence of mob violence in the city of Edinburgh, September 7, 1736. The incident arose doubtless because of anger and pain suffered by Scots after their defeat and forced union with England. A Scot named Andrew Wilson had been apprehended, tried as a smuggler, and condemned to death. The citizens of Edinburgh massed in protest and in defense of Andrew Wilson, who was a popular person. They believed he had been unjustly sentenced, and to a punishment that did not fit the crime.

During a mass protest by the citizenry, civilians were attacked by the English Captain John Porteous of the Edinburgh Guards. The English officer apparently lost his head, for he committed what history adjudges to be an unforgivable act: He ordered professional soldiers to fire upon a defenseless crowd. Some eight or nine persons were killed. It is not generally known how many were wounded. Captain Porteous was duly tried, convicted, and sentenced to death for murder, but reprieved at the last moment. Then an infuriated mob of Scots invaded the prison, captured Porteous, and lynched him. Despite efforts which the government claimed were both thorough and expeditious, no persons among that band of lynchers was ever found and prosecuted. History condemns them, *in absentia,* of course, as rioters and murderers. These incidents constitute the Porteous Riots.

Scott searched in vain for a hero in this period of turmoil in Scotland, and the ensuing terrible and decisive defeat at Culloden Moor on April 16, 1746, of the Highland Scots by English soldiers under the Duke of Cumberland. How can the great defeat of a people be conveyed? Scott must have wondered. How can the terrible, mass tragedies of history be grasped? Where is Justice in all that? Scott decided that history can only be made clear and evident as its overpowering force falls upon the individual person. Therefore historical fiction finds in this author a rationale and a reason for being.

How else could the novelist-turned-historian, or the historian-turned-novelist, reestablish order in some understandable form that will permanently clarify catastrophic events? If he spoke impersonally only of an industrial England forcing progress upon an ancient, heroic society of prehistoric clansmen in Scotland, who would read his book?

It occurred, therefore, to Scott to choose a heroine who would rise courageously, ask help of no person, and demand justice from Majesty itself. This heroine would dig a new channel for the flow of history.

The character and temper of Scotland were still little known, and it was considered as a volcano, which might, indeed, slumber for a series of years but was still liable, at a moment the least expected, to break out into a wasteful eruption (p. 395).

Escorted at the end of her journey by His Grace, the Duke of Argyle (Argyll), the heroine demanding justice had arrived on foot from Scotland to England, Edinburgh to London.

Sir Walter Scott has set for the heroine a feat perfectly suited to the strength of a young woman, his Jeanie Deans from Edinburgh. The ancient epic hero fought for his community, met champions and dragons of assorted hues and sizes, and died after having disposed of them. Henrik Ibsen dreamed of an heroic, cruel, heartless, and death-dealing Scandinavian woman who could equal Beowulf in combat and die plunged in the Baltic Sea. Scott dreamed of a commoner from another, similar warrior ethos in the north of Britain who, like the proverbial cat, could look at a queen. Scott's heroine was not only a low-class, working woman, a "commoner" she would be called, but an heroic commoner. In addition, this commoner performed what everybody must agree was an heroic deed. She managed to travel, mostly on foot, the hundreds of miles from Edinburgh to London.

When Jeanie got to London, which is a truly wide city, she managed to find lodgings with a friend, another successful commoner, who was able to assist her. Then she further managed to charm the great Lord of Argyle from Gaelic Scotland to intercede for her with the Queen of England, despite the fact that Her Majesty was not well disposed toward His Grace, even to begin with.

What was Jeanie's problem? It is easy to understand, even for a queen and a nobleman: Jeanie Deans's sister, Effie Deans, had become pregnant. Scott's plan works. Everybody has heard of the same young, innocent girl whom some fellow has put "in the family way." There is no help in any day for it. Like Tess of the D'Urbervilles after her, Jeanie will have to take her courage in hand and deal with the pregnancy, perhaps bear away the child, perhaps even kill it, and perhaps even bury it alone like the English Tess, or like the Spanish girl in a García Lorca tragedy.

While Effie Deans is ill, incapacitated, and out of action, Jeanie remains stout enough to walk to London on her sister's behalf. Effie has been accused of infanticide, tried in court, and sentenced to death. Jeanie rises to even greater heights of heroism, arguing against the courts what is a necessity in English common law: that the court must prove the guilt of the accused. Jeanie demands first that the Duke of Argyle take up her sister's cause; second, that he set up an appointment, at Windsor Castle, one supposes, between the two of them and Queen Caroline; and third, that he present her to Her Majesty. It takes Scott four pages in his Chapter XXXVII to explain to the reader the royal situation with King George II and Queen Caroline of the House of Brunswick, as related to the Porteous Riots, and that "volcano," Scotland. Scott uses an eyewitness, that same Horace Walpole who invented Gothic fiction, as his source for all this history.

The point he makes is that England is a commercial society where money, rank, and wealth dominate. Scotland is another kind—an ancient, warrior and heroical society where personal heroism and great deeds count regardless of consequence, or the devil take the hindmost. Scott's epigraph to this chapter aims another sly blow at the English queen, saying people who want to play God above lesser mortals might at least show mercy for some poor, wretched Presbyterian girl in Scotland who lies under the death sentence. . . . We can only say that the world may not consider Sir Walter Scott a great novelist, and the world is correct, doubtless: But he was a Great Scot.

Scott's Chapter XXXVII (pp. 394–406) remains today well worth reading. He tells us all about Queen Caroline, who was really a man in woman's dressing. Her face was pitted with "small-pox" scars and she was overweight, wrote Scott politely in somewhat doubtful French; the queen's graceful form was *"embonpoint."* Smallpox has been tamed now, Scott tells us (for his Edinburgh boasts an illustrious faculty of medicine) as easily as Python was conquered by the sun god Apollo. In other words, Scotland here lands some novel blows under England's belt.

Jeanie delivers an impassioned oration in defense of her poor sister, "an unhappy girl, not eighteen years of age," who must not be hanged but spared. She must be delivered by order of England's queen, "from an early and dreadful death" (p. 405). " 'This is eloquence,' said her Majesty to the Duke of Argyle." Jeanie had threatened the queen: "I would hae gaen [have gone] to the end of the earth to save the life of John Porteous." In other words, a mob could also overturn the cruel law which had condemned this Effie Deans. Scotland could rise up again, against England.

The Irish writer George Bernard Shaw applauded Sir Walter Scott, Baronet, and compared Scott's Jeanie to Ibsen's Viking women at Helgeland. Unlike them, however, Jeanie quoted the law, found the loophole, and urged that her sister's case be dismissed for lack of evidence. Where there was no proof of crime, she argued, a mistrial must be declared. Then justice would be preserved.

Christabel F. Fiske argued in the Yale University Press (1940) that Scott's historical novels related to ancient epic material even in their imagery, "epic" being virtually synonymous with "heroic." Epic material always connotes a spirit of nationalism, she found (p. ix). The literary material overlies a "solid substratum of historical fact," as here by the Porteous scandal in Edinburgh. Scott's novels contain such epic imagery in scene, plot, ethos, and characters, and feature the seer or epic bard himself. The returned heir to his kingdom (Ivanhoe) is epical, like the ancient "Miriam" or doctor (the Jewess Rebecca), the captive blonde maiden of noble birth, Edith of Plantagenet, Ivanhoe's Rowena, Amy Robsart (Alcestis) in Kenilworth, and so is religious opposition, Judaism and Catholic Christianity versus Presbyterianism and Methodism.

Scott was widely told, when in December of 1819 he published *Ivanhoe* under the pen name of Lawrence Templeton, that as an author of fiction he was finished. One can only imagine his heartache, for *Ivanhoe* was only tenth among his twenty-nine novels. The *Edinburgh Review* of 1820, the same publication that had savaged Lord Byron's first poems in 1798, opined Scott's novels contained *no actual history*. What they did originate, however, was a most successful literary structure that reigned among Scott's European and American descendants from *Ivanhoe* to Count Leo Tolstoy's *War and Peace (Voina i mir)* of 1864–69.

Scott's format in *Ivanhoe* was easy to imitate. He set one warring faction, which we may call *a,* against its enemy, which we will call *b.* All his characters but one belong to one camp or the other, all except the pale, colorless Ivanhoe, whom we will call *c.* The two camps, *a* and *b,* alternate, chapter after chapter, Saxon versus warring Norman, and after a few chapters come together when Ivanhoe *(c)* enters the action, he being related to both hostile forces. *Ivanhoe* follows three threads that envelop each other: (1) the war between Richard I and his even more dissolute and depraved brother John, fanatical persecutor of the Jews of York, (2) the love story of Ivanhoe and his colorless Saxon princess Rowena, and (3) the "degenerate" Knight Templar and his captive Jewess, Rebecca of York. Is not this history and perfectly enchanting chivalry?

One sturdy band of fans, who remain all their lives long tenderly and gratefully indebted to Sir Walter Scott, are those adults who grew up in some lost country town with nothing at all to read but the twenty-nine, very long, *Waverley* novels of Sir Walter Scott.

Scott's *Kenilworth* (1821) shows a considerable improvement in fictional techniques over *Ivanhoe,* opposing the Virgin Queen Elizabeth I as the arbiter of the realm and dispenser of justice there. Her stately, magnificent entry into Kenilworth Castle shapes the first climax of the book. Scott's helpless English heroine Amy Robsart, who had married illegally, makes no attempt to save even her own life. She had been indoctrinated, Scott explains very sympathetically, by painful but necessary lessons in submission and subservience:

> Thus, at the most momentous period of her life, she was alike destitute of presence of mind, and of the ability to form for herself any reasonable or prudent plan of conduct (Chapter XXV, p. 295 ff.).

Lacking the energy of Alcestis or of Jeanie Deans, the English heroine Amy traveled on like a woman in a dream, unable either to think or to act for herself. The "mistaken kindness" of her educators had "spared her childhood." Certainly Flaubert was inspired by this chapter to apply Scott's analysis to Emma Bovary. Thus, Amy falls down the trapdoor. All that remains for the viewer to see of her crumpled form is a heap of white petticoats. Scott says in conclusion that Amy is obviously the Daisy, the Alcestis of Greek tragedy, and Chaucer's Daisy in *The Legend of Good Women*.

In opposition, Queen Elizabeth is Astraea, the resolute dispenser of this "justice" and herself "daughter of one hundred kings." John Dryden understood Virgil's epic, and might have been speaking of Scott. Like Virgil before him, and like all Latinists, Scott also had to have worshipped Arcadia. Scott understood that "entire liberty" could not be retrieved. The queens Elizabeth and Caroline held the law in their own fists. They were Astraea from Arcadia.

Everyone raised on the *Waverley* novels as sole reading material

over the endless years of starving childhood will have his or her
favorite novel; in my case it's *The Talisman* (1825). Whereas in *Kenilworth* Scott relied over and again upon the most celebrated of medieval and Renaissance romances, here in *The Talisman* he returned once
more to the Crusades, but this time in the Holy Land itself. Whereas
in *Kenilworth* his place descriptions delineate only that castle and the
pageantry lavished upon the queen as she entered it, in *The Talisman*
Scott has written the most wonderful descriptions of the desert and of
the royal Arab Saladin and his desert horsemen that exist anywhere.
On the other hand, Scott trod most cautiously on slippery ground,
which was the utter fiasco of Richard's contribution, or lack of it, to
the Crusades, and the secret scandal of his marriage to Berengaria,
which he could not consummate. Scott wrote in his Introduction
about Richard I,

> The Christian and English monarch showed all the cruelty and
> violence of an Eastern sultan; and Saladin, on the other hand,
> displayed the deep policy and prudence of a European sover-
> eign . . .

The talisman is a charm of medicinal nature which the Muslim
sultan offered King Richard Coeur-de-Lion when the English monarch was ill. Interestingly, William Faulkner borrowed this talisman
for his one historical novel of World War I, *A Fable* (1954).

Throughout *The Talisman* Scott depends upon the male, medieval
epic, Oriental literature, including the massive Persian epic called
Shah Nameh (Book of Kings), and medieval romances. His hero Sir
Kenneth of Scotland is based upon the ancient Arthurian hero Sir
Tristan of Scotland. His colorless heroine Edith Plantagenet is therefore another Isolde and sometimes heroic. Her foil, characteristically
and as in *Ivanhoe,* is the dark, southern beauty married to King
Richard. Scott calls her Berengaria "of Navarre" and finds her idle
like medieval princesses, and mischievous. Although Scott draws very

fine portraits of the chief historical personages, he only admires Saladin and Edith Plantagenet.

When Sir Kenneth is disgraced and condemned because of a prank played by the frivolous "baby-faced" Berengaria, Edith stands by her true love and demands justice. Her harangue of Richard in Chapter XVII places justice before mercy, obliges the king to honor Sir Kenneth's services to Christendom, pleads that he was ensnared and not derelict in the performance of his military duty, that he left his post only for an instant and at the command of a certain person, that he must on no account be hanged for dereliction of duty, and that he had been forever good, valiant, and loyal. As for myself, continued Lady Edith, I am the Virgin [Astraea] who cannot fear even the Lion of England. I will not wed Sir Kenneth. He is of humble birth, but I shall remain forever true to him, even in the grave.

To be a king, Richard replies, is always to be dealing with fools, talking women, and monks.

Scott's second chapter on war and peace anticipates Tolstoy, for both condemn war in the strongest terms, Scott referring principally to its "horrors." Only the Templars dishonored themselves, Scott claimed, for failing to honor a truce. As for Sir Kenneth, he was finally discovered to be heir to the throne of Scotland. He was not hanged after all but lived to wed the eloquent Edith. Only Kenneth and Saladin function as major characters, however, both present in every scene of the book, and each hero is allowed three separate disguises. If Richard is ever the hero, he is heavily and distastefully so.

To Scott's greater glory must be held chapters I, XXII, and XXVII, which describe the desert, the lone rider appearing like a speck in the distance and gradually growing larger (an image borrowed by the cinema for the life of Lawrence of Arabia); the combat in the desert between Sir Kenneth and the Saracen warriors, Saladin awakening Sir Kenneth at dawn and leading his troop across the wasteland; King Richard and Queen Berengaria crossing the desert to their place of rendezvous—moving specks, says Scott, "on the bosom of the plain," or in that "howling wilderness."

Aleksandr Pushkin

Another brave, young heroine who acts as attorney in a case involving a death sentence comes (as if by inspiration from Sir Walter Scott via French translations of his novels) from Russia. Between the years 1833 and 1836, Aleksandr Pushkin completed his saga of Captain Mironov's daughter, *The Captain's Daughter (Kapitanskaya Dochka)*. To an American brought up on the Western, in novel and film form, Pushkin's book strikes very familiar chords, indeed.

Captain Mironov was dispatched on active duty into the wild, *eastern* frontier, across the grasslands and prairies, to take command of a log fortress. There he was to drill troops, an occupation his lady wife noted he was no good at whatsoever. Far from elegant court life in the civilized west, he had to introduce his elegant lady and lovely daughter to all the hazards of pioneers in the American West of not so long ago. They lived inside a wooden stockade, protected by ragged troops who were virtually untrained, and served by louts and drunken outcasts. The Captain, his wife, and his sweet daughter struggled to uphold the standards of courtly life in Moscow with its regiments of aristocrats and its high society.

There, far away from home, the family reside in the Belogorsky Fortress near the Yaik River, on the Kirghiz Steppes, twenty-five miles from the nearest town of Orenburg. To protect themselves from the intense cold of this frozen land, they order fur coats and lynx caps. At any moment, to compound their isolation, they expect to come under the savage attacks of Bashkirs and Kirghiz. They must resist and survive, or die for the Czar who has empowered them to act.

Probably taking a lead directly from *The Heart of Midlothian* and the

Edinburgh Riots attendant upon the Porteous murders in that city, Pushkin seizes here upon the Pugachev Revolution of 1773–75. In the first chapter the reader accompanies a young officer being dispatched to serve under Captain Mironov. As the young gentleman is driven across the vast, lonely steppes, he is almost buried by a gigantic snowstorm that blinds himself, his horse, and his driver. In that white-out they stop to pick up a huge peasant, give him a lift, and consequently save his life. That illiterate fellow turns out to be the Don Cossack, revolutionary leader Pugachev. Thus, Pushkin pitches on the even more serious history of this huge, peasant rebellion aimed at unseating the Empress and Tsarina of Russia, the popular Catherine the Great, who had ruled for over thirty years (1762–96) with her husband Peter III. Thus, instead of Scott's Queen Caroline, who is relatively or totally unknown to the reader, Pushkin substitutes one of the greatest women in history, who in truth aided the Russian expansion eastward, even as far east as Alaska. Queen Catherine meanwhile had read French revolutionary doctrine, had studied in particular French works on law, rule, and government. Thus, the Belogorsky Fortress on the eastern frontier was reinforced by a captain and then by the young Ensign Pyotr of the snowstorm. He and the poor Captain's daughter fell deeply in love.

During the young lover's absence, the Belogorsky Fortress near Orenburg fell under full-scale attack by Don and assorted Cossacks under the personal leadership of Pugachev. It is a terrible scene of savagery as the enemy break into the compound slaughtering the defenders, burning the houses, raping and murdering down to one last survivor. The townspeople filed up to kiss the hand of Pugachev, who declared himself their legal emperor. Those garrison survivors who could walk or crawl also crept up to kiss Pugachev's hand in token of enlistment under him.

Suddenly the Captain's lady was discovered, stripped naked, and driven out of her home into the circle of victorious Cossacks surrounding their wild leader. The lady's hair had fallen down around her face, but she looked up to see her wounded old husband hanging dead from the gallows. They had cut off his hair and dragged him out in the square, where he had, before dying, called Pugachev a thief and a pretender.

The Captain's lady also showed great courage. In a loud voice she too denounced Pugachev as a black villain, an imposter, and a murderer. "What have you done to my husband? He was a brave soldier doing his duty." The lady defied Pugachev, claiming he was only a renegade, an outlaw, and a pretender while the Captain was, even in old age, a gallant officer defending the realm. Calling Vasilisa Yegorovna an "old witch," Pugachev ordered her struck dead on the spot. A young Cossack slew her with one slash by his saber across her head.

The Captain's daughter was also finally found. She lay hidden in her bedroom. They stripped her of her fine clothes, dressed her in tatters, and saved her for the pleasure of the new commander. Her love, the young Ensign Pyotr, was sentenced to death. He had survived when all the others thereabouts had died or joined Pugachev. The reader must wait, of course, for Pushkin to tell him why Pugachev spared the Ensign. Pugachev also finally rescued and spared the Captain's daughter.

Catherine the Great survived this Pugachev and peasant revolution, and all had returned to normal with the execution of Pugachev. The Ensign Pyotr still lay in prison awaiting execution. At this moment, after she set her life and her dresses in order, the Captain's lovely daughter, Marya Ivanovna, set out for the royal palace of the tsarina. In her person she was a Latin personification of Justice as daughter and maid, their *Virgo filia*.

In his own spare and classical style Pushkin repeated, or rather rewrote, Scott's scene: Jeanie Deans at the castle of Queen Caroline. Marya Ivanovna journeyed alone also to Tsarskoye Selo, the tsar's residence near St. Petersburg (p. 332 ff.).

In beautiful, clean pages Pushkin describes her meeting by happenstance with Catherine the Great in the beautiful palace garden, near white swans in the lake. The Empress was walking with her little, white, English dog. Marya there in presence of the Tsarina presented her written petition in defense of the Ensign. The charges against him were absolutely untrue, she swore "to God." The truth was other, as she could testify personally, as surviving eyewitness to the attack on the fortress. The Ensign only tried to intercede in order to spare the life of his beloved, which he did. He refused to testify in court because he wished the secret of his birth to remain forever secret, and thus, he protected his mother and his father also.

The Tsarina listened quietly to the girl who warmed to her defense as friend *in absentia* of the court. Then warning her never to reveal this intercession, the Tsarina turned away. Marya Ivanovna had won. It was Pyotr who in his memoirs told the story anyway, and not Aleksandr Pushkin after all.

The next step was left to the greatest novelist the world has as yet given birth to: Count Leo Tolstoy. He rewrote and expanded Pushkin's spare novella as *The Cossacks* (1863). His hero, the young officer Olenin, gives us not only description after description of the Caucasus, but intimate knowledge of these Cossacks, their cowboy's life in their villages and in the vast expanses of the "Wild East." The hero Olenin matures there and reaches his goal, which was always philosophical and personal: to discover how to be happy in his life. Tolstoy's heroine is the young Cossack named, similarly, Maryana, who will neither desert her people nor change her life to suit Olenin.

Charlotte Brontë (1816–1855) and George Eliot (1819–1880)

The heroine of Charlotte Brontë's *Jane Eyre* of 1847 is another personification of Roman virtue, their warrior maid, *virgo bellica*. Jane began life as an orphan, shut up in a red room where she seethed with the outrage of a "revolted slave" (p. 16). The Lowood School proved to be well named because little girls were shut up inside there, or enclosed out of doors in walled gardens with no possibility even to look out at the world that must lie around them. It is not strange, considering the lives of women in the nineteenth century, that fiction should still be repeating their existences as lived in the Middle Ages.

The heroines of Marie de France in the Middle Ages view the world, and so does the poet Marie, through a narrow, Gothic window, or from the curtain wall of a castle. Women look down at other free, masculine persons. In the same way Jane Austen's famous and disillusioned heroine Catherine Morland, in *Northanger Abbey* (1818), will settle forever more for a view of the world seen not as she dreams it but only partially through the narrow windows of the Tilney home. The Abbey of the Tilneys is again well named. But Catherine Morland is no heroic heroine; she accepts both disgrace and a cloistered life. Jane Eyre from the North is a child of another mettle.

At Lowood they look upon Jane as an unsightly toad, but she sees herself privately as more alien than that. She is a "stranger bird" (p. 247), an uncommon person of stalwart strength, both moral and physical, and because she is also like Charlotte Brontë, possessed of talent. Even starvation, loathing, and flogging at this school cannot crush Jane Eyre. Her defiance only increases as their brutality rises.

As these terrible years in school go by, Jane steels herself to feel nothing, to appear "cold as a stone" before her persecutors. Dressed in her drab brown frock and pinafore, enclosed in a wet garden, washing in a pitcher of water that was half ice, forbidden to wash or brush her teeth in the morning, shivering with hunger to the point of "semi-starvation," she watches the girls around her succumb to one epidemic after another or die from typhoid fever. The public floggings of little girls drives Jane to adopt a "doctrine of endurance." Like William Faulkner's black servants a hundred years later, in the South of the United States, Jane Eyre becomes a survivor. Like them she *endures*. She also learns, when struck, how to strike back. It was "not the golden age" of her life, she has decided by Chapter VII.

Then Jane graduates. Her one consolation, and it will stand by her through all sad experiences to follow, has been her love of learning for the sake of learning. Truly, knowledge is its own reward, the only consolation in times of hardship, and the only occupation that frees the person from self-interest.

Jane finally becomes a governess at Thornfield, another house appropriately named. Here in this mansion which hides Satan, who is master here in the character of Mr. Rochester, and the mysterious woman (his mad wife) whom he has permanently shut away upstairs, Jane's principal view of the outer world is a glance downward from her narrow bedroom window.

She is in Bluebeard's Castle, she muses, or in Ann Radcliffe's Udolfo of the worst crimes, or she will die in prison like Joan of Arc. She overhears some woman's wild, insane laughter. Meanwhile she devotes herself to the education of children and reads Rousseau's educational theory in *Julie* and *Emile:* "Nobody knows how many rebellions besides political rebellions ferment in the masses of life which people earth" (p. 112). Jane realized, even shut in there as her entire life long she had been enclosed within walls of various sorts, that millions of people confronted every day a far worse and "stiller doom."

> Women are supposed to be very calm generally: but women feel just as men feel; they need exercise for their faculties, and a field for their efforts as much as their brothers do; they suffer too rigid a constraint, too absolute a stagnation; and it is narrow minded in the more privileged to say they ought to confine themselves to making puddings and knitting stockings, to playing on the piano and embroidering bags (pp. 112–13).

During her years of "stagnation" at Thornfield Jane found some inspiration, as Ann Radcliffe had done before her, in studying the various landscape paintings displayed there. They at least gave her some idea of the outside world. Meanwhile she studied to prepare for herself a Declaration of Independence based upon her rare interview with a gypsy fortune-teller: (1) She can live alone if her circumstances or her virtue warrant; (2) she possesses an inborn talent, her literary ability, which alone could bring her happiness were she reduced even to a narrow cell; (3) she will never need to sell herself; (4) her intelligence will always suffice to guide her life and control her passionate impulses; (5) her judgment will always have the last word; and (6) her conscience will bolster her, even against fire, hurricane, and earthquake.

Furthermore, Jane Eyre will later add (p. 203, pp. 222–23) her intuition that there are other ways of knowing beside reliance upon teachers, books, and reason. There are dreams, for example, and imaginings, and hypnagogic reveries, all of which were capable of both reproving and encouraging her. Then in her dealings with her employer Rochester she noticed how when he proposed to her on that Midsummer Eve in the orchard, and even as he urged Eden upon her, the rain burst forth in sheets enough to dampen her gladness, if it was really gladness. Such occurred more than once when an enigma troubled her. Once it was a rushing wind which alerted her to betrayal and danger.

The Credo she drew up for herself served as her guide for the rest of her working life (p. 319):

1. I care for myself.
2. I shall respect myself all the more if in times to come I am friendless and unsupported.
3. I intend to obey the laws of both God and man.
4. I will cling to these principles all my life long, even when I am ill, troubled, or depressed.
5. Even when my body and soul fall prey to temptation, I will remember to resist and deny them their will.
6. I realize I am guided by received opinions and determinations made by others and passed on to me, but I also realize they are all I have as intellectual wealth.

7. I now plant my foot here and vow to abide by these rules, come what may. I swear not to stray from this position.

Jane Eyre married her former employer, Mr. Rochester, and lived to bear him a son. Unfortunately Charlotte Brontë died during the first months of her own first pregnancy.

One has not had to look farther afield than George Eliot (1819–1880) to find another truly magnificent novelist who wrung hearts in *Adam Bede* (1859). There she told the pitiful story of another poor, abandoned girl giving birth to another unwanted, illegitimate baby. In George Eliot's masterpiece the heroine is named Hetty, which gives us the same impression of her we have of "Effie" Deans: a weak, silly, stupid, foolish but pretty girl. Hetty wants to rise in the world and marry the rich, local farmer, Eliot's truly local yokel. The fellow has seduced Hetty, which was no great feat, and the girl has become pregnant. She is supposed to wed a high-minded, pious gentleman, who could in no way support a pregnant bride, much less countenance one such. Hetty bears her child in the woods, out of doors, and alone. She too is, like Effie Deans, found guilty of murder. She has nobody to defend her, and doubtless she appears indefensible. Only Hetty's fiancé comes out all right. He marries a Methodist minister.

Novelists end up by being unmasked, of course, and called snide or worse, as they deserve. The harvest they reap is censure from all sides, and they richly deserve that too. They are snide. Every novelist worth his or her salt attacks society, Presbyterians and Methodists, and only partly for the fun of it.

Flaubert went to jail for using the real newspaper account of a real Madame Emma Bovary, who so hated French Normandy that she gladly took poison. Sir Walter Scott wrote his first novels anonymously, so greatly did he dread the critics' attacks and so greatly also did he fear loss of reputation. Even so, he tried cautiously enough to be raised to a Baronetcy. Mérimée hid his savage attack on society's treatment of Carmen between pages devoted to pseudoarchaeology. George Eliot of the plain and homely face was born Mary Ann Evans.

The authors of ancient epics praised the hero who volunteered to die for his king or leader. They told what a splendid funeral he received. On the contrary, the authors of the prose novel, of grand opera, and of the movies have felt free to criticize society for its ills and to champion women. Such women, with all their problems, have been our heroines.

•READINGS•

Brontë, Charlotte. *Jane Eyre*. Afterword by Arthur Zeiger, Signet Classic, New American Library (New York, 1960).

Brown, David. *Walter Scott and the Historical Imagination*. Routledge and Kegan Paul (London and Boston, 1979).

Pushkin, Aleksandr. *Pushkin, A Laurel Reader*. Edited with an Introduction by Ernest J. Simmons. Dell Publishing Co. (New York, 1961). See pp. 225–348 for *The Captain's Daughter*. Or see the previously mentioned edition, Penguin Classics, pp. 185–317.

Rosenmeyer, Thomas G. *The Green Cabinet, Theocritus and the European Pastoral Lyric*. University of California Press (London and Berkeley, Calif., 1969).

Scott, Sir Walter. *The Heart of Midlothian*. Introduction by David Daiches, Rinehart & Co. (New York and Toronto, 1948).

———. *The Talisman*. Preface and Glossary by W. M. Parker.

Virgil. *The Pastoral Poems*. Edited and translated by E. V. Rieu. Penguin Books (Baltimore, 1949).

"We've given up far too many freedoms
in order to be free. Now we've got to
take them back."

—George Smiley in John Le Carre's *The
Secret Pilgrim*

In the preceding pages we have set ancient heroines into categories
depending upon their lives, their roles, their stories, pursuits, and
functions. Many were ancient queens like Cleopatra and the Empress
Theodora, or princesses like Medea, Isolde, Electra, and Antigone.
Others were demigoddesses, hardly distinguishable from the real goddesses like Love (Venus), Earth (Ceres or Demeter), and Death (Hecate). Liberty and Justice (Astraea) were demigoddesses, with statues
still standing in their honor in our law courts and in New York
Harbor.

The ancient peoples venerated and told of their fierce women
warriors, often clad in red leather, always horsewomen, who were
matriarchs called Amazons. Their battle-hardened descendants came
from Ireland, Scotland, Norway, Iceland, North Africa, and Russia,
even as late as the Middle Ages. Still other worshipful women were
astronomers at roulette-wheel temples like Stonehenge. Others were
doctors without diplomas, so-called "witches." They followed the

ancient Medea who could revive the dead. There was also a defeated African Queen named Medusa, who could turn men into stone. Below them in honor came the illustrious Roman matron Lucrece (Lucretia), whose courage has set an example to Italy today because she saved the honor of her family and in dying founded the proud Roman Republic.

In the ancient world, and this is why we turn to it, there lived women who were famous, illustrious even, for what the Romans called *virtus,* which means manliness, honor, courage, and bravery. Others were equally memorable as enemies of the state and of society. Their acts were motivated by revenge, hatred, betrayal, and defiance. They refused, in other words, to follow custom and obey laws which they despised. Thus, as they moved down through the ages, the stories of heroines proved more and more complicated by memories of the executions and immurements of living women. The Grand Opera *Aïda* by Giuseppe Verdi (which was performed at the opening of the Suez Canal), ends with the heroine descending underground where she will suffocate, as did many of the Vestal Virgins at Rome.

The ancients had less trouble celebrating heroic men like Theseus, who founded Athens although he did not always act nobly; or Odysseus who conquered Troy, although deceitfully; and Achilles who killed Hector but prostituted the Trojan women and raped the corpse of the Amazon warrior Penthesilea. Heroes have always enjoyed license to kill and are always heroical to the degree that they win wars, rule countries, and carry off the spoils. Heroines have enjoyed an odder and usually much more tendentious kind of story.

Examples of heroic women, as we have studied them, are based upon ancient heroines. Ancient heroic women are recorded, whether in Greece, Rome, Asia Minor, Byzantium, Africa, or Western Europe before A.D. 500, and here classified according to their claims to fame. The first such candidates were women distinguished by their supposed goodness. In the classic case of Alcestis, goodness meant the willingness to sacrifice her life, to die, in fact, for her husband. Her pattern of behavior *in extremis* was perhaps accepted, although with reservation, one suspects. Not everyone, perhaps not even Euripides, believed that Alcestis actually died for her husband. Even persons who at first believed in her sacrifice of the self seemed later to become dubious. Chaucer may have calmly accepted the sacrifice of Queen Cleopatra, but also perhaps, too readily; for she probably killed herself because, defeated and alone, she preferred death at her own hands to a far worse death from her foes. In the third case, which was that of the Roman matron Lucrece, we have considered suicide most appropriate and honorable as the Romans judged it to have been. Contrary to Alcestis, Lucrece died to spare her children, to sustain her husband in his honors, and finally to rid Rome of the tyrannical Etruscan Kings. Thus, Lucrece remained forever virtuous and really, in our eyes, a good woman. Mothers prove every day that they will die for their children.

It has been fascinating to this author, then, to step into the oversized shoes of the greatest of modern followers treating these same problems from ancient myths. It is always charming to watch Fitzgerald wrestle and gnaw brilliantly away at the failed goodness of Daisy/Alcestis in Long Island. We grant, of course, that American literature takes a predominantly pessimistic view of the world. American authors are prone to adopt rather a black than a rosy view of American society. They and the French are always critical rather than admiring of the world which they have created.

What a pleasant shock it was, then, to turn to the greatest of the Russians, Count Tolstoy. He maligned a good many real and fictional women, it is true, when he chose to do so; but he held up for our esteem in *War and Peace* his Princess Maria Bolkonsky. He agreed that she was not so very lovely to look at, but she proved utterly kind, able, capable, generous, loving, noble, intelligent, educated, and good as a person. Like himself, she was a follower of a missionary religion preached by self-taught and self-appointed wandering evangelists. The princess Tolstoy loved divested herself of her real property, just as Tolstoy gave his away to his peasants also, and over the protests of his own wife. Thus, centuries later, and in the pages of Tolstoy, we found the idea of the personal goodness of Alcestis still alive.

Love stories of beautiful heroines madly in love with handsome heroes have filled, with all possible sorts of ramifications, millions and millions of pages. The ancient world was just drawing to a close when Princess Isolde was summoned to go from Ireland into Scotland and wed a wintry King Mark. His nephew and heir Tristan played John Alden here and fetched the vernal bride. But princess and hero Tristan fell madly in love, passionately, and irrevocably in love. Their folly has always been viewed as physical or sexual in nature, ergo a disguised desire for death. The reasoning has always been that since they could never marry, and since they lay together but with the drawn sword of Tristan between them, they were, in effect, killing themselves for love. Modern moralists like Simone de Beauvoir and modern theologians like Denis de Rougemont have chastised the Middle Ages for adoring this triangular story.

But what if Isolde proves now to have been a high priestess? Her fire-walking exploit, which seems to have come from an even more ancient India, has raised her status to that of a holy virgin and priestess. Modern scholars of myth and ancient languages have posited a different scenario: that Isolde's "potion" could be translated by its doublet, which is "poison." By her mother's "philter," Isolde safeguarded her virginity. The proof of this suspicion appears in her safe negotiation of the fire-walking ordeal, during which God protected her innocence. The ordeal also proclaimed her an ancient Druid priestess. As such, she was about to be outlawed and phased almost out of memory. Idem for Queen Guinevere.

Princess Isolde leads both directly and indirectly to the white goddess type of heroine and her demon lover. She will unmask him. He is another Faust who has sold his soul to the Devil in exchange for eternal youth. Or he is another Don Juan from Spain, an unholy seducer of girls. Or he is Dracula, the Tibetan bat-god. As a white maiden from the white Celtic wood, Isolde resurrects the ancient white goddess called Earth. There in an oak grove Isolde resurrects her because seeking knowledge she is a child of Earth.

The symbolism of Gothic fiction becomes transparent. Such authors posited a dark castle, which is four-cornered and facing holy Jerusalem. It stands within a garden, like that called Eden. The white heroine is another Eve standing under the tree of knowledge. Thus, Gothic fiction, especially in the hands of women novelists like Reeve and Radcliffe, broached the thorny issue of a woman and education. Knowledge comes as the result of training. Education is training of the mind.

After teaching for forty-five years in French and American classrooms (from September through June, 1937–82), I have known more young women from all backgrounds, and known their minds more intimately than a psychoanalyst. Even so, in the vexed problems of a woman's education, the author now enjoins the reader to consider two of the world's greatest authorities on the subject: Jean-Jacques Rousseau of Switzerland and Gustave Flaubert of France.

Chapter IV was concerned with the thousands of poor girls and women worldwide who turned to prostitution out of desperation, or who were sold into prostitution by their families. Two ancient examples actually cheered us, however, and offered solutions: the Greek courtesan Phryne, whose body we all know from the statue of Venus de Milo, and the Byzantine Empress Theodora of Constantinople, who still glares down, black-eyed and saturnine, from the Ravenna Mosaic. Both were prostituted from early childhood. Phryne had to have been a demigoddess to have survived such a life, to have so long conserved beauty and health. The Empress survived also, but only because of her utter loathing and hatred of all men. Once she had gained absolute power, she stripped them naked by the hundreds, confiscated their goods, and starved them to death in her underground concentration camps.

In order to show how deeply this sore, the prostitution of poor girls and women, has burned into the flesh of authors, we then turned to four among the male writers who adopted varying opinions about "fallen" women also. We chose the Englishman Daniel Defoe, the German nobleman Kleist, the French Mérimée (translator of Pushkin), and mentioned honorably the American novelist Theodore Dreiser of Chicago for his *Sister Carrie*. The English Protestant assured us that the prostitute Moll would rehabilitate herself. The German officer knew his lady's aristocratic family would avenge the Russian officer's crime against their innocent daughter. Law and family would prevail. Another French author, the son of the black dramatist and novelist Alexandre Dumas, saw that justice, on the other hand, would not prevail. His generous call-girl would die young for her sins. Above them the American Theodore Dreiser comes out clearly the winner. His fallen heroine, Sister Carrie, found work and redeemed herself honestly. Her seducer deteriorated steadily for having abandoned wife and daughter, for having deserted his business, and for having seduced Carrie. He ended a miserable beggar starving on the cold sidewalks of New York City.

As there is a crying need for women to write books and novels on prostitution, that opportunity for a great career cannot compare to the even greater need for women to write books about motherhood.

Therefore one welcomed the lofty and wise Russians, and especially Tolstoy who, as described in our Chapter I, took Euripides' *Alcestis* apart and showed us a far superior, better, nobler, good woman in *War and Peace*. Although the Russians entered the competition for best novels of the world rather late, they quickly won the title over even France, over milder England too, and over the United States. For sheer brains and then for supreme knowledge of the human heart, and a woman's poor heart at that, the Russians Tolstoy, Dostoyevsky, and Pushkin have gathered all the greenest laurels.

The world's greatest authors long ago warned the world of medicine and psychiatry that a crisis was developing among mothers in the Western countries, and especially in the United States. Educators here descried the fact that the United States was not in any way the first of countries, if ranked according to our education of women. We were more probably the last of Western countries, having apparently the lowest per capita rate of highly educated women in the Western world. And we paid scant attention to mothers and their dependent children. American mothers tend to be blamed for everything. What American mother has not been blamed for all the shortcomings of her children? What son has not blamed his mother because he has not produced to his liking? Have not teachers seen American mothers sent into treatment by Freudian psychiatry along with their sons because the latter failed to earn honor grades in private schools? Do not American children everywhere order their mothers to obey them? And furthermore, to provide for them more luxuriously? And are not American mothers frequently beaten, and purposely kept like destitute beggars?

It is no wonder that the august Nobel Prize Committee in Stockholm have granted Nobel Prizes to those authors who have written exposés about motherhood. One such recipient was the eloquent Grazia Deledda from Sicily. D. H. Lawrence also championed mothers loudly. Our own, best-beloved William Faulkner was another such recipient who added his powerful, lyrical voice from our Deep South, so resplendent among the great voices raised there for our consideration. And he established scholarships with his money for poor, black American women. One of our greatest authors here is Patrick White, praised for his long, authoritative depiction of Elizabeth Hunter in *Eye of the Storm*.

Young mothers-to-be in America in the 1990s have been refused medical advice and care and have been treated less considerately than slabs of beef. Psychologists have warned us all that when the mother has lost respect in the home, the children will run wild. We have seen that very result.

In a pagan world, where our authors have become pagan, then paganism has risen as a possible answer. Chapter VI ventures upon the terrain of ancient paganism. Paganism in our days, inasmuch as the literary critic can judge from new masterpieces penned by sharp writers, is gaining ground. For centuries now, both Judaism and Christianity, and now government, have herded women aside, and generally deconsidered them. Even our little girls perceive that they are less than second-class Americans both in school and in church. Schoolgirls out of babyhood learn fast enough to use baby talk forever, not to grow up, to bare their legs and thighs, to let their hair hide their blushing faces from the sight of their humiliation and grief. They must become sex objects. They must stay little girls who hope to be cute enough to avoid beatings. Clearly, to be safe, they must demonstrate stupidity, ignorance, and timidity. Thus, they learn not to speak, not to write, and to be present while thousands of miles away. The nightmares of little girls are usually of blood, knives, scissors, needles, murder, and revenge, which makes them even more silent and afraid.

Having suffered enough, even American career women often long to become stone and witness no more suffering of girls. Cold, hard, and numb, they would then be insensible to pain. In such ways women are returning, whether they realize it at once or not, to the old stone gods of the Neolithic Age. In Thomas Hardy's heartbreaking novel *Tess of the D'Urbervilles,* where did the heroine seek refuge after she committed murder? Where else but at Stonehenge? Had Rolman Polanski's film actually photographed that Stone Age monument in southern England, the viewer would have understood even more clearly the author's message: Women may be returning to the worship of their distant ancestors, to the old stone goddesses like Medusa. Had the message stopped there, it would have sufficed, for Hardy is a powerful author, one of the best.

Hardy has not said the last word. His message was not only reinforced, but doubled in power by David Herbert Lawrence, a novelist so magnificent and so brilliant that as a youth in World War I he was exiled, expelled forever from his native England. Critics have argued that Lawrence was England's most brilliant student of the century. And fortunately so for his patron Mrs. Mabel Dodge and for American women in general. Lawrence turned eventually to our American Indian ancestors, to that heritage which we share in common. Have we not all, as little children, combed the forests for our Native American predecessors who gave us our favorite foodstuffs and our maple syrup? The Indians gave us our native arts, our crafts, their magical names for our country, their skills in the forest, lakes, and rivers, their canoes, and our beloved land.

Because he was a very religious man, who composed books on theology, in fact, Lawrence saw the awful drudgery, the slavery to men and children, the abysmal poverty of American women's lives shut up inside ignorance and suffering with no hope of exit ever.

As eloquently as he could, this English author extolled the one escape possible, which was for women to throw in the towel, walk out the door forever, and return to the old stone gods of the Native Americans. It was they who taught us to respect our fellows, to love and preserve the land, which in their days was so beautiful. Now the white man with his unrestrained urge for more and more sex, for more and more power and money, has ruined America with over-population, exhaustion of soil and air, water, forests, and resources.

The movie *Thelma and Louise* was too long a time coming, but thankfully, come it did. In death these young women returned, as we wept, to the gods of their ancestors. We all saw them clearly as they rode away to our prehistoric Monument Valley of the Indians. Like Tess of the D'Urbervilles, Thelma and Louise preferred to die rather than to live any more in America. To them as they decided it, the megalithic stones seemed kinder than their lives had been. Therefore our debt to real women, women such as Professor Anita Hill and scenarist Callie Khouri, of *Thelma and Louise,* is immense.

Finally, to end on a braver note, some women gave us old but new lessons in courage. Women have actually been warriors, successful and winning warriors too, not only in martial France during World

War II but also in the ancient days of Norway, Iceland, Ireland, and Germany. In World War II French women joined the Resistance Army. Some even suffered torture without breaking. In Ireland the black crow and red Queen of Battle Morrigu descended fearlessly upon the male war bands, as did Queen Maeve of Connaught.

Sir Walter Scott chronicled women in Scotland who fought men in order to save their families. Henrik Ibsen in Norway recalled for us the fierce, unforgiving, heathen Viking warrior women in their world of sea battles and the frozen wastes of Arctic winter. Aleksandr Pushkin, Russia's first black writer, genially portrayed a charming, young Captain's daughter in the wild, eastern frontiers of Imperial Russia as she survived rebellion, threat of rape and death, and even finally rescued her fiancé.

Perhaps one reason for the greater respect which French men show girls and women today results from their having been taken frequently as small boys to pray to that French woman, the girl warrior, Saint Joan of Arc. Joan is beloved and still worshipped all over France as the savior of her country. Even though a young girl, Joan wore metal armor day in and day out. She carried her white banner of Orléans proudly and fearlessly. She led an army. She shared the rigors of combat. She fed her countrymen. She organized the volunteer Scots and her own people and helped them stand firm against a huge foe. She struck fear in English combatants with her brave words and her brave and daring deeds. She made good her threats. Today this Saint of France, who was burned to death at Rouen, sits in her own cathedral in Orléans. In her case, a mere girl became a demigoddess before and after death.

It is as curious a happenstance as any other that some few demigoddesses survive today in stone statues. They make us take courage as we contemplate a Return of the Golden Age. Joan of Arc is still golden and resplendent in Paris, an equestrian statue, no less, like any other celebrated Roman military hero. The prostitute Phryne is Venus de Milo in the Louvre Museum. For other demigoddesses we have films so that we can refresh our memory of the lovely faces: Elizabeth Taylor, Joan Crawford, Olivia De Havilland, Grace Kelly, Greta Garbo, who was probably loveliest of all, Rita Hayworth, Greer Garson, Merle Oberon, Marilyn Monroe, Vivien Leigh. We also have powerful women on film and forever in our memories: Glenda Jackson, Peggy Ashcroft, Bette Davis, Maggie Smith, and the beloved New Yorker Shirley Booth, who has been the most highly honored of them all.

Our last two stories from the annals of the ancient world were most familiar and most precious to us; the stone statues of Liberty and Justice. We shall not forget Liberty holding the torch of Liberty, nor Astraea and Themis blindfolded. If they can't inspire American women, then nobody can.

It used to be a truth of history that slaves had never liberated themselves.

Prima Donnas. Grand Opera

Name of Opera	Composer	Locale	Date of Presentation
1. *Alceste*	Gluck	Greece	1767
2. *Leonore (Fidelio)*	Beethoven	Spain	1805
3. *Semiramide*	Rossini	Babylon	1823
4. *Norma*	Bellini	Gaul	1831
5. *Lucia de Lammermoor*	Donizetti	Scotland	1835
6. *La Juive*	Halévy	Germany	1835
7. *La Traviata*	Verdi	France	1853
8. *L'Africaine*	Meyerbeer	Portugal	1865
9. *Mignon*	Thomas	Germany	1866
10. *Aïda*	Verdi	Egypt	1871
11. *Carmen*	Bizet	Spain	1875
12. *La Gioconda*	Ponchielli	Italy	1876
13. *Lakmé*	Délibes	India	1883
14. *Manon*	Massenet	France/Louisiana	1884
15. *Thaïs*	Massenet	Egypt	1894
16. *Louise*	Charpentier	France	1900
17. *Madama Butterfly*	Puccini	Japan	1904
18. *Salome*	Strauss	Israel	1905
19. *Elektra*	Strauss	Greece	1909

Demigoddesses

Aurora

Alcestis

Astraea

Antigone

Dalila

Medea

Cleopatra

Herodias

Salome

Hecate

Eve

Medusa

Isolde

Morrigu

Hjördis

Dagny

Lucrece

Theodora

Phryne

Rhea

Phyllis

Persephone

Penthesilea

Boudicca

Velleda

Guinevere

Virgo

Themis

Philosophy

Sibyl

Carmenta

Carmen

Libertas

Jocasta

Iustitia

Iuventa

Flora

Diana

Pieris

Pleione

Morgan le Fay

Modern Masters

Sir Walter Scott

Choderlos de Laclos

Daniel Defoe

Gustave Flaubert

Somerset Maugham

Joseph Conrad

Thomas Hardy

Count Leo Tolstoy

Boris Pasternak

Jane Austen

Theodore Dreiser

Abbe Prévost

Aleksandr Pushkin

Fyodor Dostoyevsky

Federico García Lorca

William Faulkner

Charlotte Brontë

Henrik Ibsen

Alexandre Dumas

Alexandre Dumas fils

Patrick White

Prosper Mérimée

Heinrich von Kleist

James Joyce

F. Scott Fitzgerald

Jean Jacques Rousseau

Grazia Deledda

David Herbert Lawrence

Jean Giono

Elizabeth Gaskell

George Eliot

Victor Hugo

Miguel de Cervantes

Madre Theresa de Avila

Robert Graves

Ann Radcliffe

Clara Reeve

Bram Stoker

Horace Walpole

Herman Melville

Edgar Allan Poe

Germaine de Staël

Edith Wharton

Emily Brontë

Marguerite de Navarre

Modern Heroines

Joan of Arc	Jane Eyre
Jeanie Deans	Marguerite Gautier
Moll Flanders	Lady Chatterley
Madame de Merteuil	Camille
Madame Bovary	Julie/Heloïse
Sadie Thompson	Sophie
Tess of the D'Urbervilles	Maria
Princess Maria Bolkonsky	Félicité
Anna Karenina	Carmen
Catherine Morland	Kate
Sister Carrie	Louise
Manon Lescaut	Emily
Marquise of O	Thelma
Queen Maeve of Connaught	Virginie
The Captain's Daughter	Daisy
The White Goddess	Emma
The Queen of Spades	Bernarda
The Death Queen	Addie
Bernarda Alba	Amy
Addie Bundren	Edith
Amy Robsart	Rebecca
Queen Berengaria	Jane
Edith Plantagenet	Marguerite
Rebecca of York	Tess

(Continued)

Sadie
Moll
Jeanie
Lara
Esmeralda
Mary Barton

Movie Stars from Memory

"We've come a long way. Not too long
ago we were referred to as dolls,
tomatoes, chicks, babes, broads. We've
graduated to being called tough cookies,
foxes, bitches and witches. I guess that's
progress. Language gives us insight into
the way women are viewed in a
male-dominated society."

—Barbra Streisand,
being honored at Women in Film's
Annual Crystal Awards Ceremony,
as reported by Claudia Puig,
Los Angeles Times, June 13, 1992

Star	Role	Source(?)	Film	Date
Julie Andrews	Millie		*Thoroughly Modern Millie*	1967
Dame Peggy Ashcroft	Mrs. Moore	E. M. Forster	*A Passage to India*	1984
			Madame Sousatzka	1988
	Lillian Huckle		*She's Been Away*	1989
	Barbie (Miss Batchelor)	Paul Scott	*The Raj Quartet* (Masterpiece Theatre)	1979
Mary Astor	Jennie	Theodore Dreiser	*Jennie Gerhardt*	1933
	Charlotte		*Sweet Charlotte*	1964
Lauren Bacall	Vivian		*The Big Sleep*	1946
Tallulah Bankhead		Lillian Hellman	*The Little Foxes*	1939
		Sir Alfred Hitchcock	*Lifeboat*	1944
Theda Bara	Camille	Alexandre Dumas fils	*Camille*	1917
	Cleopatra	Shakespeare	*Cleopatra*	1917
	Madame du Barry	History	*Madame du Barry*	1918
	Salome	Bible	*Salome*	1918
Brigitte Bardot	Helen	Homer	*Helen of Troy*	1956
	Babette		*Batette s'en va-t-en guerre*	1959
Ingrid Bergman	Joan of Arc	History	*Joan of Arc*	1948
	Anastasia	History	*Anastasia*	1956
	Golda Meir	History	*A Woman Called Golda*	1982
Helena Bonham Carter	Helen Schlegel	E. M. Forster	*Howard's End*	1992
Shirley Booth	Mrs. Delaney		*Come Back, Little Sheba*	1952
Leslie Caron	Gigi	Colette	*Gigi*	1958
	Fanny		*Fanny*	1961
	Golden Girl		*Goldengirl*	1979

Star	Role	Source(?)	Film	Date
Julie Christie	Lara	Boris Pasternak	Dr. Zhivago	1965
Glenn Close	Mme. de Merteuil	Chloderlos de Laclos	Les Liaisons dangereuses*	1988
Joan Crawford	Sadie Thompson	Somerset Maugham, "Rain"	Miss Sadie Thompson	1932
	Mildred Pierce		Mildred Pierce	1945
Claudette Colbert	Cleopatra	Shakespeare	Cleopatra	1934
Linda Darnell	Virgin Mary	Bible	The Song of Bernadette	1943
Danielle Darrieux	Lady Chatterley	D. H. Lawrence, Lady Chatterley's Lover	L'Amant de Lady Chatterley	1955
Bette Davis	The Waitress	Robert Sherwood	The Petrified Forest	1936
	Jezebel	Bible	Jezebel	1938
	Queen Elizabeth	History	The Private Lives of Elizabeth and Essex	1939
	Mrs. Crosbie	Somerset Maugham	The Letter	1940
	Mrs. Skeffington		Mr. Skeffington	1944
	Eve		All About Eve	1950
Geena Davis	Louise		Thelma and Louise	1991
Josette Day	Beauty	Jean Cocteau	Beauty and the Beast	1946
Olivia De Havilland	Melanie	Margaret Mitchell	Gone with the Wind	1939
	Charlotte		Hush Hush ... Sweet Charlotte	1964
Catherine Deneuve	Marie Vetsera		Mayerling	1968

*Dangerous Acquaintances (Liaisons)

Star	Role	Source(?)	Film	Date
Marlene Dietrich	Lola		*The Blue Angel*	1930
	Manon	Abbe Prévost	*Manon Lescaut*	1926
			Marlene	1984
Marie Dressler	Annie		*Tugboat Annie*	1933
Faye Dunaway	Bonnie		*Bonnie and Clyde*	1967
	Joan Crawford		*Mommie Dearest*	1981
Irene Dunne		Fanny Hurst	*Back Street*	1932
	Anna		*Anna and the King of Siam*	1946
Dame Edith Evans	The Countess	Aleksandr Pushkin	*The Queen of Spades*	1948
Mia Farrow	Rosemary	Ira Levin	*Rosemary's Baby*	1968
	Daisy	F. Scott Fitzgerald	*The Great Gatsby*	1974
Jane Fonda	Bree Daniel		*Klute*	1971
Joan Fontaine		Daphne Du Maurier	*Rebecca*	1940
	Jane	Charlotte Brontë	*Jane Eyre*	1944
Greta Garbo	Anna Karenina	Leo Tolstoy	*Love*	1927
	Anna Christie	Eugene O'Neill	*Anna Christie*	1930
	Mata Hari		*Mata Hari*	1932
	Anna Karenina	Leo Tolstoy	*Anna Karenina*	1935
	Christina		*Queen Christina*	1933
	Camille	Alexandre Dumas fils	*Camille*	1937
	Ninotchka		*Ninotchka*	1939
Judy Garland	Dorothy	Frank Baum	*The Wizard of Oz*	1939
Greer Garson	Mrs. Miniver		*Mrs. Miniver*	1942
	Madame Curie	Biography	*Madame Curie*	1943
	Mrs. Parkington		*Mrs. Parkington*	1944
Lillian Gish	Hester Prynne	Nathaniel Hawthorne	*The Scarlet Letter*	1929
	Lucy		*Broken Blossoms*	1919
	Mimi	Giacomo Puccini	*La Bohême*	1926
Melanie Griffith			*Working Girl*	1988
Rita Hayworth	Gilda		*Gilda*	1946
	Sadie Thompson	Somerset Maugham, "Rain"	*Miss Sadie Thompson*	1953

Star	Role	Source(?)	Film	Date
Audrey Hepburn	Holly Golightly	Truman Capote	*Breakfast at Tiffany's*	1961
	Natasha Rostov	Leo Tolstoy	*War and Peace*	1956
Katharine Hepburn	Jo March	Louise May Alcott	*Little Women*	1933
	Sylvia		*Sylvia Scarlett*	1935
	Rose	C. S. Forester	*The African Queen*	1951
	Mary Tyrone	Eugene O'Neill	*Long Day's Journey Into Night*	1962
	Queen Eleanor	History	*The Lion in Winter*	1968
Miriam Hopkins	Becky Sharp	Thackeray, *Vanity Fair*	*Becky Sharp*	1935
Lena Horne	Hattie	Biography	*Panama Hattie*	1942
Isabelle Huppert	The Brontë Sisters	Biography	*Les Soeurs Bronte*	1978
	Emma	Gustave Flaubert	*Madame Bovary*	1991
Glenda Jackson	Queen Mary	History	*Mary, Queen of Scots*	1971
	Ursula Brangwen	D. H. Lawrence	*The Rainbow*	1989
	Gudrun	D. H. Lawrence	*Women in Love*	1969
	Bernarda Alba	García Lorca	*La Casa de Bernardo Alba*	1936
Jennifer Jones	Bernadette	Religion	*The Song of Bernadette*	1943
	Emma	Gustave Flaubert	*Madame Bovary*	1949
	Elizabeth Browning	Biography	*The Barretts of Wimpole Street*	1956
	Catherine Barkley	Ernest Hemingway	*A Farewell to Arms*	1957
Diane Keaton	Annie		*Annie Hall*	1977
	The Mother		*The Good Mother*	1988
Grace Kelly			*High Noon*	1952
			The Country Girl	1954
			The Bridges at Toko-Ri	1955
Nastassia Kinski	Tess	Thomas Hardy	*Tess of the D'Urbervilles*	1979

Star	Role	Source(?)	Film	Date
Sylvia Kristel	Constance	D. H. Lawrence	*Lady Chatterley's Lover*	1981
	Mata	History	*Mata Hari*	1985
Veronica Lake		Crime	*The Blue Dahlia*	1946
Hedy Lamarr	Delilah	Bible	*Samson and Delilah*	1949
Elsa Lanchester	Mary Shelley (author of)	*Frankenstein*	*The Bride of Frankenstein*	1935
	Mrs. Micawber	Charles Dickens	*David Copperfield*	1935
	Katie	P. L. Traver	*Mary Poppins*	1964
Angela Lansbury	Moll Flanders	Daniel Defoe	*The Amorous Adventures of Moll Flanders*	1965
	Jessica Fletcher		*Murder, She Wrote* (TV series)	1993
Ginette Leclerc	Aurélie	Jean Giono	*La Femme du boulanger* (The Baker's Wife)	1938
Vivien Leigh	Scarlett O'Hara	Margaret Mitchell	*Gone with the Wind*	1939
	Blanche du Bois	Tennessee Williams	*A Streetcar Named Desire*	1951
	Cleopatra	Shakespeare	*Antony and Cleopatra*	1945
	Anna	Leo Tolstoy	*Anna Karenina*	1948
Gina Lollobrigida	Lucia	Sir Walter Scott	*Lucia de Lammermoor*	1946
	Empress Josephine	History	*Désirée*	1954
	Queen of Sheba	Bible	*Solomon and Sheba*	1959
Sophia Loren	Aïda	Giuseppe Verdi	*Aïda*	1953
	Cleopatra	Shakespeare, *Antony and Cleopatra*	*Due notti con Cleopatra*	1953
Shirley MacLaine			*Madame Sousatzka*	1988
Anna Magnani	Serafina Delle Rose	Tennessee Williams	*The Rose Tattoo*	1955
	The Blind Woman		*La Cicca di Sorrento*	1934
Giuletta Masina	The Housewife		*Juliet of the Spirits*	1965

Star	Role	Source(?)	Film	Date
Liza Minnelli	Sally Bowles	Bob Fosse	Cabaret	1972
Marilyn Monroe	Marilyn	Documentary	Marilyn	1963
Mary Tyler Moore	The Mother	Judith Guest	Ordinary People	1981
Agnes Moorehead	The Mother	Orson Welles	Citizen Kane	1941
	The Spinster	Orson Welles	The Magnificent Ambersons	1942
Merle Oberon	Catherine	Emily Brontë	Wuthering Heights	1939
	Lydia		Lydia	1941
Irene Papas	Empress Theodora	Procopius	Theodore, Imperatrice Byzantine	1954
	Antigone	Sophocles	Antigone	1961
	Andromache(?)	Euripides	The Trojan Women	1971
Michelle Pfeiffer	Mme. de Tourvel	Chloderlos de Laclos	Dangerous Liaisons	1988
Mary Pickford	Pollyanna	Eleanor H. Porter	Pollyanna	1920
	Annie	J. R. Lowell	Little Annie Rooney	1925
	Beatrice	Shakespeare	The Taming of the Shrew	1929
Vanessa Redgrave	Queen Guinevere	Frederick Loewe	Camelot	1967
	Isadora Duncan	Biography	Isadora	1968
	Julia	Lillian Hellman	Julia	1977
	Mrs. Wilcox	E. M. Forster	Howard's End	1992
Lee Remick	Temple Drake	William Faulkner	Sanctuary	1961
Dame Margaret Rutherford	Miss Marple	Agatha Christie*	Murder She Said	1961
			Murder at the Gallop	1963
		MGM's story	Murder Ahoy	1964
Susan Sarandon	The Mother		Pretty Baby	1978
	Casino Employee		Atlantic City	1980
	Thelma		Thelma and Louise	1991
Norma Shearer	Juliet	Shakespeare	Romeo and Juliet	1936
	Elizabeth Barrett	Biography	The Barretts of Wimpole Street	1934
	Marie Antoinette	History	Marie Antoinette	1938

*Titles changed (not Christie's titles).

Star	Role	Source(?)	Film	Date
Sylvia Sidney	Roberta Alden	Theodore Dreiser	*An American Tragedy*	1931
	Butterfly	Giacomo Puccini	*Madama Butterfly*	1932
	Jennie	Theodore Dreiser	*Jennie Gerhardt*	1933
Simone Signoret	Thérèse	Emile Zola	*Thérèse Raquin*	1953
	Witch of Salem	History	*Les Sorcières de Salem*	1956
Jean Simmons	Ophelia	Shakespeare	*Hamlet*	1949
Dame Maggie Smith	Jean Brodie	Muriel Spark	*The Prime of Miss Jean Brodie*	1969
	Judith Hearne		*The Lonely Passion of Judith Hearne*	1987
Barbara Stanwyck	The Mother Stella	Olive Higgins Prouty	*Stella Dallas*	1937
	Annie		*Annie Oakley*	1935
Meryl Streep	Sophie		*Sophie's Choice*	1982
	Karen Blixen	Isak Dinesen	*Out of Africa*	1988
	Lindy Chamberlain		*A Cry in the Dark*	1988
Norma Talmadge	Camille	Alexandre Dumas fils	*Camille*	1927
Elizabeth Taylor	Cleopatra	Shakespeare, *Antony and Cleopatra*	*Cleopatra*	1963
	Katherina	Shakespeare	*The Taming of the Shrew*	1967
Sigourney Weaver	The Boss		*Working Girl*	1988
	Dian Fossey		*Gorillas in the Mist*	1988
Mae West	Belle		*Belle of the Nineties*	1934
	Annie		*Klondike Annie*	1936
	Myra		*Myra Breckenridge*	1970
Joanne Woodward	Eve		*The Three Faces of Eve*	1957
	The Spinster		*Rachel, Rachel*	1968
	Amanda	Tennessee Williams	*The Glass Menagerie*	1987

Abelard, Peter, 83–85
Achilles, 244
Adam, 76–77
Adam Bede (Eliot), 96, 240
Admetus, King, 3–14
Aegisthus, 131
Aeneas, 53, 150–51
Aeschylus, 128–31
Aeson, 153, 155
Afallach, Ynys, 201
Agamemnon, 77, 130–31
Ahriman, 52
Ahura Mazda, 52
Aïda (Verdi), 25, 244
Albine, 58

Alceste, Queen, 15–16
Alceste (Gluck), 2
Alcestis (Alkestis), xxv, xxvi, 1–17,
    53, 56, 105, 168–69, 230,
    244–45
  in Chaucer's *The Legend of Good*
    Women, 15–17
  as fairy tale, 13
  as martyr for love, 16–17
  as model, 24
  modern portrayals, 25–26
  as myth, 14
Alcestis (Alkestis) (Euripides), 1–16,
    248
  problem of, 2, 12–13

Alcestis (Gluck), 25
Alençon, Duke of, 209–10, 212, 215
Amy Robsart, 58, 230
Anadyomene, 105
Angel Clare, 185–86
Anna Karenina, 89
Anouilh, Jean, 133
Antheia, 15
Antigone, xxvi, 78, 125, 131–34, 141, 151, 243
Antigone (Anouilh), 133
Antigone (Sophocles), 131–33
  political implications of, 133
Apelles, 105
Aphrodite (Venus), 53, 100, 105
Apollo, 2–4, 13, 17, 33, 183
Apollodorus, 1, 13
Apollonius of Rhodes, 17
Archangel Michael, 222
Argonautica (Apollonius of Rhodes), 17
Ariadne, 17, 53
Arthur, King, 54, 57, 196–97, 201
  in Isolde legend, 32, 49–50
Asclepius, 14, 182
Ashcroft, Peggy, 169, 253
As I Lay Dying (Faulkner), 165–67, 171
Astarte, 99, 188. *See also* Dido
Astraea (Justice), xxviii, 219, 221–23, 243, 253
  in Pushkin's work, 233–36
  in Scott's novels, 224, 226–28, 230–33
  in *The Talisman*, 231–32
Astrée (Urfé), 223
Athelstan, King, 203, 205
Athena, 14, 182
  Pallas, 195–96

Atlantis, 54, 73
Atlas, 182–83
Auber, Daniel François Esprit, 112
Aurora, 53–54
Austen, Jane, 69, 237
Avalon, Isle of, 55, 201
Avebury, 176

Baal, 45, 52, 99
Bad Luck, 219
Bartholdi, Frédéric Auguste, 220
Beaufort, Henry Cardinal, 210, 214
Beauty, 219–20
Beauvoir, Simone de, 246
Beelzebub, 52
Bellini, Vincenzo, 76
Beltane, 45
Beowulf, 207, 226
Berengaria, 231–32
Berg, Alban, 146
Bernarda Alba, 169–70
Bernard of Clairvaux, Saint, 84
Béroul, 32, 36
Bertrand, Alexandre, 33
Bibliotheca (Apollo), 1
Birkhead, Edith, 57
Bizet, Georges, 141–42, 145
Boccaccio, 16–17
Boethius, 220
Bolkonsky, Princess Maria, xxiv, 245–46
Booth, Shirley, 253
Boudicca, Queen, 202
Brangane, 35
Breton, André, 57
Brontë, Charlotte, 68, 236–40
Brontë, Emily, 127–28
Brown Bull of Ulster, 198, 200
Browning, Robert, 2

Brunhilde, xxiv, 205
Brutus, 23
Buchner, Georg, 146
Bull of Cooley (Cuailgne),
    197–200, 202
Bundren, Addie, 166–67
Burke, Edmund, 64
Byron, Lord, 88

Calvin, Jean, 100
Calzabigi, Ranieri, 2, 126
Camilla, 202
Camille, xxiii, 100–101, 111, 124
Camille (film), 100, 118
Captain's Daughter, The (Pushkin),
    233–36, 252
Carmen, xv–xvii, xxiii, 126
    honor of, 145–46
    meaning of name, 143
Carmen (Bizet), 140–42, 145, 152
Carmen (film), 140–41
Carmen (Mérimée), 87, 140–46,
    241
Carnac, 33, 176–79
Caroline, Queen, 227–28, 230,
    234–35
Caspar Milquetoast, 98
Cassander, 105
Castle of Otranto, The (Walpole), 94
Catherine Morland, 69, 237
Catherine the Great, xxiv, 234–36
Cato, 114
Catullus, 76
Céline, Louis-Ferdinand, 58, 94
Cerberus, 151
Ceres (Demeter), 14
Ceridwen, 154
Charles VI, King, 158
Charles VII, King, 213

Charles Bovary, 87–92
Charles of Orleans, 59–60
Charles the Simple, 206
Charon, 6–7, 151
Chastellain, Georges, 215
Chaucer, Geoffrey, 2, 219–20, 230,
    245
    Alcestis (Alkestis) and, 15–17
    Cleopatra and, 18–19
    martyr for love in works of, 17,
    19
Choderlos de Laclos,
    Pierre-Amboise-François, 83,
    93, 126, 134–39
Christ, 52
Christie, Agatha, 95, 152
Chronicle (Chastellain), 215
Chrysaor, 181
Circe, 57
Classic Myths (Gayley), 54
"Clay" (Joyce), 163–64
Cleopatra, xxiv, xxvi, 17–19,
    182–83, 243, 245
Close, Glenn, 135
Clytemnestra, 77–78, 128–31
Cocktail Party, The (Eliot), 2
Collatine, 20
Condorcet, 135, 137
Confessions (Rousseau), 82–83,
    103
Consolation of Philosophy, The
    (Boethius), 220–21
Corinne (de Staël), 69
Cossacks, The (Tolstoy), 236
Crawford, Joan, 102, 253
Creon, 131–33
Cronus, 53, 73
Cuchulain, 36, 198–202
Cunning, Willis, 202n
Cupid (Eros), 17, 106

Curie, Eve, 126
Cyclops, 54

Dagny, 204–5, 207–8
Daisy, 2, 14–16, 25–26, 196, 230, 245. *See also* Marguerite (Daisy/Violette) Gautier
Dalila, 110. See also *Samson et Dalila*
Danger, 219–20
Dangerous Acquaintances (Dangerous Liaisons) (Choderlos de Laclos), 93, 126, 134–35, 137–39
Dangerous Liaisons (film), 135
Dante Alleghieri, 47
Davis, Bette, 253
Dawn of Astronomy, The (Lockyer), 177
Death of a Character (Mort d'un personnage) (Giono), 168, 178
De Beauvoir, Simone, 246
De Casibus (Boccaccio), 17
De Claris Mulieribus (Boccaccio), 17
Deffand, La Marquise du, 94
Defoe, Daniel, 111–15, 248
De Gaulle, Charles, 209
De Genlis, Countess Stéphanie, 58
De Havilland, Olivia, 253
Deledda, Grazia, xxi, 164–65, 249
Delphi, 56, 106, 175–76, 178, 181
Delphine (de Staël), 69
Del Sol, Laura, 141
Demeter, xxiv, 14, 74, 243. *See also* Ceres
Demi-Monde, Le (Dumas fils), 123
De Staël, Madame, 69
Devil, 52
Dewey Dell, 166, 168

Diana, 57
Dido (Astarte), 17
Dis Pater, 54–55
Dr. Zhivago, 102
Doctor Zhivago (Pasternak), xxviii
Dodge, Mabel, 251
Don Juan, 95, 246
Dostoyevsky, Fyodor, 86–87, 159–60, 248
Doubleday, Frank, 101
Dracula, 246
Dracula (Stoker), 94–95
Dreiser, Theodore, 101–2, 124, 186, 248
Dryden, John, 230
Duke William of Normandy, 104
Dumas, Alexandre (fils), 58, 94, 111–12, 248
Dunois, Count, 210–11, 215
D'Urfé, Honoré, 223
Duse, Eleonora, 156

Earth Mother (Earth Goddess), 72–78. *See also* Mother Earth trees of, 74–76
Eclogue IV (Virgil), 218–19
Edith Plantagenet, 231–32
Edmonds, Rosemary, 157
Effie Deans, 240
Egil's Saga, 203, 208
Electra (Elektra), xxvi, 72, 78, 125, 128–31, 134, 243
Elektra (Euripides), 128
Elektra (Sophocles), 128, 130–31
Elektra (Strauss), 133
Eleusinian mysteries, 15, 56, 105–6
Eliot, George, 96, 112, 240–41
Elizabeth Hunter, 171–72, 249

Elizabeth I, Queen of England,
    xxiv, 222, 230
Elysian Fields, 54, 55, 151
Emile (Rousseau), 79, 82, 238
Emily (The Mysteries of Udolpho),
    58, 64–68
Emma Bovary, xv, xvii, xxiii,
    87–93, 161, 230
    death of, 89
    education of, 79, 89, 91–93
    influence of, 90
Emma (The Old English Baron), 62
Eric Blood-Axe, 203
Eros. See Cupid
Espérance, 220
Euripides, 16, 105–6
    Alcestis (Alkestis), 1–16
Eurydice, 7, 31–32. See also Orfeo
    et Euridice (Gluck)
Evander, King, 222
Evans, Mary Ann. See Eliot,
    George
Eve, xxvi, 75–77, 110
    Julie and, 86
Excalibur, 201
Eye of the Storm, The (White),
    171–72, 249

Fable, A (Faulkner), 231
Father God, 54
Faulkner, William, 58, 64, 94, 163,
    165–68, 171, 231, 237, 249
    as woman's novelist, 168
Faust, 52, 95
Faust (Gounod), 25
Fedelme, 198
Félicité, 160–65
Female Advocate, or, an Attempt to
    Recover the Rights of Women

from Male Usurpation, The
    (Radcliffe), 69
Fergus, 201
Fiske, Christabel F., 228–29
Fitzgerald, F. Scott, 26
Flaubert, Gustave, 79, 86–93,
    160–63, 230, 240, 247
    background of, 88
    as woman's novelist, 168
Fortunate Isles, 54
Frame, Donald M., 115–16
Fraser, Sir James, 33
Freedom, 221–22. See also Liberty
Freud, Sigmund, xvii, 129, 165
Freya, 188
Froissart, Jean, 16
Fuller, Edmund, 101
Furies, 129–30, 150–52

Gades, Antonio, 141
Gambler, The (Dostoyevsky),
    159–60
Garbo, Greta, xxiii, 100, 118–19,
    253
García Lorca, Federico, 169–70
Gargantua, 182
Garson, Greer, 253
Gaskell, Elizabeth, 95–96
Gayley, Charles Mills, 54
Genlis, Madame Stéphanie de,
    93–94
Gerson, Jean, 202
Gibbon, Edward, 109–10
Giono, Jean, 94, 168, 178
Gluck, C. W. von, 2, 25
God of the Witches, The (Murray),
    58
Golden Bough, The (Fraser), 33
Gorgons, 182–83

Gounod, Charles, 25
Graves, Robert, 131, 182–83
Great Gatsby, The (Fitzgerald), 26
Great Mother, 73
Greece. *See also* Alcestis (Alkestis);
    and other specific topics
Gregory, Lady Augusta, 198
Guinevere, Queen, 33, 57, 202,
    246
Gunnar, 203–5, 207
Gunther, 205

Haakon, King, 203
Hades (Pluto), 6–7, 10, 13, 74
Hamilton, Denise, 99
Hammer King, 54
Hardy, Thomas, 185–87, 250
Harold, King, 206
Hawwa, 76
Hayworth, Rita, 253
Hazard, Paul, 116
Heart of Midlothian, The (Scott),
    224–28, 233–34
Heathcliff, 127–28
Hebe, 76
Hecate, xxiv, xxvi, 57, 150, 153,
    243
    film treatment of, 169
Hector, 244
Helen of Troy, 22, 34
Heloïse, 82–85, 93–94
Henri IV, King of France, 223
Henry V, King of England, 210,
    214
Hepa, 75
Hepatu, 76
Hepit, 76
Heraea Mysteries, 15

Hera (Juno), 15, 74
Hercules, 3, 8, 10–13, 16, 53
Herodias, 110
Heroides (Ovid), 17
Hesiod, 77
Hesperides, Garden of the, 182,
    184
Hestia (Vesta), 74
Hiawatha, 197
Hill, Anita, 251
Histories (Livy), 17
Hjördis, xxiii, xxvi, 203–8
Homer, xxvii, 1, 16, 54
Hopefulness, 220
Hughes, Pennethorne, 57
Hunt, Jean, 179–80
Hydra, 151
Hypereides, 106
Hypermnestra, 17
Hypsipyle, 17

Ibsen, Henrik, 203–8, 226, 228,
    252
Iliad (Homer), xxvii, 1, 194
Inana, 75, 154
Innocent III, Pope, 107
Institutes of the Christian Religion
    (Calvin), 100
Iphigenia, 78
Isaiah, 53
Isles of the Blessed, 54, 55
Isolde, xxv, xxvi, 32, 205, 243,
    246–47. *See also* Tristan and
    Isolde legend
    fire ceremony and, 33, 49–51
    fire walk of, 246
    as sacred fire, 33
Isolde, Queen Mother, 35–36

Israel, 104
Ivanhoe, 224, 229

Jackson, Glenda, 156, 169, 253
Jane Eyre, xxiii, 68–69, 236–40
  Declaration of Independence of,
    238–40
  as a survivor, 237
Jane Eyre (Brontë), 94, 236–40
Jason, 153
Jeanie Deans, 226–28, 235
Joan of Arc, xvii, xxiv, xxvi, 57,
    63, 90, 177, 195, 202,
    209–15, 222, 224, 252
  background of, 209–12, 215
  effect of execution of, 210
  in *The Old English Baron,* 59
  prophecies about, 211
  window depicting life of,
    212–14
  women claiming to be, 210, 215
Joan of Orléans, 210–11, 215
Job, 52
Jocasta, xxvi, 77, 131–32, 168
Joyce, James, 163, 167
Julie, or the new Heloïse (Rousseau),
    79–80, 82–86, 89, 93–94, 238
  Eve and, 86
  reactions to, 83, 86
Julius Caesar, 194
Juno. *See* Hera
Jupiter. *See* Zeus
Justice. *See* Astraea
Justinian, Emperor, 100, 109–10

Kafka, Franz, 94
Kalevala, 194

Kate (Malintzi), 187–89, 191
Kelly, Grace, 253
Kenilworth (Scott), 58, 230–31
Khouri, Callie, 190–91, 251
Kinski, Nastassia, 185
Kleist, Heinrich von, 126, 133–35,
    139–40, 248
Knox, John, 100

Labraid Longsech, King, 34
La Casa de Bernarda Alba (García
    Lorca), 169–70
Laclos, Pierre-Amboise-François
    Choderlos de, 83, 93, 126,
    134–39
La Dame aux camélias (Dumas fils),
    111, 118–23
  ball scene, 122
  death scene, 123
  love is defined in, 121
  Marguerite's self-definition in,
    121–22
  opera based on, 118
Lady of the Lake, 201
La Fontaine, Jean de, 77
La Madre (The Mother) (Deledda),
    xxi, 164–65
Lancelot, 201
Lanvin, Jean, 126
Lawrence, D. H., 187–91, 249–51
Lazarillo de Tormes, 113
Le Carre, John, 243
Legend of Good Women, The
    (Chaucer), 15–19, 230
Leigh, Vivien, 253
Letters from a Portuguese Nun, 82
Liberty, xxviii, 220–21, 243, 253
Liberty, Statue of, 220

Libra, 222

Light in August (Faulkner), 168

Lily, 58

Lockyer, Sir Joseph Norman, 177

Longinus, 64

Lord of the Flies, 52

Louis IX, King of France, 107

Loyalty, 220

Lucia, Paco de, 141

Lucifer, 53

Lucretia (Lucrece), xxiv, xxvi, 17,
    104, 244–45
  in Chaucer, 19
  in *The Rape of Lucrece,* 20–23

Lum, Peter, 177–78

Mac Orlan, Pierre, 115

Mac Roth, 198

Madama Butterfly, 25

Madame Bovary (Flaubert), 79–80,
    87–93, 161–63
  criticism of, 88
  education of Emma in, 79, 89,
    91–93
  influence of, 90

Maeve (Mebd), Queen, 252
  war against Ulster and, 197–202

Magog, 196

Mala Fortuna, 220

Malintzi (Kate), 187–89, 191

Malraux, André, 138–39

Manon (Massenet), 112, 117–18

Manon Lescaut, 100–101, 111,
    113, 115–18, 124
  grace of, 116–17

Manon Lescaut (Auber), 112

Manon Lescaut (Prévost), 111, 113,
    115–20, 146

doctrine of Divine Grace and,
    116–17
  operas based on, 112–13,
    116–18

Manon Lescaut (Puccini), 112–13

Marc Antony, 18–19

Marguerite (Daisy/Violette)
    Gautier, 111, 118–23, 196
  death of, 123
  self-definition of, 121

Maria Boklonsky, Princess, 26–28

Marie Antoinette, 135–36

Marie de France, 237

Mark, King, xxv, 246
  in Isolde legend, 32–40, 43–50

Marquise de Merteuil, xxiii, xxiv,
    126, 138

Marquise of O, xxiii, xxiv, 126

Marquise of O (Kleist), 133–35,
    139–40

Mary, Virgin, 74

Marya Ivanova, 235–36

Mary Barton (Gaskell), 95–96

Massenet, Jules, 112, 117–18

Maugham, Somerset, 101–3

May Day, 45

Medea, xxv, xxvi, 57, 152–55,
    177, 243–44

Medea (Euripides), 152

Medea (opera), 152

Medusa, xxv, xxvi, 181–84, 186,
    194, 244, 250

Melville, Herman, 165

Mephistopheles, 52

Mérimée, Prosper, 86–87, 126,
    140–46, 240–41, 248

Metamorphoses (Ovid), 17

Midsummer Night's Dream
    (Shakespeare), 154

Milton, John, 64
Minerva, 195–96
Miss Marple, 95, 152
Moby Dick (Melville), 165
Moll Flanders, xxiii, 100, 111–15,
    248
Moll Flanders (Defoe), 111–15
    flight to America in, 114–16, 120
Moloch, 99
Monroe, Marilyn, 253
Montesquieu, Baron de, 109–11
Morgan le Fay, 201
Morholt, 35
Morrigu, Queen, xxvi, 196–201, 252
    Maeve and, 197–201
*Mort d'un personnage (Death of a
    Character)* (Giono), 168, 178
Mother, The. See *La Madre (The
    Mother)*
Mother Earth, 14. *See also* Demeter
    (Ceres); Earth Mother (Earth
    Goddess)
    trees of, 74–76
Murray, Dame Margaret, 58
Murray, Gilbert, 13–14
Murray, Margaret Alice, 57–58
Mylitta, 99
Mysteries of Udolpho, The
    (Radcliffe), 63–69
    characteristics of Gothic heroine
    in, 68
    as prime example of female
    consciousness at work, 65–66

Napoleon Bonaparte, 90
Napoleon I, 137
Neptune. See Poseidon (Neptune)
Nether World, 55

Niobe, 130
Noah, 74
Norma (Bellini), 76
Norman, Jessye, 152. 156
Northanger Abbey (Austen), 69, 237
Novotna, Jarmila, 118–19

Oberon, Merle, 253
Odysseus, 244
Odyssey (Homer), 54
Oedipus, 12, 77, 131, 168
Oedipus at Colonus (Sophocles), 131
Ogma Grianainech, 37
Old English Baron, The (Reeve),
    59–63
Oresteia (Aeschylus), 128–30
Orestes, 72, 128–31
Orfeo ed Eurydice (Gluck), 25, 31
Orléans, Duke Charles of, 210–12,
    214–15
Ornulf, 203–4, 207–8
Orpheus, 7, 75
Ovid, 16–17, 182

Pallas Athena, 195–96
Pandora, xix, xxvi, 72–73
Pasternak, Boris, xxviii, 102
Patrick, Saint, 195
Paul et Virginie (Saint Pierre),
    31–32, 91
Pegasus, 181
Pelléas et Mélisande, 31
Penthesilea, xxiv, 202, 244
Perceval, 196–97, 201
Persephone, xxiv, xxvi, 5, 13–14
Perseus, 182–83
Philomela, 17, 22, 130

Phryne, xxvi, 100, 103–6, 124, 247, 252
  insolence of, 105–6
  in *La Dame aux camélias* (Dumas fils), 111, 118–19
Phyllis, xxvi, 17, 74–75
Piave, Francesco, 118
Pindar, 2
Plato, 106, 151
Plowright, Joan, 169
Plumed Serpent, The (Lawrence), 187–89, 191
Plutarch, Cleopatra and, 18
Pluto, 53–54, 153. *See also* Hades
Poe, Edgar Allan, 59–60, 94, 165, 196
Polanski, Roman, 185, 250
Poliakoff, Steven, 169
Polyneices, 78, 151
Porteous, Captain John, 225, 229, 234
Poseidon (Neptune), 74, 105
Powell, Anthony, 185
Praxiteles, 105–6
Prévost, Abbé, 111–13, 115–19
Procopius, 109–10
Progress of Romance, The (Reeve), 58
Proserpina, 150–51, 153
Proserpine, 53
Proust, Marcel, 88
Puccini, Giacomo, 25, 112–13
Pugachev Revolution, 234–35
Pushkin, Alexander, xxiii, xxiv, 87, 156–59, 233–36, 248, 252
Python, 181–82

Queen of Spades, The (Pushkin), 157–59
Quinault, Philippe, 2

Rabelais, François, 88, 182, 194
Radcliffe, Ann Ward, 58, 63–69, 94, 238, 247
  deminist declaration of, 69
  on Gothic fiction, 63–64
Raimbault, R. N., 167–68
"Rain" (Maugham), 101–3
Rape of Lucrece, The (Shakespeare), 20–24
Reeve, Clara, 58–63, 94, 247
  on Gothic fiction, 58
Republic, The (Plato), 151
Rhea, 53, 72–74
Richard, King, 231
Rollo (Rolf the Marcher), 206
Romance of the Rose (Chaucer), 219–20
Rome, 73, 104
Romeo and Juliet (Shakespeare), 31–32
Rose, 219
"Rose for Emily, A" (Faulkner), 94
Rostov, Natasha, 28
Rougemont, Denis de, 246
Rousseau, Jean-Jacques, 79–86, 89, 93, 103, 135, 137–38, 178, 238, 247
  as anti-feminist, 80–81
  theory of deathless love and, 85

Sadie Thompson, 101–3
Saladin, 231–32
Samson et Dalila, 31–32
Sanctuary (Faulkner), 167–68
Sand, George, 80, 90, 112
Satan, 52
Saura, Carlos, 140
Scarborough, Dorothy, 57

Scatha, 201

Scott, Sir Walter, xxiii, xxiv, 58, 88, 90, 94, 240
  The Heart of Midlothian, 224–28, 233–34
  Ivanhoe, 224, 229
  Kenilworth, 230–31
  The Talisman, 224–25, 231–33

Secret History (Procopius), 109

Secret Pilgrim, The (Le Carre), 243

Secrets of the Great Pyramids (Tompkins), 175

Seven Against Thebes (Aeschylus), 131

Shah Nameh (Book of Kings), xxvii, 231

Shakespeare, William, 2, 31, 64, 196
  on Joan of Arc, 211
  The Rape of Lucrece, 20–23

Shaw, George Bernard, 228

She's Been Away (film), 169

Sibyl, 53, 75, 151

Sibylline Books, The, 218

Sibyls, 218–19

Siegfried, 205

Sigurd, 204–5, 207–8

Silbury Hill, 176–77

Sir Kenneth, 231–32

Sister Carrie, 124, 127

Sister Carrie (Dreiser), 101–2, 127–28, 186, 248

Smith, Maggie, 253

Solon, 103

Sophocles, 2, 131–33

Soumet, Alexandre, 76

Squire, Charles, 197

Stars in Our Heaven, Myths and Fables, The (Lum), 177

Statue of Liberty, 220

Steegmann, Mary G., 164

Stoker, Bram, 95

Stonehenge, 33, 176–79, 186, 243

Storr, Anthony, 168

Strauss, Richard, 133

Streisand, Barbra, 263

Sturluson, Snorri, 203

Taliesin, 154

Talisman, The (Scott), 224–25, 231–33

Tarquin, 20–23

Tartarus, 54, 55

Taylor, Elizabeth, 18, 253

Tess of the D'Urbervilles (film), 185–86, 250

Tess of the D'Urbervilles (Hardy), 185–88, 191, 227, 250–51

Thelma and Louise (film), 191, 251

Themis, 222, 253

Theodora, Empress, xxiv, xxvi, 100–101, 109–11, 124, 243, 247

Theogony (Hesiod), 77

Theseus, 53, 75

Thisbe, 17

Thom, Alexander, 179

Timaeus (Plato), 106

Titania, 154

Titans, 53–54, 73

Tolstoy, Count Leo, xxiv, 26, 86–87, 89–90, 229, 236, 245–46, 248–49

Tompkins, Peter, 175–76

Topping, President, 80

Toynbee, Arnold, 87

Tracking the Flood Survivors (Hunt), 179–80

Trainer, James, 59

Traviata, La (Verdi), 118

Tristan, as solar hero, 33, 45

Tristan and Isolde legend, 31–51,
    205, 231, 246–47
  capture in, 38–40
  Christian hermit in, 43, 48–49
  discovery in, 45–47
  dog in, 43–44
  dream in, 47
  escape in, 39–42
  fire walk in, 50–51
  forgiveness in, 47–49
  love potion in, 35–36, 51, 153,
    246
  oath in, 50
  origins of, 32–34
  pine tree in, 36–38

Trummel, Erna P., 14

Turgenev, Ivan, 86–88

Un Coeur simple (Flaubert),
    160–63

Urien, King, 201

Valkyries, 197, 208

Velleda of Gaul, 202

Venus, 243, 247, 252. *See*
    Aphrodite

Verdi, Giuseppe, 25, 244

Verne, Jules, 94

Vesta. *See* Hestia

Vestal Virgins, 222, 244

Victoria, 195, 202

Vikings at Helgeland, The (Ibsen),
    203–8, 226, 252

Violetta/Violet, 118. *See also*
    Marguerite (Daisy/Violette)
    Gautier

Virgil, 17, 54, 202, 218–19

Virginie, 31–32, 91

Virgin Mary, 74

Voltaire, 83

Walpole, Horace, 54, 62, 94

War and Peace (Tolstoy), 26–28,
    229, 245–46, 249

White, Patrick, 171–72, 249

White Bull of Connaught, 202

William I, King, 206–7

Wilson, Andrew, 225

"Woman Who Rode Away, The"
    (Lawrence), 189–91

Woolf, Virginia, 114

Woyzeck (Buchner), 146

Wozzeck (Berg), 146

Xenocrates, 106

Zeus (Jupiter), 4, 73–74, 222